The Daring Exploits
of a
Runaway Heiress

Center Point
Large Print

Also by Victoria Alexander and available from Center Point Large Print:

The Importance of Being Wicked
The Scandalous Adventures of the
    Sister of the Bride

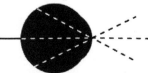

**This Large Print Book carries the
Seal of Approval of N.A.V.H.**

The Daring Exploits of a Runaway Heiress

Victoria Alexander

CENTER POINT LARGE PRINT
THORNDIKE, MAINE

This Center Point Large Print edition is published
in the year 2015 by arrangement with
Kensington Publishing Corp.

The text of this Large Print edition is unabridged.
In other aspects, this book may vary
from the original edition.
Printed in the United States of America
on permanent paper.
Set in 16-point Times New Roman type.

ISBN: 978-1-62899-573-2

Library of Congress Cataloging-in-Publication Data

Alexander, Victoria.
  The daring exploits of a runaway heiress / Victoria Alexander. —
    Center Point Large Print edition.
        pages cm
  Summary: "Lucy Merryweather has inherited a fortune—and her great-
aunt's list of unfulfilled wishes. What better way to honor her memory
than by accomplishing as many of them as possible? And with Lucy's
family an ocean away in New York, nothing stands in her way—if one
ignores the private investigator hired to spy on her"
    —Provided by publisher.
  ISBN 978-1-62899-573-2 (library binding : alk. paper)
  1. Inheritance and succession—Fiction. 2. Large type books. I. Title.
PS3551.L357713D37 2015
813'.54—dc23
                                                              2015011150

I never realized it before but family is always an important element in any story I write. As it should be I think as my family is so important in my life. So this book is dedicated to my family, those I'm technically related to and those I'm connected to by the bonds of love and friendship. You help me see the world, and you make me who I am and you have my back. I don't thank you enough but I am so grateful for all of you. So thank you and know that always, always you have my love.

To be delivered to
Miss Lucinda Merryweather
on the occasion of her twenty-first birthday

August 12, 1869
My Dearest Lucy,
I daresay you will scarcely remember me if indeed you remember me at all. Unfortunately, I will be long dead by the time you receive this missive. I have already passed my eightieth year and my time inevitably grows short. As I write this you are barely five years of age and you are already a delightful, clever child. I am confident you will be a lovely, intelligent young woman as well.

You were named after me, which has always been a source of great delight and more than a little satisfaction. Your father did so knowing, as I had no children of my own, I would no doubt leave my fortune to you. In that he was correct. Aside from a few personal bequests to friends and charitable causes, I have indeed left the bulk of my fortune to you. It shall remain in a trust until the day you receive this letter, on your twenty-first birthday. My legal advisors are every bit as clever as your father, precisely why I do not begrudge their exorbitant fees. They have done the maneuvering necessary to ensure my fortune remains under your control, even if you are married. Oh, I would like to see your father's face when he learns of that stipulation, but then perhaps I can. Hopefully, I should be looking down at him and not up.

In addition to this note, I have left you a small book, a diary if you will. When I was younger than you are now there were all sorts of, well, adventures for lack of a better word, that I wished to experience in my life. Some of them are merely silly, the musings of a young girl. Some are decidedly scandalous and some rather profound. Regardless, through the long course of my life I accomplished none of them. Even those that would have taken no effort whatsoever. So you see, my dear, what began as a list of my secret desire for adventures became a list of my heartfelt regrets.

But make no mistake, Lucy, I had a very good life all in all. My husband, Charles, was a fine man even if he wasn't the least bit adventurous, which is not a quality one usually seeks in a husband. One looks for a man solid and steadfast, as adventurous men generally do not make reliable husbands. But the day I met Charles Van Burton was the best day of my life. He was an excellent husband, a fine man, and I loved him with my whole heart and soul. Love, my dear girl, is never a regret.

When Charles died and I was free to do as I wished, I was far too set in my ways and it was entirely too late. My opportunities had slipped by and so those frivolous desires of my youth became regrets of far more significance than they should have been. It does seem a pity.

I pray you have the courage and strength of character I lacked to sally forth and pursue whatever it is that you want in life, regardless of whether the world sees it as silly or improper or unsuitable. I leave my book of regrets to you in the hopes that it will inspire you to follow your heart and chase your dreams. No matter how unconventional or even foolish they may be.

I leave my fortune to you to give you the means to do so.

Yours with warm affection,
Aunt Lucinda

Prologue

January 4, 1888
Millworth Manor

"You want to do what?" Jackson Channing stared at Lucinda Merryweather as if she had suddenly grown two heads. Which would have been most curious even here at Millworth Manor. Although from what Lucy had gathered during her stay thus far, it might not have been the oddest thing ever to have occurred at Jackson's father's ancestral estate.

"No, Jackson," Lucy said firmly, resisting the urge to heave a long-suffering sigh. She had known he would not take this well. Apparently, it was one thing for Jackson to head toward the unknown and a life of grand adventures and quite another for Lucy to do so. Regardless, he no longer had any say in what she did or did not do. She settled into one of the chairs in front of the desk and cast him her most pleasant smile. "I don't merely *want* to do this. I fully *intend* to do this."

"You intend to somehow set right the regrets of a woman you never met." Disbelief rang in his voice.

"That's not entirely true. I did meet my Great-

10

aunt Lucinda, but I was very young and simply don't remember. She died when I was five."

"Nonetheless—"

"There is no nonetheless, Jackson." Goodness, the man made her want to stamp her foot in frustration. Fortunately she had given up such childish behavior years ago. Still, it would have been most satisfying. "I was named for my great-aunt and she left me her fortune, which I received on my twenty-first birthday."

"Yes, I know that but—"

"There were no stipulations on the inheritance, if you recall. However, I also received a letter from Lucinda as well as a thin journal. A book of regrets, if you will."

"Just because she had regrets does not mean that you are under any obligation—"

"I know exactly what it does and doesn't mean, Jackson. And I do wish you would stop being so . . . so disapproving." She glanced around the Millworth library and the numerous family portraits interspersed between endless shelves of books. Each and every portrait glowered with disapproval. "Although this does seem to be the place for it."

"Lucy, I—"

"And do sit down." She rolled her gaze at the ceiling. "I hate the way you're standing behind that desk glaring at me."

"I like standing. It gives me the advantage."

"Not really." She smiled sweetly.

He huffed, took his seat, and leaned forward over the desk. "I have known you for all of your life and I have always felt, well, responsible for you." He paused. "Just because our circumstances have changed does not negate that responsibility."

"Actually, Jackson," she said in as kind a voice as she could manage. "It does."

For years Lucy and Jackson, as well as their respective families, had assumed they would one day marry. But whenever the time had come to officially announce their engagement, there had always been some perfectly legitimate reason to put it off. It had slowly dawned on Lucy that perhaps they were not meant to be together. And perhaps deep down inside, both of them knew it. The realization had brought with it a great deal of relief. She truly loved Jackson and suspected she always would, but the affection she felt for him was not unlike that she had for her brothers. And it did seem to her if one was going to marry a man, the feelings one had for him shouldn't be anything remotely brotherly.

Both their lives had changed when Jackson discovered the father he had long thought was dead was not merely alive but had no knowledge of his son's existence. And discovered as well he was heir to an English title. When Jackson came to England with his newfound father to meet his family, it did seem that fate had handed

Lucy the chance she had assumed lost forever. She had freed him from any obligation to her and set her own plan for her life in motion, at least tentatively. It was the specifics that were vague. But again fate stepped in and Lucy had jumped at the chance to accompany Jackson's mother, Elizabeth, to England. Now that she was here, she had no intention of returning home to New York anytime soon. No intention of becoming once again the placid, well-behaved daughter of a director of Graham, Merryweather, and Lockwood Banking and Trust.

"You will always be my dearest friend," Jackson said staunchly.

"As you will be mine."

Poor, dear Jackson had fallen head over heels for a friend of his family's. Unfortunately, she was as independent as she was lovely, and a few days ago both their hearts had been broken. Lucy had tried to talk to Jackson, to encourage him to go after the lady, but it was to no avail. He was as stubborn as the woman he loved. Still, Lucy firmly believed in the notion of true love and soul mates and destiny. And wasn't the mere fact that she and Jackson were not together proof of that? Lucy was confident Jackson and Lady Theodosia would eventually find their way back to each other.

However, as there seemed to be nothing Lucy could do about Jackson's life at the moment, it was time to turn her attention to her own.

"I am well aware that I am under no obligation to Great-aunt Lucinda, at least not legally, but I feel a, well, a moral obligation if you will. I was quite moved by the letter she left for me and by her regrets, but there was nothing I could do about it when you and I had our lives planned out for us. Now, everything has changed." She shook her head. "I do not want to reach the end of my life and have a list of those things I wanted to do but failed to so much as try. The very idea terrifies me. I don't want regrets of my own." She met his gaze directly. "And if I don't do this for her—for me—I know I will."

"Perhaps . . ." He settled back in his chair and chose his words carefully. A deceptively casual note sounded in his voice. "You should do those things you've always wanted rather than those someone else wished to do."

"Excellent, Jackson." She fixed him with a firm look. "And just what do you suggest those might be?"

He shrugged. "I have no idea."

"Unfortunately, neither do I." She crossed her arms over her chest and drew her brows together. "Every bit of my life has been planned and expected up until now. I've never veered from the course set out for me. Why, I never even questioned whether you and I should marry. At least not aloud."

"Nor did I," Jackson said under his breath.

"But as I am no longer expected to marry you, I'm not sure what I want to do."

"Surely you wish to marry someone someday?"

"Oh, probably someday, but at the moment . . ." She shook her head. "I feel very much like a bird who has at long last been released from its cage."

"Thank you," he said wryly.

"Come now, you know what I mean." She waved off his comment. "Now that I am free, I have no idea what I want to do with my freedom. Until I determine that, it seems the best course is to do those things my great-aunt never had the opportunity to do."

"I'm not sure that is indeed the best course. Still . . ." He studied her for a moment. "You haven't told me what these regrets of your aunt's are. I'm assuming the worst, you know. That they are all improper or scandalous or dangerous."

"Not all of them." She had no intention of telling him everything on Lucinda's long list, but she could tell him one or two items. "Some of them are a little silly and some are really rather sweet. For one thing, she always wanted to have a dog but was never able to have one as dogs made Great-uncle Charles sneeze. There are quite a few that are as innocent as that."

His eyes narrowed. "But not all of them?"

"Well, some are a bit more daring." She cast him an innocent smile. "But not substantially so."

15

"I don't believe you for a moment." He shook his head. "I don't think this is the least bit advisable, Lucy."

"Why not? You're going off to do exactly what you want. Aside from the notion of following in your father's adventurous footsteps, your plans are even less definitive than mine. Why shouldn't I do what I want?"

"For one thing, you're female," he said in a distinctly patronizing manner. She did so hate it when he was patronizing. It was the banker in him, no doubt. And even though he was now forgoing his life as a banker in favor of something far more exciting, it was obviously easier to take the man out of the bank than the bank out of the man. "For another, you have no practical experience at being on your own. Although I could hire someone to make certain of your safety, I suppose. A bodyguard or some sort of private investigator—"

"You most certainly will not! I do not need a nursemaid or a watchdog."

"I don't like leaving you here alone with no one to watch over you."

She raised a brow. "Goodness, Jackson, I had no idea you had such a poor opinion of my abilities and intelligence."

"I didn't mean that quite the way it sounded." Jackson shook his head. "You've simply taken me by surprise. I've no doubt you're probably

16

extremely capable underneath all that"—his eyes narrowed—"pleasantry."

"I am unfailingly pleasant."

"Yes, I know." He studied her for a long moment. "You're determined, aren't you?"

"I am."

"Well, I suppose you're right." He heaved a resigned sigh. "There's no reason why you can't do what you wish. And I suspect there's nothing I can do to stop you."

She cast him her sweetest smile.

"Therefore, I have no objection—"

"Oh, lucky, lucky me."

He ignored her. "However, I do have conditions."

"Conditions?" She scoffed. "I thought we had established that it's no longer your right to have any say whatsoever about what I may or may not do. I am nearly twenty-four years old, you know."

"I have the right of a good friend, as someone who cares about you. But if you would prefer not to agree to my conditions"—he shrugged—"I might feel compelled to write to your parents, or better yet, your brothers, and tell them of my concerns." It was his turn to smile pleasantly.

Lucy narrowed her gaze. She had no doubt he would do exactly that if she didn't give in to his demands. "Very well. What are your conditions?"

"One, that you restrict your pursuit of these

adventures of your great-aunt's to England and reside either here at Millworth or at Channing House in London." He held up his hand to forestall her objection. "My parents and aunt and uncle will all be traveling, so you would be as independent as you plan. Of course, the servants will be here."

Lucy bit back a satisfied smile. She was well aware that very nearly everyone in his family would be heading toward different parts of the world in the coming days. She was only telling Jackson all this in the first place because she intended to ask if she could stay on in his family's residences while they were away. She had already decided to pursue her quests in England for several reasons. First and foremost, she was here, delightfully far from home and everyone she knew. Besides, her great-aunt had always wanted to travel to England as her mother, Lucy's great-grandmother, was born here. Lucy's visit to England meant she could already cross one regret off the list. Beyond that, as this would be Lucy's first attempt at adventure of any kind, it did seem it might be easier to have grand adventures if she fully understood the language. While she had studied French and Italian, languages simply eluded her and she could do little more than ask for directions to the library or the train station. She nodded. "I can agree to that."

"And you will periodically call on my cousin, Lady Dunwell, so that someone will be assured of your well-being."

"Your cousin Beryl?"

Jackson nodded. "As everyone else will be out of the country, Beryl is an excellent choice. Her husband, Lionel, is expected to be prime minister one day. I doubt that I could leave you in better hands."

Apparently Jackson was not aware that, while Lady Dunwell and her husband were most respectable at the moment, the gossip about their past was extremely interesting and not the least bit proper. Lucy couldn't think of a more perfect watchdog. She forced a resigned note to her voice. "Very well."

"And." His tone hardened. "You will allow me to hire a companion for you."

"I don't need a companion."

"And I have been lax in my correspondence."

She narrowed her eyes. "You do realize there is a word for what you're doing?"

"I daresay there are any number of words for what I'm doing." The smug note in his voice matched the satisfied look in his eyes.

"Blackmail and extortion immediately come to mind."

He cast her a completely unrepentant grin. She could not recall ever wanting to smack that grin off his face before.

"All right." She sighed. "A companion it is then." Still, she could always discharge any companion Jackson found once he was out of the country.

Jackson paused. "You do realize once your parents find out—"

"They shall no doubt send someone to bodily haul me home." It was awkward to sail off into the unknown when your family refused to accept that you were an adult. She wasn't entirely sure how she was going to deal with that situation should— *when* it occurred. She'd always been a perfect daughter. She'd never done anything unexpected or improper in her life. It was a pity, really. If she'd had more experience with impropriety she'd probably know how to handle the repercussions of doing the unexpected. "Yes, I do realize that, which means I probably don't have a great deal of time to accomplish what I want."

"You will write to them?"

"I already have." She forced a note of indignation to her voice. "I would never want to worry them. Besides, your mother wrote to them as well." Unfortunately, as Mrs. Channing's letter had been placed on a hallway table to be posted, Lucy might possibly have dropped it into the fire. Accidentally, of course.

"And you did tell them that you are no longer accompanied by my mother."

"Goodness, Jackson." She drew her brows together. "One would think you didn't trust me."

"I didn't mean—"

"Have I ever in my entire life lied to you?"

"Not that I know of."

"And do you consider me to be a liar? Someone who prevaricates? Who hides the truth?" She pinned him with a firm look. "Well?"

"Of course not." Jackson shook his head. "I am sorry. It's . . . well . . ." He ran his hand through his hair in an endearingly familiar manner. For a moment she could see the future they had both expected. It would have been quite pleasant and it was a tiny bit sad to see it vanish. But not marrying Jackson would never be one of her regrets. "It's been a difficult few days."

"Not to mention the months preceding it." She again resisted the urge to bring up Lady Theodosia.

"Still, you're right." He shrugged apologetically. "I have no reason not to trust you."

"Thank you, Jackson." She beamed at him. Perhaps there was something to be said for having a spotless reputation after all. And it wasn't a complete lie. She had written, she simply might not have mentioned that Jackson's mother had decided to travel the world with her estranged husband in the hopes of rekindling what they once had. It was terribly romantic. And extremely convenient.

Nonetheless, even though Lucy had assured Jackson's mother she would write to her family, as indeed she had, Lucy had no doubt that at some point Elizabeth Channing would again write to her dear friend Pauline Merryweather. Said letter would surely mention Elizabeth's travels with her husband and that Lucy had stayed in England. At which point Pauline would realize she wasn't entirely certain exactly where her only daughter was or what she was doing, and there would be hell to pay. As frustrating as the slow speed of mail and transport across the Atlantic was, at the moment, Lucy was grateful. By her calculations, she had a minimum of a month to do what she wanted to do. If she was lucky, she would have far more.

She was under no illusions that she could do everything on her great-aunt's list, but it did seem to her that the worth was as much in the effort as the success. After that, Lucy had no idea what she would do, but her future certainly didn't need to be decided here and now. She had time and money and freedom.

"You are absolutely certain you want to do this?" Jackson asked.

"Aside from not marrying you"—Lucy grinned —"I have never been more certain of anything in my life."

"Again, thank you."

She laughed. She would always treasure Jackson, but they were choosing their own roads to follow. She hadn't the slightest doubt that one day he would walk his with Lady

Theodosia by his side. Precisely as it should be.

Lucy's own road was a bit less clear. Which should have concerned her but didn't. It was as exciting as it was daunting. Besides, when fate offered you a hand, you would be a fool not to take it. Adventure was where one found it, after all, and opportunities were not to be squandered.

What Jackson didn't know, what Lucy had never revealed to anyone, was that her great-aunt wasn't the only young girl to make a list of those silly or improper things she wished to do in her life.

Lucinda Wilhelmina Merryweather had long had a secret list of adventures of her own.

The Future Adventures of
Miss Lucinda Merryweather

Make an unexpected friend.
Swim naked in the moonlight.
Travel the world.
Learn to do something unexpected or
  interesting or frivolous.
Wear something shocking.
Solve a mystery.
Ride an elephant.
Beat men at their own game. Preferably for
  very high stakes.
Stand up for what I believe in.
Find unconditional love—a dog will do nicely.
  And a parrot that talks.
Fly.
See the place my mother was born, learn why
  she never speaks of her family.
Storm the sacred bastion of a gentlemen's
  club.
Dance with a prince.
Appear in a theatrical production.
Have a romantic interlude with someone I
  plan to never to see again.
Wear trousers and ride astride.
Kiss a stranger.
Frolic in a fountain.
Be painted sans clothing.
Take a lover.
Make certain the world remembers my name.

Chapter One

Cameron Effington, the youngest son of the Duke of Roxborough, resisted the urge to clench his teeth and instead adopted his most cordial expression and met his father's disapproving gaze at the far end of the dining table. "Yes, Father, my work is most satisfactory. Thank you for asking."

His father's eyes narrowed. "Well, as long as it's satisfactory."

"Father," Cam's oldest brother, Spencer, the Marquess of Helmsley, said in a low, warning tone. As the next duke, Spencer had long seen himself as the diplomat in the family.

His father had been less than pleased when Cam had taken a position with *Cadwallender's Daily Messenger* more than a year ago. But aside from the occasional disgruntled comment, the duke usually refrained from discussing his youngest son's work. Tonight, however, there was an undercurrent to his words that did not bode well.

Cam's twin brothers, Simon and Thaddeus, traded glances but wisely kept their mouths shut. It would not do for Father to turn his displeasure toward them, although admittedly they had done nothing of late to incur his ire. At least nothing Cam was aware of. His widowed sister, Grace,

Lady Watersfeld, continued with her meal, completely ignoring the potential for a family squabble that hung over the table along with the aroma of roasted beef. Two years older than Cam, Grace too had long ago learned the wisdom of not distracting Father and thus bringing her own misdeeds to his attention.

Admittedly they were more often than not quite a congenial group unless the subject arose of Cam's choice of profession—indeed that he chose to have a profession at all. Or the discussion turned to the fact that none of them was currently married, none of them had any particular prospects for marriage, and none of them seemed to be making any effort to alleviate that situation. Or the occasional indiscretion and mild scandal any of them might be involved in raised its head. Still, Cameron did give his siblings credit as they were usually most discreet. At those times, one would have thought Father's entire life had been above reproach, which was far from the truth. Although his offspring were usually wise enough not to bring up Father's less than stellar behavior in his youth.

"Jonathon," his mother said in her best Duchess of Roxborough voice, which had long struck fear into the hearts of her children and husband alike. "It is all I can do to entice my children here once a week. I shall not allow you to spoil it."

Father gasped. "I would never—"

"We agreed this was to be a cordial evening," Mother continued.

Cordial or not, dinner every Thursday at Effington House when Cam's siblings were in London was in the nature of a command appearance. While all the Effington offspring had their own private residences, a constant source of annoyance to the duke, Mother insisted her children present themselves for dinner once a week. Legitimate reasons for absence from this ritual were accepted, but woe be it to anyone who missed more than two consecutive dinners. Nonetheless, this was the first time in more than a month that all of the duke and duchess's children were seated at the table together.

Father's eyes widened in a show of feigned innocence. "I was being cordial."

"For the moment perhaps." Mother's eyes narrowed. "But I know you, Jonathon Effington. I know exactly how you think and I certainly know that look on your face."

"I don't have a look on my face," Father said under his breath, and speared a piece of perfectly cooked beef with far more vengeance than was necessary. "I don't know what's wrong with a father asking a son about his avocation."

"I believe you mean vocation, Father," Grace said in a deceptively pleasant manner. There was nothing Grace liked better than throwing fuel on the fire. As long as it was someone else's fire. "An *avocation* is a hobby, a *vocation* is a profession."

Father's brow furrowed in annoyance. "I know—"

"Grandmother is not joining us tonight?" Thad asked in an effort to change the course of the conversation. Cam cast him a grateful look. Thad too thought of himself as a peacemaker.

"I'm afraid not." Mother sighed. "She was going to retire early as she was quite done in. Some of her friends came by this afternoon and they spent a great deal of time visiting."

"And compiling lists of eligible matches, no doubt," Grace said under her breath.

"I believe all their plans and plots and schemes may well keep them young. They do have a grand time. And you, all of you"—Mother's pointed look circled the table—"should be most grateful for their efforts. One never knows where one might find a match not only suitable but perfect." Mother smiled at her husband. "Don't you agree, Jonathon?"

Father cast her a look that might well have been considered wicked if, of course, he wasn't, well, *Father*. "Cupid's arrow strikes without warning, when one least expects or desires it. And often in the most unusual manner." His gaze lingered on his wife and true affection shone in his eyes.

None of the Effington offspring knew the exact details of Mother and Father's courtship save that Mother's cousin was one of Father's oldest friends. Cam had long suspected there was more to it than that as it was obvious theirs had been a love match and just as obvious that it still was. Father cleared his throat. "Your mother is right. The efforts of your grandmother and her cronies should not be dismissed without due consideration, even if you view those efforts as meddling and manipulative."

Grandmother, the dowager duchess and matriarch of the Effington family, had recently passed her ninetieth birthday. Whereas before reaching that milestone she had often said how she looked forward to joining her beloved husband, Thomas, in the next life, now she was determined to cling to this life until she reached one hundred years or had seen all her grandchildren happily wed, whichever came first. Judging by the way her daughter-in-law was enthusiastically engaged in the same pursuit, one would have thought Mother was eager to see the old lady go.

Unfortunately, as most of Cam's cousins were older and already wed, and Grandmother resided with her only son and his wife, her matchmaking efforts focused almost exclusively on those grandchildren now seated around the table.

It wasn't as if they hadn't tried. Spencer had been engaged to the lovely Eleanora Matthew, the daughter of an earl and eminently suitable to be a future duchess. But Eleanora had succumbed to measles five years ago and it had taken Spencer some time to move on with his life. Cam was fairly certain no one else in the family, except perhaps Simon, knew that Thad had been in love with the young woman as well. Both brothers' hearts had broken when she died, although Spencer could mourn publicly and Thad's sorrow was private. This was what love did to a man.

In spite of the example set by his parents, Cam was glad he had never succumbed to that fickle emotion. Nor did he wish to. And no matter how many prospective brides Grandmother and her friends herded in his direction, marriage held no particular appeal. Fortunately, Grandmother concentrated most of her efforts on his older brothers and sister, but Cam was under no illusion that she did not have him in her sights as well.

Grace had dutifully married Henry, Lord Watersfeld, a nice enough sort, who was liked and approved by the family and most importantly the dowager duchess, who was notoriously hard to please about prospective matches regardless of how much she wanted her grandchildren to wed. While Grace did appear to care for him, it also seemed to Cam that she relished being a widow far more than she had being a wife. Grace avoided most attempts to find her a new match by declaring, as it had only been three years since Henry's death, she was still mourning, when in truth she used the freedom accorded her as a widow of independent means to pursue her own interests. Interests of an artistic nature. Something Mother knew and Father did not. Father was not overly fond of artistic endeavors.

"Being manipulative and meddling is one of the few joys left to me." Grandmother's voice rang from the doorway.

"Mother." The duke and his sons jumped to their feet. "Fiona said you had retired."

"I had but I changed my mind. I'm allowed to do that, you know." In spite of her age, her voice was strong and determined, but she leaned heavily on a carved, ivory-headed cane. She frequently complained that her mind was as sharp as ever but the rest of her was falling apart. "After a most refreshing nap I found I would rather be in the bosom of my family than in my bed. Besides, I was hungry and I hate eating alone in my rooms. It makes me feel even older than I am." Her brows drew together. "Now, are you going to make me stand here all night or are one of you boys going to come help me to my seat?"

At once the brothers moved toward her, but Simon reached her first and assisted her to a chair even as expertly trained footmen prepared a place for her.

"You needn't grin like that, Simon." Grandmother cast him a chastising look. "You haven't won a prize, you know."

31

"Oh, but I have, Grandmother." Simon's unrepentant grin widened. "Escorting you to the table or anywhere is both a delight and a privilege."

"Do not waste all that charm on me. It will do you no good as I am immune to it. You are so like your grandfather. He too was a charming rogue." Grandmother settled into her chair. "Beware of that, my boy. It is both a blessing and a curse."

"I shall keep that in mind, Grandmother." Simon chuckled and retook his seat.

"See that you do." Grandmother's gaze wandered around the table and Cam wondered exactly what she saw when she looked at each of them. Or perhaps whom she saw. "I intend to send each of you a long note tomorrow listing the assorted possibilities for suitable matches."

Grace winced. Cam and his brothers traded resigned glances. It would not be the first such note Grandmother had sent them and probably not the last.

"If you continue to make faces like that, Grace, you will be wrinkled before your time." Grandmother signaled for a footman to fill her glass with the sherry she preferred with dinner. A glass that would be kept discreetly filled until she left the table. "Marital relations are also excellent for keeping one's youthful looks and one's mind sharp."

Mother coughed back a laugh.

Father choked. "Mother!"

"Good Lord, Jonathon, when did you get so stuffy? You certainly weren't like this when you were their age." Grandmother huffed. "I have earned the right to say exactly what I want and I don't intend to curb my tongue simply because you have become something of a stick in the mud."

"I am not—"

"Besides . . ." Her eyes twinkled behind her spectacles. "One of the few thrills I have left in life is saying something shocking." She picked up her glass. "Lord knows, I can no longer do anything shocking."

"I'm certain you could if you tried," Thad said staunchly.

"What a delightful thing to say to an old woman. You, my dear boy, have become every bit as charming as your brother, although you are far more intelligent."

Simon gasped in indignation. "Not *far* more."

Grandmother raised a brow.

"I just prefer to keep my intelligence to myself," he added in a lofty manner.

"And you do it so well," Grace said under her breath.

"Intelligence coupled with charm is a potent combination." Grandmother nodded at Thad. "Use it wisely. As for whether I could still do something shocking at my advanced age . . ." She took a sip of her wine and thought for a moment. "One can only hope. I am certainly willing to try."

Laughter washed around the table, skipping over Father, who simply rolled his gaze toward the ceiling.

"Unfortunately, those opportunities for shocking behavior grow rarer as one gets older." Grandmother shook her head. "Pity really."

"Thank God," Father muttered.

"Now then." Grandmother beamed at her family. "It's not often that Fiona manages to have all of you here at once. So let us make pleasant conversation about nothing in particular while we indulge in this lovely meal Cook has prepared. Has anyone heard any interesting gossip of late?"

Mother bit back a grin. Grace choked and took a quick sip of wine.

"Mother." Father heaved a resigned sigh. "That's somewhat inappropriate, don't you think?"

"Absolutely, Jonathon." Grandmother's voice was cool but laughter lurked in her eyes. "That's what makes it so much fun." Grandmother turned toward her oldest grandson. "Spencer, I would ask you if you have heard anything of interest but you are entirely too discreet."

Spencer raised his glass and smiled. "Thank you, Grandmother."

"It was not entirely a compliment." She studied him for a moment. "But a good quality in a future duke nonetheless. I fear from Grace we may learn far more than we should. You do seem to hear all sorts of fascinating things, my dear. Things probably best discussed without the presence of gentlemen. We would hate to shock their fragile sensibilities." She leaned toward her granddaughter. "Perhaps after dinner . . ."

"Perhaps." Grace's smile was not as innocent as her tone.

"Simon." Grandmother smiled in a conspiratorial manner. "Surely you've heard something worth sharing?"

"Grandmother!" Simon gasped in feigned indignation, then grinned. "Well, I did pick up something at my club the other night. It seems a viscount, well known for his . . ."

Simon launched into a tale of good romantic intentions gone awry that would not have been nearly as entertaining had someone else been telling it. Simon was a natural storyteller, which often came in handy as he was the brother who most needed to be able to twist an incident to show himself in the best light. Although he and Thad were mirror images of each other, with the exception of Thad's need for spectacles, Simon was the more adventurous of the twins and tended to skate on the edge of scandal in direct contrast to his brother. Thad was the intellectual in the family and, if he and Simon had not taken over management of most of the family's business and investment interests, might well have become a scholar. Together, they formed a formidable team and Father was pleased.

Spencer was following in Father's footsteps, as was expected, and had a hand in everything from management of the family's estates to politics. There had never been so much as a breath of scandal about Spencer, but Cam often wondered if, like Thad and Grace, Spencer had secrets no one else knew. But Father was pleased with him as well.

Unfortunately, he was not as happy with his youngest son. Cam had dutifully negotiated the hallowed halls of education, then traveled the continent and wandered through Egypt and India. He had tried his hand at business with his brothers but it was not to his liking. He had toyed with the study of law but thought it rather dull. He had even briefly considered the church but realized almost immediately that his character was not suited for a life of unquestioned upright behavior. Indeed, for several years, he had done little more than enjoy being the youngest son of a duke with no responsibilities, no expectations, and nearly unlimited funds. Still, it wasn't particularly satisfying, which was odd as it was rather fun.

It had grown on him slowly that his greatest joy in life was putting pen to paper. Much to his surprise, he found the writing of stories to be far more enjoyable than the frivolous life he led. For the first time, Cam gave serious consideration to his future and realized if indeed he wanted one day to be as well known as Mr. Dickens or Mr. Trollope, he was going to have to have a serious plan. After all, he knew nothing of real life outside the rarified world of England's upper ten thousand. His first step toward the future was to take a position as a journalist with the *Daily Messenger*. Even though the editorial direction of the *Messenger* was still evolving and it was for the most part more inclined toward gossip and lighthearted fare than the more serious causes taken up by newspapers like the *Times* or the *Gazette*, Cam found it suited him. Not that he hadn't reported his share of murder, mayhem, and corruption. In the year since he'd begun, he'd been shocked and appalled, amused and amazed by the follies and foibles of man, and every story he wrote became fodder for his fiction. For the works he would one day write.

Cam still didn't understand why his father was so adamantly opposed to his choice of profession. After all, Grandmother had written a series of stories for *Cadwallender's Weekly World Messenger* and went on to write nearly a dozen novels of romance and adventure. Indeed, the Cadwallender and Effington families had had a close relationship since then. A few years ago, two of the Cadwallender brothers had formed their own book publishing enterprise, the *Weekly*

World Messenger had become *Cadwallender's Weekly Ladies World*, and *Cadwallender's Daily Messenger* had been launched. Still, in an effort to placate his father, and avoid undue prominence and any suggestion of favoritism, Cam used his mother's maiden name, Fairchild, instead of Effington. Even James Cadwallender, publisher of the *Messenger*, called him Fairchild. For the most part, father and son now had a sort of unacknowledged truce and simply avoided any discussion of Cam's employment.

Until tonight when Father had asked about his work. Something had obviously triggered his father's wrath and Cam suspected they were headed toward a long postponed confrontation.

When the family had finished dinner, his mother drew a deep breath. "Cameron, your father has something he wishes to discuss with you."

Father's brow furrowed. "I had planned to have that discussion privately."

"Absolutely not." Mother shook her head. "I do not intend to take sides, but I will not be left out of this."

"Nor will I," Grandmother said in a deceptively pleasant tone. Obviously she too knew what this was about.

"Very well." Father's tone was sharp. "The rest of you may leave."

"I believe I prefer to stay," Spencer said mildly.

Thad glanced at Grace and Simon and nodded. "As do we."

"As you wish." Father paused, then his hard gaze met his youngest son's. Unease clenched Cam's stomach. "I have not been happy at this rift between us. So, a few days ago, in the spirit of harmony or even perhaps compromise, I read an edition of the *Daily Messenger* for the first time."

"For the first time?" Cam said slowly.

"Good Lord, Father!" Grace stared. "He's been writing for the paper for over a year and you haven't read it until now?"

"No," Father snapped, and glared at his daughter. "I have not."

"Don't you think you should have?" Simon asked.

"The rest of us have," Thad added.

Cam stared at his father, disappointment and something that might well have been hurt rising within him. "You haven't read anything I've written?"

"I have." Mother raised her chin. "I have read every single issue since Cam began his work there."

"And I have read most of them as well," Grandmother said.

"As have I." Spencer gestured at his siblings. "We all have."

"You needn't look at me like that, any of you." Father glared. "I said I haven't read the *Daily*

Messenger. In point of fact, I have read every word Cameron has written." Father slanted Mother an annoyed look. She refused to meet his gaze. "Your mother has clipped every story, every article for me in what I now see as a most devious attempt to keep me in a state of innocent ignorance. However, three days ago I read the *Messenger* in its entirety and I now understand why she went to such great efforts to prevent that." Father's eyes narrowed. "I have never before read something as filled with slander and gossip and salacious skewing of facts and events. Something so scandalous and so . . . so *liberal*. It's appalling and not worth the paper it's written on."

"I don't think it's any worse than any other paper, Father," Spencer said.

"The Cadwallenders are an honorable family and I do not understand how they can publish this sort of rubbish."

"Admittedly there is a great deal of emphasis on scandal and gossip and sensationalism, but unfortunately, Father"—Thad shrugged—"that is what sells papers. It's what people want to read."

"It's not what I want to read," Father said firmly. "It's not what respectable members of society want to read."

"Then perhaps you would do well not to read it again," Cam said in as calm a manner as he could muster.

"Cam's work is very good, Father." Thad offered Cam a smile of support. "He is an excellent writer."

"I know that," Father snapped. "But he should put that talent to a better use."

"What would that be, Father?" Cam's voice hardened. "Should I occupy myself with the family's business interests alongside Simon and Thad and write reports on investment strategies and import regulations? Should I work with Spencer and write about the newest agricultural methods for increasing profitability of the estates?"

"Don't be absurd." Father scoffed. "You know as well as I you aren't suited for any of that. You could write books. That's respectable enough."

Cam's jaw tightened. "One doesn't just sit down and write a book. It's not that easy."

"Balderdash." Father waved off the comment. "Your grandmother did it."

"Thank you, dear," the dowager said in a wry tone.

"I don't have anything to write about." Cam drew a deep calming breath. "I have led a life of privilege and wealth. I have been well educated and have been fortunate enough to have had the means to travel. All in the comfort we are accustomed to. I think one should know the world in its fullness, the good and the bad, before one attempts to create worlds of one's own. But I know nothing of the real world and the real people in it. I know nothing of life."

"I thought we were real people," Grace murmured.

"Stuff and nonsense." Father huffed. "Your grandmother knew nothing of life and yet she—"

"She," Grandmother said sternly, "had a mother who died when she was quite young and a father who gambled and drank away the family fortune and honor. A father prepared to sell his daughters to the highest bidders to finance his vices. *She* and her orphaned sisters lived in a country house that was barely held together by little more than prayer and hope. *She* knows what it's like to have little to eat, no dowry, no prospects for improvement, and no future. I should think that would give me some sense of life beyond the privileged world we now inhabit."

"My apologies, Mother." Father grimaced. "I had forgotten about all that."

Cam stared in surprise. This was a story he had never heard before, and judging from the looks on the faces of his siblings, neither had they.

"It's best forgotten, really." Grandmother shrugged. "It was a very long time ago and most of my life has been quite lovely. But those early days taught me a great deal about life I never would have known otherwise." She turned toward Cam. "Every experience, every new person you meet, every new situation you observe is all fuel, Cameron. Muses are notoriously hungry, but if you feed them they will shower you with inspiration."

"Thank you, Grandmother."

Father stared for a moment. "That's the most ridiculous thing I've ever heard. Why, I wrote as a young man. Certainly, I never had anything published—"

"They do say certain talents are known to skip a generation, dear," Mother said pleasantly.

"Regardless, I had no need for a muse." Father snorted.

"Which explains a great deal," Grandmother said under her breath.

"Thank you, Mother."

"Don't take that tone with me, Jonathon. I am an old lady and I deserve respect if nothing else." Grandmother pinned him with a firm gaze. "I'm not saying anything you don't already know. Although I will say, your writing was better than your father's poetry." She shuddered. "Sentiment is not the same thing as good, although he did try, the dear man. And while you may have been a dreadful writer, you have been an excellent duke. The family is as sound as the Bank of England itself, thanks to your leadership, in terms of its finances and reputation. And I am extraordinarily proud of you."

Father's mouth dropped open and a stunned

look crossed his face. "I don't think I have ever heard you say that before."

"Don't be absurd, Jonathon." She picked up her sherry. "I say it all the time."

"Well, that's that then," Mother said brightly, and started to rise, her sons getting to their feet as well. "I think we should all retire to the—"

"Sit down all of you, I am not finished." Father glared and they all sat back down. "I have yet to make my point."

"I thought he made any number of points," Grace said in an aside to Simon beside her.

"Exactly what I hoped to avoid." Mother sighed. "Very well then, go on."

"I intend to," Father said sharply, then turned to Cam. "Regardless of the fact that you are writing under a different name, this reporting of yours for that disreputable rag of a newspaper is scandalous and embarrassing and puts this family in the poorest of lights." Father's tone hardened. "You will resign your position at once."

Mother groaned. "Jonathon!"

Cam braced himself. This was it then. "No, Father. I'm afraid I can't—I *won't*—do anything of the sort." He shook his head. "I still have a great deal to learn. With every word I write I am honing my craft. There is no better teacher than experience."

"I believe you've said that on more than one occasion, Father," Spencer pointed out.

44

"Well, on this particular occasion, apparently I am wrong."

Cam rose to his feet. "I am sorry, Father, but I am twenty-seven years of age. You have long bemoaned the fact that I was doing little more than drifting through my life. Now I have found my calling, my passion as it were, and there will indeed come a time when I give up my position and turn to the writing of novels, but not yet. If you cannot accept that"—Cam met his father's gaze directly and squared his shoulders—"then I fear we are at an impasse."

"Oh, sit down, Cameron, and stop being overly dramatic." Father cast an annoyed glance at his wife. "He gets that from you, you know."

"He gets all sorts of things from me," she said sharply. "But he gets his tendency to overact from you. Now, sit down, Cameron."

Cam sat.

"Obviously, I am not pleased, but neither am I surprised by your refusal. Therefore I have considered what my response would be should you decide to ignore my wishes."

"Sounded more like a command to me," Simon murmured.

"I am not about to disown you or exile you from the family or cut you off without a penny," Father said. "While four sons may seem like a great many to those who have none, I am not going to toss one aside for choosing his own path, even if I disagree with said path." He paused. "I was not aware that you seem to have something of a plan for your life in place. In truth I had feared this was yet another thing you would try your hand at and then abandon."

"I have at last found what I want to do with my life," Cam said. "It is not a passing fancy."

Father nodded. "Am I to take from what you've said that you do not intend to pursue this journalistic endeavor forever?"

"For a while but not forever," Cam said cautiously.

"And then you intend to write books?"

Cam nodded. "I do."

"And I shall be the first to purchase the first edition of your first book." Thad studied him curiously. "Do you intend to be the next Charles Dickens then?"

"Are you going to write about orphans and poverty and war with heroes or heroines who die tragically in the end?" Grace asked.

"No." Cam shook his head. "If I have learned nothing else thus far, my eyes have been opened to the fact that the world is often a dire and dreadful place beyond the gates of Roxborough Hall or the walls of fine London houses. I think what people need in this world, and what I want to do, is give them a respite from their daily troubles. I didn't know this when I began, but now I realize I want to write about the oddities and absurdities of life. I want to make people laugh or at least bring a smile to their faces, if only for as long as it takes to read a book. No, I do not intend to follow in the footsteps of Dickens, although I deeply admire his work." He drew a deep breath. "I would much rather follow in the footsteps of Mark Twain."

"You want to be a humorist?" Surprise sounded in Simon's voice. "Although I should have known. I've always found you most amusing."

"Mr. Twain's humor is delightful, but he is American and we have such excellent English writers," Grace said. "Some of them extremely amusing. Why, Shakespeare wrote a number of fine comedies."

"I don't think he wishes to be Shakespeare, Grace," Thad said with a smile.

"I like him. Twain that is." Spencer nodded. "A great deal, really."

"As do I." Father studied Cam for a long moment, a slight smile lifting the corners of his lips. "But then you knew that, didn't you?"

"Well, yes." Cam distinctly recalled his father attending a banquet for the American during his visit to England when Cam was a boy.

"You do realize if you had confided in me as to your plans in the beginning, we could have avoided all this unpleasantness."

Cam shifted uneasily in his chair. "Possibly."

"I am still not happy with your position with

the *Messenger*. If it were the *Times* perhaps but . . ." Father considered him for a long moment. "I shall make you a bargain, Cameron." Father leaned toward him. "You want to write books, then write me a book. A book that proves to me this is indeed your future and not another lark you have embarked upon. I have been impressed with your writing thus far, but a brief article where the facts are laid out before you is a far cry from a work of fiction. Prove to me this is your passion. I shall give you, what?" He glanced at his mother. "A month?"

"At least two I would think." Grandmother cast Cam an apologetic glance. "It doesn't have to be long, you know."

"And if I can't?" Cam asked.

"If you can't, you resign your position at the *Messenger*." Father's smile was decidedly smug.

"I see." Cam thought for a moment. He had not yet tried to write a book. In truth, the very thought was daunting. Still, there was no reason why he couldn't. And if he didn't believe in himself, how could he expect anyone else, especially his father, to? "And when I do?"

Father grinned. "*If* you do, I shall not say another disparaging word about the *Messenger*, nor shall I insist you resign. Indeed, I shall willingly support your efforts in whatever way you wish."

"Nor shall you throw this in his face should the rest of the world discover Cameron Fairchild is really Cameron Effington, son of the Duke of Roxborough," Mother added. "Should his work —how did you put it? ah yes—cast this family in the poorest of lights, bringing embarrassment and humiliation down upon us all."

Father hesitated, then sighed. "I will agree to that."

"Very well then, Father." Cam adopted his most confident tone. "You have yourself a wager."

"Oh, I'm willing to wager on that myself." Simon grinned.

"Simon Effington, you will not wager against your brother." Mother huffed.

"I would never do that, Mother. Besides, I think he'll pull it off." Simon chuckled. "But I am willing to bet Father can't keep up his end of the bargain."

"Really?" Father's brow rose. "And you are willing to put up your own money to back that up?"

"I'd be willing to wager, oh, ten pounds on it." A wicked gleam shone in Simon's eyes.

"As am I," Thad added.

"I'm in." Spencer nodded.

"What about you, Grace?" Father glanced at his daughter. "Are you too so lacking in faith as to your father's ability to abide by his word?"

"Oh, Father, I would never say such a thing."

Grace scoffed, then grinned. "But it does seem too good an opportunity to pass up."

Grandmother nodded. "My thoughts exactly."

"You too, Mother?"

Grandmother shrugged.

"What about you, Fiona?" The duke looked at his wife. "Are you going to join the rest of my traitorous family?"

"Of course not, dear. I said I would not take sides. Besides"—Mother smiled—"I am already planning to do something completely frivolous with the money you shall collect from our children."

"Thank you." Father shook his head in a resigned manner. "It's so gratifying to know I have the confidence of my family."

Cam glanced around the table and smiled. "That it is, Father, that it is."

It was indeed good to know his family had faith in him even if their confidence might exceed his own.

Because, while any number of ideas were constantly simmering in his head, at the moment, he had absolutely no idea what he would write about.

. . . and it does seem to me there are any number of interesting people in the world that I shall never be allowed to meet as they do not fit in the strict confines of what Mother so adamantly calls our sort of people. I should very much like to forge a friendship with someone unexpected. Someone whose social position is different than my own. Mother would be horrified by the very thought, of course, and no doubt she would disagree, but I do think such a friendship would be of more benefit to me than to the other party. Someday perhaps . . .

from the journal of Miss Lucinda Merryweather, 1804

Chapter Two

"I am curious, Miss West." Lucy sipped her tea and studied her new companion over the rim of her cup. The woman was no more than a few years older than Lucy herself. It was a delightful relief. "Where do you stand on the subject of adventures?"

"Adventures?" Miss West considered the question for a moment. "I suspect it would very much depend on the adventure in question."

"Excellent answer." Lucy grinned. "I think we will get on quite well together."

Miss Clara West had arrived at Jackson's family's house in London this morning and Lucy hadn't had time to be little more than introduced to the woman in the flurry of activity surrounding the departure of Jackson and his parents. They planned to travel together on the continent, at least for a while. Jackson had never seen anything of Europe; indeed he had never stepped foot off American soil at all until he had come to England. Their plans were uncertain after that, but he and his father had talked of going on to Turkey or Persia, Arabia or Egypt. Jackson's father, Colonel Channing, had traveled much of the world and was eager to show strange and wondrous sights in exotic and exciting locales to his wife and son. It was to be quite an adventure, although Lucy did wonder how Mrs. Channing would bear up under it all as she had never seemed particularly prone to adventure.

Jackson's aunt and uncle, Lord and Lady Briston, departed earlier today as well. They were to accompany Jackson's cousin, Lady Hargate, and her fiancé, Mr. Russell, to New York to meet the American's family. Another of Jackson's cousins, Mrs. Elliott, and her husband had left London yesterday for a long-delayed honeymoon. Which meant, of Jackson's newfound family, the only close relative remaining in London was the fascinating Beryl, Lady Dunwell.

If things hadn't been so hectic this morning, when Jackson had briefly met Miss West, he might well have reconsidered this choice for Lucy's companion. While Jackson had arranged for the hiring of Miss West, he had never met her in person. It was clear from the look on his face that he was expecting a much older lady with a dour manner and stern disposition and not a tall, slender blonde with striking blue eyes and an elegant manner. It was obvious as well that he thought she was entirely too pretty to be a companion. But she had come with excellent references from Lady Stillwell, the wife of Mr. Elliott's cousin. Regardless of how she came to be hired, Lucy had been adamant that her companion would be her responsibility, not

Jackson's, and she would provide the woman's salary. She had no intention of being accompanied by a spy paid for by the man she was no longer going to marry. He had reluctantly agreed, but then Lucy had given him no choice.

"Now then." Lucy cast Miss West her brightest smile. "Where do you suggest we begin?"

"Begin?" Caution sounded in Miss West's voice. "I'm not sure what you mean."

"It's simply that I've never had a companion before." She leaned close in a confidential manner. "Frankly, I've never really been let out of anyone's sight before. Not that my behavior has warranted watching, mind you." She straightened. "Which means I have no idea what we do now."

"Oh dear. This is awkward, Miss Merryweather." Miss West placed her cup on the table and folded her hands in her lap. "You see, I've never been a companion before."

Lucy stared for a moment, then grinned. "Then this is perfect. Absolutely perfect."

Miss West's brow rose. "Is it?"

"Oh, without question. You have no particular expectations and neither do I. I feared Jackson, Mr. Channing, would engage someone more in the manner of a watchdog than a companion, which wouldn't have suited my purposes at all. I should have been forced to discharge you as soon as I was confident he was safely out of the country. Now we can forge our relationship as we see fit. Without definition or any particular rules."

"Can we?" Miss West said cautiously.

"We most certainly can." Lucy beamed. "And to start with, I insist you call me Lucy. We shall be spending a great deal of time together and I see no reason why we should waste any of it with Miss Merryweather this and Miss Merryweather that. It is a mouthful, you know. And I will call you Clara, if that's acceptable to you."

Clara nodded, something of a stunned look on her face.

"Wonderful. We will be great friends. Indeed, it will be just like having a sister. We do somewhat resemble each other. Why, our hair and eyes are very nearly the same color, although you are so delightfully tall and I am well"—she wrinkled her nose—"not. Although I did always hope to be tall and elegant. But when you are short and blond, you are usually described as pert or cute. People tend to look at you in the same way they look at a puppy, amusing, perhaps, but not a creature you would expect much of." She shrugged. "Anyway, where was I?"

"I'm not sure." Clara eyed Lucy cautiously.

"Ah yes. I was saying we'll definitely be friends, I'm certain of that. I daresay I will need a friend. Particularly one I can share confidences and secrets with. I suppose that's the only real, well, requirement if you will, that I have for you. I need you to keep my confidences, whatever they may be. I would like your promise to keep my secrets."

"Yes, well, of course." Clara's brow furrowed. "Do you have many secrets?"

"Not yet, but I intend to," Lucy said firmly. "I have any number of friends at home, but I have never had a truly good friend before to tell my secrets to. Nor do I have a sister, but I have always wanted one." She knew she was talking entirely too fast, but she had the tendency to do that when she was excited, in spite of her mother's best efforts to curb her enthusiasm. Babbling, Mother called it. But Mother wasn't here and there was nothing more exhilarating than the feeling of freedom that had filled her the moment the doors had closed behind Jackson and his family. "I have brothers, four of them. They're all quite tall and as charming as they are handsome. But I am the youngest in the family and the only girl, and they refuse to accept that I am no longer a child. Do you have family, Clara?"

"No." She shook her head. "My mother died when I was very young and my father passed away a number of years ago. I lost my only brother as well a few years ago."

"I am so sorry for your loss." Lucy cast her a sympathetic look. "I'm not sure what I would do without my family, although they can be most annoying, and I am delighted that, at least for now, I do not have them hovering over me. My brothers are extremely protective, and they and my parents would have some sort of apoplectic fit if they realized Mr. Channing's mother was no longer accompanying me."

"Shouldn't you tell them?" Clara said slowly.

"Oh, I have, more or less. I did write to them." She waved off the question. "Admittedly, I might have been extremely vague and they might not have understood completely." She smiled in an overly innocent manner.

Clara stared.

"You see, there are things I wish to do and I can't do them under the watchful eyes of my family. Between my parents and my brothers and Jackson, of course, I have never really had the opportunity to do anything the least bit, oh, unexpected. I have never had a chance to be even a little independent. My life was entirely planned out for me and I have always been too well behaved to protest. For years it was assumed that Jackson and I would marry. And now Jackson has fallen in love with someone else and gone off to find his own adventures and I . . ." Once again the blissful sense of liberty washed through her. "I am free."

"I gather you are not particularly upset that you and Mr. Channing are not going to wed."

"Goodness, no, not in the least. In fact, Jackson and I both, through the years, found all sorts of very sound reasons to postpone an official engagement, which no one ever seemed to mind really, although admittedly, in the last year or two, my mother has been getting the tiniest bit cranky about it. After all, I am nearly twenty-four and most of the women I know who are my age have already wed and are busy producing one off-spring after another. In my mother's eyes I am perilously close to being a spinster, which distresses her but doesn't bother me at all."

"Don't you wish to marry?"

"Certainly someday, but I see no need now to rush into anything that will last the rest of my life. No." Lucy shook her head. "I am relieved for both of us and happy for Jackson that he has found someone he truly cares for even if, at the moment, they are not together. But they will be eventually. I don't doubt that for a moment. It's obviously true love and nothing can deny that, you know."

"And you were not in love with him?"

"Oh, I love Jackson and I always will. But more in the manner of a friend or a brother, and not at all in the way I think one should love the man one intends to spend the rest of one's life with." She paused. "It took me a long time to realize that, far longer than it should have, really. I suppose I always suspected it somewhere in the back of my mind, or perhaps my heart. Probably why I never insisted on an official engagement. But I have always been a dutiful daughter and, as I said, I have always done exactly what was expected of me. Marrying Jackson was what was expected. I consider myself quite lucky that fate took a hand and pointed us both in entirely different directions." She thought for a moment. "Jackson is the only man who has ever kissed me, and it was always very nice, but it should be more than merely nice, don't you agree?"

"I would think so."

"I truly believe when the right man kisses me I shall know he is the right man. Or at least I hope I will know."

"One can't always count on that." Clara chose her words with care. "I was once engaged to a man I believed was the right man, but he turned out to be a disreputable scoundrel and I was well rid of him."

"How dreadful." Lucy studied the other woman curiously. She had never known anyone who had been engaged to a scoundrel before. Her life had certainly been sheltered up to now. "Did he break your heart? Were you in love with him?"

"I fancied I was," Clara said slowly. "But when I discovered his true nature, I was more angry than hurt." She smiled in a rueful manner. "So no, he did not break my heart. But he did make it far wiser."

"I'm glad for you then. I'm afraid Jackson's heart is a bit cracked at the moment, but as I said, I am certain it will turn out happily in the end.

Still, it might take some time." Lucy sighed. "The lady in question is an independent woman and Jackson can be extremely stubborn. I quite admire that. Oh, not being stubborn, but a woman being independent. You appear to me to be an independent woman, Clara. Are you?"

Clara bit back a smile. "I'm not entirely sure what you mean by an independent woman, and I haven't a clue why you think I am."

"Well, for one thing, your bearing is extremely confident and not the least bit subservient. And from your manner it's obvious you are intelligent and educated. Your clothing is of good quality and not at all worn. It strikes me that you might not particularly need this position." At once the answer hit her and she gasped. "Good Lord, unless you have recently fallen upon hard times? Oh dear, I should have suspected as much. I am so sorry. I shouldn't have—"

Clara laughed. "No, I have not fallen upon hard times. And admittedly, I do not actually need this position. My finances are really quite sound. But there are few positions available for women that do not involve the care of children or the teaching of them, which I do not find at all appealing. I thought it might be rather interesting to be the companion of a young American. I am twenty-nine years of age and the possibility of marriage grows slimmer every day. I'd much prefer to be doing something with my life rather than sitting around waiting for some gentleman to decide to make me his wife. That does not suit me at all."

"See?" Lucy beamed. "I knew you were an independent woman."

"I have never really considered myself in that manner but I suppose I am, at that."

"Oh, we shall get along famously, Clara. I am so delighted that you are here. You can't imagine the type of companion I expected Jackson would find for me." She shuddered at the very thought.

"A watchdog you could discharge the moment Mr. Channing was safely out of the country," Clara said wryly.

"Exactly." Lucy grinned. "I'm so glad you understand. I have no intentions of allowing anyone to tell me what I may or may not do. Not anymore," she said firmly. "I am an adult, Clara, even if no one has realized that. I have my own resources, my own ambitions as it were, and I am much more intelligent than people, even my family, assume as well, but then no one suspects pert may well hide a fairly clever mind."

"I suppose not."

"Believe me, no one expects blond curls and a cheery disposition to conceal anything other than fluff and nonsense and frivolity. Which has actually served me well in the past. Now, how-ever, I am at a crossroads in my life and I find it all quite exciting. Even the fact that I don't entirely know what will happen next is exhilarating, although I do have something of a plan. But we will get to that later." Lucy cast the other woman her brightest smile. "I should apologize. I have gone on and on and scarcely given you a moment to get a word in. Surely you have some questions for me. About the position or, well, something?"

"Well . . ." Clara thought for a moment. "I was told the position was not permanent, no more than a few months at the most. Is that because you plan to return to your own country?"

"I don't plan on it, but I'm afraid that's what's going to happen. At some point my family will realize I am here alone and someone will be sent to drag me home. I have no idea how much time I have, but I should have at least six or eight weeks and hopefully longer." She drew her brows together. "I'm not sure what will happen then. I've never defied my family's wishes before and I'm not certain I have the courage to do so now. I suppose it all depends on what happens between now and then."

"You are at a crossroads, after all."

"I am indeed. Now I can get on with it. I've agreed to all of Jackson's terms in exchange for his not contacting my family." She ticked the points off on her finger. "I have engaged a companion. I promised to limit my activities to England. And I agreed to call on his cousin regularly."

Clara's brow rose. "A watchdog?"

"Not according to everything I've heard." Lucy snorted back a laugh. "In fact, I'm looking forward to knowing her better. I think she, of anyone in Jackson's family, might actually understand."

Clara nodded. "Your desire for independence."

"Yes, that and"—Lucy paused—"other things."

"Which does bring me to my next question. You said a watchdog would not suit your purposes at all. That, coupled with your question about my view of adventures and your saying you had a plan of sorts and you can now get on with it . . ." Clara's eyes narrowed. "What are you up to, Miss Merryweather?"

"Lucy," she said firmly.

"Very well then, Lucy." Clara paused. "Trust, you know, has to go both ways."

"Without a doubt," Lucy said staunchly. "I shall carry your secrets to the grave."

"And I have given you my word that I will keep yours. If we are indeed going to trust one another, then perhaps you should tell me exactly what you are planning."

Lucy hadn't intended to tell her new companion her plans. Of course, she had intended to get rid of her at the first opportunity. But she hadn't expected Clara. And certainly hadn't expected to like her. Possibly she sensed a kindred spirit in the older woman, of independence perhaps, although it was more probable that Lucy had taken an immediate liking to Clara because she was so clearly not the kind of companion Jackson had had in mind.

Why not tell her? If she had misjudged Clara, it was best to know that now. Besides, Clara might be a great deal of help.

"All right." Lucy nodded firmly. "Then there's something I should show you. I need to fetch it from my room." Lucy stood and headed toward her room. "It will only take a moment."

Lucy returned quickly, resumed her seat, and drew a deep breath.

"I too am financially stable, Clara. More than stable, really. I have a rather sizable fortune. A few years ago I received an inheritance from my Great-aunt Lucinda. I was named after her, although I've never been particularly fond of the name Lucinda." Lucy wrinkled her nose. "But Lucy does seem to suit me. At any rate, I received my inheritance on my twenty-first birthday. It was accompanied by, oh, a journal of sorts written by my great-aunt. It's not a usual type of journal. It doesn't contain passages about her day-to-day life or poorly written poetry or anything of that nature that young girls tend to write when they are revealing their innermost thoughts. What it really is, is a list of those things she wanted to do in her life. Adventures, she called them." Lucy handed the book to Clara. "Each page is titled with a different adventure and has a few paragraphs of explanation."

"Adventures?" Clara paged through the book.

"She was very young when she wrote them. Judging by the dates of the entries, my great-aunt made this list when she was between fifteen and eighteen years of age. She married my great-uncle when she was eighteen and then obviously set the book aside. And with it, those things she wanted to do. As you can see, most of them are extremely innocent. Some are a bit foolish. Some might even be called scandalous or perhaps a little improper."

"Yes, I can see that," Clara said under her breath, still turning the pages. "She does mention kisses and romantic interludes."

"The letter that accompanied the journal said that while it had started as a list of things she wished to do, ultimately it became a book of her regrets. Of things she never managed to accomplish."

"I see," Clara murmured, her gaze still on the journal.

"I thought, when I received the book, that it was frightfully sad. To get to the end of one's life, you know, and have things one wanted to do, even things that are silly or easily accomplished, and not have managed to do them, well, I thought it was a terrible shame. But at that time there was nothing I could do about it. I was expected to marry Jackson, after all. And while he really is a good man, until recently, he has never been particularly, oh, imaginative. So, I set the book aside even though Great-aunt Lucinda's regrets have lingered in the back of my mind." Lucy paused. "When I was very young, I had a list of my own—although my list was completely absurd, terribly far-fetched, and for the most part rather ridiculous."

Clara glanced up at her. "Not things easily accomplished then?"

"I wouldn't think so. Being the lady captain of a pirate ship or leading an expedition to find lost treasure in the jungles of the Amazon or traveling through the heavens on a comet are things that can only be accomplished between the pages of a novel of adventure rather than real life."

Clara laughed. "You do have a point there."

"Still, I have always found the idea of adventure, even mild adventure, to be extremely exciting. I have never had even the tiniest adventure at all." Lucy reached forward and tapped the book with her finger. "These adventures of my great-aunt's are quite tame compared with those I longed for in my youth, but unlike mine, hers are eminently achievable."

"And?"

"And since I have absolutely no idea what I wish to do with my newfound freedom, with my life, and no ideas about adventures of my own that aren't completely absurd, I intend to honor my great-aunt's life by doing those things she never did. I suppose if I were to make my own list now, it would simply be to accomplish something in my life. To have some sort of purpose." Lucy shook her head. "I keep thinking how dreadful it would be to reach the end of your days with so much undone."

"But when it comes right down to it"—Clara snapped the journal closed—"these are not your adventures. Nor are they your regrets."

"No, but if I don't accomplish them, they will be."

Clara studied her for a long moment. "You aren't really a puppy, are you?"

"Good Lord." Lucy laughed. "I certainly hope not."

Clara glanced back at the book in her hand. "This is why you didn't want a watchdog."

Lucy nodded.

"And why you intended to discharge a companion as soon as possible."

Again Lucy nodded.

"And . . ." Clara drew the word out slowly. "Why you were so pleased that I had never been a companion before."

"Exactly. A real companion, or rather, an experienced companion might well be hesitant to wholeheartedly support my quest, which I do think will be an adventure in itself."

"That is a possibility with a *real* companion."

"I would think so." Lucy grimaced. "I didn't really plan this. I'm still not sure why I brought

Great-aunt Lucinda's book along to England in the first place, but I'm fairly sure it all has to do with fate. Life is unfolding in remarkable and completely unexpected ways. Ways that I find delightful.

"You see, until I came to England, in spite of the fact that I told Jackson before he left New York that he was under no obligation to me, there was still the possibility that we might end up together. I know that's what his mother had hoped and mine expected." That she was not going to marry Jackson was another fact she had been distinctly vague about in her letter home. "As I said, I have never gone against my family's wishes. Jackson and I might well have continued to postpone our engagement until we were both too old to care."

"I very much doubt that. In spite of what you say, you don't strike me as the kind of young woman who would marry a man she didn't wish to wed."

"Thank you, Clara." Lucy smiled. "That may well be the nicest thing anyone has ever said to me."

"So this desire of yours to make up for your great-aunt's regrets is relatively new." Clara handed the book back to her.

"Yes and no." Lucy's gaze drifted to the book in her hand and her voice softened. "I have wanted to do this from the very moment I read these pages. But my life was all laid out for me and I knew it was impossible, so I did nothing about it. Looking back, I see my life as nothing more than drifting from one expectation to the next. But now, I am free to do as I please and I fully intend to do exactly that." Lucy looked up and met the other woman's gaze directly. "With your help, I hope."

Clara paused, then nodded. "I don't see why not." She turned her attention back to the journal. "As you said, some of these are really quite simple. Why do you think she never managed any of them?"

"It was a different time, of course. And she did marry at eighteen, which didn't seem terribly young when I was eighteen but now seems extremely young. After that, her life was probably too busy to concern herself with things a husband would most likely not understand or allow." She thought for a moment. "Through the course of her life, she endured two wars on American soil. I suspect when one's life is filled with, well, living, the desires of one's younger days are simply forgotten." Lucy paused and held her breath. "You will help me, won't you?"

"As I am in your employ, and I am not a *real* companion—"

Lucy winced.

"I daresay I can do nothing else. Besides . . ." Clara smiled. "I find I have to agree with you. I too do not wish to reach the end of my life with regrets. And I quite like the idea that, should I leave a journal filled with regrets, some well-meaning young woman would want to make up for them."

"Wonderful." Lucy grinned. "But I knew it the moment we started talking. Why, I already feel that we have known each other forever. Odd, isn't it?"

"You're not exactly reticent to reveal information about yourself." Clara shook her head in obvious amazement. "And I've never met anyone who has learned so much about me in such a short span of time."

Lucy laughed.

"However." Clara's expression sobered. "While ours might not be the usual sort of relationship between a companion and her employer, I do feel there are some duties that are inherent in the position."

Lucy frowned. "And they are?"

"I don't intend to be your watchdog, but part of my responsibility should be to act as chaperone. Which really is as much a question of safety and appearances as anything else."

Lucy nodded. "Of course."

"I suspect things in England are done far differently than they are in America. I understand, well, the rules here—for lack of a better word—and you do not. We can be quite stodgy, especially about public behavior. As your companion, as your *friend,* I cannot allow you to do anything that might cause you irrevocable harm, to your reputation or your person. If I judge that to be the case, I will do all in my power to stop you, even if it results in my dismissal. I need you to trust that, in that event, I am only acting in your best interest."

"As any good friend would." Lucy smiled. "Thank you, Clara."

"Furthermore, I need your assurance that you will heed my guidance in such situations."

Lucy hesitated.

"If you cannot agree to that, then I cannot, in good conscience, remain in your employ." Clara's tone softened. "And I would very much regret that as I do think you are indeed embarking upon an adventure and it would be my very great honor to accompany you."

Clara's condition did make sense. In her excitement Lucy might well be plunging ahead too hastily. After all, while the idea of accomplishing those things her great-aunt wanted to do had been in the back of her head for years, she'd never considered exactly how to go about it. Even now she had nothing specific in mind. Without someone to temper her enthusiasm, she could get into all kinds of difficulties. For one thing, she inevitably thought well of people until they proved her wrong. And while she did consider herself sensible and not the least bit impulsive, she had long had the tendency to reach unwarranted conclusions.

"I can agree to that."

"Excellent." Clara raised a brow. "I assume you wish to get started immediately?"

"Absolutely, especially as I have no idea how much time I really have." Lucy opened the journal. "Where do you think we should begin?"

"I don't think we should go in order of your great-aunt's list." Clara thought for a moment. "Rather we might start with those things most easily accomplished."

"I have already copied her regrets onto my own list—regrets set to rights. I intend to check them off as I accomplish them. I'm not silly enough to think I can do everything she hoped to do but I do intend to complete as many as possible."

"It seems to me you have already achieved one of your aunt's desires." Clara refilled both their cups from the teapot and handed Lucy hers. "You have already made an unexpected friend."

Lucy laughed and raised her cup to her new companion. "Indeed, I have. It's a most promising beginning."

Poor dear Jackson. He hadn't found her a watchdog but an independent woman, a new friend, a confidante, and what Lucy was certain he never expected, a coconspirator.

Regrets Set to Rights

Make an unexpected friend.

Chapter Three

"Come, now, Phineas, surely you have something I can use?" Cam stared hopefully at his old friend. "Something I can write for the *Messenger* as well as expand for a book."

"Nothing I can think of. Besides . . ." Phineas Chapman leaned back in the chair behind his new desk. A desk that was half the size of his previous one, necessitated by the fact that there was now yet another desk in the corner of the front room of his flat, the room that served as his main living quarters, library, and office. "You know full well my reputation rests on my discretion."

"I'm not asking you to tell me anything about an actual client." Cam scoffed. "I would never wish to jeopardize your business." He leaned toward his friend and lowered his voice. "But you and I both know you hear all sorts of things that have nothing to do with whoever is paying your fee at the moment."

"Which has served you well in the past."

"And I am most grateful." This wasn't the first time Cam had turned to Phineas for an idea.

Although Phineas was a few years older, the two men had been fast friends since their school days. Both were the youngest children of prominent families, which was perhaps what drew them together in the first place. Phineas too had had a period of trying to find his place in the world. He had flirted for a time with a life of scholarly pursuit and, even though he was unquestionably the most intelligent man Cam had ever met, he found the life of an academic too sedate and dull for him. Quite by accident, he had turned his brilliance to investigation, to the ferreting out of secrets or the locating of that which was missing, be it a person or an item of value. Phineas's reputation was such that he was now the investigator much of society turned to when time was short and discretion was called for.

"I know." The corners of Phineas's mouth curved upward slightly in the superior smile that was as much a part of him as his dark hair and sharp green eyes. "But I fear nothing of interest comes to mind at the moment, old man. You're the writer. You think of something."

"If I could think of something, I wouldn't be here asking you." Cam pushed himself up from the upholstered wing chair, one of two that sat before Phineas's desk. "I am trying. While I have any number of ideas, none of them are developed enough to be of any use. And I don't have time to waste on idle thought."

"No, we wouldn't want that," Phineas murmured.

Cam clasped his hands behind his back and

paced the room. "One can't just pluck an idea out of the air, you know. It needs to simmer as it were, in the back of your mind."

"Until it blossoms into literary brilliance?"

"Something like that." He resumed pacing. "I haven't the time to fabricate a story completely from nothing. All I need is a fact or two that I can build a work of fiction from. Kindling as it were. Something I can nurture and . . ." Cam paused in midstep and looked back at the chair he'd been sitting in. His gaze slid to its mate. "Correct me if I'm wrong, but weren't those chairs mismatched and extremely worn the last time I was here? And hadn't the leg on one been replaced with a stack of books?"

Phineas heaved a resigned sigh. "They're new."

"You're not overly fond of new," Cam said slowly, glancing around the room and wondering that he hadn't noticed the changes upon his arrival. But then he'd had other things on his mind.

It had been no more than a few weeks since Cam's last visit, but he now noted a startling change in Phineas's sanctuary beyond the replacement of the decrepit wing chairs. The walls were still covered by floor-to-ceiling shelves, but while they were usually crammed to overflowing with books and papers and anything Phineas thought of interest to himself or to an investigation, all the shelves were now tidy and well organized.

The shabby, faded velvet drapes of a nondescript hue that had long hung on the tall windows at the front end of the room had been replaced with fabric of a rich wine color. The rug on the floor was either new or had been thoroughly cleaned. Regardless, it did not look the same. Indeed, there was much more floor to be seen, which in and of itself was shocking as Phineas's reading materials, research, and collections of whatever struck his fancy, along with everything else he happened upon, were usually in disorganized drifts piled here and there. In spite of the fact that Phineas had a woman, a Mrs. Wiggins, who came in daily to clean and cook, she was forbidden to touch anything in this area. The room had always looked to be exactly what it was—the domain of an unencumbered bachelor who was more concerned with comfort than appearance. The very fact that Cam was now able to pace without dodging constant impediments should have signaled something out of the ordinary had taken place, although Cam was too caught up in his own problems to notice. At once the answer struck him. "And where is the lovely and charming Miss West today?"

"You mean the meddlesome, annoying, persistent creature I have been so foolish as to allow into my life?" Phineas snorted. "I've gotten rid of her, but only for the moment."

"She doesn't strike me as either meddlesome or

annoying. And persistence can be something of a virtue."

"One would think," Phineas muttered.

"One would also think persistence is a good quality to have in a partner."

"She's not my partner," Phineas said a bit quicker and sharper than was necessary. "She is more in the manner of, oh, an employee, I would say."

"An employee who has invested in your business, who is not paid unless you are, and receives a percentage of your fees rather than a specific salary sounds very much like a partner to me."

"I'm still not sure how that came about," Phineas said under his breath.

"Would you like me to remind you?"

"As the fault can be placed entirely at your feet, that's neither necessary nor desired."

Cam bit back a grin. He had been looking into a story about an alleged haunting and had met Miss West, a friend of the owner of the building in question. At Cam's suggestion she had then engaged Phineas's services. While the two strong-willed individuals had clashed imme-diately, they had also found a commonality of purpose and an odd meshing of their intellects. In fact, they had worked surprisingly well together. Phineas said Miss West had one of the finest minds he'd ever encountered—male or female.

The rest of her, Cam had pointed out, was every bit as impressive as her mind. A detail that Phineas appeared to ignore.

Cam wasn't entirely sure what had transpired between them, but the next time he visited his old friend, he found Phineas's enormous, beloved, battered desk had been replaced by something more in proportion with the room, a second desk installed, and Miss Clara West diligently examining and reexamining Phineas's haphazard records. She was apparently quite good with figures. That was several months ago, and it seemed the lovely and clever Miss West had proven helpful to Phineas on every investigation he'd undertaken since then. He may deny that the woman was his partner all he wished, but the simple fact of the matter was that they made an excellent team. And Phineas knew it.

Now it appeared she had been setting to rights more than his receipts and records but this room and possibly the rest of his life as well. Interesting, as Phineas did not like change, and one did have to wonder why he was permitting it. In spite of his complaints about Miss West, if he didn't want her around, she wouldn't be. His old friend might well be smitten with the lovely blonde but, as Cam had never seen Phineas smitten with any woman, it was hard to tell. He would wager Phineas had no idea either.

"On a case, is she?"

"Not exactly." Phineas heaved a resigned sigh. "I was recently contacted by a client I have worked for in the past who wanted to hire me to keep a watch on an unmarried American heiress on her own here in London. Surveillance is one thing, but this was something else altogether. I am not a nursemaid nor do I have any intention of becoming one. However, the lady who approached me has been an excellent client in the past and has recommended my services on more than one occasion."

Cam grinned. "So you didn't want to offend her by refusing this commission."

"And, as I am not an idiot, I didn't." Phineas smiled a slow, smug smile. "Nor did I accept it."

Cam raised a brow.

"My client had no interest in actually knowing the day-to-day activities of the American, she merely wanted to make certain the woman was kept from harm. I told her I would make a few inquiries to see if I could find someone willing to take the assignment."

"And?"

"And it might have slipped my mind because, as it happened, she was also charged with arranging for a companion. I told Miss West about it and . . ."

"And you've turned Miss West into a lady's companion?" Cam stared.

"Temporarily. The American is only expected to be in England for a few months. There is no one I know, and certainly no female, in whose hands she would be safer than Miss West's. She is a woman who can take care of herself." Phineas shuddered.

"Oh?" There was obviously much Cam didn't know about his old friend and his new partner.

Phineas ignored him. "It was Miss West's idea actually, and I did think it was brilliant."

"Because it removes her from your life?"

"Only briefly, but yes." Phineas drew a deep breath. "Do you smell that?"

"There was a vague hint of garlic in the hallway when I arrived, which I assumed was coming from another flat." Cam sniffed. "But no, I don't smell anything out of the ordinary."

"That, my friend, is the smell of freedom." Phineas smirked. "Freedom from female interference."

Cam retook his seat. "If you find her that unpleasant, I daresay you could sever your association, tell her her services are no longer needed."

"I didn't say she was unpleasant. Indeed, there are moments when she's quite palatable. She is impressively efficient and she does have an excellent mind, you know."

"Yes, you've mentioned that."

"She has proven to be most beneficial. She has

put all my records to rights, posted invoices to clients I had forgotten to bill, and she's been a surprisingly great help in every case I've had since she invaded my life. No." Phineas shook his head. "She is an asset I would be foolish to discard. However . . ." He smiled in satisfaction. "She began her employment with the American yesterday and I feel as if I am on holiday."

Cam chuckled. "For now."

"One doesn't need to be on holiday permanently. I would think that would be dreadfully dull after a time."

"Yes, I suppose."

"But for the moment, I shall revel in my newfound freedom and—" He straightened in his chair and stared at Cam. "That's it. That's your idea."

"A never-ending holiday?"

"Don't be absurd. I said that would be boring."

"Then—"

"Sometimes, I don't know what I see in you." Phineas rolled his gaze toward the ceiling. "I'm talking about the heiress. It's perfect for you. And the *Messenger* will love it. It will practically write itself."

"I don't think—"

"Come now, Effington. I can see the title now." Phineas waved in a grand gesture. "*The Absolutely True Adventures of a Runaway American Heiress in London.*"

"That's rather long." Cam drew his brows together. "You didn't say she had run away."

"That makes it more interesting, doesn't it?"

"Yes, I suppose it does."

"However, as far as I know, she hasn't. Run away, that is." Phineas shrugged. "But she certainly could have. It would explain why she's here in London alone."

"It would at that." Cam thought for a moment. Phineas had a good point. What was an American heiress doing on her own in London? It was unusual to say the least and well worth looking into. Perhaps this idea did have potential. "*Adventures* might not be the right word though. We don't know that she is having adventures."

"A wealthy unmarried American on her own in London? Surely just her presence here could be called an adventure." Phineas scoffed. "I know my imagination is already churning up any number of possible scenarios. First of all, one has to wonder why she is unmarried. It's my observation that wealth in a woman overcomes a great many other flaws, like age or appearance."

"Old and ugly is not what one usually looks for in the heroine of a story."

"Might I point out, you're trying to write a work of fiction as well as something for your paper. The *Messenger* has never been overly concerned with accuracy."

"There is that." While Cam did prefer not to outright lie, much could be done with implication and innuendo. He had long ago learned the difference between saying a crowd was comprised of nearly a hundred people and saying a crowd was not even a hundred strong. Both were correct but gave an entirely different picture of the proceedings. He ignored the tiny pang of conscience that jabbed him at moments like this, but then he did work for the *Messenger* and not the *Times* or the *Gazette*. Regardless, he was not going to fail at journalistic pursuits any more than he was going to fail at writing a book.

"I don't wish to use the word *Adventures* though," Cam said thoughtfully. "What about *The True Deeds of a*—"

"No, no. *True* is a mistake and I shouldn't have suggested it. Eliminating *True* leaves you a great deal of room for oh . . . creativity. *The Deeds of a Runaway American Heiress in London.*"

"*Daring Deeds*," Cam said. "Better yet—*Daring Exploits*. I like it but—"

"*The Daring Exploits of a Runaway Heiress.*" Phineas grinned. "You have to admit, that's perfect."

"It does have a nice ring to it. Still, we don't know that she's run away or that she's having exploits, daring or otherwise."

"You wanted an idea and I gave you one. Now it's up to you." Phineas's eyes narrowed slightly as they did when he had some sort of idea. "I know writing stories that are less than truthful for the *Messenger* bothers you."

"I have accustomed myself to the realities of my profession," Cam said wryly.

"But your paper also runs serials, doesn't it?"

Cam nodded. "They're extremely popular."

"Then write *The Daring Exploits of a Runaway Heiress* as a serial. As pure fiction." Phineas leaned over his desk and met Cam's gaze directly. "Don't even pretend that it's real. And use this American for your inspiration."

"My muse," Cam murmured. It was a good idea. He simply needed to convince Mr. Cadwallender of the merits of Cam's writing fiction. It would not be the first time he'd attempted to do so, but the publisher already employed several accomplished writers of fiction. "It might work."

"Might?" Phineas snorted. "It's brilliant and you bloody well know it." He grinned. "You may thank me later."

"Indeed I will. So . . ." Cam said slowly, "the only thing I need now is the name of this daring heiress."

Phineas laughed. "I can't tell you that."

"Of course you can. She's not your client."

"No, she's not. Still, it seems to me I've done enough. You should make some effort on your own."

"I intend to. Her name is just the beginning."

Once he had her name, he could locate her and observe her exploits or adventures or whatever she did that would provide inspiration.

"Besides"—Phineas shrugged—"I don't know her name. This is all Miss West's endeavor. I have nothing to do with it."

"Then perhaps I should ask Miss West—"

"You can ask her, but I'd wager you won't get any usable information. Miss West doesn't trust you."

Cam gasped. "Me? Why, I'm most trustworthy."

"Nonetheless, she is not an admirer of your work or your paper."

"She's made no secret of that." Indeed, Miss West's opinion of the *Messenger* was much like his father's.

"If she thinks you're looking for a story, she won't tell you anything. She has a very finely developed sense of honor for a woman." Phineas shook his head.

A sharp rap sounded at the door, followed immediately by the unmistakable sound of a key inserting in the lock.

"And she's back." Phineas rolled his eyes toward the ceiling.

"So much for your holiday."

"So much indeed," Phineas muttered, then lowered his voice in a confidential manner. "The means to pulling information from Miss West is not to directly ask her anything you wish to know. One never knows what one might learn in the course of casual conversation."

The door opened and Miss West stepped into the room. Both men got to their feet at once, Phineas with a show of some reluctance.

"Good day, Mr. Chapman." Her gaze slid to Cam. "And Mr. Fairchild. It's been some time since we've seen you." She nodded and proceeded to her desk.

"Far too long, Miss West." Cam smiled.

"The two of you look as if you are plotting something." Her gaze slid from Cam to Phineas. "Are you?"

"Why are you here?" Phineas asked.

She pulled off her gloves. "I am doing quite well, thank you. And you?"

"That's not what I asked." Phineas huffed. "I thought we had agreed that you would not be coming here while you are in the employ of the American."

"I don't really recall agreeing to that, nor is it something I would ever agree to." She sat down behind her desk. "However, I shall indeed be too busy accompanying Miss Merryweather to fulfill my usual responsibilities here."

Phineas slanted Cam a pointed look. It wasn't necessary. Cam had already noted the name.

"Are you enjoying your new position with the American?" Cam said politely.

"He told you about that, did he?"

"Naturally I inquired as to where you were," Cam said in a gallant manner. "Mr. Chapman told me you had taken a temporary position as a companion to an American." He paused. "I apologize if I have overstepped. If this position is confidential in nature or your activities a secret of some sort."

"On the contrary, Mr. Fairchild." She scoffed. "It's the most straightforward and least secretive venture I've been engaged in since joining Mr. Chapman."

Phineas blew an annoyed breath.

She ignored him. "I've only started today, so whether or not it will be enjoyable remains to be seen." She opened a drawer and peered down into it, rummaging through the contents. "She's a lovely woman and gives the impression of being somewhat scattered, although I suspect that hides an excellent mind. But, yes, Mr. Fairchild, I do expect it to be a most enjoyable employment. Rather like"—she raised her gaze to Phineas— "a holiday, I should think."

Cam choked back a laugh.

Phineas's eyes narrowed.

"It will be most refreshing to be around someone with a pleasant disposition for a change." She smiled and pulled a notebook from the drawer.

Phineas huffed. "I can be pleasant."

"I know you can be, you simply choose not to

be." She shut the drawer and rose to her feet. "I only came by to fetch my notebook. Now that I have, I'll be on my way."

"I assure you, I had no intention of reading it while you were gone," Phineas said. "It was perfectly safe in your desk." Phineas prided himself on never needing to write anything down. He never forgot anything he wished to remember.

"And now it is even safer." She moved toward the door.

"Might I inquire as to where you will be staying during your employment?" Cam said smoothly.

"Why, Mr. Fairchild?" She studied him coolly. "Do you intend to call on me?"

Cam hesitated, then nodded. "I had considered it."

She stared at him for a moment, then laughed. "You have not."

"He's smarter than he looks," Phineas said under his breath.

"One can only hope." She considered Cam thoughtfully. "As you have never before indicated so much as an iota of interest in me in a personal sense, I can only conclude that you have an ulterior motive in doing so now."

"Good God, Phineas." Cam glared at his friend. "What have you done to her?"

Phineas shrugged, but laughter glittered in his eyes.

"Which would further indicate to me your interest lies in my new employer." Her eyes narrowed. "Do you intend to make her the subject of one of your scandalous stories for your paper?"

Cam widened his eyes in surprise. "Not at all." He clasped his hand over his heart. "You wound me deeply, Miss West. I have long been meaning to ask if I could call on you."

Phineas snorted.

"My apologies, Mr. Fairchild. I should not have jumped to such a conclusion." In spite of her words, it was obvious from the look in her eyes that she neither believed nor trusted him. "I didn't mean to offend you."

"Think nothing of it, Miss West." Cam paused. "But perhaps, as your employer is a guest in our country, might I offer you my services as, oh, a guide of sorts?"

"Miss Merryweather has a very specific list of things she would like to see and do during her stay in England. So, while your offer is very kind, your services will not be necessary. I am well able to show a visitor the city I have lived in all of my life." She smiled in an overly sweet manner.

"The offer remains open should you decide I could be of some assistance." Cam tried to hide the note of eagerness in his voice.

"Thank you, Mr. Fairchild, but I very much

doubt that I will." She moved toward the door. "Good day. Good day, Mr. Chapman."

"Miss West," Phineas said abruptly.

She turned back. "Yes?"

"Do take care of yourself and try not to do anything foolish." His tone was brusque, but his gaze caught Miss West's and for a moment they stared at each other. Cam had absolutely no idea what it meant, but obviously these two had secrets Phineas had not shared with him.

Her gaze softened. "Thank you for your concern, Mr. Chapman. I shall be fine."

"See that you are." Phineas shuffled through the debris on his desk. "Wouldn't want to have to train someone else."

A slight smile played over her lips and she opened the door, then paused and looked back. "Oh, one more thing. Do either of you have any idea where I might be able to purchase a dog? And possibly a parrot?"

. . . and every time I ask her, the most determined, stubborn look appears on her face and she promptly changes the subject. I, however, think it's fascinating that my mother was born in another country and I should very much like to see England one day. I would also like to know why the mere mention of my mother's family is practically forbidden. It does seem to be a great mystery. I have always thought I would be excellent at solving mysteries, I'm very good at puzzles.

Solving a mystery should be on my list. A theft, perhaps of something quite valuable. Crown jewels or the like. Or, better yet, a murder. I should love to uncover a murderer and bring him to justice. Although that does sound a bit daunting . . .

from the journal of Miss Lucinda Merryweather, 1805

Chapter Four

"Clara." Lucy leaned closer to the other woman and lowered her voice. She did so hate to sound like a frightened schoolgirl and in truth she wasn't the least bit scared. On the contrary, it was most exciting. Still, she did think Clara should know. "I didn't want to say anything before, but now I'm fairly certain there's an extremely attractive gentleman who seems to be following us."

Clara pulled up short and scanned the street. "Where?"

"I don't see him now." Lucy glanced around. There were a fair number of people passing by but no one she recognized. "I noticed him yesterday and the day before, but he's very good. Every time I look in his direction, he ducks behind a carriage or steps into a doorway."

"The next time you see him, let me know at once." Clara's tone was firm. She took Lucy's arm and they started off, her pace a bit faster than before. "Come along, Lucy. It's entirely too cold to linger."

It was indeed far colder than Lucy had thought when they'd set out from Channing House. But their destination was no more than a ten-minute walk and both women agreed a carriage wasn't necessary. Lucy pushed her hands further into her fur muff, her small reticule dangling from her wrist.

They'd spent the last three days deciding on a course of action for accomplishing as many of Great-aunt Lucinda's adventures as possible. Except of course when they were busy making the acquaintance of Albert, the small Yorkshire terrier Clara had brought home. It was most thoughtful of her and something else that could be crossed off Lucinda's list. Clara said she had run into an acquaintance and discovered, in the course of their conversation, that he knew of a well-trained dog in need of a new home. If given her choice, Lucy would have preferred a dog with a bit more substance to it. Albert was extremely small, less than ten pounds, and didn't even come up to her knee. Nonetheless, it was love at first sight on all sides. He was indeed a clever little fellow and refused to leave Lucy's side, as if he knew she was his new master. Albert had been quite indignant today when they had left him behind.

"I don't like that," Clara said under her breath. "I don't like that at all."

Lucy glanced at her in surprise. "Surely we're in no real danger. It's the middle of the day, after all, and we're in Mayfair. What could possibly happen to us here?"

"One never knows," Clara said darkly. Lucy was beginning to suspect Clara was far more worldly than she appeared. "Robbery, kidnapping, seduction, murder—"

"That's enough." Lucy laughed. "You have made your point. Still, he didn't look like someone who was out to do us harm. Did I mention he was exceptionally attractive?"

"Goodness, Lucy." Clara shook her head. "A man doesn't necessarily have to look like a brigand to be one. I would wager the very best of them don't look like what they truly are. Life would be much easier if they did."

"It is a shame though . . ."

Clara slanted her a wry smile. "Because he was exceptionally attractive?"

"Well . . ." Lucy grinned. "Yes."

Lucy really wasn't accustomed to thinking of men as exceptionally attractive in anything other than a detached, objective way. After all, she was supposed to marry Jackson and whether she did or did not think of a man as handsome and dashing really hadn't mattered. Now, however, she was free. And he, whoever he was, was tall with dark hair and broad shoulders and, when he wasn't hiding in doorways, had a walk that said he was a man of determination. She didn't get more than a fleeting glimpse of his face—he was too smart to come too close—but she suspected it was quite handsome. Or perhaps she simply hoped. After all, a man of mystery should be handsome and dashing. The man watching them was certainly mysterious enough even if she was fairly certain she knew exactly who—or rather what—he was. Clara had nothing to worry about.

"This is it." Clara paused in front of the walk leading to a house too small to be accurately called grand but entirely too formidable to be called anything else. "The residence of James Rutledge, Viscount Northrup."

"This is where Lucinda's mother, my great-grandmother, was born." In her mind, Lucy placed a checkmark next to *Visit the place my mother was born.* "Shall we?"

"Do you really think this is a good idea?"

"One never knows how people will greet long-lost relatives. However"—Lucy squared her shoulders—"it is on the list." She nodded, stepped up to the door, lifted the brass knocker, and rapped it smartly against the back plate.

The door opened almost at once and a butler stared down his long nose at her. "May I help you, miss?"

"I do hope so." She cast him her brightest smile. "I have come to see Lord Northrup." She presented him with her calling card. "And this is my friend, Miss West."

"Is he expecting you?" The butler glanced at the card. "Miss Merryweather?"

"He couldn't possibly as I didn't expect to be here myself." Again she smiled.

Clara stepped forward. "Miss Merryweather has recently arrived from New York and, as she was uncertain as to the length of her stay, she did not think she would have time to pay a call on his lordship. She certainly would have made prior arrangements if she had. Fortunately her plans have changed and she would like nothing more than to pay her respects to his lordship, *her cousin.*"

"I was unaware that his lordship had any American relations," the butler said coolly.

"Then isn't this a delightful surprise for you." Lucy beamed. She had recently learned the enjoyment of saying exactly what you thought and allowing people to think you had no idea what you had just said. Because you were short and blond and perky. "My dear Mister . . . ?"

"Clarkson."

"Mr. Clarkson." Lucy leaned toward him in a confidential manner. "Would you rather have us come in, out of the cold, and be right when your suspicions are confirmed that we are not who we say we are, or refuse us entry and be wrong?" She shook her head regretfully. "I can't imagine his lordship would be happy about that."

The butler's gaze swept over them, no doubt judging the quality of their clothing and their overall appearance. Apparently, they passed his inspection.

"You have a point, miss." He opened the door wider and waved them in. "If you would be so good as to wait here."

"Thank you, Mr. Clarkson," Lucy said pleasantly.

The butler nodded and left them in the foyer

under the watchful eye of a young footman who looked more curious than vigilant.

"I have always fought to have my intelligence acknowledged," Clara said in a low tone for Lucy's ears alone. "Perhaps I would do better to rely on a brilliant smile and a pleasant demeanor."

"Oh, I am unfailingly pleasant." Lucy tried and failed to keep a smug note from her voice. "It works quite nicely."

A minute later the butler returned and ushered them into a parlor. Decorated in the furnishings of another era, there was a worn and vaguely tired air to the room. The weak winter sunlight filtering in through the tall windows did nothing to dispel the sense that this parlor had seen better days. A distinguished-looking gentleman, who appeared a little older than her father, stood near the mantel. A lady, obviously his wife, who must have been quite pretty in her youth, perched on a nearby sofa. They appeared more intrigued than forbidding and relief washed through Lucy.

"Well, well," Lord Northrup said with a smile. "Clarkson informs us I have a cousin that I am unaware of." His gaze shifted between Lucy and Clara. "Which one of you—"

"I'm Lucy Merryweather and this is my friend, Miss West." Lucy smiled. "Your grandfather's sister was my great-grandmother."

"My grandfather's sister . . ." The older man drew his brows together thoughtfully.

"It was a very long time ago," Lucy added.

"Of course," Lady Northrup said. "You remember, dear. You said your grandfather used to talk about his sister. How she had married and gone to America?"

Lord Northup nodded slowly. "Priscilla, I believe her name was." He studied Lucy curiously. "Your great-grandmother, you say?"

Lucy nodded. "I know this must strike you as being very odd, but my Great-aunt Lucinda, one of Priscilla's daughters, always wanted to know why her mother never spoke of her family. When she died she left me her, well, a journal of sorts, and one of the things she regretted in life was not knowing what happened between her mother and her mother's family. And, as I was in London, I thought I would try to find out." Saying it aloud did sound a little silly even if it was the truth. "I was hoping you could help me."

"As you said, it was a very long time ago," Lord Northrup said slowly. "Perhaps you should follow me into the library."

Lady Northrup rose to her feet. "There is something you might like to see."

Lucy and Clara traded glances, then trailed after the couple into a room lined with bookshelves divided by rich, dark wood panels. Portraits and paintings, landscapes and country scenes covered every bit of wall space, and the overall impression was one of a room nearly ready to burst with books and memories. It smelled of sweet pipe tobacco and that wonderful mustiness that can only come from very old books, better loved through the years than cared for. Unlike the parlor, this room seemed more comfortable than merely worn.

"I have always agreed with that old adage about a picture being far more effective in the telling of a story than mere words." Lord Northrup chuckled. He and his wife stopped in front of a large portrait of a family, the paint crazed with age, the gilded frame chipped at the corners as if it had been moved and hung more than once through the years.

"The shorter boy, who looks as if he would rather be anywhere but posing for a painting, is my grandfather. The taller boy is his older brother. Note how the artist caught that gleam in his eye. As if he's just waiting for adventure to present itself."

Lucy nodded and studied the painting. There was indeed a sense of restrained excitement about the figure of the older boy, as if, with very little effort, he would leap out of the painting and seize whatever opportunity came along.

"Although spirit in the heir to a title is not especially encouraged," his lordship said. "The gentleman who looks as if his cravat is tied entirely too tight is my great-grandfather, the third Viscount Northrup, and the lady who appears from her expression to have just eaten something sour—"

"Now, now, dear," Lady Northrup murmured.

"Well, she does." He grinned at Lucy. "I've thought that since I was a boy and I think the same every time I look at her. I've always wanted to commission a painter to change her expression just a bit, but apparently the original artist was quite accomplished, even if nobody remembers him now, and my wife insists tampering with his work would be wrong."

Lady Northrup's lips curved upward in a tolerant smile.

"But, as I was saying, that's my great-grandmother, and the little blond girl"—he glanced at Lucy—"that was Priscilla."

"She's lovely," Clara murmured.

"Indeed she was." His lordship nodded. "And just as lovely when she grew up. But she made the mistake of falling in love with an American."

Lucy's brow rose. "Mistake?"

"According to my great-grandfather it was more than a mere mistake, it was the gravest of sins."

"Just because he was American?" Lucy frowned in patriotic indignation. "That was rather unfair of him."

"He didn't see it that way." Lord Northrup shook his head. "You have to remember the times they lived in. He saw Priscilla's choice as a betrayal of her family and of her country. Understandable, when you think about it." He nodded toward the portrait. "The older boy, Robert, was heir to the title. Naturally, he had been trained for his position as the next viscount and, from what I've been told, would have been most successful. He was said to have had a brilliant mind when it came to the management of finances. Something that eluded my grandfather, my father, and myself. We've all had to marry well to shore up the family coffers." He cast an affectionate look at his wife. "Isn't that right, dear?"

"It is something of a family tradition." In spite of her agreement, the twinkle in Lady Northrup's eyes said their marriage was based on more than her dowry.

"A tradition that will unfortunately have to continue. Such is life these days." He heaved a resigned sigh. "But I digress. As I was saying, that adventurous streak in Robert led him to purchase a commission in the army, against his father's objections. Young men do tend to think they're invulnerable, you know."

Lucy and Clara nodded.

"He was killed during your Revolutionary War in one of the Carolinas, I believe. My grandfather said his father never got over it. He disowned Priscilla and never forgave her." His lordship shook his head. "My grandfather never forgave himself for not standing up for his sister. For allowing her to leave." He paused thoughtfully.

"I don't know if he ever wrote to her or attempted to locate her. I do know he never saw her again and that was one of the great regrets of his life."

"How very sad," Lucy said softly.

"It is always sad when families have irreconcilable rifts." Lady Northrup sighed.

"I daresay your Lucinda would have appreciated your efforts to set to rights this regret of hers." His lordship cast Lucy a genuine smile. "And I must say I'm delighted to have at last reunited two halves of my family."

Lucy stared at the little girl in the painting. "It's such a shame it couldn't have happened when they were still alive."

"Unfortunately, what's done is done." Lord Northrup shrugged. "One cannot change the past, only reconcile oneself with it."

"Now then, it's nearly time for tea. I do hope you will join us." Lady Northrup hooked her arm through Lucy's and led the group back to the parlor. "I know we are both wondering how Priscilla fared in America and curious as well about the rest of your family. It isn't often one finds an entire branch of the family one has no knowledge of."

"I don't know that tea will be enough," his lordship said wryly. "After all, it's been a hundred years or so."

"We will just have to try our best," Lucy said with a smile.

Until now, Lucy really hadn't considered that in finding the answer to Lucinda's question about her mother's family, Lucy would find an entirely new family of her own. It was as odd as it was exciting.

For the next hour, Lucy and her new relatives traded family connections, who was related to whom, family stories, and even a scandal or two. The older couple was warm and welcoming, and Lucy couldn't have been more delighted with her reception. In spite of their cultural differences, Lord Northrup and her father had a great deal in common. She suspected Harold Merryweather and Lord Northrup might end up being great friends one day. She wondered exactly how to phrase her next letter home without revealing more than she wanted her parents to know.

"Clarkson tells me we have heretofore unknown relatives visiting from America." A tall, dashing, fair-haired man strode into the room, then pulled up short. "But he failed to mention they were still here." He flashed an infectious grin. "Or that they were so lovely."

"Alfred." Lady Northrup's brow furrowed. "Do try not to enter a room as if you were an invading army bent on conquest."

"Sorry, Mother." Alfred stepped to her side and brushed his lips across her proffered cheek. "It's not everyday I learn of fresh blood in the family."

Lady Northrup winced.

Her husband chuckled. "Allow me to introduce your distant cousin, Miss Lucy Merryweather, and her friend Miss West. This is my son, Alfred."

"Miss Merryweather." Alfred moved to her, bent low and took her hand. His gaze locked with hers. "I cannot tell you what a genuine pleasure this is."

Lucy stared into his blue eyes, eyes that looked vaguely familiar. At once it struck her that Alfred's eyes were the same shape and color as her father's and her brothers' and her own. "Lucy will do."

"And you must call me Freddy." He leaned closer and lowered his voice. "My father only refers to me as Alfred on formal occasions or when I've done something he deems unsuitable. My mother, however, routinely calls me Alfred. She thinks Freddy is entirely too frivolous for a future viscount. I think it suits me. What do you think?"

"I have no idea." She studied him, then grinned. "But I think you're probably right. You do look much more like a Freddy than an Alfred."

He laughed, released her hand, and turned to Clara, taking her hand as well and staring at her as if he had just discovered a sweet he hadn't realized he'd been deprived of. "Miss West, how very nice to meet you."

"Mr. Rutledge." Clara nodded politely.

His eyes narrowed. "You're not American."

"No, I'm not."

"Miss West is my traveling companion and my dear friend," Lucy said. "My . . . my family thought it best for me not to travel unaccompanied."

"Quite right." Lord Northrup nodded.

"That would be terribly improper," Lady Northrup added.

"I see." Freddy cast a last appreciative look at Clara, then turned his attention back to Lucy. "Is this your first trip to England?"

"It is indeed." Lucy nodded enthusiastically. "I'm finding it all fascinating. We don't have castles, you know, or ancient ruins. It's all so terribly historic and old."

"We are nothing if not old." Freddy chuckled.

"You must allow Alfred to show you the sights of London," Lady Northrup said.

"I was about to suggest the very same thing." Freddy grinned. "I would like nothing better than to escort two such lovely ladies around my fair city."

"What a wonderful idea, Freddy." Lucy smiled. "That would be delightful."

The look in Clara's eyes clearly said she was not in complete agreement. One did have to wonder if it was Freddy's willingness to offer himself as a tourist guide or his obvious interest in her that Clara objected to.

Arrangements were made for Freddy to call on

them in the next few days along with promises to return for dinner before Lucy returned to America. Lucy declined both the offer of a Northrup carriage to return them to Channing House and Freddy's suggestion that he escort them, insisting that it was entirely too much trouble, they had been most kind already, and besides she did enjoy a brisk walk. She and Clara took their leave and Lucy was surprised to find it was far later than she had thought and dusk was nearly upon them.

"You didn't like him, did you?" Lucy said the moment the door closed behind him.

"On the contrary. I thought his lordship was most charming. He and Lady Northrup were far more gracious and welcoming than I expected. After all, you were a bit of a surprise."

"That's not what I meant and you know it."

"Indeed I do." Clara smiled in a wry manner.

"Why didn't you like him? Freddy, that is. I thought he was charming and rather witty as well." Lucy paused. "And he did seem to like you."

"Possibly." Clara picked up her pace and Lucy had to hurry to keep up with the taller woman's longer strides.

"He was quite handsome, really. He reminded me very much of my brothers. And tall as well. Taller than you, and I would think that would be a most attractive—"

"Lucy." Clara halted without warning and stared. "If I didn't know better I would think you were trying to make a match for me."

Lucy gasped in feigned indignation. "Why, I would never think of such a thing." Although she had thought exactly that. "But now that you have brought up the idea—"

"Now that I have, we may put it behind us and go on." Clara nodded and started off again. "I am not in the market for a husband, thank you very much."

"But you're not opposed to a husband, are you?"

"Not in principle."

"Freddy does seem like a good sort. Besides, it was obvious, from what his father said and the vaguely shabby state of the house, that he too will have to marry well. You have a fortune and he needs one and—"

"Lucy!" Clara stopped in midstep and laughed. "My financial circumstances are quite sound, but not nearly grand enough to be a suitable match for a viscount."

"But—"

"I don't know how things of this nature are done in your country, but in England the daughters of merchants, no matter how wealthy, do not marry future lords. It simply isn't the way things are done here."

"Well, that's just silly." Lucy sniffed. "Why, it's eighteen eighty-eight. We're approaching the twentieth century. It's not the Middle Ages after all. It seems to me if two people care for each other, it shouldn't matter who they are or what they have or don't have."

"Regardless, it does. All that history you are so admiring of here comes with a price. This is the way it has always been and the way it shall always be. Besides . . ." She resumed walking and shot Lucy a chastising look. "I've only just met the man and I'm not at all sure he's to my liking."

"What kind of man would you like?" Lucy adopted a casual tone. "I have brothers and—"

"Do you do this sort of thing in New York?"

Lucy drew her brows together in confusion. "What sort of thing?"

"Attempt to make matches."

"Well, no, not that I can recall." It had just seemed such a good opportunity as Freddy was so obviously taken with Clara. Still, it was probably time to change the subject. "I think that went well. I quite enjoyed our visit."

Clara slanted her a knowing smile. "It was very pleasant. In addition, you now have the answer to your great-aunt's curiosity about her mother's rift with her family. And you've seen where she was born." Clara nodded. "You may check those off your list."

"Plus I have solved a mystery of sorts. Yet another thing Lucinda wished to accomplish."

Lucy thought for a moment. "Through no fault of my own, really. Although, I suspect Lucinda had in mind a mystery of a more adventurous nature than discovering—"

Without warning a man passing by jostled them, then sprinted off.

Clara huffed. "I must say that was—"

"He took my purse! He snatched it off my arm!" Lucy started after him. "Come back here, you cur!"

"Lucy." Clara grabbed her arm. "You can't go after him."

"Of course I . . ." She huffed. "No, of course I can't. Not in these shoes. And I suppose it would be unseemly to go running down the street."

"And foolish. He might be extremely dangerous."

"Damnation, if I was a man, I'd be after him without a moment's hesitation."

"I've no doubt of that." Clara took her arm and fairly dragged her toward their destination. "But you're not a man and there's nothing you can do except return to Channing House as quickly as possible."

"He took my handbag." Lucy scowled, still looking in the direction the thief had gone. "The fiend."

"You have others."

"Well, I hope he feels his theft was worth it when he finds nothing of value except my second favorite pair of kid gloves and a few shillings."

"Yes, that will teach him a lesson," Clara said wryly.

"I should like to teach him a lesson," Lucy muttered. She'd never had anything stolen from her before. It was . . . She should probably be frightened but instead indignation gripped her along with absolute fury. How dare he?

Clara's pace was even faster than before, if possible, and in no more than a few minutes they reached the front entry of Channing House. Still, it was long enough for Lucy's ire to fade, replaced by a dreadful sense of helplessness and yes, more than a touch of fear. Good God, Clara was right. They could have been in a great deal of danger.

"Miss?" A male voice called from behind them, and both women turned. The mysterious stranger she'd seen following them now hurried in their direction.

"Good Lord," Clara murmured.

"Yes?" Lucy stared. She was right. He was handsome, with a square jaw, lips a shade full for a man but attractive nonetheless. His nose was a bit too straight and Roman for her liking, but it suited him, and his eyes were the darkest velvety brown she had ever seen. The oddest thing happened to her stomach. Still, how could he have allowed this to happen? Her annoyance returned.

"I believe this is yours." He held out her purse.

Clara raised a brow. "You gave chase to that brigand? You?"

"It seemed the least I could do." He grinned and again Lucy's stomach fluttered.

She ignored it and took her handbag. "Indeed it is. I can't believe you allowed that to happen in the first place. You're not very observant, are you?"

"I do try," he said slowly.

"You will have to try harder in the future. Especially given the exorbitant amount you're probably being paid."

"Lucy." Clara stared in confusion. "What on earth are you talking about?"

"I'm talking about Mr. . . . What is your name?"

"Fairchild, miss. Mr. Cameron Fairchild." He swept an overly dramatic bow. "And I am at your service."

"Of course you are." She scoffed. "I knew it the moment I saw you."

"Knew what?" Caution sounded in Clara's voice.

"This is the man who has been following us." She crossed her arms over her chest. "You see, Clara, Mr. Fairchild is a private investigator." She narrowed her eyes. "A watchdog."

Regrets Set to Rights

See the place my mother was born and learn why she never speaks of her family. Solve a mystery.

. . . and yet it is nice to know that I am not the only one among my close friends who has never been kissed. Although we do tend to discuss kissing a great deal. We are in agreement that one's first kiss should be special, although our mothers would say any kiss at all should be reserved for the man you wed. It seems dreadfully old-fashioned to us, but then most of the rules of proper behavior do seem both antiquated and absurd. One hopes they will change in time but that's doubtful. Nothing ever seems to change.

It would be most exciting to be kissed by someone one does not intend to marry. A dashing, mysterious stranger who would make your heart flutter and your toes curl. One would never marry such a man, of course. But I would very much like to kiss a stranger, a man I'd never met and would likely never see again. Just once as one would not want to make a habit of such outrageous behavior, for it would surely lead to scandal and ruination.

But once would be terribly romantic and yes, quite an adventure . . .

from the journal of Miss Lucinda Merryweather, 1806

Chapter Five

Cam stared at the short bundle of pretty, blond indignation. "I'm what?"

"He's what?" Miss West said at precisely the same time.

"It's obvious to me that he has been hired by Jackson to keep an eye on me. To make certain I stay out of harm's way. To keep me from doing anything that might be deemed scandalous. Or interesting." Miss Merryweather huffed. "I can think of no other reason why he would be following us."

"Why else indeed?" Miss West shot him a scathing look.

"Tell me, Mr. Fairchild"—Miss Merryweather glared—"am I wrong? Because if I am, I want to know this very instant why you have been skulking around the past few days. Following us everywhere we go. And I think the police would like to know as well." She poked him with a pointed finger. "Go on then. Are you up to no good?"

"I assure you my intentions are not dishonorable." It was the first thing that came to mind and it was the truth as far as it went.

"And have you been engaged to watch my every move?"

"I . . . um . . . well . . ." He struggled to find the right words. Her accusation as well as her appearance left him nearly speechless. He hadn't yet been close enough to get a good look at her face; Miss Merryweather was neither old nor ugly but quite lovely. Her features were delicate, her creamy skin heightened by a blush of annoyance, a few delightful freckles scattered over a pert little nose, and she had perhaps the bluest eyes he'd ever seen. In fact *delicious* was the adjective that came to mind. "I can't really say."

"No, of course you can't." She cast him a disgusted look and moved to the door. "Secrecy is a tenet of your profession, isn't it?"

Cam nodded slowly. He still wasn't sure what he should say, but at the moment absolutely nothing seemed like a good idea.

"This is exactly what Jackson threatened to do. And apparently, in spite of my objections, exactly what he's done. He said he didn't like leaving with no one to watch over me. So much for his belief in my competence." The door opened and she swept inside. She glanced back at him. "Come in, Mr. Fairchild. I am not finished with you yet."

"Nor am I," Miss West said under her breath.

Cam followed the women into the house. This was certainly not his original idea but it might serve him well.

"I should have known better than to think,

even for a moment, Jackson would accept my wishes. He gave in entirely too quickly." Miss Merryweather nodded at the footman who had opened the door and continued without pause in an impressive display of righteous anger and misassumption. "His sense of duty has always been extremely annoying. And the man refuses to accept that I am no longer his responsibility." She removed her hat and cloak and thrust them at the footman, then spun on her heel and glared at Cam. "Tell me, Mr. Fairchild, were you given a list of things to watch out for?"

"I . . . can't say, miss."

"That's fast becoming annoying, Mr. Fairchild," she said sharply, then drew a deep breath and turned to Miss West. "Clara, if you would be so good as to wait until Mr. Fairchild has removed his coat and hat, then please escort him into the parlor." Miss Merryweather's angry gaze met his. "I need a moment to myself." She nodded, raised her chin, and strode off in a magnificent manner. It was most impressive, especially given how very wrong she was.

A moment later a small terrier bounded into the entry and skidded to a stop on the polished marble floors. His little head swiveled as if he were searching for something. Finally his gaze settled on Cam, eyeing him with suspicion.

"Parlor," Miss West said firmly.

The little beast looked at her, obviously

deciding whether or not she was trustworthy, then obediently trotted after Miss Merryweather.

Cam and Miss West handed their outer garments to the footman, then she steered him in the direction Miss Merryweather had taken. As soon as they were out of earshot of the servant, she leaned close and spoke in a low tone. "What are you doing here, Mr. Fairchild?"

"Why, I'm writing a story, of course. A series of stories, really. *The Daring Exploits of a Runaway Heiress*. It has quite a catchy ring to it, don't you think?"

She stared. "Are you insane?"

"Probably." He chuckled. "They say there is a fine line between insanity and brilliance."

"Whoever says that is an idiot." Her jaw tightened. "You do realize the irreparable harm you could do by publicly exposing her in that scandal sheet of yours? Why, just the fact that she's here unaccompanied is highly improper."

"I'm not a cad, Miss West. I have no desire to harm Miss Merryweather. I am fully aware of the damage that could be done to a woman's reputation by a misplaced word. Precisely why my works will be fictitious. No more than a product of my imagination. I am simply observing Miss Merryweather for, oh, inspiration as it were. I assure you, no one will ever connect her with my work. So tell me, Miss West." He leaned closer. "I know she's up to something. What is it?"

Miss West's eyes narrowed. "Get out, Mr. Fairchild."

"Or what, Miss West?" He had her and he knew it. And in a moment she'd know it too. "Or you'll tell her who I am? That I'm not a private investigator hired to watch over her?" That alone might form the basis for his first story.

"Exactly." She fairly spit the word at him.

"That would be most distressing." He shook his head in a mournful manner. "Because if you were to reveal my secret, I should be forced to reveal yours."

Her eyes narrowed.

"While she might be annoyed by my little masquerade—one initiated entirely by her I might add—she scarcely knows me. It would be a moment of indignation, nothing more than that. Whereas you have obviously become quite close, *Clara*. If she knew you were the associate, indeed a partner of an investigator—"

"You've made your point, Mr. Fairchild." Fury blazed in Miss West's lovely eyes. "But I warn you right now, should these stories of yours cause her harm in any way, you shall have to answer to me."

He met her gaze directly and realized Clara West might well be a formidable enemy if crossed. "Miss Merryweather has nothing to fear from me, Miss West. I give you my word."

She studied him closely, then nodded. "Let us

hope that is good enough." She opened the parlor door and waved him in ahead of her, then closed the door behind them.

Miss Merryweather stood staring out the window at the deepening dusk outside, the small dog in her arms, a thoughtful expression on her face. Miss West cleared her throat. "Lucy?"

"I've come to a, well, a realization, Clara. As well as a decision." She set the dog on the floor. He immediately sat down and stared up at her in an alert manner.

"Yes?" Caution sounded in Miss West's voice.

"In spite of the fact that Jackson"—she glanced at Cam—"Mr. Channing, your employer . . ."

Cam nodded. *Who?* The name was vaguely familiar . . . Of course. Jackson Channing was the newfound American heir to the Earl of Briston. Everyone in London had been talking about it. The question now was what was the connection between that American and this American? Although it must be close if she was staying here at Channing House.

". . . hired you without my knowledge and against my wishes . . ." Miss Merryweather smiled a distinctly smug sort of smile. "I have decided to make your job easier, Mr. Fairchild."

"What do you mean?" Suspicion rang in Miss West's voice.

"Now that we know who our mysterious

stranger is and what he's up to, it seems a shame to waste him." She glanced at Miss West. "Don't you agree?"

"I'm not sure," Miss West said slowly.

"Given today's incident with the theft of my purse, it strikes me that it would not be ill advised to be accompanied by a gentleman from now on. After all, as we learned today, two ladies alone present a target for any miscreant who happens along."

"Regardless," Miss West began. "I don't think—"

"You said it yourself about the dangers to be found on London streets. He's going to be dogging our every step no matter what we do, anyway. We might as well make use of him." Miss Merryweather considered him coolly. "What do you say, Mr. Fairchild? Will you come out of the shadows and accompany us openly or do you prefer to hide in doorways in the cold?"

"I have never been overly fond of doorways and it is exceptionally cold outside," he said with a smile. This was perfect, absolutely perfect. Miss Merryweather was indeed going to make his job, and his life, much easier.

"Good." She nodded. "Clara, would you give us a moment alone? Perhaps you could write that note we discussed earlier today. You remember, to the gentleman who—"

"Yes, of course," Miss West said quickly, then

glanced at him and frowned. "Are you sure this is wise?"

"Oh, I'm certain I'll be perfectly fine. After all, his job is to keep me safe." Miss Merryweather's eyes narrowed. "Isn't that right, Mr. Fairchild?"

He nodded. It did seem the less he said aloud, the better.

"Very well, but I'll be no more than a few minutes." A warning sounded in Miss West's voice.

"I doubt we'll need much more than a few minutes." Miss Merryweather's gaze locked on his. "However, Mr. Fairchild and I do have a few things we need to discuss."

Miss West shot him a hard look and reluctantly left the room.

"She's probably listening at the door, you know," Miss Merryweather said. "I would be." She crossed the room, the dog at her heels, and seated herself on a sofa. The terrier immediately jumped up beside her, rested its head on her lap but kept his gaze trained on Cam. Cam suspected the dog was not to be trusted, small or not.

Miss Merryweather indicated a nearby chair. "Do sit down, Mr. Fairchild."

He sat.

"First of all, in spite of Mr. Channing's belief that I need a"—her jaw tightened—"a watchdog." The terrier growled softly and she absently rubbed his head. "I can assure you I am neither helpless nor stupid."

"I never thought otherwise."

"Your employer obviously did." She studied him for a long, considering moment and he resisted the urge to squirm under her scrutiny. No, it was apparent, at least to him, that she was far more clever than her delightful appearance might imply. "Given that your surveillance of my activities is no longer clandestine, I was wondering if you would consider leaving Mr. Channing's employment in favor of working directly for me. Your retrieval of my purse today was most impressive. I will pay you whatever Mr. Channing was paying you," she added.

He stared. "I'm afraid I can't do that, miss."

She blew an annoyed breath. "No, I didn't think you could. Honor among thieves and all that." She thought for a moment. "Exactly how much did Mr. Channing tell you about my plans?"

"I . . ."

"If you're going to tell me again that you can't say, you might as well hold your tongue," she said sharply, and again the dog growled. "This is my life that is being meddled with and I resent not having my questions answered."

"I can understand that."

She arched a brow. "Can you indeed?"

"I would think it would be most annoying."

She snorted. "You have no idea." She rose to her feet, gestured for him to stay seated, then paced the room. The dog trotted along at her heels. "Were you to report back to him? About my activities?"

What was it Phineas had said about the lady who wished to hire him to watch Miss Merryweather? Ah yes. "No. My charge was only to make certain no harm befell you."

"That's something at any rate." She continued to pace, then paused and looked at him. "I have no desire to have my plans interfered with, Mr. Fairchild. I could, of course, just throw you out right now, but I doubt that will stop your observation of me. You will simply go back to hiding in doorways. Am I correct?"

"I do have a job to do." It simply wasn't the job she thought.

"I suspected as much." She resumed pacing, her brows furrowed thoughtfully. He could almost see the gears and wheels of her mind working, like a fine timepiece. Whatever she was up to, it went far beyond sightseeing. This was much more intriguing than he had expected. Perhaps she really was having adventures, after all. After a few silent moments, she nodded as if she had come to a decision, and turned toward him. "It seems if I am going to accomplish what I intend to accomplish, I am going to have to trust you. Can I?"

What on earth did she want to accomplish? "I have always been most trustworthy."

"Although really, I have little choice. I can confide in you and hope it's not a mistake. Or I can allow you to trail along behind us, hopefully keeping us safe from brigands and scoundrels, and let you draw your own conclusions. Which would probably be a mistake as well." She shook her head. "I have never been fond of choosing the lesser of two evils."

He waited.

"Very well then. Let's get on with it." She moved to a side table, pulled open a drawer, and withdrew a sheet of paper. She sat back down on the sofa, the dog resuming his previous position. "My fortune is the legacy of my Great-aunt Lucinda. When she was young, before she married, she made this list of things she wanted to do in her life, adventures, she called them. She never managed them, and instead of adventures, this became a list of her regrets." She handed the paper to Cam. "I intend to accomplish as many of these as I can."

"I see." Cam scanned the sheet. Most of the items were exactly the kind of innocuous things a young girl might want. A few were profound, and indeed, if he had a list of his own, some of these same things might appear on his. And several were definitely scandalous. No wonder Mr. Channing, or Phineas's client, wanted someone to keep an eye on Miss Merryweather. "You do realize some of these will be extremely difficult if not impossible?"

"That's the challenge, isn't it?" A wicked

twinkle gleamed in her eyes, and for the first time, she cast him a genuine smile. It lit up her face and did something odd to the pit of his stomach. Good Lord, what had he gotten himself into? "And the fun."

"Fun?" He swallowed hard, trying to get some of the items regarding *romantic interludes* or *taking a lover* or *being painted sans clothing* out of his head. "Yes, I can see that."

"Do you think it's silly? My wanting to accomplish these things my great-aunt never managed?"

"It's not for me to say but, no. I don't. Some of these items might be rather foolish, but it seems to me this endeavor of yours is in the manner of repayment of a debt. Quite honorable really."

"Thank you, Mr. Fairchild."

He cleared his throat, but the idea of a luscious Miss Merryweather posing nude for a portrait refused to be vanquished. "Might I inquire as to what your family thinks of your quest?"

"They don't actually know." She shrugged in an offhand manner, as if the question was of no importance, but he would wager it was. Perhaps she was a runaway heiress after all. "It seemed best. My parents and my brothers would not share your opinion as to the honorable nature of my endeavor."

"I see." He handed the paper back to her. "What do the notations beside each item signify?"

"Miss West and I have marked them as to their degree of difficulty, and at least one, traveling the world, will have to wait for the future. But several can be combined and accomplished all at once. Why, just today I saw the house where Lucinda's mother was born and discovered the cause of the estrangement with her family, which solved a mystery as well."

He nodded.

"Others we shall be able to cross off the list with very little effort. As you can see, I have already acquired a dog. This is Albert, by the way."

Albert raised his head from her lap at the mention of his name and cast her an adoring look.

"It's a pleasure to meet you, Albert," Cam said politely.

Albert gave Cam what could only be called a look of disgust and again uttered a low growl.

"Don't mind Albert." She patted the dog fondly. "He's surprisingly protective given that we've only known each other a few days."

"Perhaps you don't need my assistance after all."

"I truly wish I didn't." She paused. "But today was . . . well, it was frightening and I would prefer not to experience that again."

"You don't strike me as a woman who would be frightened of anything."

"I don't?" Surprise widened her eyes. "Not even a little?"

"Only a fool would fail to be scared by what happened today." He shrugged. "Aside from that, no, not even a little."

"What a lovely thing to say, Mr. Fairchild. I would imagine all that charm of yours comes in handy in your profession."

He smiled. "It has."

"It must be quite exciting. Being an investigator, that is. I daresay you've been in frightening situa-tions any number of times."

"On occasion," he said cautiously.

"Come now." She scoffed. "I can't believe you haven't been involved in incidents far more exhilarating than following two women around London."

He adopted a professional tone. "Surveillance is a large part of what we do."

"Then you must have witnessed any number of fascinating and scandalous things. Tell me, Mr. Fairchild." She leaned toward him, her eyes sparkled with curiosity. "What is the most interesting thing you have observed?"

"I really couldn't—"

"Oh, I'm not asking for names. Surely you can tell me something amusing?"

Cam racked his brains. Phineas had told him about his previous cases but specifics eluded him at the moment. "Often, my client wants to know if his or her spouse is being unfaithful. Which involves the discreet observation of that spouse. But my surveillance usually ends at a door."

"That's rather dull."

"To say anything more would be highly inappropriate," he said in a lofty manner.

"Good Lord, Mr. Fairchild." She laughed. "I simply adore highly inappropriate."

"Very well then." If he couldn't remember anything from Phineas's stories, he could certainly make something up. "I do recall one occasion where I happened to be watching the wife of a prominent gentleman. Her 'friend' had gained entry to what I assumed was her bedchamber by way of a ladder placed against the outside wall. Unfortunately for him, her husband returned home unexpectedly."

Her eyes widened. "And then?"

"Then . . ." He drew the word out in the manner of a master storyteller, for effect and to give him time to think. "Then shots rang out, Miss Merryweather."

"Shots?" She stared. "The prominent gentleman shot the friend?"

"No, he missed, actually." Cam shook his head. "The gentleman in question was not a very good shot plus he was quite outraged, which does tend to affect one's ability to aim."

"I would think so." She nodded. "What happened next?"

"Needless to say, the friend was eager to take

his leave." With every word the story grew in his head.

"Naturally."

"So he . . . he scrambled out the window."

"Did he?"

"He did indeed. And unfortunately kicked the ladder away in the process." Oh, that was good. "Which left him dangling by his fingertips from the window."

"My goodness, he wasn't having any luck at all, was he?"

"It gets worse," Cam said solemnly. There was nothing better than when a story started coming to mind as if it had a life of its own. He must remember to write this one down.

"Oh . . ." She grinned. "Good. How much worse?"

"Well, you see, the 'friend' was clad"—he lowered his voice in a confidential manner—"in nothing more than his shirt and abject terror."

She gasped.

"So there he was, dangling from the window, exposed for all the world to see. His white flesh glowing in the moonlight—"

"In the moonlight?" Her brow rose. "Then this was at night? You didn't mention that."

"My apologies. Yes, indeed, it was night." He nodded. "A very dark, very stormy night."

She frowned. "But the moon was shining."

"Between the clouds," he said quickly. "The

clouds parted and a shaft of moonlight illuminated, well, parts that a gentleman would prefer not to expose and illuminate."

"Oh my." She studied him for a moment. "And what happened next?"

"He fell into the shrubbery and then scrambled off." Cam shrugged. "Never to be seen again."

"Never?"

"Well, I never saw him again." He grinned. "Nor did I wish to as I had seen entirely too much already."

She laughed. "That was delightful, Mr. Fairchild. You are an excellent storyteller."

"Yes, well . . ." He tried and failed to act modest.

"I can't wait to hear more about your exploits as an investigator."

"More?" he said weakly.

"Oh my, yes. That was most entertaining. And we are going to be spending a great deal of time together. You and I and Miss West, that is." She rose to her feet. "However, as Miss West and I have no plans to leave the house for the rest of the day, you may take your leave. Unless, of course, you don't trust me."

He stood. "You confided your plans to me, Miss Merryweather, which indicates trust in me on your part. I can do no less but to trust you as well."

"We will get on very well then." She smiled. "However, as much as I would like to trust you, and as I said I have little choice, when you return tomorrow, I would like references. While I'm certain Mr. Channing would not have hired you if you did not come highly recommended, I would like something to assure me, as well as Miss West, as she is most protective—"

"Yes, I noticed."

"That you are who you say you are."

Phineas would certainly write him a reference as would any of his brothers. And they would do so on extremely impressive stationery emblazoned with the Roxborough crest. He nodded. "Extremely prudent of you."

"Well, even if you did recover my purse, you are a complete stranger. . . ." Her eyes widened.

"Miss Merryweather," he said cautiously.

She stared at him. "We've never met before."

"No, we have not."

"One should never waste an opportunity when it presents itself, Mr. Fairchild." She squared her shoulders. "Don't you agree?"

"Yes, I suppose." He wasn't at all sure he liked the look in her eyes.

"There's nothing to be done about it, I suppose." She stepped close to him, grabbed the lapels of his coat, raised herself up on her toes, and pressed her mouth to his in a firm and shocking kiss.

Her lips were warm and soft and the most intoxicating scent of something undefined but reminiscent of summer nonetheless wafted around him and settled somewhere deep inside. Without warning she pulled away.

"There." Her voice had a charming breathless quality to it. Her eyes were bright and a becoming blush washed up her cheeks. She stepped back. "I may check that off the list."

"I . . ." He laughed. "Yes, I suppose you may."

The corners of her mouth curved upward and he wanted nothing more than to kiss her again. "Do you find this amusing, Mr. Fairchild?"

"On the contrary, Miss Merryweather. I found that"—he grinned—"absolutely delightful."

"Did you?" Her brow rose. "Oh my, this is awkward."

"Awkward?"

"Well, I thought it was cursory at best. As kisses go, I really don't think it was exceptional."

"You don't." He drew his brows together. "I must say, Miss Merryweather, I have never had a complaint before."

"No, I don't imagine you would have." She winced. "Ladies are generally polite about this sort of thing."

"But not you?"

"I was being honest, Mr. Fairchild." She shrugged. "It's not as if your affections were engaged, after all. As if this kiss meant anything. Although, admittedly"—she sighed—"I have not had a great deal of experience. But I do think I have been kissed enough to recognize an unremarkable kiss. In fact, I would say I am well acquainted with unremarkable kisses."

"That's a very great pity, Miss Merryweather."

"I have always thought so," she murmured. "But I would think when one experiences an exceptional kiss, one is well aware of it."

"And this kiss was not exceptional?"

"No." She shook her head. "Rather a shame, really. One would hope that kissing a stranger would be extremely exciting rather than merely . . . nice enough."

"Nice enough?" He stared in indignation, then laughed. "I'm afraid I have to agree, Miss Merryweather. It was adequate, no more than that. I can assure you, were I not taken by surprise, the kiss would have been far more than adequate."

"Then you need warning?"

"Not warning but, as I had no idea you were about to kiss me, I was unprepared."

"I see." She studied him curiously. "And if I had warned you, would the kiss then have become more than adequate?"

"I don't—" He frowned. "See here, Miss Merryweather, this is not the kind of conversation I am used to having with a lady."

She laughed. "Nor is it the kind of conversation I have ever had with a gentleman." She paused. "Still, I should probably apologize to you."

"For your criticism of my kiss?"

"Not at all. As I said, I was simply being honest. But it does seem to me, the fault for the unexceptional nature of the kiss was probably mine. I merely seized the opportunity presented." Her brows drew together thoughtfully. "I suspect this was not at all what Lucinda had in mind when she wanted to kiss a stranger. After all, kissing a stranger in a moonlit garden or on a dark terrace outside a ballroom would be far more exciting than a kiss in a parlor in an effort to cross an item off a list. Don't you agree?"

"I would think so, yes."

"Although, this was far safer," she said thoughtfully.

"Safe and unexceptional are exactly the comments a man wishes to hear after a kiss," he said wryly.

"Oh dear, I do hope I haven't offended you."

"Not at all," he said gallantly, but it was past time to change the topic of conversation. "Might I inquire as to your plans for tomorrow?"

She hesitated. "They are as yet uncertain, but I can't imagine we will do anything before late morning."

"Then I will return tomorrow, Miss Merryweather." He nodded and started toward the door.

"And, Mr. Fairchild?"

"Yes?"

"I will expect you to come to the door and

not hide behind carriages on the street tomorrow."

He chuckled. "I assure you, I will present myself at your front door."

"You know, Mr. Fairchild." She tilted her head and smiled at him. "You were something of a hero today."

"I simply recovered your purse."

"And modest as well. Most becoming in a hero."

He grinned. "I am at your service, Miss Merryweather."

"Excellent, Mr. Fairchild." She beamed. "This will be an adventure."

"I have no doubt of that." He smiled, nodded again, and took his leave, managing to make it out the front door and onto the street without encountering Miss West.

That went far better than he had expected. Although he hadn't expected Miss Merryweather to be aware of his surveillance. And he certainly never expected to have to rescue her purse. Nor had he expected the lovely Miss Merryweather to be lovely. All in all he hadn't expected anything about her. But she was going to make a great story.

He ignored the twinge of conscience at the thought. After all, he wasn't going to use her name. This was going to be fiction. She was simply his inspiration, his muse as it were. The story was already beginning to take shape in his head. Tonight, he would start writing.

Still, there were facts about all this he had yet to discover. Her relationship with the American, Channing, for one thing. Why she didn't want her family to know what she was doing, for another. And even more interesting: just how far was Miss Merryweather willing to go in her efforts to atone for her relative's regrets?

Regardless, in spite of his own purposes, the lady thought he had been hired to keep her safe, and the only honorable thing to do was to make certain he did just that. He could well see why Channing and Phineas's client thought she warranted watching. But she wasn't the least bit stupid. He'd realized that almost immediately. She was perhaps a bit naive, although it was wise of her to have asked him for references.

No, he would allow his fictional American heiress to get into all kinds of trouble while keeping Miss Merryweather as safe as possible. She was right. It was going to be an adventure.

And the next time he kissed her, unexceptionable would be the farthest thing from her mind.

And wasn't that interesting? Lucy sat on the parlor sofa petting a contented Albert, curled up by her side.

"Well?" Clara stepped into the parlor and closed the doors behind her.

"Well what?" Lucy asked in an innocent manner.

"You know well what." Clara sank down on the sofa beside her. "What happened with Mr. Fairchild? I saw him leave and far later than I expected, at that."

"Oh, we had a lovely chat."

Clara's eyes narrowed. "About?"

"All sorts of things. He's extremely interesting. He told me the most amusing story about one of his experiences as an investigator."

Clara's brow rose. "Did he now?"

"He's quite reticent to say anything at all about his work, but I'm certain he's full of fascinating stories."

"I'm certain he's full of something," Clara said under her breath.

"And I told him about Lucinda's list."

Clara stared. "Do you think that's wise?"

"Wise or not, it did seem the practical thing to do." She shrugged. "I would hate for him to draw his own conclusions when observing my activities and then feel compelled to report to Jackson."

"Even so—"

"Besides, I think it will be good to have a gentleman accompanying us. Especially one as dashing and handsome as Mr. Fairchild."

"Because dashing and handsome works very nearly as well as a brilliant smile and a pleasant demeanor?" Clara said slowly.

"Precisely." Lucy grinned. "And I would much

rather have that advantage working for us than against us."

"That might well be wise after all."

"I also requested he bring references when he returns tomorrow."

Clara nodded. "Very good. I should have thought of it myself."

"However, I have been giving our Mr. Fairchild a great deal of consideration." Lucy narrowed her eyes. "I am fairly certain there is more to him than appears."

"What do you mean?" Caution sounded in Clara's voice.

"I haven't been in England long, but long enough to be able to discern the difference in accents between someone expected to work for his keep and someone well educated and well raised."

"That's very good." Admiration shone in Clara's eyes. "I hadn't noticed."

"I suspect it's only because I am new to all of this that I did notice." Lucy waved off the compliment. "Beyond that, did you observe his clothing?"

"Not really."

"It's excellent quality, Clara. Remember, I have four brothers and each of them prides himself on his appearance." She smirked. "I can spot an expertly tailored suit from across a room."

"What an unusual talent," Clara said weakly.

"One uses what one has. No, Clara." She narrowed her eyes slightly. "Our Mr. Fairchild is not the man he seems to be."

"Then we would be well rid of him."

"Nonsense. Our reasons for keeping him around are no less valid simply because he's hiding something. I expect that he will be most helpful in accomplishing some of the things on Lucinda's list. Besides"—Lucy smiled slowly—"the man is a mystery, Clara. One it will be great fun to solve."

"But you already solved a mystery."

"That was entirely too easy and shouldn't count. It was practically cheating, really. And not at all in the spirit of the quest." She scoffed. "No, solving the mystery of Mr. Fairchild will be much more satisfying. Besides"—she flashed a wicked grin—"every good adventure needs a hero."

Regrets Set to Rights

Kiss a stranger.
Find unconditional love—a dog will do nicely.
~~Solve a mystery.~~

. . . the colors so vivid, the hand of the artist so exact it did seem that the elephant and his lovely rider would walk out of the gilded frame and into the gallery itself at any moment, scattering prim matrons and their disapproving husbands. The very idea makes me laugh as they were all so well behaved and proper. No one in attendance at the exhibit would have condoned the riding of an elephant and they certainly would have been appalled by the scandalous apparel of the lady on his back. Was I the only one who looked at the painting and wondered how it would feel to be an exotic princess riding a noble beast with all the world at your feet? Fanciful idea, I admit, but lovely to think about.

I am determined to ride an elephant one day. I should think it would be great fun, an adventure to remember always. I sit a horse quite well and one wouldn't think an elephant would be all that difficult. Although, just climbing up to the seat might prove daunting. Somewhat like climbing up to a roof, I would imagine . . .

from the journal of Miss Lucinda Merryweather, 1805

Chapter Six

"Well?" Lucy twirled around, reveling in the feel of cool silk swirling around her. "What do you think, Mr. Fairchild?"

Mr. Fairchild stared, his mouth slightly open, his brown eyes wide with shock or—no, it was definitely shock. Lucy bit back a satisfied grin. She'd never shocked a handsome, dashing gentleman before; in truth, she'd never shocked anyone before, but given his reaction she would definitely do it again.

"I think it's the most wonderful thing I've ever worn." She twirled again, engulfed in yards of rich blue silk trimmed with gold-threaded embroidery. "I've never worn anything so very light, like gossamer, really. Except for night-clothes, of course, but I would certainly never appear in public in nightclothes. Goodness, that would be scandalous."

Mr. Fairchild sputtered, obviously at a loss for words. She wasn't sure she'd ever seen anyone as young as Mr. Fairchild sputter. Certainly her father sputtered a great deal, usually over politics or the antics of one of her brothers. But no one had ever sputtered over anything she had done. The oddest sense of power surged through her. Mr. Fairchild's sputtering was delightful.

"It's called a sari and it's really little more than this charming blouse with its little sleeves and yards and yards of fabric wrapped around and around you. Something like a mummy." She glanced down at the garment. "One would think it would be difficult to move with all this draped around you, but it's really quite easy. And remarkably comfortable."

"Your, your arms are uncovered!" A stunned note rang in his voice.

"Goodness, Mr. Fairchild." She scoffed. "I've worn ball gowns far more revealing than this. And they are only arms, after all. When you consider it, this is really quite modest."

"But your face and your skin and your hair!" He stared. "My God, your hair!"

"I know." She patted her now black hair. "It's a wig. Isn't it fetching? I've never even imagined having dark hair and I like it. As for my arms and face . . ." She stretched her arms out in front of her and shook her hands, admiring the look of the numerous bangle bracelets on her wrists. "Clara did it. She's very clever. I'm not sure exactly what she used. It was extremely aromatic but apparently she has used it before, although one does wonder why—"

He snorted.

She ignored him. "—and she assured me it will wash away after a bath or two or possibly more. She wasn't quite sure."

"You allowed her to color your skin?" Disbelief rang in his voice. Lucy wasn't sure if it was because Clara had darkened her skin or if it was because it had been Clara doing the dying. For some reason he and Clara had not taken to each other.

"I didn't allow her; I insisted on it."

There he went sputtering again.

"With my blond hair and fair complexion, I looked completely absurd otherwise. Why, this makes perfect sense."

"Perfect sense? It makes no sense at all and might well be the most absurd—"

"Come now, Mr. Fairchild. Surely you understood doing some of the things on my great-aunt's list would call for a certain amount of disguise and even subterfuge?"

"I hadn't really considered that you would color your face and wear something so . . . so—"

"Charming?"

"Provocative!" The shock in his voice had turned to outrage. "Why, one can see every curve and every . . . It's scandalous, Miss Merryweather. Absolutely scandalous."

"And yet millions of women in India wear the very same garment every single day."

"This is not India." Indignation squared his shoulders. "This is England!"

Obviously Lucy was mistaken, but it did seem that "God Save the Queen" or some other British patriotic anthem was playing somewhere in the distance. She resisted the urge to laugh, he was so charmingly British. "But it is part of your empire, is it not?"

"Well, yes but—"

"And I am not." She smiled.

His eyes narrowed. "Where is Miss West?"

"She's gone to call for a carriage." She cast him a chastising look. "Really, Mr. Fairchild, you need to try to be more prompt. When I said late morning I fully expected you would be here no later than midmorning. Although I suppose I do need to be more specific. But another few minutes and you would have missed us altogether and then you would have thought we were trying to avoid you." She shook her head. "It would not have been the best way to begin our journey together. And it would have been most unprofessional."

"My apologies," he said sharply. "I shall try to do better."

"See that you do." She turned toward the door.

"Miss Merryweather!"

"Yes?"

"Am I to understand that you are going to leave this house in that . . . that costume?"

"It would be pointless otherwise." She smiled. "And it's more than appropriate, really. At least for today."

"But what if someone sees you?"

"Tell me, Mr. Fairchild, if you had passed me

on the street, would you have recognized me?"

"I don't think so but I might have."

"Yes, but you and I have met. As I know practically no one else in London, there's no one *to* recognize me." She nodded and started for the door.

"Nonetheless, Miss Merryweather—"

She sighed and turned back to him. "Furthermore, if you met me today and then met me a few days from now when I looked as I always do, would you recognize me?"

"Your eyes are most distinctive," he said staunchly.

"I shall take that as both a compliment and a no. Now then, if we do not hurry we will be late and that won't do." Impatience trickled through her. Clara and the carriage should be ready and waiting by now. She reached the door, then glanced over her shoulder. "Are you coming?"

"Where?" Suspicion underlayed his words.

"Where do you think I would be going dressed like this?" She huffed and started for the entry. "Come now, Mr. Fairchild. Have you no imagination?"

"I have an excellent imagination!" he called after her.

"You hide it well."

"Wait, Miss Merryweather!" His annoyed voice echoed in the corridor. "One more moment, if you please."

"Very well!" She heaved a resigned sigh and turned back to him. "What is it now?"

"This would be much easier if you simply told me what you have planned and where we are going."

"I thought I would allow you to use your powers of deduction. I must say I'm disappointed."

"My powers of deduction?"

"Isn't that part and parcel of what you do?"

His jaw clenched. "As you wish." He studied her closely. "Given the time of day, you're not going to a masquerade ball. Besides, I've never known any woman to go to such extremes of disguise simply for a ball. You are dressed in the manner of an Indian woman—"

"Princess," she said pointedly. "I am supposed to be an Indian princess, although admittedly I might not be entirely genuine—but for my purposes authenticity probably doesn't matter."

He nodded. "An Indian princess then." His eyes lit up. "You're wearing something shocking, at least for London, which is one of the items on your list. And . . ." He paused, a triumphant smile curving his lips. "And you're going to ride an elephant. Indian I would surmise."

"Very good, Mr. Fairchild, although I expected nothing less." She smiled. "You memorized my list, didn't you?"

He smiled but said nothing.

"Excellent. Now I am impressed. Shall we go?"

"You still haven't told me exactly where we're going."

"Goodness, Mr. Fairchild. I thought you would have figured that out by now." She flashed him a grin. "We're going to the circus."

Miss Merryweather did indeed look like Indian royalty from her perch in the howdah on the back of one of the largest elephants Cam had ever seen. Or perhaps it just seemed large to him, although she was probably in no real danger as long as she stayed in her seat and nothing happened to alarm the huge beast. Indeed she smiled in a serene manner and waved to the audience crowded in the tiers of seats encircling the performance ring at Astley's Amphitheatre as if she had been doing it all her life. Still, she hadn't, and he'd noted a distinct air of apprehension when she had been assisted into her seat. If she was still uneasy, she hid it well.

Cam doubted he had ever met a woman quite like Miss Lucy Merryweather, which was, in more ways than he could count, probably a very good thing. Few people—let alone women—of his acquaintance would go to such extremes to make up for the regrets of a long-dead relative. After all, she was under no obligation to do so. Her inheritance was not contingent upon it, nor had she made any promises to her great-aunt. He was right when he'd called it a debt of honor, although he doubted most people would see it that way. The fact that Miss Merryweather—he'd started to think of her as Lucy—did so spoke well of her.

That Lucy and Miss West had managed to arrange her participation in this circus today was at once impressive and mystifying. Although given Phineas's unspoken confidence in her, nothing Miss West was involved in should have surprised Cam. He and the ersatz companion now watched the parade of elephants, brightly costumed attendants, and lovely riders circling the ring. The elephants were part of a small circus with an international flavor. They had already been preceded by a parade of Egyptian camels, Arabian dancing girls, Romanian jugglers, and Chinese acrobats. It would have been most enjoyable and highly entertaining had he been entirely confident Lucy would not do something unexpected and tumble to the ground to be stomped upon by untrustworthy pachyderms.

He inclined his head toward Miss West beside him but kept his gaze on Lucy. She might be taking all this in stride, but his heart would be in his throat until she was firmly back on solid ground.

"How did you arrange this?"

"There are very few places to find elephants in London, Mr. Fairchild." Miss West shrugged. "A circus was obvious."

"And they simply agreed to allow her to take part in this exhibition?"

"For a price." She paused. "She has a great deal of money."

"And a fair amount of courage." Cam had ridden in one of those carriages strapped on the back of an elephant when he had traveled in India. He still recalled the way the structure swayed with every step the beast took. It was disconcerting and more than a little frightening. And very high.

"She knows you're not who you say you are," Miss West said abruptly.

"Did you—"

"I haven't said a word. But you should watch your step."

"Thank you for the warning, Miss West."

"You needn't thank me. I have no more desire for the truth to be revealed than you do." She shook her head. "Do not underestimate her, Mr. Fairchild. She is far more intelligent than one might think. And she is very kind. I do not wish for either of us to hurt her."

"That's not my intention." He watched Miss Merryweather start with an unexpected movement of her elephant, then regain her composure almost immediately. "She's rather remarkable, isn't she? I've never met anyone quite like her."

Perhaps there was something in his tone, but Miss West slanted him a hard look. "Don't get any untoward ideas in your head."

"Ideas?" Even from a distance he could see Lucy was enjoying herself.

"I am aware of your reputation with women, and while I may not be an experienced companion, I will not allow you to take advantage of her."

"Take advantage of her?" His attention jerked to Miss West. "I assure you, my intentions are strictly honorable. Why, the thought hadn't even crossed my mind."

"You're lying, Mr. Fairchild. I can see it in the way you look at her." Her gaze returned to the parade. "Even if you don't realize it yourself."

Admittedly, the less than remarkable kiss they'd shared had lingered in his mind. Although he had thought the feel of her lips on his, the warmth of her breath, and the close proximity of her body to be very close to remarkable. And yes, he did plan to kiss her again. And perhaps when he'd been writing his first story last night it had included a far more passionate and satisfying kiss, which was anything but unremarkable.

"Don't be absurd, Miss West. I have no designs on either Miss Merryweather's affections or virtue. And in spite of what Mr. Chapman may have said to you, my reputation with women is no worse than any other gentleman's."

She snorted. "Oh, that's a comforting endorsement."

"Don't you think you're taking this masquerade

of protective companion a bit too seriously? Miss Merryweather is of age, after all. She certainly knows her own mind and we are in agreement as to her intelligence."

"It's not a masquerade. For the foreseeable future, I *am* her companion." Her tone hardened. "She trusts me, and I take that and my current position most seriously. I will not allow that trust to be misplaced."

"Excellent attitude, Miss West. However"—he glanced at her—"you do not trust me."

"Not in the least." She huffed. "You kissed her."

"On the contrary, she kissed me."

"It shall not happen again," she said firmly.

"You'll have to speak to Miss Merryweather about that."

"I have."

"And?"

"And it's none of your business."

And wasn't that interesting? He resisted the urge to grin with satisfaction. There was no point in further annoying Miss West. Besides, Lucy and her elephant were exiting the main ring. The parade would be followed shortly by individual acts. The thought occurred to him that one of those would be aerialists performing on high wire and trapeze. He shuddered at the thought that Lucy might want to accomplish her great-aunt's desire to fly by swinging through the air. He did hope that hadn't occurred to her.

They made their way through the crowd back to the staging area, an outdoor space covered overhead by tenting attached to the building. Exotic wild beasts jostled with handlers, circus hands, and assorted performers, and the hard-packed ground was covered with sawdust and hay. Lucy had already dismounted her elephant and was in an animated discussion with the man who had been previously introduced as the head of the circus. Apparently they reached some sort of agreement. Lucy shook the man's hand, then spotted Cam and Miss West and started toward them, a satisfied smile on her face.

"I must tell you I didn't like the way the handler kept berating my elephant. Every time he smacked the poor creature, the animal would shake with fear or despair, I'm not quite sure which."

"Do elephants feel despair?" Cam asked in a mild tone.

"I can't imagine that they wouldn't." She looked back at the elephant she had ridden. "You can see it in his eyes, poor dear. His name is Hannibal, by the way. But he's old, you see, and not as quick to respond to commands as he once was, according to his handler." Lucy's expression hardened. "I took an instant aversion to him—the handler not the elephant. I think he deserves better."

"The elephant or the handler?" Miss West's brow furrowed in confusion.

"Hannibal, of course. So." Lucy drew a deep breath. "I arranged to purchase him."

"What are you going to do with an elephant?" Cam stared.

"I thought of sending him back to his native land but I'm afraid he is far too domesticated for that. I was assured that he would not fare well."

"By the people who sold him to you, no doubt." Cam couldn't quite keep a sarcastic note from his voice.

"Where will we put him?" Miss West murmured.

"Miss Merryweather, he is not a dog. Or a parrot." Cam sighed. "Your great-aunt's desire was to ride an elephant, not keep one stabled in the back garden."

"I have no intention of keeping him, Mr. Fairchild." She cast him a look that clearly said he was the one whose sanity was in question. "I simply want him to be well taken care of and cherished. He really is quite an affectionate fellow and I don't want him to be made to perform. He deserves better. I think perhaps . . ." She glanced at Miss West. "A zoo?"

"The zoological gardens." Miss West nodded. "Yes, they would like that. As, no doubt, would Hannibal." She smiled. "What an excellent idea."

"I thought so." Lucy nodded. "We need to arrange for his transport and contact the zoological gardens. The circus owner has agreed to continue to care for him until we can move him to his new home, for a fee, of course."

"Naturally," Cam said.

Lucy ignored him. "Clara—"

"I'll see to the details here and make the arrangements for him this afternoon." She handed Lucy her cloak, nodded, and started after the circus owner.

"She's exceptionally efficient." Lucy's gaze followed the other woman. "I was quite lucky to have found her. Although I suppose I really didn't find her as—"

"Why, Miss Merryweather," he said sharply. Obviously, she needed someone to keep her finances safe as well as her person. And, just as obviously, Miss West was not going to be of much help. "Why did you find it necessary to spend a great deal of money to purchase an elephant only to then donate it to a zoo?"

"Why not?" Her eyes widened in surprise. "For one thing, if I can't do something good with my money, I really don't deserve to have it. We are no better than how we treat the least among us, Mr. Fairchild. That poor animal has spent much of his life in captivity, and now that he's old, his useful days are limited. I think it's terribly sad that such a noble beast should be put in such a position."

"Agreed, but you cannot buy all the elephants in all the circuses." He shook his head. "You can't rescue them all."

"No, but I can save this one." She met his gaze

firmly. "I think this was the right thing to do and it did need to be done. I didn't want not doing it to be one of my regrets one day."

He stared at her. "I suppose one can't argue with that."

"I didn't think so," she said firmly, and handed him her cloak, then turned so he could help her on with it. "You think this was a frivolous waste of money, don't you, Mr. Fairchild?"

"Yes, I do." He helped her on with her cloak, resisting the urge to allow his hands to linger on her shoulders. "Or rather I did. No, I still do but . . ."

"But?" She turned around and smiled up at him. "You sound confused."

"You are a most confusing woman." He gazed down into her blue eyes, deep and endless, colored by summer skies and filled with life. Summer had always been his favorite season. "Yes, I think spending money on an elephant you have no use for is foolish." He drew a deep breath. "But you are as kind as you are clever. I cannot fault your motives. Or your heart."

"Thank you, Mr. Fairchild." She smiled up at him, her gaze locked with his.

The sounds of the amphitheatre dimmed, as if the world itself had faded, leaving only the two of them. His heart thudded oddly in his chest. With very little effort he could press his lips to hers. "You have a very big heart, Miss Merryweather."

"Lucy." She raised her face to his and leaned forward slightly. "You should call me Lucy."

"That would be most improper," he murmured, lowering his lips to hers. A voice in the back of his mind screamed that this too was most improper. He ignored it.

"Are you going to kiss me, Mr. Fairchild?" Her lips were a scant inch from his.

"Yes, I believe I will."

"Are you prepared then?"

"I believe I am."

"Good, Mr. Fairchild . . . Cameron . . . I . . ." Abruptly, she drew away, covered her mouth with her hands and sneezed. A second sneeze immediately followed the first and then one more. "I am so sorry." She cast him a helpless look.

"As am I," he said under his breath, even if it was probably for the best.

"My nose is itching terribly." She rubbed her nose and held out her hand. "Do you . . ." He promptly pulled out a handkerchief and handed it to her. "Thank you." She sniffed and her eyes watered. "I hardly ever sneeze, even when I'm ill." She rubbed her arms.

"Are you all right?" Miss West hurried to join them.

"I'm fine." She smiled at Cam and he could see in her eyes that she too regretted what her sneeze had interrupted. "Just a momentary reaction, I think, to all the dust in the air."

"It is rather thick in here." Miss West coughed. "I can barely breathe myself."

"I think we need to get both of you out of here at once and into the fresh air." He took each woman's arm and propelled them toward the exit. "Tell me, Miss Merryweather." A change of subject would take her mind off her nose and her eyes. He wasn't sure, but she was starting to look a bit puffy. "Were you ill at ease? On the elephant?"

"Not at all, Mr. Fairchild. I was terrified. It was far higher than I had realized and felt distinctly unstable. I had no idea riding on such an enormous beast would feel very much like being on a ship in rolling seas. But the terror was probably why it was so very enjoyable." She smiled valiantly in spite of the anxious expression crossing her face. "I do think we need to return home now however. And as quickly as possible. I'm afraid I'm reaching the end of my endurance. It's been quite an adventure and I'm sure Lucinda would have loved it. But . . ." She glanced at Miss West and winced. "Whatever we used to darken my skin"—she bit her bottom lip and her eyes watered—"is starting to itch."

Regrets Set to Rights

Ride an elephant.
Wear something shocking.

. . . and I certainly don't understand why my education seems to consist only of needlework, penmanship, the management of a household, and French. Oh, yes, and the playing of a suitable instrument. When I dare to complain about the inequity of what I am expected to learn compared to what my brothers learn, I am told it is not a lady's place to learn the sorts of things men do. Ladies should study that which will prove useful to them in the future. It's rubbish, of course, but apparently I am the only one who thinks so.

I should very much like to study the stars or ancient civilizations or anything that would not be deemed useful to me in the future. Something completely frivolous or entirely unexpected or, at the very least, interesting . . .

from the journal of Miss Lucinda Merryweather, 1804

Chapter Seven

Lucy had had a bad time of it.

While blame could not be placed on Cam— indeed, he would have stopped it had he had the opportunity—he couldn't help but feel sorry for her. She was quite miserable, at least in the beginning, and then somewhat mortified. Even the knowledge that he was right about the foolishness of it, and she and Miss West were so very wrong and, better yet, realized it, gave Cam no satis-faction whatsoever.

For the past week Lucy had been confined to Channing House at the insistence of a very disapproving doctor and her own embarrassment. It was something of a relief, really. If his job was to ensure Lucy's safety, nowhere was she safer than Channing House, and she certainly wasn't about to step foot outside its doors. Very few of her great-aunt's adventures took place in a London house. What could happen to Lucy there?

Cam had come by every day but had rarely stayed more than half an hour. He could think of no legitimate reason to linger, even though he had wanted to. He looked forward with increasing anticipation to seeing her every day and each day found himself reluctant to leave. Every minute with Lucy was a revelation and a delight.

She was nothing short of fascinating in her outspokenness and the way she looked at the world and her place in it. Whenever they could dispense with Miss West's presence, they spoke of all sorts of things. He learned she had four brothers, all engaged in various business pursuits, a bank director for a father, and a mother who sounded entirely too cognizant of proper behavior to have produced Lucy. Although, upon further consideration, perhaps only a very proper mother could have produced such a delightfully carefree daughter. But she never revealed her connection to Jackson Channing and, of course, it was not something he could ask. She was intensely curious as to the details of his alleged profession and he invented one story after another about the perilous adventures of a private investigator, each more adventurous then the last, making certain to write down whatever story he had spun after his visit. Her interest worked to his benefit and he managed to avoid saying anything that might reveal his true identity, although he did confide that he too had older brothers as well as a sister. But with every word he grew more and more uneasy with his deception.

Worse, it was no longer entirely an act. He wasn't sure when his ruse had become something akin to a legitimate position, but it had. When had keeping her safe become so important to him?

Certainly, he did not want to further arouse her suspicions by being less than the efficient investigator she thought he was. Beyond that, she had placed her trust in him and he did feel honor bound to make certain no harm came to her. He hadn't expected that. He hadn't been overly honorable for quite some time. At least not when it came to women, even if he was no worse than any other man. He cringed at the memory of Miss West's response to that.

To make matters more confusing, at some indiscernible point in the last week, perhaps when her skin color had faded to an intriguing shade of lavender, he had come to the inescapable realization that he liked her. Quite a lot really. It was something of a shock. He wasn't at all used to liking a woman. Oh certainly, he liked *women,* very much so, but aside from his sister and numerous cousins, he wasn't at all used to thinking of a woman as someone to be liked as well as desired. It was as odd and unsettling an idea as it was intriguing. Nothing could come of it, after all. She was his, well, his muse, and if she ever discovered the truth she would never forgive him. His own experiences with women, in addition to his observation of his brothers' romantic fiascos, was evidence of that.

Lucy's confinement to the house had proven most beneficial. For one thing, she hadn't been able to check on the references he had left with her. One was written by Chapman, a second by Simon, who had been curious but had enough secrets of his own that his younger brother had kept through the years to refrain from extensive questioning. For another, Cam had been able to write the first four installments of *The Daring Exploits of a Runaway Heiress* and half of a fifth, and he was quite pleased with them. They were humorous as well as adventurous. Two had already appeared in this week's *Messenger* under the pseudonym I. F. Aldrich. Which did seem wise should Lucy stumble onto the stories. Not that it really mattered. While he had freely borrowed from her quest and list of adventures, he was confident that his heroine bore little resemblance to Lucy.

Aside from that pesky matter of his conscience, all in all things were going quite nicely. Why, even that blasted dog was beginning to tolerate him. Yes, indeed, things were going well. A comforting sense of well-being filled him at the thought.

"Good day, sir," the butler greeted him.

"Good day, Clement." Cam handed the butler his overcoat. "How is Miss Merryweather today?"

"Very good, sir. She is almost her natural color again." The butler's expression didn't so much as twitch although there was a distinct hint of disapproval in his eyes. "And the swelling is nearly gone today."

Cam winced. Lucy's color had gone from brown to an odd shade of purple and then finally faded to a distinct red, no doubt as much due to intense scrubbing to remove all traces of the dye as to the concoction itself. Miss West blamed herself even if Lucy didn't. These things happen, Lucy had said. Obviously, the coloring agent hadn't agreed with her and no one could have predicted that. Still, Miss West was beside herself with guilt and remorse.

"She is in the kitchen, sir." Again, the faint glint of disapproval shone in his eyes.

"The kitchen?" Cam raised a brow. "Dare I ask why?"

"It's not for me to say, sir," the servant said firmly. "But she directed me to give the kitchen staff a half day off." Cam suspected there was a great deal more the butler wanted to say. Unease washed through him and his sense of well-being vanished.

Clement directed a footman to escort Cam through the maze of the house below stairs to the kitchen. The room was larger than he expected, ovens and stoves along one wall together with a massive fireplace, cupboards, tables, and shelves along the others. Copper molds hung on the walls, pots and pans dangled from hooks under shelves weighted with various and sundry pieces of cooking equipment. A long worktable stretched the length of the room. Windows near the ceiling let in shafts of winter sunlight. Cam had been in his family's kitchens on occasion and this one struck him as surprisingly spacious and probably well equipped. He stepped into the room and pulled up short.

Lucy sat on a stool at the center table, her elbows on the tabletop, her chin resting on her hands, and gazed up at a man standing on the opposite side wearing a double-breasted chef's coat. The cook was addressing her in an energetic manner accompanied by a great deal of gesturing. Obviously, he was not British.

Cam was not usually inclined to note another man's appearance, but in this case it was hard not to. *Greek god* was the first thing that came to mind, and given the way Lucy stared at him in a manner that could well be described as *smitten,* she thought so too. The cook took a spoonful of something from a bowl on the table and held it out to her. She opened her mouth and took the spoonful with a contented sigh. Something that might have been jealousy stabbed Cam and he shoved it aside. If it was his job to protect her, by God, protect her he would. Especially from Greek gods.

He cleared his throat.

Lucy glanced toward him and smiled a welcome. "Good day, Mr. Fairchild."

"Miss Merryweather." He strode to her side. "I hear you are much recovered today."

"Indeed I am." She tilted her face from side to side. "I am very nearly my normal color again."

"Yes, I can see that." Although she was still a shade pink, which might have been as much from the heat of the kitchen as the remains of her masquerade debacle. He glanced at the cook. "And what are you up to today?"

"Oh, I am sorry. Where are my manners?" She hopped off the stool. "Mr. Fairchild, allow me to introduce Monsieur François Vadeboncoeur."

French? Cam should have known.

A pained expression crossed the Frenchman's face. "It is pronounced Vad-eh-bon-kehr, mademoiselle."

"Yes, of course, I am sorry." She grimaced. "François—"

François?

"—this is Mr. Fairchild. My . . ." She frowned. "Why, I'm not certain what to call you. I've never had to introduce you before. What are you, Mr. Fairchild?"

"Whatever you wish me to be, Miss Merryweather," Cam said in his most gallant manner, then met Vadeboncoeur's gaze directly. "As it is my job to make certain no harm befalls you, I suppose *guardian* is as good a word as any."

"Oh?" Vadeboncoeur raised a brow. "I would not think you so feeble as to need a guardian, mademoiselle."

"Mr. Fairchild is here for my protection,

164

François. One might even call him, oh, a bodyguard of sorts."

"What a lovely job to have. Guarding the person of the charming Mademoiselle Lucy."

Lucy dimpled.

"Yes, well, it has its moments," Cam said in a crisp manner befitting a private investigator, then leaned close to Lucy and lowered his voice. "A word, Miss Merryweather, in private if you please."

"Of course." She smiled at the cook, then strode through the door into the corridor, pausing beside the stairs leading up to the ground floor. "Will this do or would you prefer to go upstairs? I doubt if François can hear us here."

"I really don't care if he can hear us or not. I simply thought it best to discuss this matter in private so as not to embarrass you."

"How very thoughtful of you." She beamed up at him. She had donned a serviceable kitchen apron, and while he had never thought of something so inappropriate as being the least bit attractive, she looked quite fetching and nearly irresistible. No doubt the Frenchman had noticed. "Although I can't imagine anything you have to say that would embarrass me. However, you do now have my complete attention."

"Where is Miss West?"

"Why, that wasn't the least bit embarrassing, Mr. Fairchild." She heaved a heartfelt sigh. "I expected far better from you."

Damnation, she could be annoying. His jaw tightened. "Miss West?"

"I insisted she take a day to herself." Lucy shook her head. "The poor dear has had every bit as bad a time of it as I have. Worse, really, as she blamed herself."

"I see." He drew his brows together. "And in her absence you thought it wise to flirt with a Frenchman alone in the kitchen?"

"Flirt?" Her eyes widened. "I was doing no such thing."

"Then what were you doing?"

"What do you think I was doing?"

"I am not going to play guessing games with you every time I arrive here," he said sharply. "There is absolutely nothing on your great-aunt's list that requires a French chef or a Frenchman at all—" Realization struck him and he gasped. "Unless you intend to take a lover or have a romantic interlude!"

She stared at him in stunned silence, then laughed.

Outrage raised his voice. "This is not funny, Miss Merryweather."

"Good Lord, Cameron, of course it is. It may well be one of the funniest things I've ever heard." She sniffed and wiped her eyes. "While taking a lover or having a romantic interlude are on my great-aunt's list, I learned my lesson from kissing a stranger." She shook her head. "We both agreed it was probably not exactly what Lucinda had in mind."

"Nonetheless . . ." He drew his brows together. "What do you mean—learned your lesson?"

"I mean when it comes to things of that nature on the list—items like kissing a stranger or taking a lover or having a romantic interlude, one simply can't grab the first opportunity that comes along. No, those things take a bit more thought and preparation."

"Preparation?" He snorted. "It looked to me as if there was a great deal of preparation already under way when I walked in."

"On the contrary, there was no preparation whatsoever. Besides, I would never hire someone to be my lover. Nor would I hide him in a kitchen. That would be extremely tasteless and tawdry and . . ." Her eyes narrowed and she crossed her arms over her chest. "The mere idea that you think I would do such a thing is insulting."

She was right. Still, why else would she have a handsome Frenchman in the house?

"I do think an apology is in order, don't you?"

"Not until you explain why that man is here."

"Jackson certainly did choose well when he hired you." She studied him for a moment, then sighed. "I don't believe I owe you any explanation at all, but I see no harm in telling you that François is here to teach me how to do something I have never done before."

"Exactly!"

"You do have an overly suspicious mind, Mr. Fairchild. No doubt a consequence of your profession." She glared at him. "One might even think you were jealous."

"Jealous?" He scoffed and ignored the voice in the back of his head that said she might possibly be right. "Don't be absurd. My job is to keep you from harm and I can tell just by looking at him that Vadeboncoeur is not to be trusted."

"Can you indeed?" She leaned to the side and peered around him into the kitchen. "How? He looks perfectly harmless to me."

"Believe me, Miss Merryweather, I know that type of man."

"He is shockingly handsome," she murmured.

"And he knows it." Cam nodded. "He is not squandering all that Gallic charm on you to no purpose. The man is dangerous, probably to every female he encounters but especially to someone as inexperienced as you."

"I'm not a child, you know." She shrugged. "Nor am I especially worried."

"Exactly my point. Why, before you can so much as call for help, he'll be taking you into his arms and sweeping you off your feet."

"Do you really think so?" she said, still considering Vadeboncoeur in the kitchen.

"I know so. Miss Merryweather!" he said sharply. "Do stop staring at him."

"I wasn't staring." Her denial might have carried more weight had she not continued to study the Frenchman with a thoughtful look on her face. "I really hadn't considered the possibility of a romantic interlude with François, but I have always heard that the French take that sort of thing differently than we do. He might well be amenable to the idea. Thank you, Mr. Fairchild, you do make an excellent point."

"I had no intention of making a point!"

"No, I didn't think you did." Reluctantly she shifted her gaze from the chef back to Cam. "François is here to teach me to make a cake."

"You can call it whatever you want!"

She snorted back a laugh. "I call it making a cake." She eyed him with amusement. "You know, one mixes flour and sugar and apparently all sorts of other things and bakes it in the oven."

"I know what a cake is," Cam snapped even as he realized he had jumped to a nearly unforgivable conclusion. Still, the situation had looked bad. "Why?"

"Because I have no idea how to do anything in a kitchen and, as I'm still not quite ready to venture out of the house, I thought learning to bake a cake would be interesting and unexpected and definitely frivolous. I shall never have to cook for myself or my family. Why, my mother never steps foot in a kitchen unless it is to instruct Mrs. Helstrom—our cook—as to the menu for dinner. And I am supposed to learn something one would not expect. Besides"—she grinned—"I like cake."

"Isn't there a cook in residence here who could teach you to bake a cake?"

"Yes, I suppose." She peered around him again. "But I thought hiring a chef would be much more fun. He comes very highly recommended."

"No doubt." He huffed. "Very well then, you have my apologies for thinking, well, what I was thinking."

"I'm not sure whether or not I wish to accept it." Her brow furrowed with annoyance. "The idea that I would have to hire someone to become my lover is not merely rude but offensive and rather hurtful as well. I thought we had come to know each other better than that. I would certainly never jump to a conclusion that painted you in an especially poor light. The fact that you seem to have no difficulty thinking the worst of me is most distressing."

"I didn't really—"

"Oh, but you did." She stepped closer and glared up at him. "Do you think I am so unappealing that I would have to pay a man to take me to his bed?"

"No, of course not." He grimaced. "I didn't mean . . . I wasn't thinking . . ." He drew a deep breath. "You are exceptionally lovely, Miss Merryweather."

"Then it's my character that you think men would have to be paid to overlook?"

"Not at all," he said staunchly. "You're quite clever and extremely interesting. You are kind and witty and have an acute sense of honor I have rarely encountered in a woman or a man, for that matter."

"Then the fault lies not with me but with you?"

"With me?" He paused, then blew a resigned breath. "I am an idiot, Miss Merryweather," he said weakly.

"None of us is perfect, Mr. Fairchild. It's important to acknowledge our own flaws so that we may strive to overcome them. You shall have to work on that." She studied him for a moment, as if she was assessing every one of his flaws and found them both numerous and irredeemable. "Apology accepted." She nodded firmly. "That's enough of that then. François insists on instructing me in the basic tenets of cake making before we actually start, and I'm beginning to suspect it will take much of the day. It's apparently far more complicated than I expected. But as I said"—a slight wicked smile curved her lips—"it will be fun."

Not if he could help it. "While the baking of a cake does seem fairly innocuous . . ." He glanced over his shoulder at the Frenchman in the kitchen. Bloody hell. Baking with Vadeboncoeur might well be anything but innocent. There was no mistaking the way the man looked at Lucy. Cake was not the only thing on the chef's mind. "Surely there is something else you could learn to do that would satisfy that item on your list?"

"Nothing I could think of." She shrugged. "At least nothing I could learn in a timely manner. Most skills take a great deal of time to master, you know."

"Perhaps but . . ." He racked his brains trying to think of something. What could she learn? "Why, you could learn a language. Or at least a few phrases."

"I daresay François could help me with that as well." She cast Cam an innocent smile. "However, every well-bred woman I know is expected to speak at least a smattering of French and Italian, so learning a language is not the least bit unexpected and is far more practical than frivolous. Besides, any number of well-meaning instructors have attempted to teach me both French and Italian and, well, my mind simply doesn't work in more than one language."

"You could learn to play tennis perhaps." Tennis was certainly appropriate. "Or be instructed in rowing or fencing."

"I already enjoy tennis, and frankly, I would much prefer to be rowed than to row. And quite a few ladies of my acquaintance fence. As do I." She smiled. "Quite well really."

"You could—"

"I could do any number of things I suppose, Mr. Fairchild." She sighed. "But this is what first came to mind and this is what I intend to learn. François is here and prepared to teach me, so unless you have any further objections, I suggest we get on with it." She considered him for a moment. "I am really quite surprised, Mr. Fairchild, given there are so many other things that I might have settled on to learn that are far more difficult, if not dangerous and even scandalous. Baking a cake is insignificant compared to some of the things that have crossed my mind." An innocent note sounded in her voice, but her eyes sparked with wicked amusement. "Would you like to hear about those?"

Without warning the unbidden thought flashed through his mind: there were any number of things he'd like to teach her as well. He ruthlessly shoved the thought aside. "Absolutely not!"

"Good, because I do love cake." She turned back toward the kitchen. "Now if you will excuse me."

"I have no intention of leaving, Miss Merryweather."

"Well, I have no intention of allowing you to linger in the kitchen glaring at François."

"It seems we are at an impasse then." He couldn't resist a satisfied smile.

"It does, doesn't it?" She stepped closer, a determined look in her eye. "Mr. Fairchild, we have already agreed that I could throw you out at any moment, which would make your job much more difficult and unpleasant as I can't believe you enjoy skulking about in the cold. I have only allowed you to join our little company because it now seems wise to have a gentleman's presence for the purposes of safety."

"You and I both know you won't throw me out." He cast her a confident smile. "We have come too far for that."

"Yes, I suppose we have." Her voice hardened. "However, I have no desire for your disapproving glare to follow my every move, nor do I intend to allow you to intimidate poor, dear François."

"When did he become *poor, dear* François?" He tried and failed to hide the indignant note in his voice, ignoring the fact that she had called Miss West a *poor dear* as well as the elephant. It was simply a phrase she used both frequently and indiscriminately. Nonetheless, when she used it in reference to the Frenchman, it made his teeth clench.

"When you became an overbearing, irrational tyrant. And an idiot."

"I am not . . . ." He sighed. "I did apologize."

"Very well." She stepped around him, opened a tall cupboard, grabbed a folded white cloth, and thrust it at him. "If you insist on staying, you'll have to put this on."

He eyed it with suspicion. "What is it?"

"It's an apron. It wouldn't do for you to be covered in flour."

He scoffed. "I'm not going to wear an apron."

"As you wish. But if you are going to be here, you too will have to learn to bake a cake."

He snorted. "I don't think so."

"Of course, if you don't believe you are up to it . . ." She shrugged.

"The greatest chefs in the world have always been men," he muttered, and snatched the apron from her hand. "I can't imagine this will be all that difficult to master."

"We shall see." She smirked.

He stared at her. "You don't think I can do this, do you?"

"Do you?"

He unfolded the apron. "You're driving me quite mad, Miss Merryweather."

"I cannot tell you how delightful I find that, Mr. Fairchild." She held out her hand. "Give me your coat."

He narrowed his eyes in suspicion. "Why?"

"Because the apron will not fit properly over a coat." She rolled her gaze toward the ceiling. "You would probably be most uncomfortable, which would make you even more irritating than you seem determined to be today."

"Fine!" he snapped, pulled off his coat, handed it to her, and struggled into the apron.

"Come along then." She nodded and marched

back into the kitchen, tossed his coat onto a chair by the door, and retook her seat. "François, your class has now grown to two. Mr. Fairchild will be joining us."

"Excellent, mademoiselle." Vadeboncoeur cast him a smug look, then turned his attention back to Lucy. "But are you certain you wish to make a cake? A cake is nothing special." His gaze met Lucy's. "But a soufflé." His voice was low and enticing, as if he was talking about something far tastier than a soufflé. "To bake a soufflé is a skill to be desired."

Lucy stared as if mesmerized. "Yes, I can see that."

"Flavored with chocolate perhaps."

Lucy made an odd sort of moaning sound. "I do so love chocolate."

Cam stared. What on earth?

"The first bite melting in the mouth . . ."

"Oh my, yes . . ." She fairly sighed the words.

"Light as the very air you breathe, an essence of flavor, the taste fit for the gods themselves . . ."

"Mmmm . . ."

"Intense and yet ethereal."

"Oh . . ." Lucy leaned forward, her eyes slightly closed.

Good God! Cam was right. The bloody Frenchman was seducing her with words of food! Enough of this nonsense was enough.

"Miss Merryweather wishes to bake a cake and a cake it shall be," Cam said crisply.

Lucy snapped out of whatever culinary spell Vadeboncoeur had cast and heaved a resigned sigh. "I do love cake."

"Then let's get on with it, shall we?" Cam removed his cuff links, set them on the table, then rolled up his sleeves and adopted a pleasant smile. "How do we begin?"

Vadeboncoeur's eyes narrowed slightly. "At the beginning, of course, monsieur." He cast a regretful look at Lucy, then launched into a heavily accented explanation of eggs and flour and Cam had no idea what else. Lucy still looked interested but no longer enthralled.

Good.

Vadeboncoeur's flirtatious manner did seem to lessen but only a bit, and Cam kept a close eye on him. Not an easy task as this whole business of baking a cake was far more complicated than Cam had ever imagined. Of course, he'd never given any real consideration to what went on in a kitchen, only to what came out of it. Separating the egg yolks from the whites alone proved far trickier than one would have thought, and he and Lucy went through an astonishing number of eggs before getting the technique right. Although Cam did question Vadeboncoeur's *technique*.

And just before the chef handed him a bowl full of egg whites and a medieval-looking instrument with which to beat them into submission, the unbidden thought struck him.

His grandmother would definitely like Lucy.

"Mr. Fairchild." Lucy leaned closer to Cam and spoke low. François, in the far end of the kitchen, had his back to them checking the ovens. "I believe you're supposed to whip those into a light and frothy consistency, not stir them as if you were trying to cool off soup."

He stirred faster.

"Goodness, Cameron." She huffed with exasperation. "François showed you how to do it."

Apparently, anything in a kitchen was as far beyond Cameron's abilities as foreign languages were for Lucy. Admittedly he did seem to be making an effort in those rare moments when he and François were not exchanging thinly veiled insults. Lucy considered it something of a miracle that neither had given in to the impulse to fling food at each other, although it was plain in both men's eyes that they were tempted. But the day was still young. They were both acting like schoolboys. Or rivals. When François had stood behind her and put his arms around her to instruct her in the proper way to separate eggs, the muscle in Cameron's jaw tightened and she wondered that his teeth didn't crack given how hard he clenched them. It was a credit to his self-control that he hadn't done something stupid but instead requested for François to show him the proper way as well. It was quite humorous, although she doubted either man would have agreed. Lucy had never had men snipe at each other over her before and it was very nearly as enjoyable as it was annoying.

Nonetheless, spending a few hours learning to do something he had no interest in and would never do again, as well as putting up with a man he obviously disliked, was the price Cameron had to pay for his . . . his idiocy. Imagine him thinking for so much as a moment that she had hired François to be her lover. The very thought heated her cheeks with embarrassment.

"You simply need to put more *wrist* into it." She shrugged. "It isn't especially difficult."

"To whip zee eggs into a concoction as light and fluffy as zee very clouds in zee sky takes a fine hand, mademoiselle," he said in his best, or more likely his worst, French-accented imitation of the chef. "One must use zee wrist and zee heart."

"Mr. Fairchild!" She gasped and tried very hard not to let him see the tiniest bit of amusement. "That was extraordinarily rude."

He cast her an unrepentant grin. "But funny. You have to admit it was funny."

"It was not the least bit funny," she said firmly, and turned away for fear he'd see her amusement in her eyes. It wasn't his imitation of the chef that was so funny but rather the very fact that he'd attempted it at all. His accent was atrocious, which did make it all the more comical.

But then she did find him more and more amusing. He'd come to the house every day during her unfortunate confinement and never once pointed out he had warned her that the skin coloring was a bad idea. It was most considerate of him.

If Cameron wasn't so terribly amusing and dashing and, when he wished to be, charming, he might not be worth the effort to keep around. But she had been far more frightened by the incident with her purse than she'd let even Clara see. The theft had brought to mind all sorts of dire and dreadful predicaments two women alone might encounter, and having a gentleman on hand seemed like an excellent idea. Still, even if she wished to be rid of him, he had been hired to watch her and watch her he was determined to do. Besides, she was becoming rather fond of him. No, in truth, she liked him. More and more each day. And just last night he had appeared in her dreams as well, which was both disconcerting and intriguing.

And she did so love his stories about his work as a private investigator. Lucy had always loved a good story. Pity she didn't believe a word of them.

It was her experience that real life was never as perfectly entertaining as something made up. And

Cameron's stories were suspiciously close to perfectly amusing. It was hard as well to ignore how he steered the conversation to one of his investigative adventures whenever it veered too close to his personal life. The man was definitely hiding something. But that touch of mystery was nearly as appealing as his brown eyes and irresistible smile.

She'd noted when she'd taken his coat that the quality of the fabric and the tailoring of the garment was well above average. And probably out of financial reach of a private investigator no matter how much he was paid for what appeared to be very little work. He was obviously well educated and, just as obviously, used to the finer things in life. His pronunciation of François' last name was impeccable even to her untrained ear and had earned him a grudging modicum of respect from the chef. He was also a bit more concerned with propriety than one might have expected. All of which spoke of a privileged upbringing.

But, regardless of his secrets, he did seem to have a sense of honor. One could tell that just by talking to him. Lucy wasn't completely certain but she suspected she was an excellent judge of character; at least, nothing had ever happened to prove her wrong, and something inside her insisted he was an honorable man. But what did an honorable man have to hide? It would be entirely convoluted to hire an investigator to ferret out the secrets of a fellow investigator. Still, the idea had merit.

Oh yes, she did indeed like Cameron Fairchild. Even so, she had lied to him. As brief and fleeting as their kiss had been, as unremarkable as she had claimed it to be, it had still done something quite remarkable to the pit of her stomach. Which did seem to bear further examination or at the very least, another kiss. He had very nearly kissed her at the circus and she had very much wanted him to. He'd not attempted it since, which was both disappointing and a relief. She wasn't entirely sure how she'd react to another kiss, although she couldn't quite get the idea out of her head. It occurred with alarming frequency whenever her hand inadvertently brushed his, or she gazed into his dark eyes or his smile reached into her soul. She slanted a quick glance at him. He was hand-some and dashing, funny and proper, no more than a few years older than she and, in many ways, all a woman might want in a man. If a woman was looking for a man—which she wasn't, of course. Still, he was a mystery and she simply adored mysteries.

Cameron leaned close and spoke softly. "Do you realize you called me Cameron? Twice by my count."

"Did I?" She shrugged. "I hadn't noticed."

He grinned in obvious disbelief.

"You needn't make anything of it. I call François by his given name."

"I thought that was significant at first and frankly, somewhat alarming. Then I realized I was wrong."

"Oh?"

"Once I heard you attempt to pronounce Vadeboncoeur, I saw that François was much more practical."

"He insisted." She winced. "He's rather sensitive about the pronunciation of his name."

"And your mind doesn't work in more than one language."

"Exactly." She paused. "I will confess, I have started to think of you as Cameron rather than Mr. Fairchild," she said slowly. "We are spending a great deal of time together, after all, and we have forged a friendship of sorts."

"I didn't expect that." He smiled into her eyes and something deep inside her fluttered. "But I find it delightful, Lucy."

She stared at him for a long moment. "As do I." She drew a deep breath. "However, I think it would be wise to restrict our address of one another to Miss Merryweather and Mr. Fairchild when in the presence of others, especially Miss West. I doubt she would find it quite as delightful."

He chuckled. "She doesn't like me."

"I'm not sure she doesn't like you as much as

she doesn't trust you." In spite of her conviction that he was an honorable man, Lucy wasn't entirely sure she trusted him either. After all, what kind of secrets did an honorable man have, anyway?

"But you do?"

"Completely," she lied.

"I suspect you're entirely too clever to fully trust anyone you barely know."

"You did say you were trustworthy."

He smiled, and again that odd fluttering caught at her. And gazing into his brown eyes, it struck her that Mr. Fairchild was wrong.

The most dangerous man in the kitchen wasn't the French chef.

Regrets Set to Rights

Learn to do something unexpected
or interesting or frivolous.

. . . most annoying that men should be allowed to retreat from the troubles of the world to a sanctuary they so innocently call a gentlemen's club. We all suspect that said sanctuary is no doubt filled with gambling and liquor and all those pastimes men find delightful but forbid to women.

It's the way of the world we live in, of course, but it strikes me, and all of my friends agree, that it's not the least bit fair. Certainly one can understand why women would be prohibited from a place of business, but a club strictly for the purposes of social interaction should not be so restricted. Although I doubt that will ever change as long as the male of the species continues to rule.

Regardless, I would very much like to see exactly what transpires in such a club. How amusing an adventure it would be to slip into those hallowed halls, especially if one could do so unobserved, like a fly on a wall. It would certainly be a scandal if one was discovered. Mother would never recover. Still, it's a delightful idea . . .

from the journal of Miss Lucinda Merryweather, 1806

Chapter Eight

"Mr. Fairchild is not going to be happy about this," Clara said mildly.

Lucy's gaze met Clara's in the large mirror reflecting the two women. "Does that concern us?"

Clara shrugged. "Not in the least."

"Yes, well, it can't be helped," Lucy said firmly. "It's not as if I actually lied to him." Lucy studied her reflection and ignored an annoying stab of guilt. Cameron would certainly see her failure to inform him about tonight's activities as a lie of omission at the very least. But only if he found out. "When Mr. Fairchild made his obligatory appearance this morning to check on our activities, I said we had no plans to leave the house this evening, and at that point we hadn't. I told him we intended to do nothing more than consider the remaining items on Great-aunt Lucinda's list and how to best accomplish them and, at that point, that was indeed our intention."

"He did look rather uneasy at that."

Lucy grinned. "Delightful, wasn't it?"

Clara laughed.

It was the truth, at that point. And Lucy really hadn't anticipated anything changing, although perhaps she should have. The day after she'd baked what turned out to be an extremely tasty cake, thanks to François, she'd received a note from Lady Theodosia Winslow. Then yesterday, she and Clara had met Teddy at the Ladies Tearoom at Fenwick and Sons Booksellers for tea and cookies and a very fruitful conversation.

"If he was better at his job he never would have simply taken my word for it," Lucy pointed out. A voice in the back of her head noted that wasn't entirely fair. But really, when all was said and done, it seemed to her he had become rather lax in his duties. He had admitted Lucy was his only assignment at the moment, and one would think he would then spend more time in her company. Still, the man trusted that she was going to be where she said she would be. It struck her that Cameron might be a bit too trusting to be a private investigator. At least a good one.

He had accompanied them to the tearoom but insisted on remaining outside in the cold carriage, which did seem silly since he could have browsed the offerings in the adjoining bookstore. But he was quite adamant about not coming in, and one did have to wonder if it was the natural reluctance of any man to enter a primarily female domain or if he was worried about running into someone he knew. It was an interesting thought Lucy filed away for further examination later, but more and more about Cameron was simply not adding up.

Teddy's note had asked how Lucy was faring

in London, although Lucy suspected she was far more interested in finding out if Lucy had heard anything from Jackson. Which indicated Teddy had not. It was a shame the two refused to compromise, but Lucy had no doubt it would all work out in the end. That was the way of true love, after all. Why, Shakespeare himself acknowledged that it did not run smoothly.

Lucy admired Teddy's independence and determination to succeed in her business of organizing and planning weddings and society events. And admired her courage as well. Lucy didn't know that she would have the strength to risk the loss of the man she loved to follow her own path. Although as Teddy had explained it, for either of them to give up what they wanted would surely lead to regret and recrimination and heartbreak. Which did indeed make sense but was a pity nonetheless.

Teddy had casually asked after Jackson's parents and about any number of other insignificant topics until Lucy bluntly pointed out Jackson had scarcely been gone two weeks now and it was entirely too soon for a letter to have reached either of them. They both left unspoken the acknowledgment that Lucy was far more likely to receive a missive than Teddy was. Although she would wager a great deal any such letter from Jackson would ask, in an entirely offhand and subtle manner, about Lady Theodosia. Lucy would then dutifully mention his inquiry to Teddy.

"I think we look adequately masculine." Lucy considered her reflection thoughtfully.

Clara snorted. "As gentlemen, I'd say we look as if we are several eggs short of a dozen."

"Not at all," Lucy said staunchly, although the male version of herself displayed in her mirror could use a little less refinement. Still, the mustache would help.

Lucy glanced down at the dog who had been sniffing the hem of her trousers since she had put them on. "What do you think, Albert?"

Albert looked up at her, sneezed, then wandered off to jump onto the center of the bed. He circled once, then lay down but kept his gaze fixed on her. The poor thing was obviously a bit confused.

That they were dressing like men at all was thanks to Teddy. During the course of their conversation, Lucy had told Teddy about her great-aunt's list. A bit edited, of course. She really didn't know Teddy well enough to predict how she might respond to some of the, oh, racier items. While Lucy wasn't about to announce her quest from the rooftops of London, she saw no need to keep it a secret from the few people she knew.

The very fact that they were now dressed like men was due directly to Teddy's delight at what she saw as a truly wonderful adventure. Yesterday, she said she might be able to help. Today, shortly after Cameron had departed, Teddy had stopped by. She was managing a social evening, dinner and the like, for the membership of Prichard's, a very exclusive gentlemen's club. This was an annual dinner honoring the club's founders, and Teddy hoped it would lead to additional business. She, of course, would not be permitted to leave the kitchen, but her reputation was such that she was more and more in demand for such events. However, Teddy's servers, all male, could freely come and go. And really, did anyone ever pay much attention to servants?

The women had decided both Lucy and Clara would disguise themselves as servers but only Lucy would actually enter the sacred sanctum of the club. Clara would stand by in the kitchen to be of assistance if assistance was needed. They had worked out the remaining details and all three women agreed the plan was as good as it was simple. Teddy had taken her leave with strict instructions as to when and where Lucy and Clara would join her. The moment Teddy left, Clara too had departed, returning an hour later with appropriate clothing, wigs, and everything else she and Lucy would need to turn themselves into passable men. They had also taken the precaution of applying the mustache adhesive they would use to Lucy's wrist to make certain it did not affect her as the skin coloring had. So far, it had no ill effects.

"All right then." Clara nodded at Lucy's reflection. "We should be off if we are to meet Lady Theodosia at the appointed hour. Are you ready?"

Lucy stared at herself in the mirror and nodded. "As ready as I'm going to be, I think."

Both women put on half masks, which had nothing at all to do with their subterfuge at Prichard's but rather with exiting the house under the watchful eyes of the butler and other servants. They then donned long, hooded cloaks to hide their clothing and cropped wigs. They would apply their mustaches in the carriage. Lucy had earlier asked Clement to summon them a cab, explaining she and Clara were to attend a masquerade and the Channing carriage was entirely too recognizable. Why, it wouldn't be any fun at all to have everyone in attendance know their identity before they had even entered the ballroom.

Clement had accepted her explanation although she was fairly certain there was a distinct glimmer of suspicion in the man's eyes. Still, in Lucy's experience, that wasn't at all unusual for the butler, at least when it came to her.

It was no more than a ten-minute ride from Channing House to Prichard's. Long enough for Lucy and Clara to apply their mustaches, but not nearly long enough for the tempest in Lucy's stomach to subside. What had her great-aunt been thinking anyway? To consider *not* invading a men's club to be a regret? Goodness, it did seem silly. Still, it was exciting, which was probably the main ingredient of any adventure.

Teddy had said Prichard's was not the oldest gentlemen's club on St. James's Street, having been founded a mere three-quarters of a century ago, and was considered extremely modern and progressive. Not progressive enough to allow women guests, of course, but progressive none-theless.

The cab dropped them off a few doors away from the club. The driver either didn't notice that his passengers now sported mustaches or didn't care. Or perhaps he had seen far stranger things among the passengers of London.

Teddy met them at the servants' entrance and hurried them inside.

"Lucien Merryweather and Clarence West at your service, my lady," Lucy said with a bow, and drew off her cloak.

"Well done." Teddy cast them an approving smile. "You can leave your cloaks behind that door. They'll be convenient there to grab on your way out, should you need to leave quickly. Now, turn around so I can get a good look at you." They turned and she examined them with a critical eye, then nodded. "You'll do. The wigs are a nice touch. I was concerned about what you would do with your hair." Her gaze skimmed over them. "As well as the rest of you."

"Thank you," Clara said with a smug smile. Lucy was beginning to realize Clara might well have as many secrets as Cameron. "We're quite, well . . . oh, confined."

"It's not easy being a man," Lucy said with a grin.

"So they claim," Teddy murmured, and led them to the door of the kitchen. "The club members attending tonight are currently in the main lounge. There's a corridor that runs from the kitchen and leads to that room, the dining hall, and several other areas. It's annoyingly narrow and is extremely busy as is the kitchen. That will make things more difficult but will serve you well. No one will notice another body or two. I already have servers in the room with trays of small glasses of a very old Scottish whisky. Apparently some sort of tradition." She eyed Lucy skeptically. "Can you act as a server? They are small trays."

"Of course." Lucy scoffed. She'd never carried a tray in her life, but she could balance a book on her head. Not the same thing, but how difficult could it be to carry a tray of drinks around a room filled with gentlemen?

"As we discussed, you'll simply circle the room once, then return to the kitchen." Teddy paused. "I realize it might not be the adventure your great-aunt wanted, but it should suffice."

"It will do nicely," Lucy said with a grateful smile. Teddy was risking a great deal to help her. If they were discovered, her reputation would be ruined. "And you have my eternal thanks."

"Appreciated, of course, but not necessary." Teddy waved off the comment. "I can think of nothing more amusing than breaching the bastion of sacred manhood unnoticed. Now then." She met Lucy's gaze directly. "If you're ready."

Lucy nodded. "More than ready."

"One more thing. You know how servers are expected to act, so this shouldn't be all that difficult, but remember not to speak unless you're spoken to directly and then say no more than "yes, my lord" or "no, my lord." And, oh, try to adopt a deeper tone of voice. Something more manly."

"I shall try," Lucy said in the deepest tone she could manage.

"Good Lord." Teddy winced. "We shall simply hope you don't have to say anything." She squared her shoulders. "Let's do this, shall we?" She pushed open the door to the kitchen and stepped into the room, Lucy and Clara at her heels.

Teddy was right. The kitchen was chaotic, overly warm, and filled with cooks, assorted assistants, and men dressed exactly as Lucy and Clara were. Teddy directed Lucy to a tray, gave her a look of encouragement, and sent her toward her fate.

Lucy kept her head lowered and followed two

servers down the corridor and into the club lounge. Her heart thudded with apprehension and she had to force herself to stay calm. She wasn't sure what she had expected—murals of mythological satyrs and maidens cavorting was probably too much to hope for—but the lounge was every bit as, well, unexceptional as any room designed with gentlemen in mind usually was. Gas sconces and low-burning lamps lit the dark-paneled room. Comfortable-looking leather chairs and sofas were arranged to encourage private conversations. Evenly spaced forbidding portraits, probably of notable club members or past presidents, and more than likely deceased, hung on the walls and glowered down on the proceedings. Glowered down on her. Lucy shivered and ignored the disquieting thought. She drew a deep breath and dutifully circled the room, offering her tray to those gentlemen with empty glasses.

While the members ranged in age, the majority did seem to be older, some extremely old. Probably original members who would have some sort of apoplectic fit at the thought of a woman's presence defiling the place. She bit back a grin at the thought. Lucy moved from group to group and no one gave her a second look. She avoided eye contact and tried to be as efficient, discreet, and invisible as possible. There was a reason why no one paid any heed to servants. Still, she couldn't help but overhear conversations that were, for the most part, not worth overhearing. While most of the discussions dealt with any number of topics men found fascinating and women considered boring, one gentleman was saying the most impertinent things about the wife of a man across the room, and Lucy regretted she couldn't linger to hear more. Still, that was the most interesting thing she heard. Great-aunt Lucinda would have been so disappointed.

All but one of the glasses on her tray were taken far quicker than she had expected. Good. She could make her way back to the kitchen now and she and Clara would soon be on their way home. Relief washed through her along with a distinct sense of satisfaction. She could check one more thing off her list.

She offered her tray to another group of gentlemen. Much to Lucy's relief, a hand reached for the last glass. In her haste to escape she made the fatal mistake of glancing up.

And into the startled dark brown eyes of Mr. Cameron Fairchild.

Cam stared over the rim of his glass. For no more than a fraction of a second he absolutely refused to believe his eyes. But this was exactly the sort of thing Lucy would do. Damnation, the American was maddening.

She cast him a weak smile under the most

absurd mustache he had ever seen, then turned and briskly moved away. Oh no, this was not going to be that easy for her. He downed his drink and handed the empty glass to Thad by his side.

"Take this for me." He thrust the glass at his brother, his gaze fixed on Lucy's retreating figure. "I have to go."

Thad's brow rose. "Go where?"

"I'm not sure, but it's important."

Thad glanced at Father, Simon, and Spencer a few feet away. "Father won't be happy. He's quite fond of this place, especially since Grandfather was one of the club's founders."

"He shall have to add it to the list of all else that he is not happy about in regards to his youngest son." Cam slanted his brother a quick glance. "Surely you can come up with something clever to cover my absence."

"I'm sure I could." Thad sipped his drink. "Tell me why I should."

"Because . . ." Cam really didn't have time for this. "Because I'm working on a story."

"Oh, well, in that case." Thad grinned. "Do tell me it's another installment of *The Daring Exploits of a Runaway Heiress*."

Cam's attention snapped to his brother. "Those are written by Mr. Aldrich."

"Who just happens to write in your style with your voice?" Thad scoffed. "Not to mention the fact that I. F. Aldrich is an anagram for Fairchild and you have always been fond of anagrams."

Cam sighed in resignation. "Does anyone else in the family know?"

"Not that I'm aware of. Why?" Thad studied him closely. "What are you hiding?"

"I don't want my, well, my source to know I'm the writer."

"Your . . ." Thad's mouth dropped open in surprise. "You mean to tell me there's a real runaway heiress? I thought she was fictional."

"She is for the most part. But there is someone I am basing the character on. Inspiration as it were." Cam chose his words with care. "And I much prefer no one know that. Especially her."

"I can see why." Thad chuckled.

"So will you help me?"

"On one condition."

"What?" Cam snapped.

Thad smiled in a wicked manner. "I want to meet her."

Not bloody likely! "I can't promise you that, but possibly."

"I'll accept that." Thad nodded. "One more thing."

"What is it now?" Cam said impatiently.

"I'm just wondering." Thad sipped his drink. "How many names do you intend to have anyway?"

"As many as it takes." Cam nodded and hurried after Lucy.

She was mere steps away from a door disguised among the paneling as to be nearly unnoticeable when he caught up with her.

He grabbed her elbow and bent to speak low into her ear. "Escaping, are we?"

"I have no idea what you mean, my lord," she said in a deep voice so ridiculous he would have laughed under other circumstances.

He guided her toward the door. Without warning it opened and he came face-to-face with another man. Taller than Lucy, with a mustache every bit as ridiculous as Lucy's, this one's blue eyes widened at the sight of him.

Cam groaned. "I should have known." He steered Lucy through the open door and growled at Miss West. "How do we get out of here?"

"Follow me," Lucy's coconspirator said, and led them down a corridor bustling with servers, allegedly men, but he wouldn't wager on it. Not tonight.

They passed by a door leading into the kitchen and Cam caught a glimpse of Lady Theodosia Winslow. He ducked his head to escape her attention, but it appeared she was busy with other matters. He had managed to avoid her at the tearoom—he certainly didn't want to run into her now. She was obviously in on this masquerade, but the last thing he wanted was to have his own charade revealed by a lady his family had known for years.

No one said more than a word or two of direction until they had safely exited the building. Both ladies had long cloaks that served to hide their improper attire, something to be grateful for. He hailed a cab, fairly shoved Miss West into it, then gave instructions to the driver.

"We'll follow in the next cab," he told her in a hard tone. "I should like to have a few words with Mr. Merryweather."

Miss West huffed. "I don't think—"

"Apparently not!" He slammed the door and signaled to the driver.

A minute later he hustled Lucy into a second cab, then took the seat facing her. Long minutes ticked by. He wasn't sure when, if ever, he'd been so furious with a woman and he wasn't entirely sure why. He really should have expected something of this nature. In truth, this was very much the sort of stunt his sister would have pulled, especially if she were encouraged by the regrets of a dead relative. Grace would have done it without so much as a by-your-leave and considered it a grand adventure. He shuddered at the thought of Grace and Lucy ever combining forces.

"Good evening, Mr. Fairchild," Lucy finally said in an overly pleasant manner.

"Good evening?" Pity it was too dark in the cab for her to see him glaring at her. *"Good evening?"*

"I believe we've established that." She paused. "Lovely weather we're having, don't you think?"

"It's late January in London. It's cold, it's damp, it's foggy, and snow is in the air. So, no, Miss Merryweather, I do not think it's the least bit lovely."

"Lucy," she said firmly.

"What?"

"We agreed to call each other by our given names. If you intend to chastise me, I much prefer Lucy as it is so much more cordial than Miss Merryweather."

"I have no intention of being cordial."

"I was afraid of that." She sighed. "Miss Merryweather it is then."

A few minutes of stony silence later they arrived at Channing House. He helped her from the cab and she started toward the door.

"Might I suggest that you remove that . . . that piece of fur from your upper lip before we go in."

"You don't like it." She patted the mustache. "I thought it was quite fetching."

"I assume that is Miss West's doing."

"Clever, isn't it?"

He narrowed his eyes. "Given your experience with her skin dye, are you certain it will come off?"

"You are skeptical tonight, Mr. Fairchild." Her tone was a shade less pleasant than it had been in the cab. She peeled off the mustache and in the light cast by the street lamp he could see her wince. "There. Is that better?"

"Much."

"Have you ever kissed a woman with a mustache, Mr. Fairchild?" She fluttered her lashes at him.

"Not that I can recall. And certainly never deliberately."

"What a shame that you missed your opportunity then." She smirked and turned toward the door.

"I do hate to miss an opportunity." He grabbed her, pulled her into his arms, and stared down at her. *"Miss Merryweather."* Before she could protest he pressed his lips to hers. For a moment she hesitated, then kissed him back, hard and with a great deal of fervor. At last she pulled away and gazed up at him.

"If that is how you intend to chastise me in the future, Mr. Fairchild"—her voice was breathless and she made no move to leave his embrace— "I cannot promise to restrain from activities you find objectionable."

"You are driving me mad, Miss Merryweather."

"Then I have accomplished more than I expected this evening." She pulled away from him and moved to the door. It opened at once and she swept inside as if she were wearing the grandest of ball gowns instead of men's attire. She nodded at the butler and continued into the house.

He followed, handed his hat and coat to Clement, and called after her. "In the parlor if you please."

"That's where I was going," she tossed back over her shoulder.

"Has Miss West arrived?" he asked.

"A few minutes ago, sir. She's in the parlor." The butler paused. "Might I ask if there was a problem, sir? This is rather early to be returning from a masquerade. We didn't expect the ladies for quite some time yet."

"It's later than you think, Clement." Cam nodded and headed after Lucy. "Much, much later."

He reached the parlor doors just as Miss West was leaving. She cast him a scathing look, then took her leave. Why on earth should *she* be annoyed with *him?* He had done nothing. At least not yet.

He stepped into the room and closed the door behind him. "Well?"

"Well?" Lucy crossed her arms over her chest and he couldn't help but notice how becoming the man's apparel was on her. The black trousers and coat certainly never looked that enticing on a man. "What have you to say for yourself?"

"Me?" He stared. "What do I have to say for myself? I have nothing that needs explaining. You are the one who lied to me about your plans for this evening."

"I did nothing of the sort." She scoffed. "When I told you we had no plans to leave the house, it was entirely accurate. It was only later that we decided to, well . . . seize the opportunity presented to us. Surely you can understand that as you do so hate to miss an opportunity."

"Not nearly as much as I hate having my words thrown back at me."

"Then perhaps you should choose your words more carefully in the future."

She was baiting him, no doubt to defuse his justifiable anger at her rash behavior. An intelligent man would ignore it.

"We need to talk, Miss Merryweather, about your behavior." Apparently, he was not as intelligent as he thought. "In your desire to accomplish the items on your great-aunt's list of regrets, you put yourself, Miss West, and Lady Theodosia in an untenable situation."

"Only if we were discovered." She pulled off her wig and shook out her hair, combing her fingers through it. Blond waves fell to below her shoulders. He had never seen her hair down before, and combined with her attire, the overall effect was, well, tantalizing. "We weren't."

He ruthlessly shoved aside the image of all that fair hair fanned out over a pillow. This was not the time. "I discovered you."

"But you know me. You do not count. I, however, believe this evening's activities were well worth the risk."

"Only because you were not discovered!"

She smiled.

"We really need to discuss your actions past and future!"

"No, Mr. Fairchild." Her voice hardened. "We need to discuss yours."

"Mine?" He stared. "What have I done?"

"Overstepped, Mr. Fairchild. You have overstepped."

"Overstepped?" He stared, then winced. "You're right, of course. My apologies. I should not have taken such liberties."

"Liberties?" Her brow furrowed in confusion, then her expression cleared. "Oh, the kiss you mean? You needn't apologize for that. If I had objected, you can be certain I would have said so at the time."

"And you did kiss me back." He smirked.

A becoming blush colored her cheeks. "That is not the topic under discussion and not what I was referring to."

"Then I don't understand." He drew his brows together. "How have I overstepped?"

"You have gone entirely too far." She stepped closer and met his gaze firmly. "You, *Mr. Fairchild,* are the employee of my former almost fiancé, who through some misplaced sense of responsibility or perhaps guilt, has taken it upon himself to hire you to make certain I come to no harm. As admirable as his intentions were, my actions are really no longer any of his concern. Which brings me to you."

"Oh?"

"I thought it was best if we dispensed with subterfuge and allowed you to accompany us. For convenience, safety, and the fact that it is extremely cold out. My opinion on that has not changed. However"—her eyes narrowed—"you are not my father, my brother, my husband, or my fiancé. You have neither the right nor the privilege of chastising me. Nor do you have any right whatsoever to tell me how I may or may not behave."

"I did think we had become friends," he said staunchly.

"As did I, but the fact remains that you are being paid to keep me from harm, to protect me, if you will."

"Part and parcel of that is keeping you from doing anything that is fraught with the potential for scandal or, in some cases, even danger. I cannot assure your safety if you do not keep me informed as to your plans."

"That, Mr. Fairchild, is no concern of mine." She shrugged. "Perhaps if your charge is to watch my activities, you should do a better job of it. Why, one would think you had never done this sort of work before."

His mouth dropped open.

"You're not very good at this, are you?"

"Not very good . . ." He glared. "I have never had a complaint before."

"I thought we had established not hearing a complaint does not necessarily mean you know what you're doing. And I would think a good private investigator, when charged with the well-being of a . . . oh, a subject I suppose, for lack of a better word, would certainly do more than make a brief appearance once a day."

And even that had been difficult given his duties at the *Messenger*, although admittedly, Mr. Cadwallender was so pleased with the response to *Daring Exploits* thus far he had given Cam far more freedom to follow his own course than he'd had up to now. "I trusted you!"

"A good private investigator would not have trusted so easily."

"You struck me as very trustworthy." He narrowed his eyes. "And I am an excellent judge of character."

"Really?" She sniffed. "I hadn't noticed."

"I'm very good at what I do!"

"Again, I hadn't noticed. Although I suppose it's neither here nor there at the moment."

His jaw tightened. "Now that we have dispensed with your critique of my job performance, perhaps we can return to the subject at hand. Your behavior tonight, regardless of whether or not your deception was discovered, was dangerous, scandalous, and somewhat childish."

Her eyes narrowed slightly.

"In point of fact, most of the remaining items

on your great-aunt's list are dangerous, scandalous, and childish."

"Are they?" she said in a deceptively calm manner. He ignored it.

"They are indeed. These escapades of yours are bound to end badly." He wasn't sure where the words were coming from, although he certainly meant them. "Therefore, as a representative of my employer and because you are without the sensible influence of a father, brother, husband, or fiancé . . ." A voice in the back of his head screamed for him to shut up but he couldn't seem to stop himself. "I must take it upon myself to insist you cease this ludicrous quest of yours at once."

"And you are speaking for the gentlemen in my life, are you?"

"I'm certain if they were here—"

"But they are not here, Mr. Fairchild. And simply because one has hired you does not mean you may speak in his stead."

"Perhaps not, but as we have become friends—"
She snorted.

"—I feel it's my duty, my responsibility if you will, to stop you from this course you have so blithely set for yourself before it's too late. Before you have become mired in scandal and indiscretion and who knows what else."

"Your responsibility is to save me from myself?"

"I wouldn't have put it that way, but yes, that's not entirely inaccurate. I don't want to see you make a mistake that will affect the rest of your life!"

"And you are the judge of such things?"

"Yes! Bloody hell, Lucy, whether you like it or not, I, and every other man, are indeed the judge of such things!"

She chose her words with care. "I do appreciate you not wanting me to make a mistake but unfortunately I have already made at least one."

He scoffed. "Just one?"

"When I suggested you accompany us rather than slink from doorway to doorway in a futile effort to avoid my notice . . ." She smiled pleasantly. "I see now that was a mistake. One I intend to rectify immediately." Her tone hardened. "I suggest you leave, Mr. Fairchild, and do not bother returning. You may consider our agree-ment terminated. We no longer require your accompaniment. Miss West and I will be fine on our own."

He stared. Surely she wasn't throwing him out? "But—"

"Now." Her smile didn't slip for so much as a moment, but her blues eyes flared with anger.

"But—" But what? "It's cold outside."

"Then you should dress warmly as you lurk in the streets wondering what *escapade* I shall embark upon next. Where we are going. What I intend to do. Even"—a smug smile curved her lips—"which door we are using to leave the house."

"Very well," he snapped. "But don't for a minute think I will shirk my responsibilities simply because you are making me uncomfortable."

"On the contrary, Mr. Fairchild. You have now made it all much more of a challenge. It's going to be a great deal of fun outwitting you, although I can't imagine it will be all that difficult."

He was too angry to think of a coherent response. "Good evening, Miss Merryweather."

"Good evening, Mr. Fairchild. Do try not to lose any necessary body parts to the freezing cold."

"Miss Merryweather!" Good Lord. What kind of woman said such a thing?

"I should have known the first time you sputtered that you had a tendency to be stuffy."

"I most certainly do not," he said in a haughty manner that rivaled any tone his father might have taken. Damnation, the blasted woman was turning him into his father. "I shall try my best to survive the elements, Miss Merryweather. Thank you for your concern." He nodded and took his leave.

The instant the sharp cold night hit him he realized he had indeed overstepped. He should have been smarter. He should have kept his mouth shut. He never should have let his own sense of responsibility turn him into the protector she had assumed him to be. He never should have let these feelings of, well, affection overcome his own goals. But damn it all, she believed his job was to keep her safe and keep her safe he would. Whether she liked it or not.

And realized as well it was indeed damnably cold outside.

"What happened?" Clara said the moment she stepped into the parlor and closed the doors behind her.

"Weren't you listening at the door?"

"That was my original intention, but that blasted butler didn't take his eyes off me, so I was forced to simply pace in the corridor." Clara huffed in exasperation. "Well?"

"I threw him out." Lucy shrugged.

Clara's eyes widened. "Permanently?"

"That very much depends on him."

"You threw him out because . . . ?"

"Because he was acting like my father or one of my brothers or Jackson." Lucy clenched her jaw. "And he has no right to do so."

"I see." Clara paused. "And if he did have that right?"

"Clara." Lucy met the other woman's gaze firmly. "I have spent my entire life behaving exactly as I was expected to behave. Which includes bowing to the wishes and guidance of the men in my life. These last few weeks have been, well, liberating I suppose. I am an adult with financial security and my own mind. I see no reason to bow to the wishes of any gentleman ever again."

"How very . . . progressive of you."

"It doesn't feel especially progressive. But it does feel right."

Clara nodded. "And where does that leave you and Mr. Fairchild?"

"I'm afraid there is no me and Mr. Fairchild."

"But you would like there to be."

It would be silly to lie. Clara wouldn't believe her anyway. Lucy sighed. "Perhaps."

"I thought you liked him."

"I do. Very much." Lucy was still shocked by just how much. "And I'm fairly certain he likes me. But . . ."

"But?"

"But I don't know that I can care for a man I don't completely trust. And while I do feel that he is quite trustworthy, as I am a far better judge of character than he, there is still the matter of whatever it is he's hiding." Resolve hardened her voice. "And why."

"I see."

"Furthermore, I am not at all pleased to be accused of lying by a man who is so obviously not revealing the complete truth himself. A question that becomes more and more interesting all the time. One does have to wonder why a man who has to work for a living is present at an exclusive gentlemen's club looking very much like a guest or a member."

"Yes, I suppose," Clara murmured. "So what happens now that you have divested us of Mr. Fairchild's company?"

"Now we continue on with our plans and wait for Mr. Fairchild to apologize."

"You think he will?"

"I know he will. We have already established he is not who or what he appears. But the man is definitely a gentleman, Clara. And, as he conducted his initial surveillance so poorly that I noticed him almost at once, we can surmise as well he is fairly new to the world of private inquiry. As such he would hate to fail on what is so obviously one of his first assignments. Besides, I have a strong suspicion that he is an honorable man. He has taken payment to provide a service and he will feel honor bound to provide that service. Beyond that . . ." She smiled. "Mr. Fairchild does not like the cold."

Regrets Set to Rights

Storm the sacred bastion
of a gentlemen's club.

Chapter Nine

"Tell me, Lucy." Lady Dunwell, Beryl, sat on the sofa in the Channing House parlor and sipped her tea. "Are you familiar with *Cadwallender's Daily Messenger?*"

"No, I'm afraid not." Lucy thought for a moment. "Although I have become quite fond of *Cadwallender's Weekly Ladies World* since I've been in England."

Beryl had called on Lucy shortly after Clara had left on an errand. Her visit was a welcome respite from Lucy's constant perusal of the street outside Channing House in a futile search for a tall, dashing figure lurking in the shadows. If Cameron was there, his skills in surveillance had vastly improved, although she doubted it. It was already afternoon and she had fully expected him to make an appearance before now, hat in hand, well-phrased apology on his lips. Or barring that, lurking outside in the shadowed doorways and stairwells that lined the street.

"Is it a newspaper?"

"It is." Beryl nodded. "And a most salacious one at that. Full of gossip and scandal and innuendo. In spite of that, no *because* of that"—Beryl smiled in a wicked manner—"I simply adore the

Messenger and read it every morning. It's most entertaining as well as informative and a far more interesting way to start the day than with the *Times*."

"I can well imagine," Lucy said absently. As much as Lucy was fascinated by Jackson's cousin and did want to know her better, it was hard to keep her attention from straying.

One would think Cameron would have seen the error of his arrogant ways after a night's rest, but perhaps the man needed more time. Men were such an unreasonable lot.

"It also runs the most compelling fictional stories."

"I shall have to read it then." Lucy smiled politely.

"Yes, you should." Beryl studied her closely. "Especially since I believe a current series of stories is about you."

"Me?" Lucy stared. "What on earth do you mean?"

"I could be wrong, of course." Beryl pulled a handful of clippings from her bag and handed them to Lucy. "Before he left, Jackson told me there were things a relative had regretted not doing in her life that you were now determined to do."

"I don't know what that has to do with this." Lucy paged through the clippings. "*The Daring Exploits of a Runaway Heiress*?" She glanced up at Beryl and grinned. "I would like to be a runaway heiress having daring exploits, but why do you think this is about me?"

"For one thing the heiress is American, from Philadelphia, I believe."

"But I'm from New York."

Beryl waved away the comment. "Goodness, dear, here in London no one cares where in America she is from, nor will anyone note it. The only pertinent fact is that she is American."

"Still, I'm sure I'm not the only American heiress in England at the moment."

"I doubt there are many others on a quest."

"What kind of quest?" Lucy asked slowly.

"It's something of a hunt, really. Miss Mercy Heartley—that's the heroine's name—must find a series of objects detailed in the will of a late relative. Once she retrieves all the objects, she will earn the right to her inheritance and she can then be independent." Beryl's brow drew together. "I'm not sure I have all the details right, the plot does seem overly complicated, but it's something like that."

Lucy stared for a moment, then laughed. "That's not at all what I'm doing."

Beryl reached over and tapped the clippings with her finger. "But there are distinct similarities."

"Well, yes, I suppose there are. Both the fictional Miss Heartley and myself are from

America and we are both trying to accomplish something here, but her purpose is to achieve her inheritance. I am already financially independent. Nor have I run away." She ignored the thought that her family might think differently, but really she hadn't run away. She'd already been in England when she had decided to make up for her great-aunt's regrets. "Beyond that, there are very few people who know of my plans and those who do can be trusted to be discreet." She shrugged. "I really don't think it's anything more than coincidence."

"Possibly." Beryl heaved a disappointed sigh. "Then you're not having daring exploits?"

Lucy laughed. "I'm afraid not." She paused. "But I am having some interesting adventures."

"*Interesting adventures* does not sound nearly as much fun as *daring exploits,* but I suppose one takes what one can. Do these interesting adventures have to do with your great-aunt's regrets?" she asked casually.

"Jackson didn't tell you what was on her list of regrets, did he?"

"No, the blasted man did not." Beryl's brow furrowed in annoyance. "While he did tell me about the list—he did have to make my role as erstwhile guardian palatable after all—he said he couldn't remember the exact details."

Lucy laughed. "He didn't tell you because he didn't know."

"He certainly concealed that pertinent fact. In spite of his lack of knowledge, or perhaps because of it, he was concerned about your becoming embroiled in scandal or worse. I told him it was really none of his business, and certainly none of mine. Still, I did agree to be here should you need me."

"And for that you have my gratitude." Lucy stood up and crossed the room to fetch the list of Lucinda's desires from the drawer in the side table, then returned to her seat. "Would you like to see the list?"

Beryl scoffed. "Of course I would. It's been all I could do to keep from asking outright. One does try to be polite, you know." Beryl accepted the list from Lucy and studied it. "I assume the check marks are for those you have already accom-plished." She looked up, her eyes wide. "Dare I ask which gentlemen's club you managed to breach?"

Lucy grinned. "It's probably best that I not dis-close that."

"Probably. I might be tempted to mention it when I find some member of said club says something annoying in the course of casual conversation at some event or other." Beryl's attention returned to the list. "One can see why Jackson thought it was necessary to have some-one watch over you," she said under her breath. "I knew the man was smarter than he appeared."

Beryl continued to study the page before her.

"Well?" Lucy held her breath.

"Well . . ." Beryl looked up, her eyes twinkling. "These are delightful, simply delightful. What a perfect excuse for improper behavior. I should have thought of it myself. Do you intend to accomplish all of these?"

Lucy nodded. "As many as I can before I am forced to return home."

"You do realize some of them will be impossible? At this time of year, frolicking in a fountain or swimming naked in the moonlight is extremely ill advised."

Lucy grinned. "Those may have to wait until spring."

"Do you plan to take a lover then?"

"Well . . ." Lucy still wasn't certain how she felt about that particular regret along with the one about a romantic liaison. "I don't plan not to. After all, I am nearly twenty-four and the likelihood of marriage does grow slimmer. That is to say I'm not especially opposed to taking a lover." Good Lord, it was hard to sound like a woman of the world when one wasn't.

Beryl's brow arched. "You've never had a lover, have you?"

"Not exactly."

"My dear girl, there is no *not exactly* about it. Either you have or you haven't." Beryl eyed her knowingly. "And I would wager you haven't.

Nor, would I imagine, do you have a great deal of experience with men."

"I have been kissed." Lucy grimaced. "But no, I've never had a lover and I'm not sure how I would go about finding one suitable or even if I want one, really." She leaned toward Beryl and lowered her voice in a confidential manner. "It does seem that is a door that once walked through, cannot be walked through again."

"Indeed." Beryl's tone was somber but there was a definite gleam of amusement in her eyes. "Therefore one should hesitate, or at least give due consideration, before crossing that particular threshold."

"Absolutely." Lucy nodded. "And I did learn my lesson from kissing a stranger. That sort of thing can't be planned. I mean you can't simply point at a man and say, 'He'll do.' "

"I do know all sorts of gentlemen who would be more than willing . . ." Beryl wrinkled her nose. "Although, I suppose that is not at all what Jackson had in mind when he requested my looking out for you."

Lucy laughed. "I would think not."

"However, I can help you with some of these if you like. For one thing, you are supposed to dance with a prince. I know several princes and more than a few pretenders." She thought for a moment. "It is a dreadfully slow time of year unfortunately, but there is a ball the day after tomorrow given by the ambassador of some tiny little country in the Balkans, I think, and I am fairly certain an Austrian prince I am acquainted with will be in attendance."

"That would be perfect." Lucy beamed.

"Excellent. Now then, as for some of these other items . . ."

By the time Beryl took her leave, she and Lucy had come up with several good ideas and quite a few that were completely absurd. Even so, Beryl's visit did serve to take Lucy's mind off Cameron's absence.

It was entirely possible the man had taken her at her word and was not going to return. It was for the best, really. Nip this thing—whatever it was—right in the bud before it went any further. After all, it was no more than some amusing conversation, a few shared adventures, and two mere kisses, one of which was no more than adequate. The other . . . She could still feel the press of his lips against hers, the tingle that suffused her at his touch, and the heretofore unknown desire that had curled her very toes. She couldn't wipe the memory of that kiss, or the memory of his smile and his laugh and even the way he sputtered in indignation, from her thoughts. The annoying man had invaded her every waking moment and most of her dreams as well. Dreams that were far more intimate than her waking life had ever been.

No, it was definitely for the best that this end before it went too far. Before she did something terribly ill advised. Before she let all these new feelings he aroused in her overcome her good judgment. Before she did something really foolish.

Before she fell in love.

". . . and now I don't know how to proceed." Cam paced the floor of Phineas's flat, not as easy as it had been on his last visit. Phineas was apparently taking advantage of Miss West's absence to return to his beloved state of disorder. "I tell you I can't sleep, I can't eat, and I can hardly think well enough to put pen to paper."

"As this only happened last night"—Phineas chuckled—"I can hardly wait to see your state a week from now."

"A week?" Cam scoffed. "I shall surely be mad in a week. I cannot allow this to continue. I must do something."

"I see." Phineas studied his friend silently.

"I could use more than that." Cam glared at the other man. "A bit of advice from a disinterested bystander would be appreciated."

"I'm not the least bit disinterested." Phineas smiled. "In fact, I find this all most amusing."

"I'm glad someone is amused," Cam snapped.

"Very well then. In gratitude for that amusement I will give you the benefit of my opinion on this matter." Phineas settled deeper in the wing chair and considered the question. "But I'm not sure you're going to like it."

"I rarely do," he said sharply. "Go on."

"It seems to me that you have all you need from Miss Merryweather."

Cam stopped in midstep. "All I need?"

"Your original purpose was to use her as your inspiration for your stories for the *Messenger* and the compilation of those stories into a book. You now know about the list of her late relative's regrets, you've witnessed firsthand her attempts to rectify some of those, and you've taken that information and spun it into stories loosely based on your observations." He chuckled. "And might I add, I do appreciate the name of your fictional heiress. Miss Mercy Heartley is very nearly an anagram for Miss Lucy Merryweather."

"It would have been perfect if not for an extra *R* and that damn *U* and *W*," Cam muttered.

"But no one else will ever realize it. You've gone to great pains to make certain her identity is concealed so she'll not be harmed by your actions." Phineas shrugged. "Your stories are practically writing themselves. You were looking for inspiration and you have been inspired. So, as I said, at this point you no longer need her."

Cam stared.

"Therefore whether she wants you around or not is immaterial. You have what you wanted. I say you extricate yourself from this web of deception you've spun while you still can. There's no need to continue this charade of yours."

"No need." Cam snorted. "There's every need. You don't know her, Phineas. She's remarkably stubborn and reckless—"

"And yet still clever enough to have managed quite a few of the items on her great-aunt's list."

"Oh, she's smart, she's very smart. She has a diabolical mind hidden beneath that blond hair and those sapphire eyes, and all that pleasantry. Her intelligence is not in question, but she's been lucky thus far. Very lucky." His jaw clenched. "That luck cannot last forever. She needs someone to watch over her. To make certain this quest of hers does not ruin her life."

Phineas quirked a brow. "Does she?"

"Without question. The very thought of those things that still remain undone on her great-aunt's list . . ." Cam shuddered at the thought of *romantic interludes* and *taking a lover*. "Left to her own devices she will surely come to ruin. I cannot allow that."

"Why? She's not your responsibility."

"Oh, but she is. At least it feels as if she is." Cam blew a long breath. "I don't quite understand it myself, but somewhere along the way this stopped being something I was pretending and became a real obligation. I'm not sure how or why—"

"I have my suspicions," Phineas murmured.

"But I feel honor bound to make certain Lucy—"

"Lucy is it?"

Cam ignored him. "Comes to no harm."

"Because?"

"Because that's what she expects of me."

"And?"

"And I don't wish to disappoint her."

"Because?"

"Because I care for her, damn it!" The import of what he said slammed into him along with equal parts panic and denial. "What I mean to say is that we have become friends. And of course, one has a certain amount of affection for one's friends."

"Of course."

"Do not read more into my words than I intended."

Phineas scoffed. "Never."

"She's a friend, almost a . . . a sister," Cam said staunchly.

Phineas snorted back a disbelieving laugh. "A sister?"

"A sister," Cam said firmly. "Nothing more than that."

"I never imagined otherwise." The twinkle in his friend's eyes belied his words. Cam ignored it.

"The question now is how do I get back in her good graces?"

"That's the question?" Phineas shook his

head. "And I thought the real question was why."

"I have answered that," Cam said sharply.

"Not to my satisfaction, and I suspect not to yours either."

Cam opened his mouth to reply but Phineas waved him off. "Regardless as to the why, if you insist on continuing your relationship, such as it is, with Miss Merryweather, you must take the path every man in such a situation has taken from time immemorial." Phineas paused. "You must apologize, promise to do better and, of course, grovel."

Cam scoffed. "I'm not going to grovel."

"Unless you prefer to observe her from a distance and not be privy to her plans and intentions . . ." Phineas shrugged. "There is no other way. And you know it as well as I."

Cam thought for a moment, then blew a long breath. "You're right. There is no other option."

"I know I'm right." Phineas smirked. "I am very nearly always right." He thought for a moment. "Admittedly, there is one other choice."

"And what would that be?"

"You could tell her the truth."

Cam grimaced. "Yes, I suppose I could." He drew a deep breath. "And I should. I don't like deceiving her."

Phineas grinned. "You do like her then."

"I said I liked her."

"You more than merely like her."

"Don't be absurd." Cam ran his hand through

his hair. And when it came right down to it, wasn't that really the crux of his dilemma? "Possibly, I suppose. I don't know."

"I've never seen you unsure about your feelings for a woman before."

"I've never encountered a woman like Lucy Merryweather before." He shook his head. "I've never had the desire to protect a woman before. Nor have I ever had so much as a twinge of conscience at not being completely truthful with a woman. And I've certainly never cared whether I disappointed one or not."

"And now you do."

"Bloody hell, Phineas." Cam sank into a chair and stared at his friend. "I do at that."

A sharp knock, followed immediately by the sound of a key in the lock, caught their attention.

"Oh, this will add to the discussion." Phineas chuckled.

Cam winced. He didn't want to see Miss West any more than Phineas did. "Were you expecting her?"

"I am never expecting her. But it's been more than two weeks since she was last here, so I suppose I should have." Resignation sounded in his friend's voice but it didn't strike Cam as entirely legitimate. Was it possible that Phineas actually missed the woman?

The door opened and Miss West sailed into the room. "Good day, Mr. Chapman."

Both men rose to their feet.

"Good day, Miss West," Phineas said. "What a delightful surprise."

She scoffed, then turned her attention to Cam. "And Mr. Fairchild as well. Excellent." Her eyes narrowed. "It will save me the trouble of running you to ground."

"Clara." A warning sounded in Phineas's voice. She ignored him.

"And good day to you too, Miss West," Cam said.

Miss West cast him a withering glance. "Do sit down, gentlemen." She pulled off her gloves. "I have something to say to Mr. Fairchild and I don't want the two of you looming over me while I do it."

As neither man was more than a few inches taller than Miss West, looming seemed impossible. Still, Phineas and Cam exchanged glances, then obediently sat.

Miss West glanced around the room. "Have you insulted Mrs. Wiggins again, Mr. Chapman?"

"I would never insult Mrs. Wiggins," Phineas said indignantly. "But she does have a tendency to be rather thin-skinned. I simply told her there was no longer any need for her to waste her time in this room."

"Of course you did." Clara rolled her gaze toward the ceiling. "Well, I haven't the time to waste on you at the moment either. I don't intend to stay long."

"For which you have my undying gratitude."

"No doubt." She settled in the chair behind her desk and turned her attention to Cam. "I shall be brief. I have decided to tell Miss Merryweather the truth. About everything." She met Cam's gaze firmly. "I cannot continue to deceive her. It's simply not right."

"I see." Cam thought for a moment. The truth about everything would include his deception. He couldn't allow Miss West to reveal that. "And which truth would that be?"

"What do you mean *which truth?*" Her brow furrowed. "The truth is the truth. Period."

"It's not quite as cut and dried as that." He studied her. "You say you cannot continue to deceive her."

She nodded. "Nor do I intend to."

"Yet, it seems to me you have already told her the truth about your experience as a companion. Have you not?"

"Well, yes but—"

Cam continued. "And are you or are you not legitimately employed as her companion?"

"I am but—"

"Has anyone else employed you to watch or protect her?"

Miss West's gaze shifted to Phineas, then back to Cam. "No, of course not, but—"

"Does your business relationship with Mr. Chapman, past or present, have anything whatsoever to do with your current employment?"

She paused. "Other than leading me to the position in the first place, no, not really."

"Then I don't see deception on your part at all."

"He's got you there," Phineas said.

"Perhaps you're right, in some sort of convoluted, morally questionable way," she said. "But the fact remains that you are deceiving her and I am a party to your deception."

"Point to her," Phineas murmured.

"I know and I apologize for putting you in that position. And, as much as I hate to admit it, you're right as well." Cam heaved a heartfelt sigh. "I am deceiving her and I too have decided it's not right."

Suspicion shaded her tone. "You've decided that, have you?"

Cam nodded. "I have. It has weighed heavier upon my conscience with every passing day."

"He was just saying as much before you came in," Phineas said helpfully.

"Was he?"

Cam drew a deep breath. "Are you going to tell her about me?"

"I fully intended to but . . . the fact that you have a conscience at all is something I didn't expect." Miss West drummed her fingers on the desktop. "She likes you, you know."

"Does she?"

"Quite a lot, I suspect." Miss West blew a

frustrated breath. "I would like to tell her but I have no desire to be the one to inform her that this man she regards as honorable and a gentleman is in fact only interested in the stories he can write about her."

"That might have been true in the beginning but . . . I like her as well." Cam shrugged in a helpless manner. "I beg you not to tell her."

She studied him closely. "Give me one good reason why I shouldn't."

He met her gaze directly. "Because I should be the one to tell her."

She narrowed her eyes. "When you say you like her—"

"She is the most remarkable woman I have ever met," he said simply. "She has worked her way into my, well, affections I suppose."

"I knew it." Phineas cast him a smug smile.

"And I do not want to lose her." Even as he said the words he realized the truth of them. Blast it all, could he possibly be in love with the maddening American? Surely not. Still, he'd never been in love before and it did explain why he was so determined to save her from herself.

She stared at him for a long moment, no doubt assessing his sincerity. "I have absolutely no reason to believe you."

"No, you don't."

"And yet . . ." She threw her hands up and sighed in resignation. "It seems I do."

"Thank you."

"Oh, don't thank me." She shook her head. "I am the least of your problems. If you don't think of some brilliant way to get out of this mess, she will never forgive you."

"I realize that." At once it struck him that he would do very nearly anything to prevent that. If this was indeed love, one would think it would be far easier.

"One can only hope, my lord, one can only hope."

"Yes, well—" He stared for a long moment, then drew a deep breath. "How long have you known? Did Chapman tell you?"

"I would never!" Phineas huffed, then stared at Miss West. "How did you know?"

She cast them both a pitying look. "There was no need for Mr. Chapman to tell me. I discovered your true name and position shortly after I met you. It wasn't especially difficult."

"I told you she was brilliant," Phineas said in an aside to Cam.

"Indeed you did," Cam said under his breath. And she would make a far better ally than enemy. "That's probably something else I should confess to Miss Merryweather."

"I would think so." She eyed him closely. "As I see it, you need to reveal everything to her as soon as possible, before she finds out some other way. She already realizes you're not exactly who, or rather what, you say you are. You have my word I will not tell her the truth about you." Her gaze locked with Cam's. "But I will not lie to her if she asks me a direct question."

"Something like, 'Do you know Mr. Fairchild is a reporter and the son of a duke?' you mean?" Phineas asked in a deceptively innocent tone.

"Sarcasm, Mr. Chapman, is not appreciated."

"On the contrary, Miss West. Sarcasm is always appreciated." Phineas smirked. "At least mine is as it is infused with wit and tempered with wisdom."

She stared at him for a moment, then shook her head in a long-suffering manner and continued. "You might also wish to reconsider any stories you may be planning to write about her."

"Stories I may be planning?" Cam said slowly.

"You told me at the start of all this you were going to write stories based on Miss Merryweather." Her brow rose. "Dare I hope you have found a more appropriate subject?"

"No, I haven't." Cam resisted the urge to trade glances with Phineas. Apparently Miss West was not aware that four installments of *Daring Exploits* had already appeared, including one in today's *Messenger*. "Nor would I imagine I could ever do so."

"No, Miss Merryweather is indeed unique. And while she hasn't been especially secretive about her activities, she does not want them shouted to the world either. If you do intend to pursue her affections"—she pinned Cam with a hard look—"I would suggest you find your inspiration elsewhere."

"Although he had planned to write his stories strictly as fiction," Phineas said mildly. "He is surprisingly skilled at his craft, Miss West. I daresay he is good enough to make certain no one would identify Miss Merryweather as the lady in his stories. Should he write them, that is," he added.

"I imagine Miss Merryweather would." Miss West shook her head. "While you may well be able to explain your deception thus far and gain her forgiveness, I doubt that she would ever be able to forgive you using her for your own purposes. She would see it as a betrayal of her trust."

"I shall keep that in mind," Cam said slowly. She was right, of course.

"Very well then." Miss West rose to her feet and started toward the door. "One more thing."

Cam stood. "Yes?"

"Do not take my willingness to keep your secrets and allow you to tell her the truth as so much as the slightest encouragement as to some sort of match between you and Miss Merryweather. I still do not trust you. However, as you pointed out"—her assessing gaze slid over him—"you are not substantially worse than any other man, although I do think she could do better. But she is a grown woman and well capable of making her own decisions. And when it comes to affairs of the heart, even the most intelligent among us usually refuses to listen to reason."

"The last thing I would ever want to do is hurt Lucy," Cam said staunchly.

"What we want does not always reconcile with how things turn out in the end, my lord." She pulled on her gloves. "You should know she expects you to apologize for your high-handedness last night."

"And I fully intend to do so." Cam nodded. "However, I also reserve the right to tell her the truth when I think the moment is most opportune."

"It's not something he can just blurt out, you know," Phineas pointed out. "Timing, in a situation like this, is crucial."

"Nonetheless, the longer his deception continues, the less likely she is to forgive him."

"There is that," Phineas murmured.

"Very well then." She stepped to the door. "I anticipate seeing you soon, my—Mr. Fairchild."

Cam nodded.

"As for you, Mr. Chapman."

Phineas got to his feet. "Yes?"

"Do allow Mrs. Wiggins to tidy up on occasion." Her tone was firm but a definite twinkle shone in her eye. Hard to believe but there it was. "I would hate to find you swallowed up by disorder upon my return."

Phineas bit back a grin. "Faith, Miss West. One must always have faith."

"And a broom would be helpful as well." She opened the door. "Good day, gentlemen." She took her leave, snapping the door closed behind her.

"It seems to me," Phineas began slowly, "that if she is unaware that you have already begun writing and publishing your stories—"

"Then Lucy is unaware of them as well." Cam nodded. "That is a relief."

"Then do you plan to stop writing them?"

"Absolutely not." Cam scoffed. "They've been quite well received and were not written by me, after all, but by Mr. Aldrich."

"Ah, yes, that makes all the difference."

Cam raised a brow. "Miss West was right about sarcasm, you know."

"Then appreciate this." Phineas crossed the room to his desk, opened the bottom drawer, and pulled out two glasses and a bottle of Scottish whisky. "There's a flaw in your thinking."

"I don't see one." Cam accepted a glass, Phineas filled it, and both men retook their seats.

"First of all, and as much as I hate to admit it, Miss West was right." Phineas took a long sip of his whisky. "Whereas your fictional interpretation of Miss Merryweather might fool the world as a whole, she might be able to identify herself in your stories. I daresay Miss West could as well."

"Nonsense." Cam scoffed. "There are distinct differences between my fictional heiress and Lucy."

"They are both American and both are on some sort of quest initiated by a dead relative."

"They are entirely different." Cam waved off the comment. "Mercy is trying to gain her financial independence so that she is not forced to marry a lout who only wants her for her money. Lucy already has financial independence. Her quest is more of a moral obligation."

"And in the second installment didn't our fictional heiress disguise herself as a harem girl and ride a camel to become part of a sultan's traveling entourage in order to find one piece of the puzzle she is looking for?"

"A camel and a harem girl are entirely different from an elephant and an Indian princess," Cam said firmly.

Phineas's brow rose.

"Admittedly, there might be some similarities. . . ."

"Some?" Phineas snorted. "Parallels is more accurate."

Cam ignored the sinking feeling in his stomach. No, Phineas was wrong. Lucy was sufficiently disguised. "Besides, as few people in London know Lucy and fewer still know of her quest, I am confident no one will connect my fictional heiress with Lucy."

"Except, of course, Miss Merryweather herself. And very nearly as bad"—Phineas raised his glass—"Miss West."

Cam grimaced.

"So in this confession you intend to make to Miss Merryweather . . ." Phineas studied his friend with barely concealed amusement.

What kind of friend took pleasure in the dilemmas of another? Cam brushed aside the fact that he would be doing exactly the same thing if their positions were reversed.

"You're not going to tell her about the stories?"

"I don't see why I would. It would simply be adding fuel to the fire. Telling her my real name and that I'm not an investigator but a writer is enough fuel to deal with already, thank you."

"So when it comes to ambition versus affection . . ." Phineas eyed him thoughtfully. "It would appear ambition wins."

"I wouldn't put it that way." Although Phineas did have a point.

"It seems to me if you're going to eliminate the rather pertinent fact of your stories from your revelation, there is only one thing you can do."

"I know." Cam tossed back the whisky in his glass. "Make sure she never finds out."

. . . and it did seem disingenuous to us that nude sculptures carved in antiquity and paintings of ladies clad in nothing more than a few scarves and an enigmatic expression are considered art, yet woe be it to any female who dares to show so much as an ankle in public. My friends and I have all agreed, should the opportunity ever present itself, we shall, each and every one, have a portrait painted in which we are wearing little more than a smile and a knowing look. And in that way, we shall become art. Which is really quite exciting.

Although I will confess that I cannot foresee a time when I would be brazen enough to allow even an artist, who has no doubt seen hundreds of nude females, to observe me without clothing. I doubt that I have the kind of courage to pose under such conditions and certainly would be mortified to have such a work displayed in public.

Still, perhaps if one's features were suitably disguised, it would be a remarkable adventure to be immortalized, to live forever, in a work of art . . .

from the journal of Miss Lucinda Merryweather, 1806

Chapter Ten

The butler directed Cam to the conservatory in a tone that should have given Cam pause, but he was far too concerned with rehearsing both his apology and his confession. Neither one was yet to his satisfaction, which was why it had taken until midafternoon before he finally arrived at Channing House. He had already learned to expect the outrageous from Lucy but he had never expected this.

It took him a moment to realize exactly what he was seeing. The conservatory soared nearly two stories. The outside walls were paneled with glass framed in iron, the floor paved with an intricate pattern of red and blue tiles. Condensation beaded on the glass. Moisture hung heavy in the air, pleasantly warm and scented with the rich smell of earth and the vague sweetness of flowers. Wooden benches here and there bordered a wide pathway leading to a large palm that grew nearly to the ceiling in the center of the room. A myriad of tropical plants competed for space amid lush greenery and exotic blossoms.

Several feet in front of the palm, slightly off to one side, a tall, dark-haired man stood before an easel, paintbrush in hand. A stool by his side was littered with paints and rags and all sorts of artistic paraphernalia. From the door, it was impossible to see exactly what he was painting.

Cam stepped into the conservatory and only then saw past the artist.

Lucy reclined on a blue brocade chaise, her elbow resting on the chaise's arm, her head turned over her shoulder, her knees bent and stretched out to one side. Her blond hair was loose and drifted in waves to the middle of her back—*her naked back.*

"Good God, Miss Merryweather!"

Her shoulders tensed, then relaxed. "Good day, Mr. Fairchild," she said brightly. "I would know that outraged, indignant voice anywhere."

"Are you mad?" He started toward her.

"I can hear you approach, Mr. Fairchild. Do not take one more step," she said in an unyielding tone tinged with what might have been a touch of panic. "As you can see, I am posed quite carefully. I would be most embarrassed should you see more than I would prefer."

"I have already seen a great deal!"

"Then consider yourself fortunate and turn around. At once, Mr. Fairchild!"

"Very well." He huffed and turned.

"Your timing, Mr. Fairchild, is abominable," she said coolly.

"My apologies!"

"Jean-Philippe has taken great pains to get me into this pose—"

Cam snorted.

"And I have taken great pains to make certain he did not see more than was necessary. It took longer than I expected, as he is extremely difficult to please for a man who is being paid for a service."

"Thank you, mademoiselle," the artist murmured in a heavily accented voice.

Another Frenchman? Where did she find them?

"Aside from arranging me to his liking—"

"No doubt," Cam muttered. What was the woman thinking?

"—he rearranged greenery and fiddled with shading and angles and positions for what seemed like forever. I can't tell you how many times he repositioned this chaise in order to get it just right."

"One cannot simply throw paint on a canvas and hope for greatness, mademoiselle," the artist said absently.

"Yes, of course," she said, and Cam could hear the smile in her voice. "I would hate to go through all that again, Mr. Fairchild, simply because you have deigned to make an appearance in a flurry of shock and righteous indignation."

Cam clenched his teeth. "Again, my apologies."

"Accepted, although you don't sound the least bit sincere." She paused. "You may turn around now."

"Thank you," he snapped, and turned.

Lucy stood in front of the chaise, tightening the sash of what looked like a long men's dressing gown. The silky fabric was patterned in hues of greens and blues, complementing and blending with the colors of nature in the conservatory. In truth, in that garment with her hair caressing her shoulders, the American looked like some sort of magical forest creature made of shadows and light who would fade into the foliage at any moment and disappear. He realized the robe had been draped low on her back when he had first seen her and had covered most of her legs. Most but not all.

She glanced at the artist, who ignored the interruption and was busy applying paint to canvas in a haphazard manner.

"I should have known this was your next *adventure,*" Cameron said sharply. The artist threw him a condescending look and Cam gasped. "You!"

Lucy's gaze shifted between the two men. "Do you know each other?"

The artist shrugged.

"Of course I know him! Bloody hell, if you were so determined to be painted sans clothing you could have found a genuine artist!"

"I assure you, monsieur, I am quite genuine," the Frenchman said under his breath, not bothering to pull his attention away from his painting. "And very, very good."

Lucy grinned.

"I hope you paint better than you bake!" Cameron snapped.

"I do not bake," the man muttered.

Lucy stared. "What on earth are you talking about?"

"I'm talking about how you managed to find the one Frenchman who can bake as well as slap paint on a canvas." Cameron crossed his arms over his chest. "At least I hope you are getting your money's worth!"

Lucy shook her head in confusion. "What?"

"The resemblance, mademoiselle," the artist pointed out. "You noted it yourself."

"Oh, for goodness' sakes, of course." Lucy sighed. "Allow me to introduce Monsieur Jean-Philippe Vadeboncoeur—"

"Vad-eh-bon-kehr, mademoiselle," the artist said in a long-suffering tone. "Vad-eh-bon-kehr."

Lucy grimaced. "My apologies. Jean-Philippe is François' brother."

"He certainly looks like the chef!" Although now that Cam had a better look at him, he realized the artist was a bit older. And probably much more experienced at the seduction of young women.

"I have two other brothers as well, monsieur." Vadeboncoeur stepped back from his work, studied the canvas, then continued to dab. "We bear a striking resemblance to each other and to our father." He glanced at Lucy and a wicked smile shone in his eyes, then his attention returned to his work. "My mother says it is most convenient."

Lucy choked back a laugh.

"This time, Miss Merryweather, you have gone too far!" Cameron huffed. "And please do me the courtesy of putting some clothing on."

"Englishmen." Jean-Philippe sniffed.

"I am more than suitably clothed, given the situation. And I quite like this." Lucy glanced down at the robe. "It's no worse than the sari."

"That's not saying much!" Cam couldn't remember the last time prurient interest had dueled with honor and honor had won. "Good Lord, Lucy." He strode toward her, shrugging off his coat. He wrapped it around her, jerking her closer to him in the process. "That's not much better but . . . but . . ." His gaze locked with hers. His hands still gripped his coat and he stared down at her. He hadn't realized just how intimate their position was. There was nothing between him and that delicious body of hers but the merest sigh of silk that clung to every curve, molded against her, and whispered upon her skin.

She stared up at him, the oddest look in her eyes. Of recognition or realization or awareness. As if she too knew the sudden and unrepentant longing, the ache of desire that surged through him, twisting his stomach and wrapping around his soul.

"I am nearly finished with you, mademoiselle," Vadeboncoeur said.

The moment between them shattered and they jerked away from each other as if one or the other of them was ablaze.

Lucy cleared her throat. "Oh?"

"I will soon have all that I need of you." The artist picked up a rag and wiped his brush, his gaze still focused on the painting. "A few hours, no more."

"Are you nearly finished then?" she said.

He scoffed and gestured at the work. "No, no, there is much still to be done. The plants, the leaves, the way the light filters through the window and dances on the foliage and caresses the skin. But I will soon have enough to continue without you." He nodded. "Such brilliance leaves me weary and parched. I must refresh myself. I shall be no more than a few minutes, then we will continue. Monsieur." He nodded at Cameron, then strode out of the conservatory in search of refreshment.

"His English is better than his brother's," Cam noted. But like his brother, he too had the look of a god. A god somewhat older and probably more experienced and no doubt extremely skilled at—

"Why are you here?" Lucy asked the moment Vadeboncoeur disappeared from sight.

He drew a deep breath. "I came to apologize."

"And yet your attitude today is precisely the same as it was two days ago."

"Yes, well, that's to be expected, isn't it?"

"Is it?"

"Damn it, Lucy." He ran his hand through his hair. "This isn't some little lark, some silly antic. That man saw you *naked!*"

"Oh, he did not." She paused. "Not much of me, anyway."

"Have you no modesty?"

"I have a great deal of modesty. Why, I am probably the most modest person I know." She huffed. "Let me tell you, Cameron Fairchild, it's not particularly easy to pose without clothing. It takes a great deal of courage."

He stared. "Courage?"

She nodded. "Yes, courage. At least in the beginning. But after a while . . ."

His eyes narrowed. "After a while?"

"After a while one realizes the artist is not really looking at you."

"Come now." He scoffed. "No man in his right mind would not be looking at you, *naked,* if given the chance."

"Why, thank you, but that's not what I mean." She thought for a moment. "He certainly looked at me but with no more salacious interest than he would give a bowl of oranges or a vase of flowers. Once you realize that you are simply a subject like any other"—she raised a shoulder in a casual shrug—"then any sense of embarrassment goes away."

"How delightful for you." He glared. Had she no idea of the seriousness of all this? "Do you realize this is the sort of thing that destroys a woman's reputation?"

"Only if people know about it and no one ever will. Besides, women pose for paintings all the time."

"Well-bred, respectable, young women do not pose for paintings without their clothes on!"

She cast him an annoyingly wicked smile. "Which is what makes it an adventure."

"Which is what makes it scandalous!"

"Nonsense." She waved off his objection. "Scandal is in the eye of the beholder. Besides, I intend to keep the painting, not have it displayed in a gallery."

"Which doesn't mean no one will ever see it!"

"Which means no one will see it unless I wish them to. And even if they do, it will make no difference." She paused. "Would you like to see it?"

He would like nothing better. "Absolutely not."

"Come now, Mr. Fairchild, don't be so stuffy. It's art after all." She strode over to the easel and studied the painting. "I think it's quite extraordinary. Or at least it will be when it's finished." She glanced at him. "Are you sure you don't want to see it?"

"No!" *Yes!*

Her attention returned to the portrait. "Even now there's something about it that's quite, oh . . . provocative."

"To say the least!"

"I should tell you that I chose Jean-Philippe because of his artistic style." She continued to inspect the work. "François had told me his brother was an artist, and yesterday Jean-Philippe came by to show me some of his work." She glanced at Cam. "You would have known that if you had been here."

He stared. "You told me not to come back."

"And yet here you are."

He hesitated. "Taking off your clothes is not the only thing that requires courage."

"I had already decided to forgive you. You can't help who you are, no man can. I have brothers, you know. It's the very nature of your gender to be arrogant and overbearing and somewhat asinine." She returned to her perusal of the painting. "In that you are no different than any other man."

He stared. "Thank you?"

"Jean-Philippe considers himself something of an impressionist. Although he feels his work is progressing further beyond the mere depiction of a subject than even the impressionists went. Or something like that. It was a bit difficult to understand exactly what he meant; he did tend to go on and on, until I saw his work. That's when I decided he was the only artist I could trust for this."

"Trust?"

She pulled her gaze from the painting. "Are you certain you don't want to see it?"

"Oh, very well." He blew a resigned breath and joined her.

For a long moment he could do nothing but stare at Vadeboncoeur's interpretation of a partially nude Lucy.

"He's calling it *American Dreamer*, which doesn't seem entirely accurate. I've always thought of myself as rather practical and sensible. But it does look a bit like a dream at that." She glanced at him. "I can't read your mind and for once your thoughts don't show on your face. Tell me, what do you think?"

"I'm not sure what to think," he said slowly. It was not at all what he expected.

The canvas was covered with dabs and dashes and dots of paint in what looked like a random manner. He took a step back, then another. The shapes took form the farther back he stood. It was definitely a woman in a lush, tropical setting, but it was indeed no more than an impression, a feeling perhaps of beauty and serenity and sensuality. It was obviously unfinished but was already most evocative, reminiscent of the works of a Monet or a Renoir, but not as refined and yet striking in a raw, abstract sort of way. More a vision than a truth, a dream more than reality.

"It's unique," he said at last.

"It is at that." She laughed. "When Jean-Philippe visited yesterday he showed me two works. One was a portrait, nicely done and quite realistic. He says one has to do what one must to pay one's bills. The second was the same woman painted in this style. He paints portraits to make a living. This . . ." She nodded at the painting. "This is the work of his soul. This is where his passion is."

Cam nodded. "And this is what you wanted?"

"What I wanted was to cross off Great-aunt Lucinda's desire to be painted without clothing. But I am not stupid, Cameron."

"I never thought you were."

"I realize the dangers inherent in pursuing this quest of mine. I have no desire for scandal to ruin the rest of my life. You've said nothing on that topic that I have not thought of myself."

"Again, my apologies for not giving you the credit due you."

"Now *that* was sincere." She smiled and returned her gaze to the canvas. "In her journal, Lucinda thought it would be a great adventure to be immortalized forever as art as long as one's features were suitably disguised."

"That you have achieved."

"And better yet, I like it, very much." She considered it thoughtfully. "It strikes me as, oh, I don't know, pure emotion if you will, captured in color and movement. A fanciful idea, I suppose."

"Not at all." The more he studied the work, the more it called to him. "It strikes me in much the same way. It's all light and shadow, variations of hues and shades and makes no sense when examined too closely. But step back and you get a, well, an impression of something remarkable."

She raised a brow. "Then you do like it?"

"God help me, I do." He grinned. "So." He adopted a casual manner. "Now that you can cross this off your list, what do you plan next?"

"I have been giving that, and you, a great deal of thought." She stepped away from the painting and drifted aimlessly along the path encircling the palm.

"You have been giving me a great deal of thought?" He wasn't sure if that was good or very bad.

"I have." She nodded. "While I have acknowledged that you cannot help your attitude when it comes to women, because we are so weak and fragile and lacking in intelligence."

"I never said—"

She pinned him with a hard look.

It was no use arguing with her, especially when she was more than a little right. He sighed. "I did come to apologize."

"And?"

"And, well, apparently, I will have to continue to apologize."

"Will you?"

"You said it yourself—it's in my nature. Because as much as you don't think you need someone to watch over you, I am certain you do. Which reminds me." He glanced around the conservatory. "Where is Albert? I expected him to be nipping at my heels the moment I stepped foot in here."

She sighed. "He doesn't seem to like Jean-Philippe, so he's confined to my rooms for now."

"Good dog," he murmured. "And where is your cohort in scandal?"

"If you mean Miss West, she was here until shortly before you arrived. Then I sent her off on an errand."

"Dare I ask what kind of errand?"

"You can ask, but half the fun of any adventure is the element of surprise," she said with a wicked gleam in her eyes.

He ignored her. "What I'm attempting to say is that I suspect I will continue to annoy you because, in what I believe is your best interest, I will continue to try to make you see reason when it comes to these regrets of your great-aunt's. And I shall do so in my arrogant, high-handed manner."

"I expect nothing less." She leaned over to inspect a large tropical blossom. A hibiscus, he thought.

"You may throw me out as many times as you want but I shall continue to return."

She nodded. "Because it's your job."

"Because it's the right thing to do."

"Oh?" She moved to another plant and rubbed a velvety leaf between two fingers.

He trailed after her. "And because we've become friends."

"There is that," she said under her breath, and continued to wander slowly from one plant to the next, making her way around the palm in the center of the room.

"And because, well, I . . . I like you."

She smiled.

He drew a deep breath. "I like you a great deal, Lucy."

She bent to take a sniff of an elegant blossom he couldn't identify. "Go on"

He could use a little encouragement but apparently that was not going to happen. "It's because I like you that I think this course you're set upon is . . . well, you know my thoughts on that."

"Indeed I do."

"I want only the best for you." The oddest note of desperation sounded in his voice. "If you have any feelings for me—"

"Feelings?" Lucy straightened, her eyes wide.

He grimaced. "I am sorry. I shouldn't—"

"No, no, it's quite all right." She waved off his apology. "I was simply surprised, that's all." She moved to the chaise and sank down onto it, casting him a weak smile. "Actually, this is exactly what I was thinking about. Well, not exactly this, but something like this. Or perhaps not at all. Although—"

Good Lord, the woman was babbling. He'd never seen her babble before. It was rather endearing. Obviously, she was taken aback by his comment.

"—somewhat, I think. Your wanting what's best, that is. And the truly charming, if overbearing, compulsion you have to make certain I am, well, protected, I suppose. Of course, some of that is your job but"—she drew a steadying breath—"at this point, it appears there is only one sensible thing to do."

"You'll give up this absurd quest?" Had the woman at last come to her senses?

She stared at him. "Two things then."

He narrowed his eyes and sat on the chaise beside her. "I'm afraid to ask."

"If you're so concerned about what sort of mischief I might become embroiled in, perhaps you should help me accomplish the items on my list rather than leaving me to my own devices." She smiled in an innocent manner, but a note of triumph rang in her voice.

"Help you?" He stared for a long moment. He was right. She did have a diabolical mind. "You want me to assist you to do what I don't think you should be doing at all?"

"I thought it was a brilliant idea."

"*Brilliant* isn't the word I would use." Still, it was not a bad idea. If he was the one to plan how to accomplish the remaining items on her list, she certainly couldn't go off on these little adventures without him. It would, in fact, make his life easier.

"Unless of course, you'd prefer not to." She shrugged "Or you're not up to the task."

He raised a brow. "Is that a challenge?"

She smiled in a smug manner. "It would appear so."

"I'm more than up to the task," he warned.

"One can only hope." She grinned and held out her hand. "Then we have an agreement?"

"We do at that. You have my word I will do everything I can to assist you in your absurd quest."

She laughed.

He took her hand and for a moment wanted nothing more than to pull her into his arms and knew if he did, he might not let her go. His gaze met hers. "There is a great deal I need to say to you, Lucy."

"Is it important?"

"Yes."

"Then I don't think this is the time." She paused. "I have something I wish to say to you as well. But this is not the time for that either."

"Why not?"

"If we are going to discuss important matters, then I would much prefer to do so fully dressed."

He laughed. "Would you?"

"I would." She nodded. "I feel entirely too, well, free I suppose, without my usual layer upon layer of clothing." She shook her head. "I'm afraid that sensation of liberty would not serve me well in a discussion of important matters. I am beginning to suspect women are made to wear garments like corsets in the first place to restrict our sense of freedom. It's awfully difficult to do anything improper in a corset."

"I had no idea."

"That is a relief."

He laughed. "You may well be the most delightful woman I have ever met."

"Am I?" Her gaze searched his. "What makes me the most delightful woman you have ever met?"

"Any number of things." He considered the question. "You have a tendency to make the most outrageous comments. You're clever and amusing. You know your own mind. You have a deep sense of honor. You're independent and you have the courage to follow your own path."

"All of which drives you mad."

He hadn't realized it before, but she was right. The very things that made her so captivating were the very things that drove him to distraction. He chuckled. "So it would seem."

"Goodness, Cameron." She considered him curiously. "Do you realize you know everything about me and I know very little about you?"

"On the contrary, I don't know much about you at all."

"Then we should add that to the list of important matters we need to discuss." She glanced at their hands, then her gaze met his. "You do realize you are still holding my hand."

"Do you want me to let it go?"

"No," she said with a sigh. "I like you too. Quite a lot, really. Awkward, isn't it?"

"Or perfect."

"It has been my observation," she said slowly, "that perfection is only found in tales of fiction. Life is not as tidy as a story. In life everything does not always end well."

"It can."

She tilted her head and smiled up at him. "There is more than a little of the dreamer in you as well, isn't there, Cameron?"

He smiled slowly. "Perhaps."

"I like that. It almost makes up for that tendency you have to be stuffy."

He started to argue, then thought better of it. "It's good to know you think I have some redeeming qualities."

"Some." She laughed and gently pulled her hand from his. The oddest sense of loss washed through him. "However, if you are truly going to help me, there are some conditions."

He drew his brows together. "What kind of conditions?"

"First, you need to accept that I am of age. I am an adult fully capable of making my own decisions and my own choices, whether or not you agree with them. While I am willing to listen to reason, this is my quest and my life."

He hesitated.

"If you cannot accept—"

"No, you're right of course." Still, if he were now helping her instead of blindly following in her wake, he was confident he could steer her away from anything too potentially scandalous. He nodded. "I can agree to that. Anything else?"

"I will keep you informed as to any new endeavors I plan; however, I will not track you down to do so. If you wish to be informed as to my comings and goings, you need to provide me with an address where you may be found."

"Of course." He could certainly give her his address. He had purchased the modest house some years ago when he realized being in his father's presence more than necessary would inevitably lead to disaster. "Is there more?"

"Yes." She considered him for a moment. "When you were being so incredibly irrational after we returned from Prichard's the other night, you said that you had trusted me and implied I had betrayed that trust."

"Did I?" Unease washed through him.

"You know full well you did. Trust, Cameron, has to go both ways."

"Of course."

"As well as honesty."

"That goes without saying." An annoying voice in the back of his head pointed out he had not actually been honest with her. However, as he had every intention of rectifying that minor discrepancy, he ignored it.

She clasped her hands together in front of her. "I have trusted you up to now. Can I continue to do so?"

He nodded. "Without question."

She stared at him thoughtfully, as if expecting him to say something more. Or trying to decide if he was indeed worthy of her trust. This might be the perfect opportunity to tell her everything. Although Vadeboncoeur would return any minute as would Miss West. And this wasn't something that would bear an interruption. Besides, he still wasn't quite sure exactly how to say what he needed to say.

"Well," she said at last, the vaguest hint of disappointment in her voice. "There's no need for you to stay. Clara will return shortly and Jean-Philippe said we would be finished in a few hours."

"I have no intention of leaving." He stood and strolled over to one of the benches beside the pathway.

"What are you doing?"

He picked up the bench and moved it to a

position where he could see both the chaise and the artist's easel. "I have always wanted to watch an artist at his craft."

She laughed. "You have not."

"Consider it a new desire then." He seated himself on the bench and smiled. "In hopes of, I don't know, broadening my horizons, shall we say. And perhaps becoming less stuffy in the process."

Her eyes narrowed. "Don't you trust me to be alone with him, Mr. Fairchild?"

Once again, her great-aunt's desire for *romantic interludes* flashed through his mind. "I trust *you* implicitly."

"Then it's Jean-Philippe you don't trust?"

He snorted. "Not for an instant."

"Oh, come now." She huffed. "I am not going to allow some silly Frenchman to seduce me."

"I never thought—"

"You most certainly did."

"Well, he is handsome and probably charming—"

"Oh, he is most definitely charming. But did you think me so shallow as to succumb to a bit of charm and a handsome . . ." She paused. "Well, *extremely* handsome face."

"No." He scoffed. "Of course not."

"Furthermore, I am nothing if not sensible. Certainly I may, on occasion, jump to an inaccurate conclusion. I might even be a bit reckless, but I am not impulsive. I do not make important, significant decisions without due consideration."

He nodded. "Nor should you."

"And even you must admit that everything I have done thus far has been well thought out and equally well planned."

"Yes, I suppose it has."

"Make no mistake, Cameron Fairchild." She met his gaze directly and there was a distinct challenge in her eyes. "Should I decide to allow anyone to seduce me, it will not be because I am some silly, vapid female prone to swoon into the bed of the first man to whisper passionate phrases into my ear."

"I should hope not."

"Furthermore, if I were to permit someone to seduce me it will be for no other reason than because I wish to be seduced. Which means we are no longer talking about the seduction of one person by another but something much more mutual. Even democratic, if you will."

"I see." He stared at her for a long moment, then smiled slowly. "And will that be well thought out too?"

Behind him he heard the artist return to the conservatory. Lucy smiled a welcome, then leaned close and spoke low into Cam's ear. "Goodness, Cameron. It already is."

Regrets Set to Rights

Be painted sans clothing.

. . . discussion turned to an article Father had read on the scientific uses of balloon flights. He called it complete and utter nonsense. I then mentioned how I would very much like to fly in a balloon. One would have thought I had uttered the worst sort of blasphemy. Mother gasped and said such a thing would be most improper for a lady, adding that discussions of this nature had no place at the dinner table. Father declared he would never permit a daughter of his to do something so completely absurd and further stated that man was not meant to fly. As much as I wanted to point out man was already flying and that I had indeed read of a French girl, no older than myself, who was piloting balloons, I wisely said nothing. Father would have just said something rude about the French having no sense whatsoever anyway.

I cannot imagine anything more exciting than floating through the heavens with no particular destination in mind. I doubt that I will ever be allowed to do such a thing. As Mother said, proper young ladies don't. But then proper young ladies never seem to do much of anything of interest. I am quite tired of being a proper young lady. I would much rather be daring and courageous and a seeker of adventure.

But adventure too is forbidden to women. My life is destined to be completely unexciting and excruciatingly proper. Still, I can dream, and in that at least I can do whatever I wish. And perhaps one day I too can rise above the earth to see the world as those very few brave souls have done . . .

from the journal of Miss Lucinda Merryweather, 1805

Chapter Eleven

"I'm not sure how you managed to arrange this," Lucy said, forcing a bright note to her voice. "And so quickly as well."

"Yesterday you challenged me to help you complete the tasks on your great-aunt's list." Cameron grinned. "Correct me if I'm wrong, but wasn't flying one of those you had yet to accomplish?"

"Indeed it is," she said weakly, trying very hard not to let her gaze stray over the edge of the gondola of the balloon that was taking them ever upward and probably to their doom.

Fortunately they were tethered to the ground and would rise no farther than the length of the rope. A rope that did seem to be unreasonably long. The gondola itself—and she preferred to think of it as a gondola rather than a creaking, insubstantial wicker basket more suited to the storage of yarn than the carrying of people—was square in shape and no more than five or six feet across, adequate for perhaps four inhabitants, although she and Cameron were alone on this ascent. Unfortunately, the limited space meant anyone who might not wish to watch the earth rapidly growing smaller beneath them, someone who might prefer to curl up in a small ball on the floor and pray for an end to this particular adventure or at the very least a swift and painless death, was unable to do so. No, such a person had little choice but to bravely face her fate and smile and pretend that she was having a wonderful time.

To make it worse, it was shockingly cold up here. Lucy could no longer feel her toes. She pushed her hands further into her fur muff and hunched her shoulders. Her nose was numb as well. Cameron was not the only one who was not fond of the cold. Once again, she wondered at Lucinda's lists of regrets. Had her great-aunt put no thought into the practicality and the sheer terror of any of them? Someday perhaps there would be means of flying—machines possibly like trains with wings—that did not expose travelers to the cold and a view of the far distant ground through woven wicker, but today was not that day. "I didn't think it was possible to go up in a balloon in weather like this."

"Actually, according to Carswell, the aeronaut who mans this balloon—"

Who had wisely remained on the ground with Clara.

"—as long as the winds are calm, winter isn't a bad time at all to ascend."

"Except of course for the bitter cold."

"Oh, it's not that bad." Cameron drew a deep breath. "Really rather invigorating, I think." He turned away from her and braced his hands on the rail of the gondola. "And the view, Lucy. My God, the view is magnificent. You can see all of London from here."

"I prefer seeing it from the ground, thank you," she said under her breath. Certainly she'd been a bit uneasy when she'd ridden Hannibal, but she'd attributed that to the sway of the animal and not the height of her seat. Now, she knew better.

Lucinda Wilhelmina Merryweather was deathly afraid of heights.

"Did you say something?" Cameron asked over his shoulder.

"No, nothing, nothing at all." She absolutely was not about to let him know how truly terrified she was. After all, this was her adventure. Besides, she was an American and they were made of sterner stuff than to let something as minor as sailing far above the rooftops of London turn them into quivering rabbits. Although a rabbit wouldn't be so stupid as to let his little paws leave the ground. Lucy promised herself to never again leave the solid earth behind. "How did you manage this?"

"The army, the Royal Engineers to be exact, has a balloon division." He scanned the horizon as if he were a captain at the helm of a grand ship. "And I know someone who knows someone. It really wasn't all that difficult to arrange."

"And yet most impressive." Would they ever stop their ascent? Surely the rope had reached its limit by now. Unless the rope had come loose. Or the aeronaut had forgotten to tie it. Or his heart had failed and he was lying dead on the ground leaving them to continue to shoot ever higher until they lost sight of the earth altogether. Her already uneasy stomach twisted at the thought.

She was being silly, of course. She drew a calming breath.

Nothing of that sort had happened. They simply hadn't reached the end of the rope yet. Nothing would go wrong. They were in the competent hands of someone who had something to do with the Royal Engineers, which did sound encouraging. Why, they would be back on the ground before they knew it. She would tell Cameron how delightful it had been and thank him for helping her check another regret off her list. In the meantime it might be better to think of something—anything—that did not bring to mind the all too vivid idea of dropping like a stone from the heavens.

Admittedly, if she hadn't been in fear for her life at the moment, her thoughts would be filled with trying to work out the mystery that was Cameron Fairchild. Indeed, she'd thought of little else but him since he'd left her yesterday. He'd stayed watching Jean-Philippe paint long enough for Clara to return and then had finally taken his leave. But he had given her an address where he could be reached should she need him. Tonight, she would attend the ambassador's ball with Beryl and Lord Dunwell. Tomorrow, she would do a bit of investigating of her own. It was past time she found out exactly who or perhaps what Mr. Fairchild was. At this point, it was more than simple curiosity on her part. She absolutely refused to give her heart to a man who wasn't completely honest with her. But oh, dear Lord, how she wanted to.

She hadn't expected that, certainly hadn't planned on it, but then she hadn't planned on a less than competent private investigator or watch-dog or bodyguard or whatever he really was. Hadn't planned on endless brown eyes or the endearing way his jaw clenched with indignation or, for the first time in her life, someone who didn't see her as a dutiful daughter or a perky, brainless, fair-haired little sister or the future bride of Jackson Channing. Someone who seemed to see her for her. It was as disconcerting as it was wonderful.

"The army came up with the idea in the first place from your civil war." He glanced back at her. "Did you know that Confederate forces used balloons to safely observe battles and track forces on the ground?"

"I had no idea," she said faintly. Frankly, she'd rather be shot at.

The last thing she wanted to talk about was the history of balloon flight. Still, it was better than nothing, and anything would serve to take her mind off their imminent demise. "How on earth do you know all of this?"

He chuckled. "I am a repository of useless information."

As most educated, well-bred young men who had no financial need to seek eventual employment tended to be. Yet another clue as to the truth about Cameron. Still, as confident as she was of his honorable nature—and surely she would know somewhere deep down inside if he were truly a deceitful cad—she did need to have her confidence confirmed. After all, an expected engagement to Jackson and growing up with four brothers did not give her true experience with men and certainly not with deceitful cads. Besides, she suspected a man could be deceitful and not be a cad. There might be all kinds of valid reasons why a man would be less than perfectly honest with a woman. Still, it was extremely annoying. Yesterday she had given Cameron any number of hints about honesty and trust and yet he still hadn't told her what he was hiding. Of course, it was entirely possible he wasn't hiding anything, but she doubted it. There were too many tiny clues that indicated the man was not what he appeared.

And with every passing day it was more and more important to learn the truth. Because with every passing day her heart, which seemed to have no understanding of the impracticality of falling for a man one couldn't trust, was urging her to toss caution aside and fling herself headlong into his arms and his life and, God help her, his bed.

Whatever had possessed her to speak to him of seduction and in a most risqué manner? She had never in her life been that, well, brazen. Worse yet, she had enjoyed it. There was something quite satisfying about seeing a look of shock on a man's face at a suggestion of impropriety. Especially a man who didn't expect it. Although she was every bit as surprised as he. Certainly it could in part be attributed to her lack of proper clothing. It was amazing what going without a corset did for a woman's candor. But one could only blame so much on one's underpinnings or lack of them.

And then he had spoken of feelings and said he liked her and there was a definite look in his eyes that said he more than merely liked her. She really hadn't expected that either, although she sup-posed she had hoped, somewhere in the back of her mind where she was reluctant to admit it. Still, as much as she did seem to be falling into some sort of vast abyss, she wondered now if he was falling as well. That thought too was both wonderful and disconcerting. But mostly wonderful.

"It's only been in the last ten years that progress has really been made in the field."

"How fascinating." She thought for a moment. She'd realized from the beginning he was well educated. What better time than now to find out more. "Is this an interest of yours? Balloon flight, I mean. You seem to know a great deal about the history of it. Was this part of your studies? At a university perhaps?"

"No, just something I picked up here and there." He glanced back at her. "You really should come here and see the view."

"I can see it quite well from here, thank you." She adopted a casual tone. "Where did you study?"

"Oh, I—"

Without warning the balloon jerked, abruptly stopping its upward motion. Lucy uttered a short shriek, sank to the floor of the gondola, and buried her face in her hands.

"Lucy?"

"Good God! We're going to die! I knew it! I knew it all along!" Sheer terror swept through her. "We'll plunge to the ground! We'll be smashed into a thousand pieces!"

"Lucy!" Cameron grabbed her hands, pried them from her face, and pulled her to her feet. "Don't be absurd. We've simply reached the end of our rope."

"The end of our rope?" Her voice rose. "*The end of our rope?* I don't want to be at the end of our rope! I don't want to be at the end of anything! I have a great deal left to do in my life! I've scarcely even begun!"

"Lucy," he said firmly, gripping her shoulders and staring into her eyes. "We're perfectly all right. Nothing is going to happen."

"I don't call falling from the heavens nothing!"

"We're not going to fall." He shook her shoulders slightly. "Trust me, I will never let anything hurt you."

"Really?" Fear sharpened her voice. A tiny, rational part of her mind noted that he was probably right. She ignored it. "Unless you plan to sprout wings and fly us back to the ground, I don't see that there's anything you can do to stop it! We're about to—"

He yanked her into his arms and crushed his lips to hers. She struggled against him and pulled free.

She sucked in a deep breath. "We're going to hurtle to our deaths! There's nothing you can do to stop—"

Again, his lips claimed hers. He held her tight against him until she stopped fighting. Until the warmth of his mouth on hers, the heat of his body pressing against her, surrounding her, eased her panic. At last he raised his head from hers. "We are not going to plummet—"

"Plummet?" Terror widened her eyes and she stared up at him. "I never said plummet! Oh God, Cameron, I don't want to plummet!"

"We are not going to plummet." His arms tightened around her and his hand pressed her head against his chest. "Nor are we going to plunge or hurtle or fall—"

She moaned.

273

"And we will certainly not be smashed into a hundred pieces."

"A thousand pieces." She shuddered.

"Breathe, my sweet girl, just breathe."

For a long moment or forever he held her tight and she clung to him and little by little her terror eased.

"This is rather disconcerting." A smile sounded in his voice.

"Don't even think of letting me go," she warned. "I don't care about propriety or anything else at the moment, but if you let me go, Cameron Fairchild, I swear to you—"

"I promise, I won't let you go." He chuckled. "It's not that. Holding you in my arms is delightful. I've simply never seen you as anything other than completely courageous before."

"I'm not especially brave when it comes to things like imminent death."

"Few of us are."

"I don't think I like adventures that include the actual risking of one's life."

"Some people think that's the only true kind of adventure." Amusement sounded in his voice.

"Men no doubt." She huffed. "And utter idiots."

He laughed.

"This is a dreadful adventure."

"It's hard to enjoy if you're terrified. I had no idea you would find this frightening."

"Neither did I."

In spite of her fear, his words and his embrace comforted her. "You're not scared at all, are you?"

"Not really. I'm finding this quite exciting. But I am truly sorry that you are."

"It's most embarrassing," she murmured against his chest.

"We're all scared of something," he said gently, and her heart warmed.

"What are you scared of, Cameron?"

He thought for a long moment. "Failure, I suppose. Not living up to expectations. Being a disappointment to those I care about."

How very interesting. She looked up at him. "I can't imagine ever being disappointed in you."

He smiled. "Thank you."

"But you're not a very good private investigator, are you?"

"You do realize a man with lesser confidence than I would be offended at your continued criticism of the way I do my job." His brow furrowed. "Why do you keep mentioning that?"

"It seems worth mentioning." She sighed. "I do apologize if I have offended you. But if you cannot be honest with, well, friends, who can you be honest with?"

"You do have a point." He paused. "And you? What are you afraid of, Lucy? Aside from heights, that is."

"Apparently I'm afraid of dying before my time," she said wryly.

He laughed. "I assure you, that will not happen today. I told Carswell we only needed to stay up for a few minutes. As soon as I release some of the gas in the balloon, we'll start to descend. As the rope slackens, he'll reel it in. We'll be back on the ground in no time." He paused. "Lucy."

"Yes?"

"If I am to do that, you are going to have to let go of me."

She shook her head. "Oh, I don't think so."

He chuckled. "I wouldn't mind staying up here forever with you in my arms, but at some point we're going to get very hungry."

"Well then, it can't be helped, I suppose." She released him with a reluctant sigh.

He cast her a confident smile, then turned and reached up to adjust a valve. A soft hiss of escaping gas sounded and they slowly started to descend. "This will take a few minutes. We don't want to drop too quickly."

"What a terrible choice." She blew a frustrated breath. "Die a thousand deaths in a slow descent to solid ground or plummet and die only once."

"Let's take a thousand, shall we?"

"I have to confess, going down makes me just as uneasy as going up." She hesitated. "However, I would feel much safer if . . . well . . ."

He grinned and slipped an arm around her waist. "Is that better?"

"Not entirely. But this is." She stretched up to

meet his lips with hers in a kiss long and slow and as heavenly as their surroundings. And when she drew back to gaze into his eyes, the flutter in her stomach was no longer due to the movement of the basket. "Now, Mr. Fairchild." She smiled. "*Now, this is indeed an adventure well worth having.*"

"I cannot agree more." He chuckled. "So, tell me, what else are you afraid of, Lucy Merryweather?"

"You're just trying to keep me from thinking about our imminent demise."

He laughed and his arm tightened around her.

"I'm afraid of being forced to fit into expectations that no longer seem to suit me," she said without thinking. "I'm afraid of molding my life to the requirements of others and losing my soul in the process."

He stared down at her.

"And I'm afraid of reaching the end of my life with regrets."

"Well, we can't have that." He grinned, drew her closer, and kissed her once again.

And I'm very much afraid of falling in love with a man who will inevitably break my heart.

Without warning a line from her great-aunt's letter to her flashed through her mind.

Love, my dear girl, is never a regret.

Regrets Set to Rights

Fly.

. . . and it is a singular pity that a girl in this country cannot be a princess. Worse yet, there is not even the slightest opportunity to so much as meet a prince.

Father will go on and on about throwing off the yoke of oppression and liberty from tyranny and so on and so forth, and while I do under-stand why we prefer not to have a king, princes and princesses are an entirely different matter and would be great fun. Especially princes. Why, very nearly every story I've ever read includes a handsome, dashing prince who dances with the heroine at a grand ball, wins her heart, and sweeps her away to live her life in a magnificent palace. That doesn't sound the least bit oppressive or tyrannical but rather quite, quite lovely.

Still, I shall never have the chance to be swept away by a prince as I shall probably never meet one. And that too is a pity as a dance with a prince is the stuff a girl's dreams are made of . . .

from the journal of Miss Lucinda Merryweather, 1804

Chapter Twelve

Lucy Merryweather had the remarkable ability to make him gasp with shock or sputter with indignation. Tonight, she simply took his breath away.

Cam had thought she looked like a magical forest creature in the conservatory. Now she looked like their queen.

Her gown was blue, the color of crystal clear ice in a frozen pond, and turned the blue of her eyes deeper and more vivid. The bodice dipped in a scandalously low V that at once annoyed and delighted him. The whole thing was held up with tiny lace sleeves that could be snapped with one flick of a man's fingers. His stomach tightened at the thought.

He stood in the shadows of an arched colonnade that ran along one side of the ballroom discreetly watching her dance with one gentleman after another, including one who must have been royal given the ornate, medal-covered sash he wore diagonally across his chest and the way everyone who crossed his path bowed before him. Cam smiled. Obviously, Lucy could check *dance with a prince* off her list. There was really no need for him to be here.

Cam's time would be better spent writing. But

he had never written anything so quickly in his life. Every time he sat down at his desk he was like a man possessed. His pen fairly flew across the page. Five installments of *Daring Exploits* had already appeared in the *Messenger*, two more were written and scheduled. He had added a few pertinent secondary characters and while he wasn't sure how Lucy's quest would end, Mercy Heartley would be successful in gaining her inheritance. Better still, he had written and rewritten the completed installments into book form.

No, there was no need for his presence tonight. Lucy was in the capable hands of Lady Dunwell, and no one knew the tricks of men better than Beryl Dunwell. But ever since Lucy had said that she would be here, he couldn't get the idea of dancing with her out of his head. A single dance was all he wanted. Silly, of course. One would think he hadn't held her in his arms only a few hours ago or felt her warm body next to his or kissed her. But there was something about dancing with a woman, something about the way the music filled your soul and the way two moved as one, that had always seemed special and deeply romantic.

Besides, it was his experience that women were always a bit more amenable to things like confessions and the complete truth if a little romance was mixed in. The dance floor was the one place he could truly get her alone, without the constant presence of Miss West. He would much prefer to tell Lucy everything without the other woman's forbidding presence. Although admittedly, he'd had a few missed opportunities.

He had intended to tell Lucy the truth about his deception yesterday when he came to apologize. But finding her nearly naked had swept that from his mind. Then he had planned to confess everything when they were floating above London. He had never expected her absolute terror nor that the way to ease her fear was to hold her in his embrace and kiss her over and over again. He grinned at the memory. He was nothing if not helpful.

It wasn't difficult for him to arrange to be here tonight. His family always received invitations to events like this. Depending on the importance of the event, and whether the duke and duchess were otherwise engaged, one of the duke's children would be sent to represent the family. Tonight it was Spencer's turn, although Cam had yet to see his older brother and didn't especially want to. Spencer would wonder why Cam had deigned to make an appearance at the sort of function he usually avoided and Spencer could be relentless when he wanted to know the truth of a matter.

His oldest brother wasn't his only concern. Cam hadn't realized what a mistake this was until after his arrival. Everywhere he turned he saw someone he knew. And while it would be wiser to leave now, certainly he could avoid unwanted encounters long enough to have one dance. If he swooped in on Lucy right before she was about to step on the dance floor—

"Is that her?" A glass of champagne appeared before him.

Cam resisted the urge to sigh in frustration and instead forced an innocent tone and took the glass. "Is that who?"

Spencer stood by his side, surveying the dancers. "The American."

Damnation, he might as well confess all. It was impossible to have secrets in his family. "How much do you know?"

"Oh, I should think I know quite a lot." Spencer sipped his wine. "Let's see. I know Simon wrote you a letter of reference extolling your qualifications as a private investigator."

"Yes, well, I can explain that—"

"And I know that you are I. F. Aldrich, the author of a series of extremely popular stories about a runaway American heiress. And while the stories are fictional, apparently the heiress is not. That information is thanks to Thad."

"I shall have to remember to thank him myself."

Spencer chuckled.

Cam glanced at his brother. "Does anyone else know?"

"I doubt it. I daresay I'm the only one with all the pieces." Spencer shrugged. "Mother is following the *Daring Exploits* with bated breath. I'm fairly certain she has realized it's your work, but she hasn't mentioned it. And Father is back to reading only those parts of the *Messenger* Mother clips for him."

"Good."

"However, as I said, I am the one with all the pieces." He paused. "But I do think congratulations are in order."

"For what?"

"Your stories are proving to be remarkably popular. Not surprising as they are most entertaining. I suspect the book will do even better." He glanced at his brother. "Given the timing of the heiress stories, I'm assuming you intend to compile them into a book."

"That was my plan," Cam said under his breath.

"Was?" Curiosity sounded in his brother's voice. "And has something changed?"

Cam hesitated.

"Ah, I see." Spencer chuckled in that wise, older brother way he had. "It's the girl, isn't it?" His gaze scanned the dancers. "Which one is she?"

"The one in blue." Cam nodded. "Dancing with the tall, thin fellow."

"Of course. She's quite lovely," Spencer murmured. "Does she have a name?"

"Miss Lucy Merryweather."

"The name is familiar." Spencer's brows drew together. "American banking, I believe?"

Trust Spencer to know a business name even from another country.

"Her father."

"I see." Spencer paused. "You know, it's been a long time since you confided in me. Should you wish to do so now—"

"She thinks I'm a private investigator who has been hired by an old friend she was once supposed to marry to keep her out of trouble."

Spencer frowned. "Have you?"

"No." Cam scoffed. "No, I was trying to learn more about her and she jumped to this conclusion, and it seemed in my best interest so I didn't correct her. Besides, I needed inspiration. A muse as it were."

"Oh, that sounds good." Spencer nodded. "I would stay with that if I were you. A woman would much rather be thought of as a muse rather than think she had been shamefully misled for the sake of literary success."

Cam slanted him a wry glance. "It's not going to work, is it?"

Spencer shook his head. "I wouldn't think so."

"I'm going to have to tell her the truth, aren't I?"

"If you were hoping I'd say no, I'm afraid you're talking to the wrong brother." Spencer chuckled. "Telling the truth is usually the right thing to do."

"I've already come to that realization. I'm just trying to find the right moment."

"Ah yes, the right moment. Timing is critical in a situation like this," Spencer said in a knowing manner. "Tell me something, Cam. What happens then? Or rather, what do you hope happens then?"

"I hope she forgives me, of course."

"And then?"

"And then . . ." Cam blew a long breath. "I don't know. Bloody hell, Spence." He ran his hand through his hair. "I don't know anything. I can't think about anything but her."

Spencer studied his brother curiously. "You're serious then?"

"I don't know that either."

"I see." He paused. "It shows, you know."

"What? My confusion?"

"How you feel about her. That she is uppermost in your thoughts. Your stories, *Daring Exploits*, may be far closer to the truth than you care to admit."

"Don't be absurd." Cam scoffed. "I've taken great pains to disguise her completely."

"Have you?" Spencer's brow rose. "Your . . . Miss Heartley, is it?"

Cam nodded.

"Let's see, how did you put it? Ah yes. You describe her as having hair the color of burnished gold, with fragile features, a mere slip of a woman who looks as if she would blow away in a strong wind but with a determination and will forged of iron."

"Your point?"

Spencer nodded at Lucy. "How would you describe Miss Merryweather?"

"Well, her hair is certainly not burnished gold." He studied Lucy for a moment, not that he needed to. He could describe her with his eyes closed. "It's much more of a, oh, a bright gold, I would say, newly minted, not as red as a burnished gold. And her features are not fragile but rather fine and delicate. Yes, she's short in stature but deliciously curved in all the nicest places and she certainly doesn't look as if she would blow away. As for the rest of it . . ." Good God, Spencer was right. There, on the dance floor, with a few minor alterations, was Miss Mercy Heartley. Still, no one unacquainted with her would ever connect the very real Lucy Merryweather with the fictional Miss Heartley. "You only recognize her because you know Miss Heartley was based on a real woman. No one else will."

"Are you trying to convince me or yourself?"

"Both," Cam muttered, and sipped his champagne.

"As for the story itself, your heroine is on a quest to gain her inheritance." Spence's gaze fixed on Lucy. "Is Miss Merryweather on a quest as well?"

Cam blew a long breath. "You could say that."

Spencer nodded. "And did Miss Merryweather ride a camel?"

"It was an elephant."

"And dress as a man at a gentlemen-only sporting event?"

"It was Prichard's." He glanced at his brother. "The night we were all there."

"The ever sacred, never to be defiled Prichard's?" Spencer stared in disbelief.

Cam winced. "I'm afraid so."

Spence laughed. "She certainly does have spirit."

"At the very least." Cam smiled.

"Let me ask you something else. The rest of the characters in *Daring Exploits*, are they based on reality as well? Or are they fictional?"

"Fictional," Cam said firmly. "No more than a product of my imagination."

"Interesting." He paused. "Then let me ask you this. Strictly as an ardent devotee of the story, mind you."

"Yes?"

"The gentleman who has been following your heroine, who was originally employed by the man who wants her to fail so she will be forced to marry him, who started out intending to thwart her efforts but is now helping her . . ."

"Yes?"

"He's fallen in love with her, hasn't he?"

"Of course he has." Cam scoffed. "Readers

like nothing better than a good love story."

"And what happens when he tells her he was working against her in the beginning?"

Cam paused for a long moment. "I don't know."

"That's the crux of it all, isn't it?" Spencer nodded. "You might want to work out that little plot detail before you go much farther."

"He runs the risk of losing her if he tells her."

"My dear younger brother." Spencer cast him a sympathetic look. "He will absolutely lose her if he doesn't."

"Why, Mr. Fairchild." Lucy widened her eyes in mock indignation. "Perhaps you are unaware that I had promised this dance to someone else?"

"I was completely aware of that." He grinned and whirled her around the dance floor to the glorious strains of a Strauss waltz. "But as he was not as quick as he should have been, he missed his chance."

"It seemed to me you gave him little opportunity." Indeed, Cameron had cut in front of her next partner in an impressive display of determination and efficiency.

"Exactly my plan."

"You didn't mention you would be here tonight."

"How could I pass up the chance to dance with you?"

"Well, I am an excellent dancer." She grinned.

"Due in no small part to any number of lessons my mother insisted I and my brothers take. You dance quite well yourself, Mr. Fairchild."

"My mother too insisted her children know the proper way to dance."

She studied him closely. "So your only purpose here is to dance with me?"

"Exactly."

"And is it living up to your expectations?"

He executed a perfect turn and she followed him flawlessly, almost as if they had danced together always. As if they were always meant to dance together. It was as delightful a thought as it was confusing. But then what about Cameron Fairchild wasn't?

"It is more than meeting my expectations." He grinned down at her. "My thanks to your mother."

"She would be thrilled to know that at least in this I am meeting her expectations," she said wryly.

"Come now, surely you haven't been a disappointment to her?" He shook his head. "I can't imagine that."

"In little more than a month, I will be twenty-four years of age. And, as I am not yet married, I am indeed a great disappointment." She thought for a moment. If she truly expected honesty from him, perhaps she needed to be completely honest herself. "From very nearly the day I was born I was expected to marry your employer."

His eyes widened in surprise. "Jackson Channing?"

She nodded. "My grandfather and his great-grandfather founded Graham, Merryweather, and Lockwood Banking and Trust. His grandfather is president and chairman of the board, my father is a director of the board. I believe both families had dreams of a banking dynasty."

Curiosity shone in his eyes. "What happened?"

"We grew up, I think." She shrugged as best she could in his arms. "Both Jackson and I kept coming up with very sound reasons to put off our engagement. I finally realized we were doing so because, in spite of our families' wishes, neither of us truly wanted to marry the other. Make no mistake," she added quickly, "Jackson will always be my dearest friend even if he cannot seem to get over the idea that he has some responsibility for me."

"That explains quite a lot," Cameron said under his breath.

"It certainly explains his hiring of you and his asking his cousin, Lady Dunwell, to keep an eye on me as well." She sighed. "As annoying as it is, I suppose it's understandable given he probably is feeling somewhat guilty about me. You see, when he discovered the father he thought was dead was very much alive and came here to England to meet his family, he fell in love with the woman he was fated to be with."

"So much for the dynasty." He chuckled.

"You may call it fate or whatever you wish, but things turn out the way they're supposed to in the end, Cameron," she said firmly. "I truly believe that."

"Tell me, Lucy." Caution sounded in his voice. "You were not disappointed that he had found someone else?"

"Goodness, no." She laughed. "I was relieved. You see, I've always done exactly what I was supposed to do."

"Have you?" He cast her a disbelieving look.

"I most certainly have. I've never been involved in scandal or trouble of any kind for that matter. I have always been the perfect daughter. And I'm afraid I probably would have married Jackson and been a perfect, dutiful wife." She smiled into his dark eyes. "But I am very grateful that is not to be my fate."

His brow rose. "Don't you want to marry?"

"Every woman wants to marry, but I'm in no particular hurry. I am having entirely too much fun at the moment."

He laughed. "I am well aware of that."

"I'm not especially looking for a husband." She studied him for a moment. "And, as turnabout is fair play, might I ask you the same question? Do you wish to marry?"

"I'm not opposed to marriage but I haven't given it much thought." He chuckled. "Even if I was considering it, I would never let my grand-mother know. She is determined to find suitable matches for all of her grandchildren, although she's finding it a daunting task."

"A stubborn lot, are you?"

"That does seem to run in the family." He grinned. "But Grandmother doesn't just want us to marry; she wants us to find love."

"How very modern of her."

"Not really. She married for love as did my parents. That too runs in the family."

"So what you're looking for is love?"

"I wouldn't put it quite that way, but as I don't intend to marry for any other reason, I suppose you're right." He smiled. "But I'm not actually *looking* for anything. It seems to me the most interesting things in life happen when you're not really looking for them."

She nodded. "When they strike you unawares."

"Exactly. One minute, your life is perfectly acceptable. You're doing what you want to be doing, pursuing your own goals, chasing your own dreams. And the next . . ." His gaze met hers and the world around them slowed, faded.

She held her breath. "The next?"

"And the next minute"—his gaze searched hers—"everything has changed."

She swallowed hard. "Everything?"

His hand tightened around hers. "And nothing will ever be the same again."

"No, it won't, will it?"

For a long moment her gaze locked with his. The music continued around them. Their steps didn't falter—they moved as one. But in the endless depths of his eyes she saw the reflection of her own cautious excitement and growing awareness.

And with awareness came resolve. It was time to stop waiting for him to be honest with her and ask him outright what he was hiding. Given the things he had said to her, the way he made her feel, the way he obviously felt, the time for secrets was past. She drew a deep breath. "Cameron—"

"Blast it all," he muttered, and she realized the music had ended. He quickly escorted her off the floor. "My apologies, Lucy. This has been a delightful and most informative dance but I'm afraid I must take my leave."

"Now?" She stared in disbelief.

"Unfortunately." He took her hand and raised it to his lips. "I have another matter to attend to."

"You do not. You—" She gasped and glared at him. "You're escaping, Mr. Fairchild. I can see it in your eyes."

"Not at all, Miss Merryweather." His tone was clipped, brisk. "But I must be off."

"Yes, well, the work of a private investigator never ends, does it?" she said sharply, yanking her hand from his.

"About that . . ." His gaze slid past her and he

shook his head. "Tomorrow, Lucy, we shall speak more tomorrow." He turned and fairly sprinted away as if someone, or something, was hard on his heels. The truth, no doubt.

"Nothing will ever be the same again," she said under her breath. "Ha!"

"Miss Merryweather, may I have the honor of this dance?" a voice said behind her.

She drew a calming breath, adopted her most pleasant smile, and turned. At once her mood brightened. "Freddy! How delightful to see you."

"I was afraid you would not remember me," Freddy said with a wry smile.

"I would never forget you. Especially as you and your parents are my only relatives here in England."

"The only ones you know, at any rate. There are others but . . ." He shuddered. "We do try not to mention them."

"How very remarkable." She leaned closer in a confidential manner. "We have those on my side of the Atlantic as well."

"Do you think they're the same ones?" He frowned as if seriously considering the idea. "They simply spend their lives traveling the seas from one continent to the other, embarrassing unsuspecting relations?"

"I wouldn't be at all surprised."

He laughed and offered his arm. "Shall we?"

"I'd be delighted." She took his arm and he

led her back onto the dance floor. "But I am quite annoyed with you, you know."

"Me?" His eyes widened. "What have I done?" The first notes of another waltz sounded in the air.

"Nothing, Freddy." She heaved a heartfelt sigh, placed one hand in his, the other on his shoulder. "Nothing at all. Except that you did say you would call on us and show us the sights of London and you failed to do so."

"On the contrary, Lucy." Indignation rang in his voice. "I called on you several times but you were always out. With the exception of one day when I was told you were indisposed."

"Oh, yes, well." She wrinkled her nose. "My apologies then."

"No, I'm the one who should apologize." He shook his head. "I failed to leave a note or my card. But only because I did want to see you in person and it's terribly easy to ignore a card."

"Then we'll say that we are both at fault and leave it at that."

"Agreed." He smiled. "And are you enjoying our great city?"

"London is remarkable." She returned his smile. "I may well be having the best time of my life."

"You've already seen all the sights then?"

"Some." Most from the point of view of a bird. She pushed away the thought. "I doubt we could ever see them all."

"And have you met anyone interesting?"

"Well, I am getting to know Lady Dunwell better. She is extremely interesting."

"True enough." He chuckled. "You certainly are in demand here tonight. I could barely fight my way through the crowd. I saw you dancing with Effington a minute ago. I could have sworn he saw me but I must have been mistaken."

"Who?"

"Effington. The chap you danced with right before me. I haven't seen him recently. I wonder what he's up to these days."

It was all Lucy could do to keep from stumbling through the steps of the dance. "What did you say his name was?"

"Effington. Cameron Effington. Actually Lord Cameron Effington. He's the son of the Duke of Roxborough."

She stared.

Freddy raised a brow. "Don't tell me you weren't properly introduced."

"A dreadful breach of etiquette, I know." She plastered a pleasant smile on her lips. The son of a duke? *A duke?* She wasn't entirely sure, but she suspected a duke was rather significant. Why on earth would the son of a duke be working as a private investigator?

"But one easily forgiven," he said gallantly.

"Thank you, Freddy." The last thing she wanted to do at the moment was make idle chatter with Freddy or anyone. She needed to consider this new bit of information. Still, one did hate to be rude. Her mother had once told her that men loved to talk and if a lady kept a smile on her face and nodded now and then, a gentleman scarcely ever noticed if she was indeed paying attention. It was advice that had come in handy on any number of occasions.

She favored him with a pleasant smile. "Tell me, Freddy, how are your parents?"

"Quite well, all things considered. Oh, Father has . . ."

Unless Cameron's father, *the duke,* had disinherited him. No, she discarded that idea. While he'd been extremely vague about his family, she'd had no sense of a rift. She searched her mind trying to think of everything Cameron had mentioned, but aside from a few bare facts—he had three older brothers and an older widowed sister—there was not much to recall.

". . . and naturally Mother has been talking about putting together a small soiree to introduce you to . . ."

Unlike in America where most wealthy men expected their sons to follow in their footsteps in choice of a profession, it was her observation that sons of wealthy noble families in England rarely had any actual profession at all. That Cameron did was decidedly odd.

". . . rather eager, really, to know more, and I must say, I think it's an idea . . ."

Odder still that he wasn't using his real name. It did seem like a great deal of trouble given that Cameron didn't seem to have a particular passion for investigation, but then she had already surmised that he hadn't been at it for very long.

"We dance together beautifully, Lucy. I think we make an excellent pair."

"We do dance well together," she said absently.

Perhaps he didn't want his family or anyone to know until he had made a success of himself. He had spoken of failure and being a disappointment to those he cared about. It was entirely possible that he wished to succeed on his own without having to rely on his family's name and influence. How very . . . independent of him. And admirable.

"I'm not one to beat around the bush, Lucy. When I have something to say I come right out and say it."

She nodded. To want to stand on one's own two feet and make something out of one's life was commendable. Why, even her father would find that impressive.

"My parents think, and I have to say I agree with them, that it would be an excellent idea if you and I were to marry."

"What?" Her attention jerked back to her partner and she nearly stumbled.

"Oh, not right away of course," Freddy added quickly. "We would probably want to get to know each other a little first."

She stared. "That would be advisable."

"And really, isn't that what marriage is for? To get to know each other."

"I suppose but—"

"You do like me, don't you?"

"Well, yes but—"

"And we do seem to get on well together."

"Thus far, but we've had no more than one conversation and a single dance." She shook her head. "Hardly enough to begin a serious discussion of marriage."

"I know marriages that are based on far less," he said staunchly.

"I do not intend for mine to be one of them." She adopted a firm tone. "Good Lord, Freddy, don't you want more than that?"

"But we do have more. Much, much more." His tone was earnest. Too earnest. "Why, the first time I saw you, I knew you were the only woman in the world for me."

"The first time you saw me, you looked at Miss West as if she were the only woman in the world for you."

"A momentary lapse, nothing more than that. You've conquered my heart, Lucy. I cannot eat, I cannot sleep. You're everything I ever wanted and more. You are in my thoughts day and night. Please end my suffering and say you'll be my wife."

She stared at him for a moment, then choked back a laugh. "I don't believe any of this."

"None of it?" Disbelief crossed his face.

"I'm afraid not."

"Not even the part about you being everything I ever wanted and more?" A hopeful note sounded in his voice.

"As flattering as that was." She shook her head. "No."

"Or the part about you being in my thoughts day and night?"

"Again, no."

"Oh dear." He winced. "I've mucked it up then, haven't I?"

"I can't say since I have no idea what you're thinking or what brought all this about." She studied him curiously. "Why on earth would you ask me to marry you?"

He grimaced. "It wasn't actually my idea."

"Whose idea was it?" she said slowly.

"My parents, but I thought it was an excellent idea," he added.

She chose her words carefully. "Why would your parents, and you, think it was an excellent idea?"

"May I be perfectly honest?"

"Now *that* would be an excellent idea at this point."

"Well, this is awkward but . . ." He paused to choose his words. "The family finances are not what they once were. The only real way to shore them up is for me to marry well. You're an heiress and . . ."

She stared. "You want to marry me for my money?"

"I'm so glad you understand. I was afraid you wouldn't." He blew a relieved breath. "Although it is something of a family tradition, you know. Rutledges have almost always married for money." He paused. "But affection has inevitably followed. My parents are very happy with each other."

"I would imagine one would feel most affectionate toward someone whose money has rescued one's family," she said dryly.

"See here, Lucy." He huffed. "I do like you. And I think we would have a very nice life together. We have a manor house and a castle in the country," he added in a tempting manner.

She raised a brow. "And is this castle comparable to your house here in London?"

"Admittedly it's a bit run-down." He grinned. "But it's quite scenic for a ruin. Little more than a pile of stones, really. And I did think a castle would be appealing to an American."

"Even Americans want their castles to be more than a scenic pile of stones."

"Do they?"

"I'm afraid so."

"What a pity," he murmured. "I was counting on the castle."

"Freddy," she said in as kind a tone as possible. "Aside from everything else, regardless of how distantly we're related, I can't possibly think of you in any way other than how I think of my brothers. And when I marry, I want to feel more than the kind of affection one feels for a brother."

"I see." He paused. "Any chance you'll change your mind?"

"I wouldn't wager on it." She shook her head. "I am flattered, really I am, but I'm sure there's another heiress out there for you."

"England is remarkably short of heiresses." He heaved a resigned sigh. "And believe me, I've looked. In this country, property and money are usually passed to male offspring. Women are simply expected to marry well."

"Then obviously you're going to have to expand your horizons." She thought for a moment. "You, and your parents of course, should come visit America after I return home. I know a fair number of eligible young ladies who would suit your needs quite nicely."

He brightened. "So you really think so?"

"I really do." She paused. "How concerned are you with appearance?"

"I'm not overly concerned with it," he said slowly, "but there are the children to consider."

"Nonsense, a pleasant disposition is much more important than looks."

Freddy smiled weakly.

"Now that I think about it, right off the top of my head I can name several suitable young ladies, and their mothers, who would be more than willing to trade an inheritance for a castle, no matter how ruinous, and a title. They would get a title, wouldn't they?"

"Eventually—after Father is gone, that is—I'll be Viscount Northrup. My wife would then be Viscountess Northrup, also referred to as Lady Northrup."

"Lady Northrup has a lovely ring to it."

"Are you sure you don't—"

"I am positive, Freddy," she said firmly. "Besides, I think of you as I do my brothers, and the least a sister can do is help you find the wife you're looking for."

"All right then." He cast her a reluctant smile. "I've never had a sister." He grimaced. "Never particularly wanted one."

"Then this will be a new experience for you." She beamed. "Now, Freddy, tell me everything you know about Lord Cameron Effington."

Regrets Set to Rights

Dance with a prince.
Solve a mystery.

303

Chapter Thirteen

"This has now gone entirely too far." Beryl marched into the Channing House dining room brandishing a fistful of newspaper. Albert immediately bounded from his spot at Lucy's feet to wiggle and leap around Beryl's skirts in a frenzy of canine welcome. Beryl scooped him up without so much as a pause in her step or her discourse. "Something must be done, Lucy. And I cannot simply pretend I am unaware of the situation. While that is tempting, apparently I feel some sort of moral obligation—oh." She spotted Clara and pulled up short. "I beg your pardon. Clement told me Miss Merryweather was in here and I assumed she was alone."

"That's quite all right." Caution edged Clara's voice and she rose to her feet. She glanced at Lucy. "There are things I could be doing."

"Do finish your breakfast. It doesn't really matter to me if you stay or go. You're Miss West, aren't you?"

Clara nodded.

Beryl dropped Albert onto a chair beside Lucy's, where he sat quite properly, as if sitting in a chair at the dining table was his due. Beryl nodded her approval. "Oh good, there's food left. I'm never especially hungry in the morning but lately I've been famished." She dropped the papers onto the table, then moved to the sideboard and filled a plate, glancing back at Lucy. "Does she know?"

"Does she know what?" Lucy said cautiously.

"About those." Beryl took the chair next to Albert and nodded at the papers on the table.

Lucy stared. "I doubt it as I have no idea what you're talking about."

"I'm talking about those blasted stories." Beryl took a bite of coddled egg, then sighed as if she'd never tasted anything so good.

"Stories?" Clara said slowly.

"The ones in the *Messenger*."

"There are stories in the *Messenger*?" Clara's voice rose.

"Oh yes, those." Lucy shrugged. "I really haven't had the chance to read them."

"You haven't read the ones I gave you last week?" Beryl set her fork down and stared with disbelief. "Why ever not?"

"Quite honestly, Beryl, they slipped my mind. I've been, well, busy."

"I cannot imagine being that busy." Beryl signaled for a footman to bring her a cup of tea. "I would strongly suggest you read these right now. I no longer have even the slightest doubt that they are based on your activities."

"I can't imagine how they could be." Lucy

moved her plate to one side and picked up the clippings.

"I can," Clara said under her breath.

Lucy shuffled through the papers, reading a line here and a line there. Not much but enough to realize the truth of Beryl's charge. A heavy weight settled in the pit of her stomach. "Good God, you may be right." She glanced at the older woman. "How could this have happened?"

"We'll probably never know." Beryl accepted the cup, then took a sip. "But people do overhear things. Especially servants, and they are notorious for not being able to keep a secret. Why, some of my very best information has come from what my servants learned through their chats with servants of other households."

Lucy paged through the clippings. "These stories aren't entirely accurate."

"I daresay they don't need to be. But close enough, I would think. This writer has taken your adventures and twisted them into slightly different stories." Beryl plucked the clippings from Lucy's hand and shuffled through them. "In this one"—she handed a clipping to Lucy— "he has taken your elephant and turned it into a camel, your circus into a harem. He's even had you dying your skin. Right there." She tapped her finger on the page. "He calls you a dark-haired beauty with the look of the stars in her blue eyes, bright against her dusky skin."

"The man certainly knows how to turn a phrase," Lucy murmured. "It's quite flattering, really."

"And here, he has changed your gentlemen's club to a sporting event." Beryl thrust the rest of them at Lucy. "Your chef and your artist have been altered to twin brothers, one who instructs the heroine in fencing and the other who sculpts a nude likeness. And both brothers have lascivious intentions toward her."

"They are rather wicked, aren't they?" Lucy said, reading a few lines describing the lustful intentions of the brothers. She would certainly have to read more of this later.

"They are indeed. Neither of them have the least bit of honor and both of them have only one thing in mind." Beryl paused. "I must admit I do like that part. It adds a nice touch of, oh, lurid excitement, I would say. Puts the heroine in a bit of jeopardy."

"Lady Dunwell!" Clara gasped. "You're talking about Miss Merryweather!"

"No, Miss West, I'm not," Beryl said firmly. "It's not actually real, you know. And I'm certainly not encouraging Lucy to follow in the footsteps of a fictional character. However . . ." She turned her attention back to Lucy. "The author of these, a Mr. Aldrich, has also taken those regrets you've yet to rectify and written about them as well."

Lucy stared at the papers in her hand. Those items she had not yet gotten to, especially the ones about lovers and liaisons, flew threw her head. She was almost afraid to ask. "Which ones?"

"Here." Beryl again took the clippings, found the one she wanted, and handed it back to Lucy. "This one has our heroine frolicking in a fountain in a lighthearted moment as well as misplacing her clothes and swimming naked in the moonlight. In the Thames!" Beryl snorted. "Of all places."

Clara groaned. "Good Lord."

"I know. It's utter nonsense, of course." Beryl shook her head. "For one thing, no one misplaces their clothing in such a situation. Why, one makes very certain one knows exactly where one's clothing has been left to forestall situations exactly like this."

Lucy and Clara traded glances.

"And the Thames?" Beryl grimaced. "Who in their right mind would swim in the Thames? All sorts of disgusting, vile things are seen floating in the Thames. And you absolutely never want to be in that river naked." She shuddered.

"Still, as you said"—Clara smiled weakly—"it is fiction."

"Thank God." Beryl drew a deep breath. "Nonetheless, I think it's time to do something, take some precautions as it were."

"Past time," Clara muttered.

"What do you mean by precautions?" Lucy drew her brows together.

"While you haven't been exactly secretive about your activities, I do assume you want to preserve your anonymity."

Lucy nodded. "That would be preferable."

Beryl met Lucy's gaze directly. "I think you need to leave London."

"Leave London?" Lucy shook her head. "Absolutely not. I'm not ready to go home. I've managed no more than half of the items on my great-aunt's list." She set her jaw firmly. "I started out to accomplish something and barring difficulties due to the time of year and various moral questions, I intend to finish what I started. Or as much as I can. And I cannot do it in New York. Why, I know entirely too many people and—"

"I'm not suggesting you leave England, only London, and you have nicely made my point," Beryl said. "The more people you meet in London, the more who might possibly connect you with the imaginary Miss Heartley."

"But I haven't met many people."

"Nor are you hiding under a rock either. And might I point out you met a great many people just last night. It's only a matter of time before people put two and two together and get you." Beryl plucked a piece of toast from the rack on the table and slathered it with clotted cream. "These stories have become extremely popular and there is already a great deal of speculation as to whether or not they are indeed fiction. People"—she aimed her butter knife at Lucy—"are talking."

"Even so—"

"Let's look at this rationally." Beryl leaned forward. "Even eliminating Miss Heartley's fictional exploits or your real adventures, there are similarities between the two of you that you cannot deny. How many runaway American heiresses do you think there are in London anyway?"

"I have not run away." Lucy's jaw tightened.

"Not in the strict definition of the word, but a young woman in London without her family might well appear to have run away."

"I suppose but—"

"And appearances, my dear, are everything. Aside from that, there is a distinct physical resemblance between the two of you."

"Which certainly could be explained by simple coincidence," Lucy said.

"Of course it could." Beryl waved off the comment. "But it won't be. I'm talking about speculation and gossip here, neither of which relies more than vaguely on the facts of a matter." She took a bite of her toast. "I'm not trying to tell you to give up this quest of yours. I'm not even saying you need to be more discreet. You've been most circumspect thus far. I'm simply suggesting that, at this point, you return to Millworth for a while. Out of sight, out of mind and all that."

Lucy thought for a moment. She had been entirely truthful when she'd told Cameron she had no intention of allowing scandal to ruin the rest of her life. If a bit more discretion was needed now, given these newspaper stories, then there really was no choice.

"There are several things on your list that could be accomplished quite efficiently at Millworth," Beryl pointed out.

"It's not a bad idea, Lucy," Clara said quietly.

"No, it's not." Lucy drew a deep breath. "You're right, Beryl. There's no reason why I can't continue my efforts at Millworth. But it does feel as though I am now indeed running away."

"Nonsense." Beryl scoffed. "You're simply being sensible. Believe me, it is far easier to avoid scandal in the first place than have to repair one's reputation."

"Of course. Still . . ." Lucy narrowed her eyes. "I would like to know who this"—she glanced at the clippings—"Mr. Aldrich is and how he came by his information."

"I daresay that's probably impossible to discover." Beryl shrugged in an offhand manner. "And you know how these things happen. We've already mentioned the servants, plus there were the people at your circus, the chef, your artist, all of whom could have overheard something.

And . . . well . . ." She grimaced. "You never know when one might have said something, in complete innocence and without thinking, in the course of casual conversation at some sort of social gathering. Nothing specific, mind you, but *something* might have been said to lead *someone* else to assume the stories aren't entirely fictional."

Lucy stared. "You said something to someone?"

"Possibly, but certainly not deliberately," Beryl added quickly. "You know how it is. Someone has an interesting tidbit of information and, well, if you have something much better it's nearly impossible to keep it to yourself. But I do make it a point never to reveal names."

"That's something anyway," Clara said under her breath.

"Regardless," Beryl continued. "The people I might perchance have mentioned something to would never give that information to a writer. They would simply spread it amongst themselves."

"What a relief," Lucy said wryly.

Beryl pinned her with a firm look. "You should have been more definitive, Lucy. If you had said your activities were secret I never would have said anything to anyone. I'm very good at keeping secrets. And really the more I think about it, the more I am reasonably confident I didn't say anything. Except of course to Lionel, but then I tell him nearly everything these days. There was a time when I didn't and now I'm trying very hard not to keep secrets from him. But Lionel is the soul of discretion. He always has been, really. Quite prudent, you know, for a man in politics."

"Oh, I don't think this is your fault." Lucy waved at the clippings. "There are any number of other people who could have overheard some of this and passed it on to this writer. Although the detail is unsettling." She picked up a clipping and studied it. "I wonder if Mr. Fairchild can find out who this Mr. Aldrich is and how he came about his information."

Beryl's brow rose. "Who is Mr. Fairchild?"

"Oh, well, he's not really Mr. Fairchild. He's Mr. Effington. Or rather, I suppose, it's Lord Effington. No, Lord Cameron Effington."

"He's what?" Clara stared.

"I was going to tell you right before Beryl arrived."

Beryl's confused gaze slid from one woman to the next. "What are you talking about?"

"Lord Cameron Effington is working as a private investigator under the name of Fairchild. Jackson hired him to well, I don't know—guard, protect, watch over me. Something absurd like that. And then my purse was stolen and he recovered it and, as I knew he'd been following us, it seemed best to have him accompany us rather than lurk in the shadows."

Beryl's brow furrowed. "Jackson didn't hire a private investigator. I did."

Lucy sucked in a hard breath. "You?"

"One wouldn't think that was the most important point in that particular revelation," Clara said under her breath.

"Or at least I tried to. But the investigator I usually employ, Phineas Chapman, said he didn't do that sort of thing. Although he did say he'd make a few inquiries to see if there was someone who might be willing to take this on. I do wish he'd told me he had found someone." Beryl sighed. "I suppose now I will be billed at some point."

"You hired him?" Lucy stared.

"So it would appear." Beryl stabbed a piece of bacon.

"Why?" Lucy frowned. "I could understand why Jackson might hire a . . . a watchdog, but why would you? You of all people should understand that just because you're female doesn't mean you can't take care of yourself."

"Of course I understand that." Beryl huffed. "But I didn't know you at all at that point. And Jackson did not seem overly confident that you would do well on your own."

Lucy snorted.

"He did ask me to keep an eye on you, and well, frankly, even though I agreed, it really wasn't the sort of thing I do. You understand. So I thought I would hire someone to do it. Although I didn't realize I actually had." Beryl took a bite and chewed thoughtfully. "Jackson also asked me to help find a companion for you and Chapman did recommend"—her gaze flicked to Clara and brightened in recognition—"Miss West, of course."

Clara looked decidedly uneasy. Good Lord, it was worse than Lucy had expected.

"Clara," she said brightly. "I believe it's your turn for confession."

"I'm afraid so." Clara clasped her hands together in front of her on the table and drew a deep breath. "Mr. Chapman told me you were seeking a companion. As the duration of the position was not expected to be more than a few months, I thought it would be, oh, interesting. And indeed it has proved to be far more interesting than I imagined."

Lucy nodded.

"It was, as well, the perfect way to allow Mr. Chapman and myself a respite from each other." Clara's eyes narrowed. "We are frequently at odds with one another. He can be a most exhausting man."

"I suspected something about you was . . . unusual," Lucy said. "I realized nearly from the beginning there was more to you than first appeared. Not many people know how to dye skin or can acquire male clothing at a moment's notice."

"One learns all sorts of skills when one works with Mr. Chapman." Clara paused, then met Lucy's gaze. "You should know, I never reported to anyone about your activities. While I've been in your employ, you have been my only employer."

"I never doubted it. At some point, Clara, you have to depend on your own instincts, your own intuition, your heart as it were," Lucy said firmly. "I knew the moment I met you I could trust you. I have to trust someone and, well, I choose to trust you."

"Thank you," Clara said simply.

"You work with Phineas Chapman?" Beryl asked curiously.

"In a manner of speaking." Clara paused. "Actually I have invested in his business, so I am really more of a partner, although he would deny it." She smiled in a decidedly smug manner. "But Mr. Chapman has no head for figures."

"Why?" Beryl stared. "I've known the man and his family for years. He's brilliant, and he does have the most amazing green eyes. Indeed he's quite dashing but he's also decidedly, oh, different."

"As am I, Lady Dunwell," Clara said. "The answer to your question is really quite simple. At the time, I thought it sounded like an adventure."

"And was it?" Doubt sounded in Beryl's voice.

Clara smiled. "It still is."

Beryl considered her curiously, then smiled in approval. "Good for you, Miss West."

"Very well," Lucy said abruptly. "We'll go to Millworth."

"Excellent." Beryl nodded. "We should leave this afternoon. And I've decided to go with you."

"That's not necessary."

"It is if I'm going to help you with a few more things on your list. Besides, I could use a respite in the country myself. I've been feeling a bit out of sorts lately."

"Very well then. I'll instruct my maid to pack and we will plan on leaving this afternoon. In the meantime . . ." Lucy pushed her chair back and stood. "I believe I'll pay a call on the publisher of *Cadwallender's Daily Messenger.*"

"I'm not sure that's wise," Beryl said thoughtfully, taking another piece of toast. "Wouldn't it be better for him to simply suspect you exist rather than to know for certain?"

"Possibly, but if there is already speculation about a real American heiress then that ship has sailed, hasn't it?"

"Still—"

"I've spent my entire life allowing events to unfold as it were. I'm not going to sit around and wait to see what happens next. This is my future at stake, after all." Lucy thought for a moment. "I simply want to make sure he understands that should my name become connected with his paper's stories, I will be very, very angry."

"Oh, and he wouldn't want to annoy you." Beryl scoffed.

"My dear Beryl, perhaps you've forgotten that I have a great deal of money. My mother taught me that one should only use money as a last resort but one should not hesitate to use it when necessary. My mother taught me many things that I paid no real attention to." She smiled. "This is not one of them."

Beryl stared at her for a moment, then grinned. "My, you can take care of yourself. Oh, this will be fun."

"You'll come with me then?" It certainly wouldn't hurt to be in the company of Lady Dunwell, wife of the prominent Lord Dunwell.

"As much as I would enjoy it . . ." Beryl shook her head. "I can't. I do have to arrange for our travel and I need to discuss with Clement whether he and some of the staff here should accompany us or if we can make do with the staff in the country and . . . well, the truth of the matter is . . ." She wrinkled her nose. "Lionel and I have made certain promises to each other in recent years about avoiding so much as the appearance of impropriety. He does hope to be prime minister and, if that is what he wants, I want that for him. For me to accompany you to a newspaper office—"

"Say no more." Lucy held up a hand to stop her.

"I understand completely. Clara will come with me and, as I expect Mr. Fairchild—"

"Cameron Effington, you said?" Confusion colored Beryl's face.

Lucy nodded. "He can accompany us as well."

"Let me see if I understand this." Beryl's brows drew together. "Lord Cameron Effington, the youngest son of the Duke of Roxborough, has been acting as a bodyguard, watchdog, guardian, whatever you wish to call it—"

"He's a private investigator," Lucy offered.

Beryl nodded. "And he's using the name Fairchild?"

"Exactly."

Beryl's brow furrowed. "That name sounds vaguely familiar."

Clara stared. "When did you find this out?"

"At last night's ball. Freddy Rutledge told me." Lucy drummed her fingers on the table. "It certainly does answer a lot of questions."

"And brings up even more, I suspect. Why would the son of a duke be masquerading as a private investigator?" Beryl said thoughtfully.

"Oh, I don't think he's masquerading at all. I think he's trying to make his own mark on the world. He's not very good, entirely too trusting, really, but one gets the impression that he's new at it. I have no doubt he will be quite successful." Lucy beamed. "Isn't it wonderfully independent and ambitious of him?"

"Yes, I suppose. Although a more conceivable possibility might be that he's run through his trust funds—all the Effington offspring have trusts," Beryl said in an aside to Clara.

Clara nodded.

"He's squandered all his money and now he actually has to work for a living." Beryl shook her head in a pitying manner. "He wouldn't be the first, although to give the man his due, most young men in that situation simply live off their families or live on credit against expectations until they find some suitable match whose dowry will restore their fortunes."

"How terribly rude of them," Lucy murmured.

"Perhaps, but it's not at all uncommon."

Cameron would never do such a thing. He simply wasn't that type of man. Still, the fact that he hadn't actually been hired was disconcerting.

"I suspect he knows Chapman," Beryl continued. "In fact I would be surprised if he didn't. Which explains why he took the job I had offered Chapman." Beryl paused. "I do wonder how much I'm paying him."

"Are you going to tell him you know who he is?" Clara asked.

"Oh, let's not." A few minutes ago, Lucy would have said she absolutely intended to tell Cameron she knew he had been using an assumed name. Now she wasn't so sure. Not now that Beryl had raised the idea of a man who had lost his fortune looking for a wealthy wife. What better way to get into the good graces of a young woman with money than to portray yourself as her protector? Her guardian? Her knight straight from a fairy tale? She pushed the thought aside but it was impossible to ignore.

Nor could she ignore the very real possibility that if Cameron was acquainted with Chapman, might Clara not know him as well? And if Clara knew him, did that mean she too was in on his deception? And if so, to what end?

Regardless, it had always been apparent that Clara neither liked nor trusted Cameron, for whatever that was worth. And Lucy had indeed trusted Clara from the beginning. If she was wrong . . . well, she refused to think about that. About the possibility that her intuition, her instincts, were flawed or had failed her altogether. She was as confident of that as she was of Clara's loyalties. Clara was a good, honorable woman and her friend. Clara would never betray her.

As for the idea that Cameron was engaged in an elaborate plot to marry Lucy for her money, why, it was utter nonsense. There were far easier ways to gain her affections than by arguing with her at every turn. She had no doubt that she'd spent enough time with him to know what kind of man he really was. And one did need to rely on one's instincts. If one couldn't trust oneself, who could one trust?

Admittedly, this revelation about his identity didn't entirely explain everything about Cameron Fair—Effington. In fact, it brought up more questions than it answered. Given that he'd said he would talk to her today, and in a manner that indicated said talk was of some importance, she'd rather not let him know what she knew, at least for now.

"No," Lucy said coolly. "I would much prefer to see how long it takes him to finally tell me the truth."

Chapter Fourteen

"We're going where?" Cam forced a casual tone and ignored the sense of impending doom that settled in the pit of his stomach.

"Fleet Street," Lucy said briskly. "The offices of Cadwallender and Sons, the firm that publishes a somewhat questionable newspaper called *Cadwallender's Daily Messenger.*"

She adjusted her hat in the mirror in the front foyer. Apparently, she and Miss West had been about to leave without him. Fortunately, he had arrived just in time. If Lucy was going to see Mr. Cadwallender, it meant only one thing. The surreptitious glares of disgust from Miss West reinforced his suspicion.

Lucy's gaze caught his in the mirror. "Have you heard of it?"

"Vaguely." He shrugged in an offhand manner, belying the panic threatening within him.

Miss West coughed or choked, one couldn't be sure, although the sound had a distinct edge of disdain.

"It seems they are publishing a series of stories written by a Mr. Aldrich—"

"Have you heard of *him?*" Miss West asked in an overly pleasant manner.

He shook his head. "I don't believe so."

"No doubt," Miss West said under her breath.

"Stories about a runaway American heiress." Lucy blew a long breath. "Stories that sound suspiciously like they are based on my activities."

"Really?" he said with feigned astonishment.

"Hard to believe, isn't it?" Sarcasm dripped from Miss West's voice. Lucy slanted her a sharp glance.

Good Lord, just how much did Lucy know? And how much did she suspect?

"So . . ." He chose his words with care. "You're going to talk to the publisher?"

"I am indeed." She tucked an errant strand of hair under her hat, then nodded in satisfaction.

"Do you think that's wise?"

Again her gaze met his in the mirror. "You're the second person today who has asked me that."

"Which would indicate to me that this particular course is not especially wise."

"Perhaps not." She turned toward him and cast him a brilliant smile. "But it's what I intend to do."

"Still, you might want to reconsider."

"Excuse me, miss." The butler stepped into the foyer. "I know you are eager to be off as soon as you return from your errand, and Eloise, the maid who is packing your things, had a question for you. It will only take a moment."

"Of course." Lucy nodded and followed Clement out of the foyer.

The moment she was out of sight, Miss West moved toward him with the barely concealed animosity of an avenging angel, her voice low and venomous. "You need to tell her everything."

"I intend to," he snapped. "How did she find out about the stories?"

"How did you think she wouldn't?" She stared as if she'd never seen an idiot before. "They are in a newspaper, for God's sake."

"You didn't see them!"

"No, but Lady Dunwell did." She clenched her teeth. "And there's gossip, my lord, about whether or not the heiress in your stories is truly fictional or if she's real."

"They are doing well if people are talking about them," he said more to himself than to her.

Miss West's eyes widened in outrage.

"I didn't mean that the way it sounded," he said quickly. "I will tell her everything at the first opportunity."

"Well, you'd better hope that's soon." She pinned him with a hard look. "The longer you wait, the more likely it is she will find out everything on her own. *Everything*. And that will serve neither of you well."

"I know that but . . ." He ran his hand through his hair. "The moment has to be just right."

"That moment might well be too late." She shook her head in a pitying manner. "I gave you

325

my word that I would not tell her about you, but the time is fast approaching when I may have no choice but to—"

"Are we ready?" Lucy swept back into the foyer. "I really do want to get this over and done with. And we don't have any time to waste if we're going to take the afternoon train."

"Why are we taking the afternoon train?" he said slowly.

"*We* are not. Miss West and I have been invited by Lady Dunwell to join her at Millworth Manor. And I see no reason for you to accompany us."

"No, I suppose not." He studied her closely. She was obviously annoyed at him for some reason. If she knew that he was the author of the stories, surely Miss West would have said something. And Lucy would be far more than merely annoyed. No, there must be something else wrong.

"Didn't you say last night that you had something you wished to discuss today?" A challenge shone in Lucy's eyes.

"I . . ." No, this wasn't the right time, especially not with Miss West glaring at him. He really did need to find a way to get rid of her. He shook his head. "It can wait."

Lucy's eyes narrowed. "Yes, that's what I thought. Very well then." With that she nodded to the footman at the door and strode out of the house, Miss West at her heels. Cam trailed behind.

He had absolutely no idea how this outing would end, but he was fairly confident for him it would not end well.

Stepping into the offices of Cadwallender and Sons Publishers would have been somewhat intimidating if one wasn't filled with righteous indignation. Housed in a large building on Fleet Street, which was, according to Lucy's copy of *Collins' Illustrated Guide to London*, an area filled with newspaper and printing offices and literary associations, the offices of the assorted Cadwallenders themselves were on the first floor. The overall impression was of an enormous room divided into partitioned spaces by half walls, about four feet in height. Tall enough to give the illusion of privacy without going so far as to actually provide it. Each space contained a desk and chair and most were occupied with gentlemen. Some were busy on typewriting machines, others talked on telephones, but the majority seemed to be scrambling around as if whatever they were doing could not wait another moment. A row of decidedly worn and uncomfortable-looking chairs lined the walls on either side of the entry door and faced a long, wooden counter in what served as some sort of reception area. There was a sense of immediacy here, the feeling that everything was critical, heightened by the faint thrum of machinery and a cacophony of urgent voices. Under other circumstances, Lucy would have found it all fascinating.

In the center of this fortress of journalistic endeavor, some of the half walls supported glass windows to create enclosed, separate spaces. Lucy, Clara, and Cameron were shown to one of these, the private—although private did seem a relative term—domain of the publisher of *Cadwallender's Daily Messenger*, Mr. James Cadwallender, as opposed to the publisher of *Cadwallender's Weekly Ladies World*, a Mr. Matthew Cadwallender. Apparently there was also a Cadwallender Brothers Publishing, which published books. Beryl said she had heard there was something of a split among the Cadwallender publishing brothers. She had also mentioned that she thought the Cadwallenders had long been connected to the Duke of Roxborough's family, although she didn't know if that was personal or business. Beryl had then remembered that Cameron's mother was a Fairchild, which explained his choice of name.

In the hour or so since Beryl had left, Lucy had found herself growing more and more annoyed at Cameron. Not because he hadn't been honest about his name—she could easily see any number of legitimate reasons for that—but because she couldn't get the idea of him wanting her for her money out of her head. It was like some sort of incessant noise, the constant drip of a faucet, that refused to be ignored. The worse thing about it was that it was entirely possible. Perhaps by going to Millworth and putting some distance between them, she could at least sort out her feelings about him and who he was and what he might really want from her. It was past time to accept that she might well be in love with the man. At the very worst her heart would be broken; at the very best it would all be an amusing misunderstanding. Fortunately, she had other matters to deal with first.

Lucy sat in a chair facing the desk of Mr. James Cadwallender. Clara perched on a chair beside the door to the glass-enclosed office, and Cameron stood nearby.

"Mr. Cadwallender," Lucy began after the publisher had resumed his seat. "I'm sure you're wondering why I am here."

"That did cross my mind, Miss Merryweather," Mr. Cadwallender said politely. He was some ten years older than she, with dark brown hair and eyes an interesting amber color. And, at any other time, she would have quite appreciated his dashing appearance. Today, she had other things on her mind. "How may I be of assistance?"

"It has come to my attention that you are currently featuring in your newspaper a series of stories about a fictional heiress."

"We are." He nodded. "They are becoming quite popular."

"Yes, I have heard that as well. Unfortunately, I have also heard some rather distressing speculation."

His brow rose. "Have you?"

She nodded. "There are rumors that your heroine is not fictional but rather based on a real person."

He stared in feigned astonishment. "I had no idea."

"Shocking, isn't it? Worse yet, it does seem that, on occasion, the stories might be reflective of my own life."

He gasped. "I find that hard to believe."

"As do I." She paused. "I'm certain this is nothing more than mere coincidence. Goodness, Mr. Cadwallender, I have certainly not run away, nor am I having daring exploits. I only wish I was. I fear my life is really quite sedate."

"I doubt that, Miss Merryweather," he said with a smile.

"How very nice of you to say." She cast him a brilliant smile. "And even if I were having daring exploits or mild adventures for that matter, I will tell you, I would not mind the chronicling of them."

"You wouldn't?" he said slowly.

"Oh my, no. They are written in a most amusing manner. I find them extremely entertaining. Your Mr. Aldrich is quite skilled."

"I'll tell him you said so."

"However." She leaned forward slightly. "As I said, there is speculation, rumor, that sort of thing. You must understand, London is not overrun with American heiresses, therefore if your readers are wondering if indeed your stories are based in fact, well . . ." She shrugged in a helpless manner.

"I see your point."

"While I am confident the young woman in these stories is not meant to be me, and any resemblance is no more than an odd quirk of fate, there are a few, oh, slivers of truth here and there in the stories. Vague similarities to my own life that, while no more than coincidence, could cause me great personal concern."

His brows drew together. "Are you asking me to stop the publication of the *Daring Exploits*?"

"Why, Mr. Cadwallender." She widened her eyes in a show of indignation. "I am an American and we are firmly committed to the basic principle of a free press. I would never tell you not to publish anything."

"Then—"

"I simply request that you speak with your Mr. Aldrich and ask him to, I don't know, expand his imagination perhaps, make his heroine's exploits more far-fetched and improbable to make very certain your readers do indeed realize his stories are complete fabrications."

He scoffed. "I would never tell a writer of fiction what he should or shouldn't write."

"Come now, you and I both know that's not true." She paused. "Mr. Cadwallender, perhaps I am not being clear." She forced a cool smile. "You see, the biggest difference between the heroine of your stories and myself is that I already have my inheritance." She lowered her voice in a confidential manner. "And it's most impressive. Why, I could buy this building out from underneath you. Or purchase a competing newspaper and drive you out of business. It's my understanding that the current climate for newspapers like the *Messenger* is quite competitive and rather, oh, cutthroat. Is it not?"

His eyes narrowed and he nodded.

"I however have no desire to do that. At the moment. But should my name ever be connected with these stories, at the very least, I shall bring all the power and the wrath of the most unpleasant solicitors in both America and England down upon your head." Good Lord, she sounded like her mother. She shook her head in a mournful manner. "I will be dreadfully sorry, of course, but this is that important to me."

"I wouldn't think something like this would concern you at all," Mr. Cadwallender said slowly.

"One wouldn't think, but it has been pointed out to me that this is a potentially scandalous situation." She wasn't sure why this was so important to her. She did think she had left any concern about propriety behind her when she'd decided to stay in England. Apparently, she was wrong. The entire idea of being the heroine in a story of her own misadventures there for all the world to see turned her stomach. "And I would prefer to avoid that."

"I see." He studied her calmly. "As far as I am concerned there is no connection between the characters in *Exploits* and any living person. But I will speak to Mr. Aldrich."

"That will do nicely." She drew a deep breath. "I will be eternally grateful."

"You know, I might have done exactly the same thing had you simply asked for my assistance," he said with an offhand shrug.

She considered him for a moment, then grinned. "You would not."

The publisher chuckled. "Probably not."

She rose to her feet and extended her hand. "Good day then, Mr. Cadwallender."

He stood and took her hand. "Coincidence or not, Miss Merryweather, you strike me as having all the makings of a fictional heroine."

"Why, Mr. Cadwallender, what an utterly charming thing to say." She favored him with her brightest smile. "I shall make you a bargain. Should I ever decide to have daring exploits worthy of print, I will give your newspaper exclusive rights to my very real story."

"Then I can only hope you do indeed have

daring exploits." Mr. Cadwallender's eyes sparkled with amusement.

They exchanged a few more pleasantries, then Lucy led the others back through the maze of desks and workers toward the entry.

"Do you really have the money to do that?" Clara asked in a low voice beside her. "Buy the building or another newspaper?"

"I have no idea as I don't know what a building or a newspaper would cost." Lucy shrugged. "It's possible, I suppose, but I doubt it."

"Don't you think Cadwallender will realize that?"

"No doubt." Lucy nodded. "But he'll also realize that I probably do have the funds necessary to make his life a legal hell."

Clara stared in amazement. "And you seem so pleasant."

"Oh, I am." Lucy cast her a smug smile. "It's what makes me dangerous."

Clara grinned.

"Excuse me, ladies," Cameron said behind them, and they turned. "I seem to have left my gloves in Mr. Cadwallender's office," he said smoothly. "In fact I have an errand to run, so you needn't wait for me. I'll join you at Channing House to escort you to the train."

"That's not necessary," Lucy said in a clipped tone.

"Yes, it is." He smiled, turned, and headed back to Mr. Cadwallender's office.

Lucy watched him for a moment and her heart twisted. As much as she wanted to believe in him, to trust him, it was becoming harder and harder. She turned and started for the door. "One does wonder what he's up to."

"What do you mean?" Clara asked.

Lucy narrowed her eyes. "Mr. Fairchild was not wearing gloves."

"Do you care to explain any of that?" Cadwallender leaned back in his chair.

"I'd prefer not to." Cam shifted uneasily in his chair.

"That's what I thought." Cadwallender considered Cam thoughtfully. "She doesn't know you're I. F. Aldrich, does she?"

"No."

"I gathered as much from the way she introduced you as Mr. Fairchild." He paused. "Is she actually engaged in daring exploits?"

"No, not at all." It wasn't a complete lie. Lucy's adventures weren't nearly as daring as his fictional heiress's exploits.

"As she seems to think your stories are about her, I'm not sure I believe you. But I'd rather take you at your word than risk her displeasure. Still, if her real activities are better than the ones you're writing, it might be well worth it." He thought for a moment. "Just how close are your stories to her life?"

Cam blew a long breath. "She's inspiration as it were. I based the character on Miss Merryweather. Nothing more than that, really. Aside from the fact that she is in London without her family, although she has certainly not run away and she is accompanied by a companion—"

"The lovely Miss West," Cadwallender murmured. "I suspect there's an interesting story that could be inspired by her as well."

"One about an annoying, suspicious termagant, perhaps."

Cadwallender chuckled.

"As I was saying, beyond a few details here and there, the stories are entirely fictional."

"She seems to think differently."

"She is mistaken," Cam said firmly.

"I see. So tell me this." He straightened and leaned over his desk. "Who does she think you are?"

Cam grimaced. "She thinks I am a private investigator hired to keep an eye on her while she's here."

Cadwallender stared. "That's brilliant. More of my reporters should use that."

"I'm afraid it wasn't deliberate. It was an assumption on her part that I chose not to correct."

"Well, that's neither here nor there at this point, I suppose. I assume you can do as she asked and make *Daring Exploits* more adventurous and bold."

"Of course I can but—"

"In truth, that will probably make it even more popular," the publisher said thoughtfully. "I hadn't anticipated that. Not that it isn't well written, but one can never predict the appetite of the public. To be perfectly honest, I was originally thinking *Daring Exploits* would be more of a filler than anything that would catch on. For that you have my apology."

"Thank you but—"

"Of course we've been bringing them out entirely too quickly. That was a mistake."

"Mr. Cadwallender."

"There should be no more than one a week, even one a month," Cadwallender continued without pause.

"I want to end this," Cam blurted. "*The Daring Exploits*, that is."

"Are you mad?" Cadwallender stared in disbelief. "This is just beginning to build up steam. Why, it could run for a year or more."

"No," Cam said firmly. "The story was never intended to run forever. The heroine has a finite number of objects she has to acquire and once she does, the story is at an end."

"Nonsense. Throw more obstacles in her path."

"No, the story has run its course. I have three more installments nearly finished and I've already started on the ending."

"You realize you're throwing away a promising

start to what might be a very notable career. You're good, Fairchild. I'm afraid I underestimated your talent."

"Thank you, but I have no intention of throwing away anything." Cam drew a deep breath. "I have an idea that I think you'll like."

Cadwallender's eyes narrowed. "Oh?"

"I propose to introduce a new character in the last installment, a brilliant private investigator with a beautiful and equally brilliant assistant. And then continue the stories with the new characters."

"Go on."

"Together they get into all kinds of difficulties and solve any number of cases, mysterious or dangerous or amusing. The possibilities are endless. In addition, there's an element of romance between the investigator and his assistant."

"That never quite comes to fruition," the publisher murmured.

"If it proves popular, and since it's really an extension of *Daring Exploits*, I suspect it could indeed go on for months."

"Even a year or more."

"And we could call it"—Cam paused—"*The Perilous Adventures of a Private Investigator*."

Cadwallender's brow furrowed in thought. The man was intrigued by the idea—Cam could see it in his eyes. And why not? It was a brilliant idea.

"I like it," Cadwallender said at last. "If I can't have a runaway heiress, a brilliant private investigator and a beautiful assistant might be the next best thing."

"Excellent." Cam breathed a sigh of relief. Now that this was settled, he did indeed have an errand to run, which with luck and fortuitous timing, would get Miss West out of the way. Then Cam would follow Lucy to Millworth Manor. What better place than the country to confess all and beg forgiveness?

"I am curious about the ending."

"I'll wrap up the loose ends, award the heroine her inheritance, and introduce the characters for *Perilous Adventures*. It's very nearly written already."

"That's not what I'm wondering about. I'll wait to read that when you turn it in. I have no doubt it will work out well. But tell me, Fairchild, which story ends best?" Cadwallender considered Cam curiously. "The one with the fictional heiress you've been writing or the one with the very real Miss Merryweather you have apparently been living?"

"Quite honestly"—Cam blew a long breath—"I have no idea."

. . . and while I shall admit it only to myself, it is perhaps no more than jealousy. I am relegated to a sidesaddle, a distressing, awkward contraption no doubt created by a madman, and forced to ride in a sedate and extremely boring manner. Whereas men are permitted all the joy that a well-bred steed can provide.

I was reminded of this unfair fact of existence again today when we rode to that charming glen near the river for a picnic with some of our country neighbors. The young men among us took every opportunity to race like the very wind itself at a speed that quite took my breath away.

One day, I am determined to don trousers and ride astride. Of course, it shall have to be a day when I find myself quite alone . . .

from the journal of Miss Lucinda Merryweather, 1805

Chapter Fifteen

"I understand Father isn't in." Cam dropped the brown leather portfolio onto his father's desk in the Effington House library. "I'm on my way to catch a train to the country and I want to leave this for him."

"He's expected back any minute." Spencer straightened in his chair behind the desk and set down his pen. While he had his own residence, he spent a great deal of time here engaged in family concerns at the desk that had been exactly where it was now for generations. The desk that would one day be his together with all the responsibilities that went along with it.

As always, Cam noted a pang of gratitude that he was not the firstborn son. Aside from management of the Effington estates and oversight of family business investments, Spencer had any number of private interests as well.

Spencer's gaze flicked from his brother's to the folder and back. "What is it?"

"That, my dear older brother"—Cam plopped down in the chair in front of the desk and grinned—"is my book."

Spencer's expression brightened. "I knew you could do it. Congratulations, Cam. I never doubted you."

"That's one of us." Cam chuckled.

"Come now, you had the confidence of everyone in the family."

"Except Father."

"Nonetheless, you've accomplished what you set out to do and far earlier than the deadline Father set."

"Once I had inspiration"—he shrugged in an offhand manner—"it moved surprisingly quickly."

"Excellent." Spencer beamed with pride. "Now what?"

"Now I am going to the country for a few days to confess all to Lucy."

"You haven't done that yet?" Spencer said slowly.

"I haven't had the chance." Cam tried and failed to hide the defensive note in his voice. But saying he hadn't had the opportunity—which wasn't entirely inaccurate—sounded much better than admitting his courage was lacking as well. "She left three days ago to accompany Lady Dunwell to Millworth Manor. I needed to finish this and make a few arrangements before I could follow her."

"What kind of arrangements?"

"Nothing of significance, just a few matters to take care of." The most critical was convincing Phineas to send a telegram to Miss West requesting her to return to London on some pretext or other. "And deciding exactly what I want to say."

"Have you?"

"Not quite yet." Cam shook his head. "But I'm confident the words will come when the time is right."

Spencer stared as if his brother had completely taken leave of his senses. "That sounds like a plan. Not a particularly good one, but I suppose you'll make do." Spencer cast him a pitying look, then turned his attention to the portfolio. He flipped it open, withdrew the manuscript, then hesitated. "May I read it?"

"Yes, of course." Cam shrugged as if he didn't care one way or the other and wasn't in truth pleased that his oldest brother wanted to read his work. "Although, for the most part it's very much what ran in the *Messenger*. I had to make a few changes, adjustments as it were, to make it cohesive and complete, but I'm pleased with it all in all."

Spencer picked up the first page. "I gather it's ready for publication."

"I hadn't really thought about publication."

"Well, you have had other things on your mind. Multiple identities do tend to keep one busy." Spencer replaced the page and flipped through the manuscript. "Why don't you leave this in my hands?"

"I was going to have you give it to Father," Cam said slowly.

"Absolutely not." Spencer scoffed. "You should

be the one to give it to him. However, I have an idea on the best way to do just that."

"Oh?"

"Wouldn't it be much more, oh, I don't know, impressive to hand Father a bound book rather than a stack of pages?"

"Impressive?"

"All right then . . ." Spencer chuckled. "Pointed. Triumphant. Victorious." There was little the duke's children liked better than to prove their father wrong, unless of course it was winning a wager with him. Neither happened often.

Cam shook his head. "I don't have time to look for a publisher."

"Fortunately for you, you don't need to." Spencer settled back in his chair. "Do you remember a few years ago when two of the Cadwallender brothers decided they would much rather publish books than periodicals?"

Cam nodded. "Vaguely."

"They needed an influx of funding and I wanted an investment that was, oh, more speculative than usual. So I became a very silent partner in Cadwallender Brothers Publishing." He met his brother's gaze firmly. "They are always looking for good books."

"That's a very generous offer." Cam chose his words carefully. "But I would prefer to have this published on its own merits rather than because my brother owns part of a publishing firm."

Spencer's brow rose. "I'm surprised you're not jumping at the idea."

"Apparently I have some moral standards I was not aware of," Cam said wryly.

"You misunderstand me, Cam. I'm not talking about one brother doing a favor for another. I'm talking about a potentially profitable business endeavor." Spencer's tone hardened. "When I said I am a silent partner, I meant it. I have no say in what the brothers choose to publish. The literary world is not where my expertise lies. However, this"—he patted the manuscript—"this is certain to be successful. The story has already proven to be popular. The book should be as well. Strictly as a business venture, I want Cadwallender Brothers to have the first chance at this book." He leaned forward in his chair. "Leave this to me. Allow me to give it to Benjamin Cadwallender. I would double the wager I made with Father that he'll jump at the chance to publish this. And I'd wager as well, he'll do it quickly. Why, I would imagine he'd have it available for sale as soon as the last installment runs in the *Messenger*. Strike while the iron is hot, and all that."

Cam stared at his brother. This was what he had wanted after all. Still, he hadn't imagined it actually happening.

"You could have this book in hand and available for sale before the deadline Father set for you," Spencer said in a tempting manner. "And wouldn't it be so much more gratifying to present him with an actual book rather than a stack of papers?"

Cam chuckled. "It would indeed."

"Then . . ."

"Then . . . I leave this in your capable hands." Cam rose to his feet. "And I need to be on my way if I am to catch the next train to the country."

Spencer nodded and stood. "To claim the heart of the fair Miss Merryweather?"

"I hadn't thought of it that way." But wasn't that exactly what he intended to do? "Yes, I suppose I am." He stared at his brother. "Blast it all, what am I doing?"

"I would have thought you might have determined that by now." Spencer studied him curiously. "Or realized it. Have you?"

"I . . ." He blew a long breath. "Bloody hell, I'm in love with her."

Spencer laughed. "You needn't sound so shocked by it."

"I am shocked. I didn't think . . . I never imagined . . ." He paused to pull his thoughts together. "I have always thought that I would know the right woman for me the very moment I saw her."

"And did you?"

"I didn't realize it at the time." Cam thought back to his first meeting with Lucy. She had been so very indignant and determined and wrong and completely and utterly endearing. And then she had kissed him. And he realized now what he hadn't then, that nothing would ever be the same again. "But perhaps I did."

"Grandmother will be pleased." Spencer chuckled. "I gather you're talking about marriage?"

"I hadn't really considered that either, but it does appear to be the only way to keep her in my life. And it no longer seems like a lifetime sentence," he added sheepishly.

Spencer nodded slowly. "But rather a gift to treasure."

Cam smiled. He should have known Spencer of all people would understand. For the first time, Cam understood the depth of sorrow that Spencer had known when the woman he loved had died. Losing Lucy, even due to his own stupidity, would devastate him. Good God, this was indeed love.

"I'm going to bring this to Cadwallender right now." Spencer put the manuscript back in the portfolio and got to his feet. "Why don't I drop you off at the station on the way?"

Cam nodded at the portfolio. "I thought you were going to read it first."

"I don't need to. I've read every installment thus far. I have no doubt the rest of the story is every bit as good." He put the portfolio under his arm and circled the desk to join his brother.

Cam stared. "You have that much confidence in me?"

"I always have," Spencer said simply. They started toward the door. "Sometimes, I wonder . . ."

"About?"

"Father." Spencer paused. "Before he challenged you to write a book, in spite of your various failed attempts at assorted things to do with your life—"

"Thank you. I had almost forgotten that."

Spencer ignored him. "I would have thought he was your most ardent supporter."

"He has an odd way of showing it."

"Yes, he does," Spencer said thoughtfully. "I hope I do as well when my turn comes." He shook his head as if clearing it. "Although I daresay you'll be a father and a husband long before I am."

"With any luck," Cam said under his breath.

"Come on, you can rehearse what you want to say to Miss Merryweather in the carriage."

"Thus far I haven't gone much beyond 'I'm sorry, can you forgive me?'"

Spencer clapped his hand on his brother's back in a show of support or perhaps condolence. "Yes, well, one has to start somewhere."

It wasn't until Cam had departed the train after the hour-long trip from London and was in a hired carriage on the last leg of the journey to Millworth that he was struck by a realization he should have had earlier.

If he still hadn't found the right words to explain about the installments of *The Daring Exploits of a Runaway Heiress* in the *Messenger*, how in the hell was he going to explain away a book?

One could say it was not in the spirit of the quest.

Lucy cantered or trotted or flew across the frozen fields, hills and valleys of the Millworth estate with renewed confidence in her own abilities, helped in no small part by the excellent training and fine disposition of the horse she'd been given from the Millworth stables. Albert scampered along on the ground beside the horse or, as often as not, led the way. She wouldn't have thought such a small dog would have been able to keep up but he was a terrier after all. And he was having as grand a time as she. It had been years since she'd donned men's trousers and ridden astride beside one or more of her brothers. This was on Lucinda's list and Lucy could certainly have simply checked it off and considered it a regret long ago made amends for, but where would be the fun in that? This was too good an opportunity to pass up.

There was an exhilaration in riding astride, a sense of freedom and being one with the horse that was impossible to achieve in a sidesaddle. Pity she had forgotten that, but then it had been a very long time. In their childhood, she and her brothers had spent several summers in the country with two of her mother's aunts. Both women were widowed and neither had children of their own. For a few magical years, the Merryweather children had joined an assortment of cousins for a summer of questionable discipline, lax rules, and a true holiday from expectations. It had been a splendid time for all concerned, except perhaps the collected nannies and governesses who had been in charge of the herd of rambunctious children. Mother and Father, and the aunts and uncles who were the parents of their summer companions, traditionally joined them at the beginning of the season and then again at the end.

Mother would have been shocked if she had known her daughter was riding astride like an ill-mannered hellion. Even then, Mother had had plans for Lucy that did not include improper behavior. Lucy grimaced at the thought of what Mother would think of her activities now. Eventually, she would have to confess some of what she had been doing, carefully edited of course. Obviously confession was good for the soul only because it was so awkward to manage. Still, she had time and she certainly wasn't going to worry about that now. The sun was sinking low and with it the temperature. She would much prefer to be nice and warm at the manor rather than riding on property she wasn't familiar with in the dark. She turned the horse back toward the stables. There was nothing like a solitary ride to help one think, and she did have a great deal of thinking to do. And what better time to do it than now, when she was gloriously alone.

Clara had been called back to London this morning. Apparently Mr. Chapman had fallen gravely ill or had been in some sort of accident— Lucy wasn't sure and neither was Clara. It was the confusion as much as anything that had sent her back to town. Clara said Mr. Chapman was never vague. Lucy suspected Clara's concern was more than that of one colleague for another. But as much as Lucy liked and trusted her, Clara was an exceptionably private person and Lucy wasn't sure that she knew her at all.

On the other hand, she was certain that she knew Cameron well enough to have confidence in the type of man he was. As she'd told Clara, one did have to rely on one's own instincts, one's own heart. Or maybe she simply hoped she was right, because in the three days since she'd last seen him she'd realized a few important facts. First of all, she missed him. She hadn't gone this long with-out seeing him since they'd first met.

Secondly, nothing about the man made sense. If he was indeed trying his hand at private investigation, he wasn't very good at it. On the other hand, he was excellent at storytelling. The tales he told of his misadventures as a private investigator were quite entertaining, even if she didn't believe a word of them. They were entirely too amusing and far too perfect. While life was often amusing, it was never perfect. No, although she now knew his real name, he was still hiding something. She could be wrong, of course, and she did hope she was.

And third, even if he was interested in her money, well, she certainly had enough for them both. If he loved her, she might well be able to forgive whatever brought them together in the first place, although the very idea of someone wanting her only for her fortune did make her stomach turn. Perhaps she should simply give all her money to charity? She grinned. And wouldn't that serve him right if indeed he wanted her for her money?

But did he love her? It struck her as a rather important question given that she had realized in recent days that she did indeed love him. It did not seem like a particularly good idea, but then there it was and there was nothing she could do about it. The very idea of a life without him tore at her heart. She would have thought she'd be shocked by the revelation—she had never expected love—but it seemed so natural, so right. As if it was meant to be. Fate and all that.

Odd, that she had started her quest because she was no longer going to marry the man she had been expected to wed and was nearing the end with the one man she wanted to spend the rest of her life with. Pity that love simply wasn't enough.

She had long ago decided she couldn't love a man she didn't trust, but it appeared her heart was not as stalwart and sensible as her head. Still, one did have to have a certain amount of faith. And what was love, after all, but faith? She was confident that Cameron was a good and, for the most part, honest man.

Now all she had to do was get the blasted creature to prove it.

Cam paced the floor in the Millworth Manor parlor where he'd been left to wait by the butler. Clement hadn't so much as twitched an eyebrow when Cam had arrived, bag in hand, and announced he would be staying for a few days. But then the man was exceptionally well trained. And it wasn't as if Cam and Lucy would be residing in the manor alone. It was not only filled with servants but the lovely and terrifying Lady Dunwell was here as well, and Clement had pointedly mentioned Lord Dunwell was expected later this evening.

Cam had never thought of Beryl Dunwell as being anything other than fascinating before now. A few years ago, both she and her husband, while publicly discreet, made no great secret of their numerous affairs and escapades either. Cam was fairly certain at least one of his older brothers had had some sort of liaison with her, although it might have been nothing more than a flirtation and could well have been with her twin sister. Cam couldn't remember the details if indeed he ever knew them, and it wasn't something he could ask. Especially as, according to gossip, Lord and Lady Dunwell had apparently given up their days of indiscretion for the more respectable, if exceedingly rare, life of connubial bliss. Still, there was nothing more sanctimonious than a drunkard who had sworn off drink and Cam was grateful he had not yet run into her.

No, he needed all his courage and his wits to finally confess to Lucy. He would make a clean breast of it. Tell her everything. He was a writer, by God. Surely the words were there somewhere, even if he hadn't been able to quite find them yet.

Cam could start with his name. That was fairly simple. Then casually mention his love of writing. And his longtime friendship with Phineas. And why he'd been following her originally . . . He rubbed his hand over his forehead and resisted the urge to groan.

"What are you doing here?"

Lucy did not sound happy to see him. It was not an auspicious beginning. He braced himself, turned, and tried not to stare.

"You needn't look so shocked, Mr. Fairchild." Lucy pulled off her gloves. "It isn't the first time you've seen me in men's clothing."

"No, but . . . this is . . ." This was a far cry from

the loose-fitting attire she'd worn to play server. These trousers clung and caressed her legs, her long and shapely legs, before disappearing into battered men's boots that reached nearly to her knees. She wore a close-fitting jumper underneath a too large men's coat, a woolen scarf wrapped around her neck. Her hair was disheveled, her blue eyes sparkled, and her face was flushed from the cold. The overall effect was one of bundled temptation, and longing swept through him. It struck him that he had exactly the same reaction very nearly every time he saw her in something completely inappropriate. Or rather every time he saw her at all. "Suffice it to say that is rather more revealing than your costume at Prichard's."

"Do you really think so?" She pulled off her scarf and glanced down at her clothes. "I thought it was all quite fetching in a lovely bohemian sort of way. My mother would be appalled, which makes it all the better. Lady Dunwell loaned these clothes to me. Apparently, she used to wear them on occasion."

"That explains it then," he murmured.

She glanced at him sharply. "You haven't answered my question. Why are you here?"

"Well, I thought you might need me and . . ." This was ridiculous. He drew a deep breath. "I missed you, damn it."

"Did you? Isn't that interesting." Her tone softened. "I expected you two days ago."

"I had matters to attend to." Perhaps she wasn't as annoyed with him as he had feared.

"I see." She trailed her fingers over the back of the sofa. "Matters involving your . . . work?"

"One could say that." He paused. This was Lucy after all. Kind, generous, sensible Lucy. Surely she would understand. Best to get this over with. "And there are matters that we should . . ."

She moved toward him, a challenge in her eyes. "Matters we should what?"

"Discuss. Talk about . . ." But what if she didn't understand? What if she hated him? Perhaps this wasn't the best time after all. "Um . . . consider."

"Oh?" Her brow arched upward. "What kind of matters?"

"Well, you know, matters . . ." Had his tie suddenly grown tighter?

"Matters?" Her eyes widened, her voice rose, and she stepped closer. *"Matters?"*

"Well, yes." He swallowed hard. "Matters . . ."

"Good Lord." Impatience rang in her voice. She stared up at him. "Why don't you just say whatever it is you have to say?"

"It's nothing, really," he said weakly, and shook his head. No, if there was any chance at all of a future with her, if he didn't want to lose her, this had to be handled correctly. The time had to be right and the words had to be right.

"You drive me mad, *Mr. Fairchild.*" She glared at him.

"I—"

"I was told we had a guest." Lady Dunwell's distinctive voice sounded from the door.

"Apparently." Lucy cast him a disgusted look, then stepped away. "Beryl, allow me to introduce *Mr. Fairchild*. Mr. Fairchild, this is Lady Dunwell."

"Ah yes, *Mr. Fairchild*." Lady Dunwell moved toward him, the pleasant note in her voice belying the wicked look in her eyes. "I've heard so much about you." She held out her hand. "You're the investigator charged with keeping an eye on our dear little Lucy."

Was it possible she didn't recognize him? Certainly she was closer in age to his brothers, and socially she and Lord Dunwell moved in more political circles, but she and Cam had met on any number of occasions. Admittedly he might well have been beneath her notice, and while there was a chance she didn't remember him, it did seem unlikely. He doubted he could be that lucky. Still, he would be an idiot to point out that they had met, which would lead directly to the revelation of his name. No, far better to keep his mouth shut.

Cam took her hand. "Good day, Lady Dunwell."

"I assume I'll be getting an invoice from you at some point." Her gaze bored into his.

"An invoice?" he said cautiously.

"For your services." She withdrew her hand and her eyes narrowed.

"I realize discretion is part and parcel of what you do," Lucy said with an exasperated sigh. "But you could have told me you weren't hired by Mr. Channing but were working for Lady Dunwell."

"I was not at liberty to disclose the name of my employer," he said without thinking. But it seemed the right thing to say as he had absolutely no idea what they were talking about.

"I do wish Mr. Chapman had told me he had found someone to accept the job I had offered him."

"Oh, yes, well . . ." Cam's mind raced. Of course. Lady Dunwell had been the unnamed client who had wanted to hire Phineas to keep an eye on Lucy. He adopted a puzzled tone. "My apologies, Lady Dunwell. I thought he had."

"Not to my knowledge, but I've been a bit scattered of late. I'm certain it's nothing more than a simple misunderstanding. In my experience Mr. Chapman has never been particularly good with the more practical points of dealing with his clients." Lady Dunwell's gaze pinned him firmly and he resisted the ridiculous urge to squirm. "Don't you agree?"

Cam nodded. "That has always been something of a problem for him."

"Lucy." Lady Dunwell addressed Lucy but kept her gaze firmly fixed on Cam. "Your maid is drawing a bath for you. I told her I would have a bite sent up as supper won't be for hours."

"That will be lovely." Lucy blew a relieved breath. "It was a wonderful ride but I am more than ready to bathe and get ready for this evening. And I am famished."

This evening? What was happening this evening?

"You wouldn't want to keep the gentlemen waiting." Lady Dunwell chuckled. "They get quite impatient when they're ready to play."

Ready to play what?

Lady Dunwell turned to Cam. "I assume you'll be joining us, Mr. Fairchild?"

"Joining you for what?" he said carefully.

"Lady Dunwell has invited a neighbor and his friends for cards and a late dinner tonight." Lucy grinned. "I'm told the stakes can get quite high on occasion."

Beat men at their own game. Preferably for very high stakes.

"Of course." He nodded.

"Lord Fairborough and several of his cronies have a rousing evening of cards every month. They've done so for years. My father plays with them when he is in residence. I invited them to play their games here tonight and permit Miss Merryweather and I to play as well. Lord Fairborough was quite taken with the idea as he and his friends are fond of poker and they do enjoy playing with Americans. Admittedly, he did balk at the idea of playing with a woman.

359

However, when I pointed out she was a guest in our country, had a great deal of money she was willing to lose, and was young and pretty, his lordship agreed it was his patriotic duty and he was not one to shirk his responsibilities to the Crown." She chuckled. "Lady Fairborough was pleased as well. I don't think she's especially fond of hosting her husband's monthly venture into gaming. Nonetheless, one thing did lead to another and . . . well . . ." She shrugged.

"I had no idea Miss Merryweather knew how to play poker," Cam said.

"I suspect there are all sorts of things I know that you have no idea about," Lucy said coolly.

Lady Dunwell smirked.

Cam's gaze shifted from one woman to the other. There was something here that he was missing.

"Is that all then, Mr. Fairchild?" Lucy's challenging gaze locked with his.

"Well yes, I think so."

Her eyes narrowed. "Nothing more you wish to say?"

"Not at the moment," he said weakly. He'd never thought of himself as a coward, but apparently he was. Even so, he was not about to confess everything in the forbidding presence of Lady Dunwell. Apparently there was a thin line between caution and cowardice.

"Very well then." Lucy huffed. "I look forward

to playing with you, *Mr. Fairchild.*" She turned and strode from the room.

Lady Dunwell stared at him for a long, considering moment and it was all he could do not to shift from foot to foot. "What are you up to, Cameron Effington?"

So much for the hope that she had not remembered him.

"I have no idea what you mean, Lady Dunwell." He forced an innocent note to his voice.

"You may have fooled Miss Merryweather but you can't fool me."

"I am not trying to fool anyone."

"I don't believe that for a moment." She dismissed his comment with a wave of her hand. "I think there is far more to all this, to your actions, than appears at first glance. Miss Merryweather seems to think you are nobly pursuing a vocation in an effort to make your own way in the world, stand on your own two feet as it were. She thinks you're ambitious and determined and all those things Americans find so admirable." Lady Dunwell's eyes narrowed. "Are you?"

Bloody hell, how much did Lucy know? "In a manner of speaking, yes."

"She further thinks your family is not pleased, which is why you're not using your real name—"

"She knows that?"

"Of course she knows." Lady Dunwell scoffed. "Good Lord, Effington. You cannot appear in a ballroom with hundreds of people, most of whom know you or know of you or your family, dance with a woman and expect that someone will not say something."

He grimaced. "That was a mistake."

"I'm so glad you realize it. And private investigation? Really, Effington." She shook her head in a disbelieving manner. "Surely you could have come up with better than that. Phineas Chapman was no doubt destined to ferret out mysteries from birth. From what I've heard, even as a child he was a bit unusual. But you? You can't even keep your identity secret."

"This was not exactly planned."

"I should hope not. One would hope an actual plan would be better thought out, although even a bad plan is better than no plan at all. Do you have a plan?"

"Not yet."

"Why am I not surprised?" She studied him closely. "Do you care for her?"

"Yes." He squared his shoulders. "Very much so."

"I was afraid of that, although it certainly does answer a lot of questions. However, if you hope for anything to come of your affection—and I am hoping your intentions toward her are honorable . . ."

He nodded.

"I can't say I trust you, which might not be fair

as I don't really know you at all. I do, however, know your brothers and I do know your reputation—"

"No worse than anyone else's," he pointed out.

"That is not a recommendation." She cast him a disgusted look. "As I was saying, while I don't entirely trust you, ultimately it doesn't matter."

"It doesn't?"

"I'm not the one whose trust you need to earn. Therefore, I would strongly suggest you come up with a definite plan."

"I am trying."

"Try harder," she snapped. "You need to tell her the truth, all of it, and I suspect there's quite a lot to tell. She needs to hear it from you. The longer you wait—"

"I am more than aware of that," he said sharply.

"Oh, well, as long as you're aware of it." She rolled her gaze toward the ceiling. "There's some very nice Scottish whisky in the cabinet by the window. You look as if you could use something to strengthen your courage."

He was about to argue that his courage didn't need strengthening but thought better of it.

"I have a great deal to do before the guests arrive." She started toward the door. "There's no dinner tonight, but we are having a late supper. You might want to get yourself a bite to eat. I'm assuming you brought something appropriate to wear this evening."

"I did."

"It's nice to know you haven't abandoned good manners in your quest for, well, whatever it is you're looking for." She paused and studied him for a moment. "I am extremely fond of Lucy. You might want to keep that in mind as well."

In spite of the mildness of her tone, there was a distinct warning in her words.

"I shall," Cam said.

"See that you do." She nodded and again started for the door. "I do hope you brought money with you. It might be an expensive evening."

He grinned. "Not if I win."

"I, for one, would not wager on you." She scoffed, opened the door, and took her leave.

Cam found the whisky and poured himself a glass. Lady Dunwell was right. He could indeed use this. He took a grateful swallow.

If Lucy knew about his name it was entirely likely she knew everything, at least judging from what Lady Dunwell had said. Actually, upon reflection, Lady Dunwell really hadn't said anything of substance. He wasn't sure if she, and therefore Lucy, was talking about his work for the *Messenger* or his alleged profession as a private investigator. It certainly wasn't something he could ask her to clarify. But if Lucy knew every-thing, why hadn't she said anything? She was not the kind of woman who would keep something like that to herself.

Unless she was toying with him. He sipped the whisky thoughtfully. Waiting until he got in deeper and deeper before pulling the rug out from underneath him, probably as retribution for his less than completely honest behavior. Brilliant and diabolical. That was the woman he loved. Very well then. He'd play her game. It would be a challenge, it would be fun, and he'd win.

He'd bet both their hearts on it.

Regrets Set to Rights

Wear trousers and ride astride.

. . . as it does seem to me that my friends, and admittedly I am among them, are continually complaining about the way of the world in regards to men and women. For whatever reason men do not seem to understand that being born a female does not mean being born without a brain. Quite honestly, we know just as many stupid men as we do unintelligent females. Perhaps more as women, no matter how witless, do tend to be much quieter.

I would dearly love to beat a man at a game he considers his own, be that a game of chess or backgammon or cards. Father says the greater the risk, the greater the reward, and I should like to play for something significant. For stakes that are more than a mere token but substantial and important. Such a wager would not be out of greed but rather the heartfelt desire that whatever man I best in such a manner would well and truly know his loss.

As the victor, I would want, more than any-thing else, for him to remember always that he had lost something of true value to a mere woman.

I know I would never forget . . .

from the journal of Miss Lucinda Merryweather, 1806

Chapter Sixteen

Lucy's gaze met Cameron's over the table. She did so love it when he looked as if he couldn't quite believe she knew what she was doing. Not completely shocked but definitely doubtful. Hadn't the poor dear learned anything about her by now? Mother had indeed turned her into the perfect daughter, but one didn't grow up with four brothers without learning a few things in spite of her mother's best efforts. Things like riding astride and playing card games deemed unsuitable for ladies.

She and Cameron sat at a table with Beryl's husband Lionel, Lord Fairborough, a Mr. Wilcox, a Sir Edwin Parker, and a Lord Larken. In the hour or so that they'd been at the table, Lucy had realized Cameron was good but a relatively cautious player, which did surprise her, although given his concern about propriety, it probably shouldn't have. But somehow she had expected him to be less thoughtful and more brash in his playing. Perhaps it was the influence of the older gentlemen, who were, for the most part, more enthusiastic than they were skilled, but then they had said at the beginning their games were not intended to be terribly serious but were more for the enjoyment of playing and the companionship of like-minded friends. Lucy had always been excellent at all kinds of cards, and while it had been years since she'd played poker, it did seem to be coming back to her. Thus far, the wagers had been relatively insignificant, with winning and losing hands more or less evenly distributed among the group. Lucy couldn't help but be a bit disappointed. She had expected much more significant wagering after all, and given the disgusted looks on the older gentlemen's faces, they agreed with her.

"We might as well be playing with pennies. I blame the ladies for this," Sir Edwin muttered, then realized what he'd said and flashed Lucy an apologetic smile. "I don't mean you, my dear."

"He means Lady Fairborough and the wives of the other gentlemen," Lord Fairborough said with a sigh of resignation. "They aren't usually present, you see, and I'm afraid we find being in the same room with them somewhat daunting."

"Dampens the spirits and all. Damnably hard to have a good time with your wife sitting at the next table where she can see exactly how much you're wagering," Mr. Wilcox said under his breath. "And how much you're losing."

"Even worse." Lord Larken smirked. "How much you're winning."

The other gentlemen chuckled in a wry manner. As Beryl had explained it, when she'd invited Lord Fairborough to have his friends play at

Millworth, while Lady Fairborough hadn't been at all unhappy at the move, she had expressed a sort of wistful disappointment that the evening was only to be for the gentlemen as it had been months since there had been any kind of social gathering at Millworth. And wasn't it a pity not to take advantage of Beryl being in residence at the manor for something more social than an evening of cards for old men? Particularly as Beryl was such an accomplished hostess. Beryl related all this with a perplexed expression and admitted she wasn't at all sure how it had happened, but Lady Fairborough was far cleverer than Beryl had ever suspected. One thing had led to another and before she had realized it, a straightforward evening of poker had become a card party with no fewer than a dozen people. Three tables had been set up in the gallery, although only two were being used as all the men present had chosen to play poker.

"I suspect we can do something about that." Lucy cast a smile around the table and played a card. "As we are about to go into supper, perhaps the tables can be rearranged while we eat. One placed in the parlor for the ladies' games, and ours in the library. Will that do?"

"Admirably, Miss Merryweather." Lord Fairborough beamed. "And, might I add, an excellent idea."

"Thank you, my lord."

"And I see the signal for supper," Lionel said. "Just in time to save me from attempting to bluff my way through a most disappointing hand."

"I should think you would be used to bluffing," Sir Edwin said mildly. "Given your position in politics and all."

"Admittedly, it's a skill that has come in handy on more than one occasion. But unfortunately, not tonight." Lionel laughed and tossed his cards on the table. "I am, however, optimistic that a little sustenance and a move to a more favorable surrounding will change my luck entirely." He nodded at Lucy. "I'll mention your suggestion about the tables to Beryl."

"I pass," Mr. Wilcox said at Lucy's right.

"I could certainly use a little more luck myself." Lucy sighed and laid down her cards. "I too pass."

It was apparently a common sentiment as the three remaining players passed as well, leaving Cameron to collect this hand's meager winnings. The gentlemen stood, Cameron quickly circling the table to help her with her chair.

She rose to her feet and he leaned closer and spoke softly for her ears alone. "You're not planning on fleecing these old men, are you?"

"Well," she said thoughtfully, "I'm not *planning* on it."

He chuckled. "You never fail to surprise me."

"Why?" Her brow rose. "Because I know how to play poker?"

"Because you play to win."

"Goodness, Cameron, why wouldn't I? Don't you?" She gazed into his eyes and once again it was as if the rest of the world faded away. She drew a steadying breath. "We have to stop doing that."

"Doing what?"

"You know perfectly well what. Gazing into each other's eyes as if nothing and no one existed except for you and I. It's happened on more than one occasion. Why . . ." She met his gaze firmly and raised her chin. "One might think we were in love."

He stared as if he had no idea why she would say such a thing. Her heart plummeted and her stomach lurched. Good God, what had come over her? Certainly she did want to know if her feelings were returned, but she might as well have come straight out and asked him. Judging from the startled look on his face, like a rat caught in a trap, the idea hadn't so much as crossed his mind. And wasn't that humiliating?

"Silly idea, of course. Why, we barely know each other." She adopted a crisp tone. "Now, if you will excuse me, I would like a bite to eat." She nodded, turned, resisted the need to flee, and willed herself to walk in a serene and sedate manner to the dining room.

A light supper of cold meats and cheeses and assorted other dishes had been arranged on the sideboard. As this was a fairly impromptu gathering, an informal meal was to be expected, but Beryl and the Millworth kitchen staff had done an outstanding job. Still, as appealing as the offerings appeared, Lucy had little appetite. Regardless, she stood at the sideboard and filled her plate.

How could she have been such a fool as to have fallen in love with a man who was so clearly not in love with her? A man who wouldn't even give her his real name? She was not a stupid woman, but bringing up the mere suggestion of love with him was not one of her brighter ideas, although she really hadn't given it much thought. She had opened her mouth and the words had simply fallen out of their own accord. In spite of his reaction, and completely aside from the fact that he'd taken every opportunity presented him to kiss her and quite thoroughly at that, it was hard to believe she was the only one who had been aware of those moments of, well, magic.

"I apologize if I upset you." Cameron's voice sounded behind her.

"Goodness, Mr. Fairchild." She drew a steadying breath, plastered a polite smile on her face, and turned toward him. "Don't be absurd. What on earth would I be upset about?" *Except for the fact that I very nearly told you I was in love with you. Oh, and that pesky business about you lying to me from the first moment we met.*

"I'm not sure," he said slowly, his gaze searching hers.

"Really? Nothing comes to mind?" It was all she could do to keep a smile on her face. "Nothing at all?"

He drew his brows together. "I can't think of anything."

"Come now, Mr. Fairchild, surely you're smarter than that."

He smiled weakly. "Apparently not."

"Apparently," she said in a sharper tone than she had intended. "If you will excuse me, I see Lady Fairborough and I did promise to sit with her." She nodded smoothly and walked away, surprised she could do so given that her unsteady knees threatened to give way at any moment. And why on earth did she want to do nothing so much as to throw herself onto Lady Fairborough's motherly shoulder and weep?

She took a chair beside the older lady, greeted the others at the table, and allowed the conversation to ebb and flow around her, while feigning a great deal of interest in the food on her plate. Somewhere between the sliced ham and some sort of savory pudding it struck her that she wasn't being entirely fair. Even the most brilliant of men did tend to be, well, stupid when it came to matters of the heart. Hadn't she seen it time and time again with her brothers? There was every chance the blank look on his face had nothing to do with how he really felt. Still, she was not about to go down that path again. If the man was in love with her, he should damn well do something about it.

Right after he confessed his deceits.

He was an idiot. There was nothing more to it than that. At least when it came to Lucy. Cam had suspected as much but now he had solid proof.

Lucy had presented him with the perfect opportunity and he'd let it slip through his fingers. When she'd looked directly into his eyes and said that one might think they were in love, he should have done something other than gape at her like, well, an idiot. He should have said something clever and charming and romantic. Or he should have taken her hand and kissed it and looked deeply into her eyes without saying a word. Even a simple smile would have sufficed. There was no need to declare himself right then and there, but there was a need to do *something*. She had simply taken him unawares. He was not prepared, but then he hadn't been especially prepared since the moment he met her. It was unsettling, to say the least. A woman had never caught him unprepared before. He'd always been quick with a reply guaranteed to melt even the most resistant heart. But with Lucy he could barely remember his own name. Any of them.

This was getting out of hand. He had to do

something. Anything. Without warning it struck him. He absolutely had to win her heart before he told her the truth. And not just her heart but her hand as well. And why not?

Marriage to Lucy wouldn't be a penance but an adventure. She was the woman he wanted to spend the rest of his life with after all. Besides, one would think it would be easier to forgive a man you loved, a man you intended to marry. It was the only chance he had if he didn't want to lose her. How to go about it was the question. But Lady Dunwell was right. Even a bad plan was better than no plan at all, and while he didn't have an actual plan, at least he now had a goal and an idea. By the time they'd returned to the tables, he'd made a few arrangements.

Admittedly, his efforts might be futile as she was even more annoyed with him now than she had been earlier today. She'd refused to look in his direction at all through supper. They'd resumed playing over an hour ago at a table set up in the library, without Lord Dunwell, who said he'd had enough for one night. Even though Lucy had returned to her seat directly across the table from Cam, where she couldn't help but meet his eyes inadvertently, her gaze never settled on his for more than a fleeting instant. It was obvious that she didn't, at the moment, want anything to do with him.

"I do feel compelled to apologize, Miss Merryweather." Lord Fairborough shuffled the cards. "Usually, this is quite a rousing evening and Lady Dunwell had said you were looking forward to games with a little excitement. I did promise her as much. But tonight I'm afraid we're all rather staid and somewhat dull."

"It's the influence of the ladies," Mr. Wilcox said darkly. "I find it hard to enjoy myself unabashedly without thinking that my wife is aware of my every move even from another room."

"It's so much more entertaining when none of us pays any attention to how many glasses of port or whisky we've had. No one notices the lateness of the hour. And no one is concerned with how much they wager or even how much they lose." Sir Edwin heaved a heartfelt sigh.

"We will confess to you, Miss Merryweather, that we had intended for this to be a rather high stakes game," Lord Larken said in a confidential manner. "According to Lady Dunwell, you have a tidy fortune and we could all use a nice influx of cash at the moment. She had also implied that you were something of a, well, a madcap heiress and would find playing for high stakes most amusing."

"Like the girl in those stories running in the *Messenger*," Sir Edwin said.

Cam choked, then quickly grabbed his glass of whisky and tossed back a swallow.

"I never read the *Messenger*." Lord Fairborough scoffed. "Although I will confess my wife does." "Damnably funny stories." Sir Edwin chuckled. "About an American heiress trying to win her inheritance."

"It does sound amusing," Lucy said pleasantly. "I will make it a point to read it. However, I can assure you that no one has ever before referred to me as madcap."

"Lady Dunwell certainly implied it." Lord Larken cast an annoyed look at his friends. "So naturally we assumed that you would lose. We never imagined you actually knew how to play."

The other gentlemen nodded.

Lucy's eyes twinkled with amusement. "I apologize for disappointing you. But I hope you realize"—she leaned closer to the older man— "the evening is not yet over. I could still lose and possibly a significant amount as well."

"Would you?" Sir Edwin asked in a hopeful manner.

"Parker," Lord Fairborough said sharply, and cast him a chastising look.

"Gentlemen." Lucy's eyes widened in feigned surprise. "Were you planning to, oh, what's the word? Fleece me?"

A wave of protest washed around the table.

"No, of course not." Lord Larken scoffed.

"We would never do such a thing." Indignation that didn't ring quite true sounded in Lord

Fairborough's voice. "Not deliberately anyway. But you never know what might happen."

Cam stared in disbelief. These gentlemen were older than his father and should certainly have better things to do than conspire to win a game of chance with a young American.

"But that is the risk when you play, my dear," Mr. Wilcox said in a fatherly manner that, oddly enough, did sound most sincere.

"Goodness, gentlemen," Lucy said pleasantly. "If you had wanted to take all my money you certainly should have bet more of your own."

"Oh, but we couldn't." Sir Edwin jerked his head toward the closed door. "You understand."

"Any other night we would, of course. Why, we routinely throw caution to the winds," Lord Fairborough added.

Cam doubted it. Although he was grateful to Lady Dunwell for arranging the evening. It might not be the high stakes game Lucy's great-aunt had envisioned, but it was far safer than any he had ever partaken in and should allow Lucy to cross this regret off her list.

"And we do apologize for the stakes being so paltry tonight." Lord Larken shrugged apologetically.

"It can't be helped, I suppose, and it's probably for the best." Lucy favored the gentlemen with a brilliant smile. "The idea of wagering a large sum of money does sound quite exciting, but the thought of losing a large sum doesn't sound like any fun at all. Although I suppose that risk is the lure of playing for high stakes."

"I doubt that the highest stakes are truly monetary," Cam said without thinking.

Her gaze snapped to his. "Oh?"

"You mean when a man bets something of value." Larken nodded. "Say his horse or his house."

"I've known men who have wagered ships," Mr. Wilcox said in a disapproving manner. "And lost them."

"Balderdash." Sir Edwin scoffed. "No man in his right mind would ever wager a ship. A ship can take you places unimagined and exotic." A wistful look crossed the older man's face. "Be a bloody shame to lose a ship."

"That's not really what I meant," Cam said slowly. "Actually I was thinking of something more esoteric."

Lord Fairborough's brow furrowed. "What are you talking about, young man?"

"Yes, Mr. Fairchild," Lucy said coolly. "What are you talking about?"

"Well." Cam thought for a moment. "If you gentlemen could wager to win anything, anything at all, what would it be?"

"I'd like a castle in the Swiss Alps," Lord Larken said promptly. "Or on the coast of Spain. That would be quite nice."

"No, that's not what he means at all. That's something that can, with enough money, be purchased." Lord Fairborough considered Cam. "You're speaking of things that can't be bought."

Cam nodded. "Exactly."

"Well then . . ." Lord Fairborough paused. "I'd like to be able to do the things I used to do without the aches and pains and discomfort that now seem to accompany nearly everything I attempt."

Sir Edwin nodded. "I'd quite like to relive my younger days." He grimaced. "One would hope I'd do a better job of it now."

"Hair," Mr. Wilcox said firmly. "I'd like my hair back. I used to have a fine head of hair."

"I'd like to look in a mirror and not have the face of an old man I barely recognize looking back at me." Lord Larken shrugged. "The price, I suppose, for being older and wiser."

"We've noticed the older part, Larken," Lord Fairborough said with a grin, "but none of us have noted you growing any wiser through the years."

"And if we had, we've probably forgotten it." Sir Edwin chuckled.

"As interesting as all your ideas are, gentlemen"—Lucy's speculative gaze lingered on Cam—"I suspect they're not exactly what Mr. Fairchild had in mind. Am I right?"

"I was thinking more in the realm of possibility than fancy," Cam said. "Something you could actually win."

"Something like wagering to win a dance with a lovely woman," Lord Fairborough said.

"Or a kiss." Sir Edwin grinned. "I remember wagers of that sort. Admittedly, it was a long time ago."

Lord Larken sighed. "For all of us."

"You could wager for information," Mr. Wilcox said thoughtfully. "Particularly information that would assist you in making a decision. Perhaps regarding, oh, I don't know, an investment or something of that nature."

"Or your next step." Lord Larken nodded. "What path you should take."

"As long as that information was truthful," Lucy said mildly.

Sir Edwin snorted. "Well, it would have to be, wouldn't it? You certainly wouldn't wager for a lie. What would be the point?"

"What indeed?" Lucy murmured.

"One question," Lord Fairborough said abruptly. "You could wager for the answer to one question."

"Just one?" Cam asked.

"If it was a good question," Mr. Wilcox said.

"Is one enough?" Lucy said.

"Possibly." Cam paused. "If it was the right question."

"And if the answer was honest." Lucy studied him. "But that's the trick of it, isn't it? Honesty, that is."

"And should be part of the wager," Cam said.

"One honest answer wagered on one hand or the turn of a card."

"It's an interesting idea, Mr. Fairchild. But then one would have to be confident in the honesty of the party one wagered with." She shrugged. "And that, I would think, is exceptionally hard to do."

"I suppose one does need a certain amount of trust." Cam's gaze meshed with hers. "And faith."

"One would be far better off relying on experience than faith. Faith is so easily shattered. And if it's only one question, then it should be a very important question." Her eyes narrowed. "If, in one's experience, the other party has already been deceitful, why one would then be extremely foolish to expect better. Faith and trust, Mr. Fairchild, need to be earned."

"Trust perhaps, but faith . . ." He shook his head.

"It seems to me faith doesn't require any sort of proof," Sir Edwin said in an aside to Lord Larken. "Isn't that the very definition of faith?"

"It's rather sad when one doesn't have faith in one's fellow man," Larken said under his breath. "To be expected I suppose, the way of the world and all, but sad nonetheless."

"Nonsense, my lord," Cam said. "What's sad is the cynical way we all look at the world."

"He's got you there," Mr. Wilcox said.

Cam leaned forward slightly. "I would trust that everyone at this table would give me an honest answer to a single question."

"Then you are far more trusting than I." Lucy paused. "Let me ask you this. What if someone at this table had misled you before? Lied to you? Deceived you?"

"I say, we've scarcely met the man," Mr. Wilcox said to Lord Fairborough beside him.

"I don't think she's talking about us," his lordship said thoughtfully.

Lucy ignored them, her gaze still locked with Cam's. "Would you still trust that they would give you an honest answer?"

Cam chose his words with care. "I suppose it depends on the reasons for the deceit."

"What if you didn't know the reason because the person in question had yet to be forthright with you?"

"It seems to me that brings us back to faith."

"Ah, but isn't faith difficult to maintain when honesty is in question?" She shook her head. "I know I would be extremely hard-pressed to have even the tiniest bit of confidence about the answer given by someone who has already lied to me."

"What if he had a very good reason?" he asked.

"What if he didn't?" she shot back.

"She's got him there," one of the older gentlemen murmured.

"You're right." Cam's gaze bored into hers. "What if he didn't have a good reason? What if something had seemed like a good idea in the beginning but he had subsequently realized he had been an idiot? And what if he then deeply regretted his actions?"

"Assuming he did indeed regret his actions, his deceit, his *lies*—"

Lord Larken winced.

She continued without pause "—perhaps he would need to prove it."

"Prove what?" Mr. Wilcox asked.

"His regret, I think." Lord Fairborough's gaze shifted between Cam and Lucy.

"Correct me if I'm mistaken, but this strikes me as somewhat personal," Lord Larken said quietly. "Should we leave?"

"Probably." Lord Fairborough nodded. "But Lady Fairborough and the other ladies will want to know every word of this."

"You do have a point," Sir Edwin murmured. "Besides, it would be like leaving a play before the end."

"How would he prove it?" Cam asked, ignoring the older men.

Lucy shrugged. "I would think if he was as clever as he thought he was—"

"He's an idiot, remember?"

"He's smart enough to manage deceit and deception," she snapped. "And if he's that clever, surely he can think of a way to now atone for his mistakes. Perhaps, oh, I don't know, a full confession? Complete and utter honesty?"

"And groveling," one of the others said under his breath. "Never underestimate the importance of groveling."

"As in an honest answer to a single question?" Cam said slowly.

She scoffed. "I don't know that one answer to one question is enough at this point."

"It is if it's the right question."

"Oh, come now, Mr. Fairchild." Her brow rose. "The *right* question?"

"I know I only have one," he said quietly.

"Well, I have half a dozen at the very least," she said sharply.

"One is all you need."

"Is it?" She stared at him, then blew a long breath. "Very well then, one question it is."

"I'm assuming the rest of us are no longer playing," Sir Edwin said with a pleasant smile.

Lucy's gaze snapped to the older man. A blush washed up her face and her eyes widened in horror. "Good Lord, my apologies. I don't know what came over me. I simply wasn't thinking. I, oh dear . . ."

"No apologies necessary, my dear," Lord Larken said smoothly. "You were simply swept away by the drama of the proposed wager."

"Exceptionally high stakes will do that," Sir Edwin added.

"And while this does seem to be a private matter . . ." Lord Fairborough said, "and the polite thing might be for us to take our leave, we're afraid at this point—"

"We think it would be most unchivalrous of us to do so," Mr. Wilcox said staunchly. "After all, you're a guest in our country."

"And some of us have daughters your age." Sir Edwin shrugged. "Leaving now would feel like abandonment. And we couldn't do that."

Lord Larken nodded. "And if this person has been dishonest with you"—as if of one mind, all four gentlemen fixed Cam with threatening looks—"why, it's our duty as honorable gentlemen to, well, defend you."

"It's really not necessary, but thank you," Lucy said.

"Consider it moral support then," Sir Edwin said.

"I would welcome moral support," Cam said under his breath.

"Apparently, you don't deserve any," Mr. Wilcox said mildly.

"Nonetheless, we insist on seeing this through with you to the end." Lord Fairborough met Lucy's gaze, a kind note in his voice. "Are you certain you want to do this, my dear?"

"Goodness, my lord." She shrugged in an offhand manner. "It's merely a single question. I certainly have nothing to hide." Her gaze shifted to Cam. "I, for one, have never been less than honest."

"Never?" He cast her a skeptical look.

"Never," she snapped.

"Never is an absolute, Miss Merryweather," Cam said. "I doubt that anyone at this table can truly say they have never done anything that was less than honest."

"Oh, I think we can all *say* it," Sir Edwin murmured.

"Very well then." Lord Fairborough pushed back his chair, stood, and moved to the desk that dominated the far end of the library.

"You should probably decide exactly how you're going to go about this," Mr. Wilcox said. "Will it be another hand or simply the highest card drawn?"

"Whatever Miss Merryweather wants is fine with me," Cam said. She was surprisingly good at cards, but he was at least her equal. A cut of the deck for the highest card was nothing more than luck. Although, luck did seem to be with him tonight. While he was certain nearly everyone here knew of his father and his family, he had never met any of them. Still, one couldn't count on luck.

"The greater the risk, the greater the reward." A firm note sounded in Lucy's voice. "I am willing to risk honesty on a single draw of the card. Are you sure you are?"

"As you said: the greater the risk . . ." He shrugged.

Lord Fairborough returned with a few sheets of Millworth stationery and fountain pens. He set them on the table and sat down. "Each of you will write your question, fold the paper once, then again, and keep it until a winner is decided."

"This is absurd." Lucy glared at Cam. "You know that, don't you?"

"I think it's perfect." He smiled.

She studied him closely, then drew a deep breath. "I don't know why *I'm* nervous about this."

"One does wonder," he said mildly. "As you have never been less than honest."

She held out her hand for the paper as if she was a surgeon reaching for an instrument, her gaze never wavering from his, challenging and calculating. Diabolical and brilliant. "And I have nothing to hide."

"We all have something to hide." The low murmur came from one of the older gentlemen.

Lord Fairborough obediently placed the paper and a pen in her hand, then passed a second sheet and pen to Cam.

Cam stared at the blank page for a moment. There were any number of questions that came to mind. She knew his real name, but what else did she know? This was his chance to find out. Still, if he had only one question, he hated to waste it. He scribbled down the one question that took precedence over anything else, waited for the ink to dry, then folded the paper.

Lucy smiled in an all too confident manner, folded her paper, and placed it on the table.

Lord Fairborough shuffled once again, then positioned the deck in the center of the table. "I would suggest Miss Merryweather draw first." He glanced at Cam. "If you're amenable to that."

Cam nodded. "I have no objection."

"Very well." Lord Fairborough fanned the deck out on the table. "If you please, Miss Merryweather."

She didn't hesitate for an instant but reached out and selected a card from the middle of the deck. She glanced at it, then placed it faceup in front of her.

The jack of diamonds.

"Your turn." Lucy smiled in a smug way. Certainly it was a high card, but it wasn't the highest. He still had a chance.

No, one couldn't count on luck, but one might be able to count on fate. He drew a deep breath, selected a card, and stared at it.

Or faith.

He met her gaze directly and slowly laid his card on the table. The ace of clubs.

"Very well then." She heaved a resigned sigh. "Give me your question."

Cam handed the folded sheet to Lord Fairborough, who handed it to Lucy. She unfolded it impatiently, glanced at the question, and froze. She stared at the paper for a long moment before that familiar look of determination and resolve settled on her face. "What an interesting question, Mr. Fairchild."

"I thought so," he said coolly.

"And something of a pity as well."

"Is it?"

"It is indeed." She met his gaze directly and smiled. "As I have absolutely no intention of answering it."

Chapter Seventeen

"I say, Miss Merryweather, you did agree to the wager," Sir Edwin said firmly. "You do have to answer the question."

"Unless, of course, you don't know the answer," Lord Fairborough said helpfully.

"That's it exactly." She cast his lordship a grateful smile. His excuse was acceptable even if not entirely accurate. Nonetheless, like a drowning man, she'd cling to anything that floated her way. "I can't possibly answer a question if I don't know what the answer is."

"Or you're simply saying you don't know what the answer is." Cameron studied her intently. "Although I suspect you do."

"You may suspect whatever you wish, Mr. Fairchild," she said sharply, clenching her fists in her lap. "The fact is I don't, at this particular moment, know the answer to your question, so obviously I cannot answer it."

Lord Larken's gaze shifted between the two of them. "Perhaps we might know the answer if you told us the quest—"

"No!" Lucy and Cameron said in unison.

"Oh, I see." Mr. Wilcox nodded in a knowing manner. "It's that kind of question, is it?"

"It's the kind of question that is not at all in

the spirit of the game," she said firmly, in a tone that sounded uncomfortably like that of her mother. She drew a steadying breath and forced a bright note to her voice. "Do forgive me, gentlemen. I am not usually one to renege on a promise or a wager, but under the circumstances . . ."

"Not that we know what the circumstances are," Sir Edwin murmured.

"I suppose this sort of thing happens on occasion—not that it ever has to me before, of course—but then nothing like any of this has ever happened to me before and . . ." Good God, she was babbling. This is what that blasted man had reduced her to. She hadn't babbled in, well, days at least. "It is regrettable but . . ." She shrugged and cast them a brilliant smile. "There you have it."

"Have what?" Mr. Wilcox's bushy brows drew together in confusion.

Cameron studied her as if he could read her mind. The slight knowing smile playing on his lips did nothing to ease her growing panic. She needed to escape that smug look before . . . well, before she did or said something. Something stupid or rude or wrong. Like scream at him about what a heartless, callow beast he was. Or, better yet, smack him.

"Now, if you will excuse me." She got to her feet and picked up the paper with the question she'd written. The last thing she wanted was for

Cameron to read that she could come up with nothing better than *What are you hiding?* which had seemed rather clever and all-encompassing when she'd written it, but not quite as insightful now.

"Again my apologies." She nodded, took two steps, then swiveled back and snatched his question off the table as well. She wasn't going to leave that for anyone else to read either. "Good evening, gentlemen."

"I don't suppose you'll tell us what the question was," one of the gentlemen asked behind her.

"Absolutely not," Cameron said.

Another gentleman sighed. "I didn't think so."

Lucy tucked both folded papers beneath the waistband of her gown, bemoaned for perhaps the thousandth time the lack of pockets in evening dresses, and was barely out of the library before Cameron caught up with her. She wasn't sure how she felt about that and, aside from justifiable anger, she certainly wasn't sure how she felt about him. At least not at this very moment. She hadn't expected him to follow her, but then what about Cameron Effington was expected?

"How could you?" she said through clenched teeth. "What kind of question was that?"

"I thought you wished for high stakes." He signaled to a nearby footman.

She stopped and stared at him. "This was not what I had in mind." She started off again. Lucy had no idea exactly where she was going, but it was an enormous house and she could probably stalk through it for hours. "That question wasn't in the spirit of the game."

"You said that right before you stomped off."

"I did not stomp off." At least she had tried not to stomp off. "I thought I made an exceptionally graceful exit, all things considered."

"My mistake, of course you did. Your composure was admirable, all things considered. Why, aside from that air of angry indignation that surrounded you, you appeared almost serene."

She clenched her teeth. "Good."

"However, I disagreed then and I disagree now. My question was entirely in the spirit of the game," he said at her heels.

"It was personal!" She picked up her pace.

He pulled up next to her. "It was indeed."

"You had no right to ask it."

"I'm afraid I have to disagree with that as well."

"Imagine my surprise." Again she stopped and turned to him. "Are you going to follow me through this entire house?"

"That's my plan." He grinned in an unrepentant manner that would have been charming at another time. Now, it was infuriating.

"Your question was . . ." She struggled for the right word. "Not the sort of thing you expect an answer to in front of virtual strangers. It was the wrong place and the wrong time to ask me something like that. It was private and personal and—"

"Don't forget important." He accepted her cloak from the footman. "I thought it was important."

"Ha!" She scarcely noticed him helping her on with her cloak. He was right though—it was important. At least to her. But what did it really mean to him? "One does not frivolously wager on important questions."

"I didn't wager on the question," he said mildly, accepting his coat from the footman and putting it on. "I wagered on the cards. I wagered *for* the answer."

"It's the same thing." She waved off his comment.

"No, actually, it's not." He took her arm and steered her down the corridor. "Although I suppose now we're getting into semantics, which will serve neither of us well."

"I scarcely think—"

"Suffice it to say, an opportunity presented itself and I took advantage of it."

She snorted. "Indeed you did." She braced herself. "Are you trying to humiliate me?"

He laughed. "Good Lord, no."

She glared at him. "This is not funny."

"Oh, but it is." He released her arm, opened a door, and grinned. "It's extremely funny and you would realize it if you weren't so busy being indignant. And annoyed."

"That question was completely unfair."

He nodded. "Probably."

"Furthermore, it's not the kind of question that should be asked to only one party."

"I agree."

"If one party answers, the other party should as well."

"Absolutely."

"The fact that you agree with me does not negate the . . . the *unsuitable* nature of the question!" She huffed. "Particularly in the setting in which it was asked."

"So it's not the question itself that has you so irate, but the arena in which it was posed?"

"I am irate about it all," she said in a lofty manner, but he might well have been right. Nonetheless, she was not going to admit it to him. "And justifiably so."

She raised her chin and stepped through the doorway, the frosty February night air pulling her up short. "Good Lord, it's cold out here." She glanced around. She'd never been on the terrace before and she really couldn't see much now. Clouds drifted across a pale crescent moon. The terrace was little more than shadows and darkness, and a hint of snow was in the air. "What are you doing? Why are we out here?"

"I'm changing the rules." He stepped away from her, farther onto the terrace, as if he was looking for something.

She wrapped her cloak tighter around herself and scoffed. "You can't change the rules."

"Why not? You did." He vanished in the shadows.

"I couldn't answer your damned question because I don't know the answer," she called.

"And I am supposed to believe that because you have never been less than honest?" His voice drifted back from what she assumed was the far end of the terrace.

"Yes," she snapped, and ruthlessly ignored the voice in the back of her head that pointed out that might not be entirely true.

"Well, I don't believe you, Lucy Merryweather."

"That is not my concern." She sniffed. "Where are you anyway? I find speaking to a disembodied voice, in the dark, in the cold, rather eerie and extremely disconcerting."

"Right here." The strike of a match sounded and fire flamed, illuminating Cameron. He lit a gas lamp perched on the stone balustrade of the terrace.

She narrowed her eyes. "What are you up to?"

"You're the second woman today who has asked me that question."

"Which should tell you something."

"Possibly." He chuckled. "As I said, I am changing the rules."

"You can't—"

He held up a hand to quiet her. "I most certainly

can, but *rules* might not be the right term. Perhaps it's the regret that needs to change."

"You can't change a regret." She really didn't want to be the least bit curious, but she was. "You can make amends for it or atone for it, but you can't simply change it."

"I'm not going to change it, I'm going to substitute one regret for another."

"You can't do that either."

"And yet I intend to." He moved along the balustrade and lit a three-armed candelabra positioned a dozen feet or so from the lamp. "I promised to assist you in accomplishing those things your great-aunt never managed. I think we can both agree that our wager tonight elevated what was a rather lackluster game into the realm of high stakes, can we not?"

"Well, yes, I suppose." Even if she did hate to admit it.

"So you may check that off your list."

"Possibly." Although she really couldn't since she had played but certainly hadn't won. Worse, his question kept repeating itself in her head. There were several reasons she could think of as to why he would ask such a thing. One was to embarrass her, and he had denied that. As for any other reasons, well, when one looked at it in a calm and rational way, as difficult as that was, they weren't all that dire.

"I have been considering the remaining items

on your list." Cameron continued to move around the perimeter of the terrace. "There are some that can't be accomplished at this time of year."

"I realize that." She pulled her cloak tighter around her. "Can't we discuss this inside? It's entirely too cold, if you haven't noticed."

"My, you do get cranky when you're cold." He chuckled.

Her jaw tightened. "Go on."

"It struck me that swimming naked in the moonlight is one of those things that sounds delightful but might not live up to expectations." He shot her a pointed look. "Believe me, I know."

"Do you?" Perhaps it was the cold or the fact that he could be so amusing, but her anger had definitely dimmed. What was he up to?

"First, there's the choice of the appropriate location. There is a pond on the grounds here." He circled behind her and she had to turn to keep him in sight. "Did you know that?"

"I did." She nodded. "There was ice-skating there at Christmas."

"So I thought skating in the moonlight might serve the same purpose." He lit a third lantern sitting on a bench near the manor wall.

"Did you?" She resisted the urge to smile. "Dare I ask if you intended skating to be accomplished naked as well?"

"Believe me, I did consider it but, as you have

pointed out before, I am not overly fond of the cold. And I couldn't expect you to skate naked if I was not going to skate naked. It seemed, well, inconsiderate."

"How very thoughtful of you."

"Thank you. I thought so." He continued his progress around the terrace, stopping here and there to light a candle or a lamp. She wondered how many there were and how he had managed to arrange for them. "And then I realized there was very little light tonight." He glanced up at the moon. "The full moon was over a week ago. This is a very feeble, waning crescent tonight."

"That does create a problem if one is attempting to swim or skate in the moonlight."

"It also makes navigating to a pond on unfamiliar grounds on a cold night exceptionally difficult. So I thought a terrace would do just as well."

She raised a brow. "For skating?"

"Come now, Miss Merryweather." He shook his head in a chastising manner. "I am changing the regret, remember?" He lit another candle, then glanced around in a satisfied manner.

The lamps and candles glowed in the sharp night air as if touched by magic. In spite of the cold, or perhaps because of it, the terrace took on the feel of a place of enchantment, a winter palace. A place of dreams and illusion and romance. A place where anything could happen.

"I gather this is your attempt to provide a substitute for moonlight?"

"Exactly." He grinned. "And a damn fine job I've done too."

"It is possibly somewhat impressive," she said grudgingly, and smiled in spite of herself. "As I don't see that we can swim or skate here, what else are you changing?"

"I was hoping you'd ask." He turned and signaled to someone out of sight. A moment later the strains of a violin drifted around them.

Sheer delight washed through her and she wondered exactly when she had stopped being angry with him.

"I would imagine that your great-aunt would have quite regretted not dancing on a crisp night under a pale moon in an enchanted setting had she passed on the opportunity, don't you agree?"

Lucy blew a long breath and admitted defeat. "I know I would."

"Excellent." He grinned. "Miss Merryweather, allow me to introduce myself," he said with a formal bow. "I am Lord Cameron Effington and I should very much like the honor of this dance."

Her breath caught. "This is silly."

"Yes, I know. It seems to me you're rather fond of silly on occasion."

"Yes, I suppose I am." She sighed in resignation and stepped into his arms. A moment later they were circling the terrace, the cold forgotten. "How did you arrange all of this?"

"One learns how things work and who to ask for what when one grows up in a household like this," he said in a matter-of-fact manner. "If you're especially lucky, you discover a member of the household staff plays an instrument, in this case a violin, and can be convinced to play while standing in an open doorway."

"My, that was lucky."

"It was indeed. I was prepared to hum."

She laughed.

"I have been surprisingly lucky tonight." He paused. "You approve then?"

"Goodness, Cameron, it's wonderful." Even nature conspired in the spell Cameron had wrought. The pale moon peeked out from behind dark-edged clouds like a celestial goddess stealing a look at the mortals below. The night itself was still, without even a suggestion of a breeze. The music floated on the air and drifted into Lucy's soul. It was indeed magic. And he had done it all for her. Her heart fluttered. "And, well, perfect."

"I'm glad you like it." He paused. "I knew I needed to do something, something grand and perfect, once I learned from Lady Dunwell that you discovered my real name at the ball."

"I can't imagine this was easier than simply confessing your deception."

"You'd be surprised," he said under his breath. "I suppose confession might be easier when one starts out with a clear deception in mind. In my case, one thing simply led to another and before I knew it, well, it was messy and convoluted and I had no idea where to start. But I didn't plan to deceive you."

"Thank you for saying so." She paused. "I really didn't think you had."

"That's something, at any rate."

"Goodness, Cameron, I have always thought that I was an excellent judge of character." She shook her head. "I would hate for you to prove me wrong."

His hand tightened on hers. "As would I."

"Believe me, I do understand the expectations placed on children by their parents and their families."

"Expectations?" A cautious note sounded in his voice.

"Yes, of course. To be, to do exactly what we are supposed to be and do."

"Ah yes." He led her through a flawless turn. "You were supposed to be part of a banking dynasty."

"Which was never my desire, by the way. It seems to me one can choose to do what other people and society itself has decided is appropriate or one can follow one's own path, no matter how difficult it may be." She shrugged. "Although it's much easier simply to do as expected."

"Not upsetting the cart as it were."

"Exactly." She nodded. "Even if everyone else thinks we're foolish or choosing the wrong path. But you could have confided in me, you know." She gazed up at him. "Ambition is admirable. I would never fault you for wanting to succeed on your own."

He grinned. "How very American of you."

"I am very American," she said primly. "I can't imagine how difficult choosing your own way in life would be for the son of a duke. To go against one's family's plans and wishes."

"Oh." Surprise sounded in his voice. "Well, yes."

"I suspect a private investigator is not what your father envisioned for you."

"No, he most certainly did not," he said slowly.

"Which is why you use the name Fairchild."

"I have always used Fairchild professionally." His tone was measured. Even now that the truth was out, the poor dear was watching his words.

"It seems to me if you are doing what you want to do in spite of your family's objections, then you must prove their objections wrong."

"And how would I do that?"

"Why, by being the very best private investigator you can, of course," she said firmly, and resisted the urge to point out that he hadn't been very good at his chosen profession thus far.

"That certainly makes sense." He smiled weakly. "Particularly as my family tends to be very accomplished. My oldest brother is brilliant in matters of finance and management. He will make an excellent duke one day. My two other brothers excel in the family's business pursuits. And my sister is pursuing the arts. Painting and sculpture and whatever else strikes her fancy at any given moment. My mother is aware of Grace's work but my father has no idea."

She nodded. "It is more difficult for women."

"Indeed it is. Not all women are as strong-minded and independent as you, although you and Grace would get along quite well."

"Well, as much as I hate to admit it, independence is fairly new to me as is the idea that I'm the least bit strong-minded. I like to think I was simply waiting for the right time to . . . to burst forth."

He grinned. "Like a caterpillar."

"Not exactly the example I would have chosen, but I suppose so." She thought for a moment. "I am trying very hard to be the woman no one expected me to be and I find it"—she searched for the right words—"exhilarating. It suits me. I like it very much. It's suspiciously like fun. And I am having a great deal of fun."

"I have noticed that." He chuckled. "I'd like you to meet my sister and my mother and grandmother as well. You'd like them and they would certainly like you."

"What a lovely thing to say."

"Not at all. I can't imagine anyone not liking you." He smiled down at her. "May I confess something to you?"

"Yes, of course." She breathed a sigh of relief. It was past time for his confession, although she wasn't sure what was left to confess. She already knew about his name and his family connections. And understood as well that his choice of profession wasn't something his family approved of. That was not the least bit unexpected. Beyond that, unless he was going to confess an interest in her money, and she doubted that, she couldn't imagine what other secrets he might have.

"I quite enjoyed our dance together at the ambassador's ball."

"As did I."

"It seemed to me as if we had danced together before. Or always." He held her a little tighter. "As if we were fated to dance together."

"You thought that, did you?" she said lightly, as if it was of no consequence. As if it didn't make her stomach knot and her heart thud. As if it wasn't quite wonderful.

"Will you?"

"Will I what?"

"Will you dance with me always?" His gaze met hers. "Will you dance with me for the rest of your days?"

She stumbled and stopped short. "What are you asking?"

"I'm asking you to spend the rest of your life with me." He drew a deep breath. "As my wife."

"As your what?"

"My wife." He cleared his throat. "I'm asking you to marry me."

"Cameron." She stared. "I don't know what to say."

He smiled. "Yes is always a good answer."

"I hadn't really planned on marriage," she said slowly. "At least not yet."

"Neither had I. But then I hadn't planned on you either." He chuckled. "But one should never waste an opportunity when it presents itself."

"And I am an opportunity?" *Because I have money?* She tried and failed to ignore the thought.

"You, Miss Merryweather, are a gift." He took her hands in his. "A treasure I neither expected nor sought. I further suspect that you, Lucy Merryweather, are the love of my life."

"Oh my." Her heart caught.

"I don't want to reach the end of my days with regrets. You and your quest have taught me that." He shook his head. "Losing you would be a regret I would take to my grave."

"Love is never a regret," she murmured. And dear Lord, she did love him.

His expression sobered. "There are still some things I need to tell you."

She gazed into his eyes and surrendered. "I don't care."

"But—"

"Very well." She pulled her hand from his and crossed her arms over her chest. "Are you married?"

His eyes widened in surprise. "No."

"Betrothed?"

He shook his head. "No."

"Are you engaged now or have you ever been engaged in criminal conduct?"

"Let me think." His brow furrowed. "No, I don't believe so."

"Are you going to break my heart?" she said abruptly, and held her breath. "I would like to know that in advance."

"I might ask you the same thing."

She stared into his dark eyes. "The last thing I would ever want is to break your heart."

"Good." He took her hand and pulled it to his lips. "Because I would rather cut my own heart out than break yours."

She smiled. "A simple *never* would suffice."

"Then never it is." He paused. "But, Lucy, there are things we need to talk about."

She placed a finger on his lips to quiet him. "Tonight, they're not important. You made this a place of magic for me, for us, and I don't want anything to spoil it."

"Neither do I." He smiled. "Then will you marry me, Lucy Merryweather?"

"I . . ." She wanted nothing more than to say

yes. To throw her arms around him and press her lips to his. To tell him that she loved him and would love him forever. But some small, reasonable part of her urged caution. She chose her words carefully. "I do need to think about it before I give you an answer."

His eyes widened in surprise. "You do?"

"Of course I do."

He stared and dropped her hand. "What is there to think about?"

"Why, obviously there are any number of matters to consider." She ticked the points off on her fingers. "My family and yours, for one thing. Where we would live, for another. Whether or not I would continue my quest, of course. All sorts of practical matters that need to be addressed."

"I don't care about practical matters."

"One of us should."

"I have no desire to be practical."

"Frankly, neither do I." She pulled a deep breath. "But if this were any other decision, particularly one this important, you would be the first to tell me to give something like this due consideration. In fact, you would be most irate if I didn't."

"I have given it due consideration," he said staunchly.

"Due consideration on both sides." She shook her head. "I am not going to be swept away by a romantic gesture no matter how wonderful. Marriage is for the rest of our lives. It shouldn't be taken lightly."

"I'm not taking it lightly. I've never asked anyone to marry me before." His tone sharpened and he stared at her. "I've given this a great deal of thought."

"I haven't." Admittedly, when she'd realized she wanted to spend the rest of her life with him, it had occurred to her.

"Hasn't it crossed your mind before now?"

"Marrying you?"

"You needn't say it as if I had asked you to swim an ocean or fly to the moon or do something completely absurd."

"Not at all but—"

"But." His eyes narrowed. "You think I'm beneath you."

"Don't be absurd." She scoffed.

"Until recently you thought I was nothing more than a . . . an inept private investigator."

"Do remember in the future that you were the one to use the word *inept.*" Her tone hardened. "Not I."

"You would never consider marriage to a man who had to work for a living."

She stared in disbelief. "That's neither fair nor true. And even if it was, if I was that . . . that *shallow,* the fact that you are the son of a duke would negate that objection, wouldn't it?"

"One would think," he snapped.

"Under your reasoning, why, I should jump at the chance to marry you."

"Most women would." He shrugged in an offhand manner, as if the idea of any woman not leaping to accept his proposal was so far-fetched as to be unbelievable.

"I am not most women. I would never marry anyone because of what they are." Her eyes narrowed. "I am more concerned with who they are."

"You know who I am." His jaw tightened. "I am the man who has done everything in his power to keep you from ruining your life with scandal and improper behavior. I am the man who has gone out of his way to help you in your silly little quest."

She gasped. "Silly little quest?"

He ignored her. "I am the man who has made certain you did not fall prey to unscrupulous French cooks and artists bent on seduction!"

"I would never—"

"I am the man who just foolishly asked you to marry him!" He glared at her. "Bloody hell, Lucy, I am the man who loves you!"

"You're also the man who deceived me from the moment we met," she pointed out. He had absolutely no right to be quite so indignant. "As well as the man who didn't trust me enough to tell me the truth!"

"You know the truth now."

"Through no fault of yours!"

"I intended to tell you!"

"Intentions, Mr. Fairchild or Effington or whomever you are calling yourself tonight, scarcely count if they never come to fruition!" she snapped. "You had any number of opportunities to confess."

"Yes, well, admittedly that might have been a mistake on my part."

"Might have been a mistake?" She pulled a steadying breath in an effort to calm herself. It didn't help. "I am not inclined to make a decision at the moment on your generous offer of marriage. I shall consider it and give you my answer in the morning." She turned and stalked toward the door.

"What about my other question?"

"Answering one will give you the answer to the other," she called over her shoulder, and continued into the manor, avoiding the library and the parlor and heading straight to her rooms.

She almost expected him to follow her and wasn't sure if she was disappointed by his failure to do so or grateful. They were both saying things they didn't really mean and it was probably best to part now before either of them said something that was truly unforgivable.

Besides, while she had done what she was certain was right a few minutes ago, now she wasn't sure if she had been extremely sensible or had just made the biggest mistake of her life. The horrible heavy weight squeezing her heart indicated the latter. Still, try as she might, she wasn't entirely confident he wasn't still hiding something.

But Cameron had said he loved her and she did love him. And while she truly believed love was never a regret, she couldn't help but wonder if, sometimes, it might well be a mistake.

Regrets Set to Rights

~~Beat men at their own game.~~
~~Preferably for very high stakes.~~

. . . and there is a great deal of gossip about her. Mother says, should I encounter her, I am not to so much as bid her good day. Which does seem rather silly, as though her scandalous ways are somehow contagious.

From what I have heard, she is not at all regretful of her indiscreet dalliances. I would never say it to anyone, as it might imply approval on my part, but I suspect she is having a great deal of fun. And indeed, it does seem to me that taking a lover, or in her case apparently, one after another, would be rather exciting. Not that I ever would, of course. No, I am too well bred and too cognizant of proper behavior to do such a thing.

Still, it would be fun to have a lover one day. Or perhaps nothing more than an evening of indiscretion, a romantic interlude, with someone I plan never to see again. How very wrong and terribly exciting and yes, quite an adventure . . .

from the journal of Miss Lucinda Merryweather, 1806

Chapter Eighteen

Lady Dunwell was wrong. A bad plan was not better than no plan at all.

Cam poured another glass of whisky, took a fast swallow, and resumed pacing the floor of his room, trying to determine exactly what had gone wrong. He'd attempted to sleep but knew full well it was unlikely if not impossible. Lucy had said she'd have an answer for him in the morning and he couldn't be certain what that answer would be. Especially given how they'd left each other.

He was extremely proud of the enchanted winter setting he'd created on the terrace; aside from the lack of falling snow, it was a scene straight from a snow globe. The rest of the evening was filled with missteps and mistakes. For one thing, he never should have wagered that blasted question, but the opportunity had been too good to resist. All he wanted to know was if she loved him. And really, what man in his position wouldn't? A simple yes was all that was required. If she loved him, he could certainly find the courage to tell her everything. If she didn't, well, it scarcely mattered.

But Lucy was right. What was he thinking? It had been the wrong place and the wrong time. He should have saved that particular question for the terrace. After he'd let the magic he'd arranged do its work. He should have taken her in his arms, declared his love, and only then asked if she felt the same.

He'd never before gone to such romantic lengths for a woman and, regardless of how the evening had ended, he was quite pleased with his efforts and the result. Lucy had loved it. But asking her to marry him then was, at least in hindsight, not his wisest move. That had not been planned. No, his plan was simply to enchant her. And then to tell her everything. Of course, he had suspected that she already knew it all. That he wasn't a private investigator hired to watch her but a journalist for a somewhat scandalous paper using her life as the basis for his stories. Unfortunately, he was wrong. He should have realized she didn't know the worst of his deception when he'd arrived at the manor and she wasn't furious with him. That was a clue he shouldn't have missed.

He had tried to tell her and he would have if she hadn't stopped him. At least he thought he would have. He still didn't have quite the right words, but he had been confident that they would come when necessary. Not that he had said anything right from the moment he'd asked her to marry him. Yet another part of his vague and not very clever plan, although he hadn't intended to propose at that particular moment. The words simply slipped out of his mouth. While in hindsight, it might not have been the brightest thing to do, at the moment he said the words they had felt, well, right.

He certainly never considered that she would want to think about it. No, he was fairly certain she was in love with him even if she hadn't yet admitted it. Surely one couldn't feel the way he did if those feelings weren't shared. He supposed it was possible that he could be entirely wrong. After all, unrequited love and heartbreak had long kept poets busy. No, he refused to think about that possibility. He knew her well enough to know how she felt about him. Because if he was wrong, then she had lied. She would indeed break his heart.

He blew a long breath. He really couldn't fault her for not giving him an immediate answer. But he had been, well, stunned. Once again, she was right. Given any other significant decision, he would have indeed urged her not to do anything rash, to consider her answer and everything that went along with it. It was practical and sensible and he didn't care. He wanted her to be swept away. God knows, he was.

She was right as well when she had charged that he had never told her the truth. That she had discovered it through no fault of his. He paused in midstep. Perhaps that was the real reason for her hesitation to accept his proposal. Perhaps she suspected there was still something he was hiding.

And in spite of his efforts tonight to tell her everything, he wasn't entirely certain he would have managed it.

There was only one thing to do. He was a writer, by God, and if he couldn't find the right words to say, he could certainly put the right words to paper. He tossed back a bracing swallow of whisky, then sat down at the desk in the alcove of his room. He selected a piece of stationery, picked up a pen, and considered exactly what to say. The simple facts of the matter would be best, coupled with his heartfelt apology and a vow to spend the rest of his life making up for his deception. He drew a deep breath and started to write.

If he wanted Lucy in his life, by his side for the rest of his days, he was going to have to win her trust as well as her heart. And hope he wasn't too late.

She was sure of it now—she had indeed made a dreadful mistake.

Lucy wrung her hands in front of her and paced her room. She had attempted to sleep but that was futile. The very effort was pointless. How on earth could she sleep when she might have lost the man she loved? And *lost* wasn't even the right word. Why, she had practically thrown him away. She had simply thought it was a good idea not to leap into acceptance of his proposal but to deliberate about it in a calm and rational manner. And then say yes.

Surely he wouldn't be deterred by a minor obstacle like her very sensible desire to rationally consider his proposal. But he had not been at all gracious about it. No, he'd been quite irate and had made a few comments that were definitely uncalled for. Not that she could blame him. She heaved a heartfelt sigh. If their positions were reversed, she too would have been upset. Her heart twisted. It was obvious that she had hurt him. Which only increased her dismay. It was simply her attempt to be sensible even if sensible was the last thing she wanted.

She'd always thought she'd know the right man the first time he kissed her. And in spite of the critique she'd given that kiss, she wondered now if indeed she did know. Because in ways too vague to express in words, somewhere deep down inside, it had been more than a little wonderful.

She had to set this to rights.

But there was still something he was hiding. He had tried to make some sort of confession last night, but obviously it wasn't of any real importance as he certainly hadn't tried very hard. It had been her observation that when a man had something really important to say and had, at last, worked up the courage to say it, he'd let nothing deter him. Besides, her married friends agreed that it was not at all uncommon for men to use the occasion of a proposal to confess all sorts of minor misdeeds, as if by doing so they could wipe the slate clean and start anew.

Even so, there remained a niggling sense of unease that there was a matter of significance he had yet to reveal. And dishonesty did not seem the best way to start a life together. She had meant it when she said she didn't care and that it wasn't important, but that had been in the romance of the moment and really she did care. But did she care enough to allow whatever he concealed to ruin their future and break both their hearts?

Absolutely not.

Resolve swept through her. If he couldn't find his way clear to confess everything to her, she might simply have to beat it out of him. Goodness, she had ridden an elephant and breached a gentlemen's club. She could certainly wring the truth out of the man she loved.

But first, she had to tell him how she felt. She couldn't let this wait until morning. By morning he might have decided she wasn't worth the trouble. Which either meant he didn't love her enough to fight for her or he was too badly hurt to forgive her. Good Lord, this was so much more complicated than the years when she was going to marry a man who didn't make her toes curl and her heart flutter.

She'd write him a note and slip it under his

door, where he would find it first thing in the morning. Lucy sat down at the small ladies desk on the far side of the room, took a piece of Millworth stationery from the paper rack, and stared at the blank page for a long moment. There were any number of things she could say but perhaps at this point brevity was best. Yes, indeed, it wasn't necessary to write more than one word. She picked up the pen and wrote with a flourish.

Yes.

That would do. She got to her feet, tightened the sash of her robe, sent a quick prayer heavenward, and moved to the door. It was somewhere in the wee hours of the morning. She had no idea of the actual time; there was no clock in her room, which she found most disconcerting and vowed, as she had every night since she'd returned to Millworth, to ask for one.

She pulled open the door, stepped into the hallway, turned, and came face-to-face with Cameron.

"What—"

"I was leaving you a note," he said quickly, waving a folded sheet of stationery.

She stared at him. "I was about to bring you a note."

He studied her carefully. "This strikes me as a good sign."

"I suppose that depends on what our notes say," she said slowly.

"You do have a point but I—"

"Goodness, Cameron, if we are about to embark on a long discussion, we can't do it here in the hallway in the middle of the night." She stepped back into her room and gestured for him to join her. "Don't stand there—come in."

He hesitated. "I don't think I should."

"Why? Do you intend to ravish me right here and now?"

He bit back a smile. "I don't intend—"

"And I don't think we can sort out our differences in the hall where anyone might see or hear us." She grabbed his sleeve and yanked him into the room. "Good Lord, Cameron, are you trying to ruin me?" She gently closed the door behind him.

"Actually, I was trying to avoid it."

She stared at him and at that moment made a decision. "Pity."

His brow rose. "What?"

Her courage faltered. "Here." She thrust her note at him. "Read mine first."

"Very well." He took the note, unfolded it, and studied it for far longer than it took to read a single word.

"Well?" She tried and failed to hide the impatience in her voice. And the hope.

"Well," he said slowly, and his gaze met hers. "Is this the answer to the question I won or the one I asked?"

"I told you the answer to one would give you the answer to the other." She held her breath. "Well?"

"Well." A slow, wicked smile spread across his face. "You have excellent penmanship."

Once again, she resisted the urge to smack him. "I've always thought my S's were a little weak."

"Your S's are perfect." He glanced at the note, then back at her. "So, you do love me?"

She nodded. "I'm afraid so."

"And you will marry me?"

"There are still practical details to consider but . . ." Her heart caught in her throat. "Yes."

"Good God, Lucy." He pulled her into his arms and gazed down at her. "I thought I'd lost you."

"I thought I'd lost you as well." She swallowed hard. "Isn't it customary, in situations like this, for the prospective groom or rather the intended groom to kiss the future bride or—"

"Sometimes you talk entirely too much." He grinned down at her. "Have I ever told you that?"

She shook her head. "I don't recall."

"However, in this particular case, you are absolutely right." His lips met hers in a kiss tender and warm and surprisingly restrained. The man really was trying not to let this go too far.

Desire washed through her and with it need and longing. She slid her arms around his neck and pressed herself closer against him, and her mouth opened to his. So much for restraint. His tongue teased hers, the sensation both odd and exciting.

He tasted of whisky and desire, as intoxicating as any spirit. Heat pooled between her legs.

He pulled away and stared down at her. "Good Lord, Lucy."

She grinned. "Yes?"

He pulled a deep shuddering breath. "I should go."

"Oh." She reached up and brushed her lips across his. "I don't think so."

"Lucy." He groaned. "You have no idea what you're doing to me."

She rolled her hips tentatively against his and could feel his erection through his nightclothes and hers. Her breath caught. She was well aware of this part of a man's body, but it had never been pressed against her in such an intimate and arousing manner, as daunting as it was intriguing. Was this what she did to him? The oddest sense of power surged through her. How delightful.

"Actually, Cameron." She pulled his head back down to hers. "I'm quite aware of what I'm doing to you." Her lips pressed to his and her tongue dueled with his. His arms tightened around her, her breasts flattened against his chest, her hips pressed tighter against the hardness beneath his clothing. Dear Lord, she wanted him and all that wanting him meant.

The increasing desire within her lent a frantic edge to her actions, sweeping away any sense of self-control. She slid her hands down the front of his dressing gown, over hard planes of his chest evident under the fabric of his nightclothes, and continued downward. Her hand trailed over the flat of his stomach and fumbled with the knot of his sash.

His hand caught hers. "Lucy." His gaze bored into hers. "Do you know what you're doing?"

"Absolutely not." She leaned forward and kissed the base of his throat. "I've never done this sort of thing before."

"Now is not the time . . ."

"I think now is the perfect time." She brushed his hand away and gazed up into his eyes. "Do you love me?"

"Yes."

"Do you intend to marry me?"

"Without question."

"Soon?"

"As soon as humanly possible."

"Excellent." The knot loosened. "I may not have given the idea of marriage any consideration but I have thought about this." She pulled the sash free and tossed it aside. "In fact, it has come to mind rather frequently."

"Oh?" He swallowed hard.

"Haven't you?"

"Constantly."

She paused and stared at him. "Are you nervous?"

"No." He scoffed. "Of course not."

"You have done this before, haven't you?"

She pushed his dressing gown off his shoulders.

"Yes, of course." Indignation sounded in his voice, but he shrugged out of his dressing gown nonetheless and let it drop to the floor.

"Pajamas, Cameron?" She stared at the loose-fitting, striped silk shirt and trousers. "How very progressive."

"I suppose. I like them. Nightshirts make me feel like a little boy."

"This is lovely," she murmured, and ran her hands over his silk-covered shoulders and down his arms. "You don't feel like a little boy." She gathered the edges of the silk shirt in her hands and pulled it over his head. His chest was hard and muscled. A smattering of hair covered his abdomen and arrowed down to disappear beneath the silk trousers. She sucked in a sharp breath. "And you certainly don't look like one."

"Lucy!"

"Surely you're not embarrassed?" She ran her hands lightly over his chest, reveling in the hot feel of his flesh and the way his muscles tightened beneath her fingers.

"No, but . . ." He drew in a shuddering breath and she had the distinct impression he was doing everything possible to keep himself firmly under control. Oh, that would never do.

"I wouldn't think so." She trailed her fingers along the indentation between his silk trousers and his waist. "This is not new to you after all."

"You, however, have not done this before."

"This what?" She leaned forward and flicked her tongue over his nipple."

"Good Lord." He grabbed her shoulders and took half a step back.

She stared up at him. "In spite of my obvious enthusiasm at the moment, no, of course I haven't."

"That makes it . . ."

"Extremely exciting." She cast him a wicked smile.

"Yes, but." He huffed. "There's a great deal of pressure, you know, when a man is taking a lady to bed for the first time."

"Goodness, Cameron." And he thought she talked too much. "I don't see why."

"Aside from the obvious reasons, you weren't especially complimentary the first time we kissed."

"The first time you said you weren't prepared." She shrugged out of his grasp, moved closer, and slid her hand over the front of the tented silk covering his arousal. "You seem well prepared now." The silk was no more than a whisper and she ached at the feel of him beneath her hand. "Extremely prepared."

"Lucy." He groaned and grabbed her hand, then guided it beneath the waistband and down the trousers to his erection. "Feel what you have done to me."

"Gladly." Her hand closed around his member, hot and hard and thick. It throbbed in her hand as if it had a life of its own. Shivers of need fluttered through her. She teased him, stroked him, running her fingers along his hard length, and savored the thrill of touching him so intimately.

He rested his head on her shoulder and murmured against her skin. "There's no going back now, you know."

"Good." She hesitated, then whispered, "I would like to see you. All of you."

He groaned, then straightened. "I have no desire to be naked by myself." A wicked gleam shone in his eyes. His gaze locked with hers and he quickly untied the ribbons of her wrapper.

"You don't?" It was her turn to swallow the lump in her throat. Up till now she had felt rather like the seducer and had relished the excitement of exploring him and watching him melt beneath her touch. Now the tide had apparently turned. Cameron had at last given up all attempts at restraint, and she suspected she was about to be seduced and quite thoroughly at that.

"Absolutely not." He whipped her around and pulled off her robe. He kissed the back of her neck and slid his hands along her sides and over the curve of her hips, leaving a trail of awareness in his wake.

"I suspect you're no longer nervous," she said weakly. Odd how she had been perfectly confident in what she was about to do a minute ago; now, she wasn't quite as sure.

"I never was." A faint growl sounded in his voice. Without warning he gathered the fabric of her nightgown in his hands and pulled it up and over her head. The night air enveloped her, cooling her heated flesh, and she shivered with anticipation as much as the cold.

He pulled her back against him and she realized he had managed to rid himself of his silk trousers. His erection nudged between her legs and, good Lord, she felt her own moisture slick against him. How very . . . erotic. He wrapped one arm around her waist, his free hand cupped her breast, and she gasped.

"Lucy," he murmured against her neck.

She melted back against him, losing herself in the way his hand felt on her skin, holding her breast, his fingers teasing her tightening nipple. Her eyes closed, her back arched, and she rested her head against his chest. She'd never so much as suspected that a man's hand on her breast would feel so incredible.

His hand trailed downward, across her stomach, and she shivered with the intensity of his caress. With every touch her flesh ached for more. She pushed his hand lower, wanting him to touch that part of her now throbbing with need, wondering if she had a heretofore unsuspected wanton nature or if every woman at this point felt this way. Not that she cared or that it mattered. Not now.

He slipped his hand between her legs and held her, cupped her. She could feel her wetness on his hand. She had touched herself on occasion, even though it was most certainly a sin and she would surely burn in hell for it. She had always considered the risk of eternal damnation to be worth it as the sensations were so exquisite. But nothing had quite prepared her for someone else's touch, someone else's hand, someone else's fingers sliding over her. She sucked in a short breath and held it, her attention, her very being, focused on that part of her that ached for his attention. His fingers explored the folds of her flesh, then slid over that point of acute sensation, slowly and deliberately, and she marveled that her legs continued to support her. She could die quite happily like this, lost in a world of utter sensation. A world where she existed only in the touch of his hand and the heat of his body behind hers.

He slid a finger into her and she gasped. Then another, then withdrew and pumped his fingers in again, each thrust better than the last. Behind her, his breath was labored and she realized as intoxicating as this was, it was not enough. Not for him and certainly not for her. She wanted more.

She pushed his hand away, then turned in his embrace to face him. "Cameron, in a strictly practical sense . . ." Goodness, her voice was breathless. "This is far more awkward than it has to be."

His eyes were glazed and dark with passion. "Is it?"

"Not that it's not extremely, well, arousing but . . ." She glanced at the bed. "Perhaps—"

He laughed, scooped her into his arms, and carried her to the bed. "We wouldn't want it to be awkward."

He dropped her on the bed and stood grinning over her.

"No." Her gaze slid from his eyes to his, well, his arousal, and it looked much larger than it had felt. She reached out for him and pulled him down onto the bed with her. "Awkward is not at all what I had in mind."

He pulled her into his arms and his hands wandered over her, skimming along her sides, caressing her stomach, teasing between her legs. He traced the line of her jaw with his lips, then kissed her neck, her throat. His mouth moved ever lower, tasting and teasing with his lips and his teeth and his tongue. He took one breast in his mouth and tugged gently with his teeth and she moaned and lightly bit his shoulder. Her hands caressed the back of his neck and traced aimless patterns on his shoulders and his back and his buttocks, and she reveled in the feel of the planes and valleys of his body. Of hard, firm flesh and well-defined muscle and the searing feel of his naked skin pressed against her own.

His hand again slid between her legs, his fingers

caressing and exploring. She wondered if he could feel her throb against him. She slipped her hand between their bodies and found his erection and squeezed him, stroked him. His breath quickened with need, her blood coursed through her veins, and she wanted—no—needed more.

She shifted to wrap her legs around his. "Cameron, I want . . ."

"You," he whispered, and positioned himself between her legs. "Only, always you."

He eased into her slowly and tenderly, as if he was afraid she would break. In spite of her desire, she braced herself. She had never done this before, after all. It was her understanding that there would be, well, pain, and she was not overly fond of pain. But she had been assured that any distress would ease fairly quickly. There was a mild stinging, nothing overwhelming, and she wondered if riding astride had made a difference. She had heard that. Still, a certain amount of discomfort was to be expected obviously when a rather large, hard part of his body was invading a relatively uncharted part of hers.

He slid into her, deeper. She angled her hips toward him and wrapped her legs around his, urging him on. He paused for a long moment, allowing her to adjust to the feel of him inside her. Strange and odd and somehow rich. The intimacy, being one with this man, was as powerful as the physical sensations and she uttered a silent prayer of gratitude. She had never suspected it would be this intense, this feeling of being filled with him. As if their souls were bound as completely as their bodies.

He slid back the tiniest bit, then pushed into her again and her breath caught. Again he pulled back, then thrust forward. And again. And with each thrust the most remarkable feeling of pure pleasure grew. And need. Aching and relentless. Slowly, she met his thrusts with her hips, rocking against him. And then she moved faster and he moved in kind.

Together they rocked harder and faster. Desire, need, tension coiled within her, like a spring being wound too tight. He pounded into her and she met each thrust with her own, arching upward to meet him. To welcome him. They moved as one in a rhythm as natural as breathing, as right as forever. The muscles of his back strained under her fingertips. Her legs tightened around his, urging him on.

Faster and harder they moved, climbed, seeking, searching. His heart thudded against hers. Her body throbbed around him. An ever increasing, ever faster, ever tightening whirlpool of sheer ecstasy and unbridled sensation.

And something inside her stilled and then erupted, exploded in waves of absolute pleasure that shuddered through her body and arched her back and seized her very soul. And his body too quaked and shuddered and he strained against her and called out her name.

And they collapsed together, arms and legs entwined, bodies pressed together, their breathing still fast and labored, their hearts beating as one. For a long moment they could do nothing but lay wrapped around each other and she marveled at the sheer exquisiteness of what they had shared and what they had found. And knew being one with him was not merely the joining of their bodies but the coupling of their hearts.

At last, with a shared reluctance, they untangled themselves.

"My." Lucy stared at the ceiling and tried very hard not to giggle. Good Lord, if she was going to hell simply for touching herself, there was probably somewhere entirely worse for this. But well worth it. "You certainly were prepared."

Cameron snorted back a laugh. "Thank you?"

"Oh, it was a compliment." She rolled over, folded her arms on his chest and rested her chin on her hands. "Most definitely a compliment."

He chuckled and wrapped his arm around her.

"Is it always that delightful?" She gazed into his dark eyes. "Although admittedly, in the beginning it was a tiny bit uncomfortable, but all in all well worth doing."

"It's usually a great deal of fun, yes." His tone was solemn, as if it was a question of great merit, but his eyes twinkled.

"Oh good. I'd hate to think it was only fun the first time."

"It gets even better."

"Something to look forward to then."

"We have all sorts of things to look forward to." His tone sobered. "You never did read my note."

"And I would like to. I expect it contains all sorts of words of apology and even some groveling."

"Perhaps some," he said slowly.

"Then it can certainly wait until morning, can't it?"

He looked at her for a long moment, then smiled. "Yes, I believe it can."

"We have all the time in the world, you know."

"The rest of our lives," he said softly, and her heart swelled.

"Now then, Cameron." She shifted and slipped her leg between his. "My married friends say there are all sorts of interesting things that can be done between a man and a woman when—"

He choked. "Lucy Merryweather! What kind of friends do you have?"

She widened her eyes innocently. "Just the ordinary kind."

He raised a brow. "Do proper ladies in America frequently discuss this sort of thing?"

"Well, certainly not in public." She thought for a moment. "Or around their mothers, although one would think to be a mother you would have to

435

know something about this sort of thing. However, my mother would faint dead away were I to so much as broach the subject of relations between men and women."

He snorted back a laugh.

"And definitely such a subject would never be spoken of around fathers or brothers or other family members. Goodness, we'd all be mortified. And not around husbands." She cast him a wicked look. "The discussion is not always favorable."

"Good God." He groaned.

"I never thought you were naive enough to think that women did not discuss this sort of thing. I gather men do all the time."

"That's different."

"Is it?"

"Yes," he said firmly.

"Why?"

"Because we're men." Even as he said the words the look on his face was more than a bit chagrined.

"You do realize how stupid that sounds."

"Yes, I do."

She laughed, then shifted to allow room for her hand to slide down his chest and over his stomach to his, well, she wasn't entirely sure what to call it. *Erection* or *arousal* perhaps? She'd heard a few terms but they were all rather distasteful or just silly. *Penis* was entirely too medical, *cock* entirely too coarse, and *manhood* just plain stupid. *Erection* or *arousal* it was then.

She caressed him lightly. "You do realize that not all men are quite this quick to oh, what's the word? Recover, I believe."

"No?"

"Well, not from what I've been told." She swung her leg over his, shifted to rest her knees on either side of him, then straightened and grinned down at him. "It does seem a shame to waste it."

He smiled slowly. "It does indeed."

He grabbed her waist, raised her up, then slid her back onto him. She shivered with the delight of feeling him slide into her.

"Cameron." She squeezed her muscles around him and watched the expression on his face, a grimace of pure pleasure. She raised up, then slid back down on him. "I like this."

He gasped. "Yes, well, so do I."

"I like watching your face when you're inside me."

He thrust upward and she gasped. "I like watching your face too."

His gaze locked with hers and he thrust again and she rocked her hips against him. And hunger swelled between them and passion once again erupted, frantic and unrelenting and explosive. They drove into each other faster and harder, as if neither could get enough of the other. And when again that remarkable feeling of overpowering release claimed them both, it was as if their very essence had been spent, drained, exhausted by passion and joy and love. Nothing, nothing she had heard, nothing she had read, had truly prepared her for this, for the complete and utter joy of being one with a man. The man you loved.

Just before sleep claimed her, still curled in his embrace, she thought it would probably be best if he returned to his room before dawn, although she did hate to let him go. She'd never felt quite as warm and delightful and, well, loved as she did with their naked bodies entwined. But it would be most embarrassing if he was caught in her room. Although, really when one thought about it, it didn't matter. The servants at Millworth had probably stumbled across far worse through the years. And Clara wasn't here—Lucy wasn't sure how she'd explain this to Clara. And Beryl would probably be amused.

Besides, Lucy was an independent adult—no—an independent woman. If she wished to take a lover, there was nothing to stop her.

Especially if that lover was the man she intended to spend the rest of her life with. She snuggled against him and wondered exactly what was in his note. And wondered as well why she really didn't care.

Was there anything better in life than starting the day by waking up next to the man you loved? Cameron looked so delightfully tousled and warm from sleep, and quite, quite perfect. Even his nose.

"Are you staring at me?" he murmured, his eyes still closed.

"I am." She leaned over and brushed her lips across his forehead. "Good morning, husband-to-be."

His eyes flicked open. "For someone who needed to give due consideration to a proposal not twenty-four hours ago, you certainly have taken this engaged business to heart."

"Well, I'm a changeable sort," she said primly. "You'll have to get used to that." She rolled over and sat up.

He reached for her and tugged her back down beside him. "I suspect there are any number of things I shall have to get used to."

"Do you know I've never slept naked before?" She lifted up the covers and glanced down at her nude body. "I like it. It feels so free and decadent."

He laughed. "Well, then I shall make it a rule not to allow you to have any nightclothes."

"A rule?" She raised a brow. "For me?"

"Would it help if I refuse to allow myself to wear any nightclothes as well?"

She thought for a moment. "I believe I could accept that."

"As much as I hate to say this, I should go back to my room." He grimaced and sat up, swinging his legs over the side of the bed. "Hopefully, I can do so undetected, but it is much later than I had planned."

She shook her head in a mournful manner. "I am so sorry that I ruined your plans."

"My plans rarely seem to work out the way I expected," he said wryly.

"Plans change." She sat up, leaned over, and kissed the back of his neck. He did have a wonderful neck. "Oh, and I would like to see that note of yours before you leave."

He turned toward her, the oddest look in his eyes. "About that . . ."

Without warning, pounding sounded on the door. Before she could say a word the door swung open and Beryl burst into the room, Clara a step behind her.

"Lucy, your—" Beryl pulled up short and stared. Clara nearly smacked into her.

Clara gasped. "Good Lord."

"Bloody hell, I was afraid of this." Beryl groaned. "Although I suppose I should have expected it."

"Good morning," Lucy said brightly, clasping the covers closer around her. "Clara, you're back."

Clara choked.

"You remember . . ." Lucy paused. Lord Cameron did seem terribly formal given the circumstances, and Mr. Fairchild was no longer really accurate. "Cameron."

"Good morning, ladies," he said pleasantly, as if he had met them properly attired at breakfast and not sitting naked on a bed beside an equally naked woman he was not married to.

"Do you know who he is?" Clara stared.

"Yes, of course." Lucy shrugged. "We all knew that before we left London. He's Lord Cameron Effington."

"Also known as Mr. Fairchild." Clara shot a disgusted look at Cameron. "Also known as I. F. Aldrich."

"Aldrich?" For a moment she had no idea what Clara was talking about. Then the truth slammed into her, stealing her breath and twisting her heart. She scrambled out of bed, pulling the bedspread with her, and stared at him. "You're the one who has been writing those stories about me? It's been you all along?"

Cameron's eyes widened. "Lucy, I can explain—"

"Of course, I should have seen it myself." Beryl clapped her palm to her forehead. "I read the *Messenger* nearly every day. I should have realized this Fairchild was that Fairchild. I read his stories all the time."

"I tried to tell—"

"Explanations are the least of your problems at the moment," Beryl said sharply. "Lucy . . ." She paused. "Your mother is here and"—she winced—"your brothers."

Regrets Set to Rights

Take a lover.

Chapter Nineteen

"My what?" Lucy stared in horror. "How can my mother possibly be here? Are you sure?"

"Aside from the fact that there is a distinct family resemblance, she introduced herself as Mrs. Merryweather and said she was your mother?" Beryl huffed. "Why no, I'm not at all sure."

"Good Lord." Lucy wrapped the bedspread tighter around her and tried to pace. The last thing she needed at the moment was to have to deal with her mother. And her brothers. "How many brothers?"

Beryl stared. "How many do you have?"

"Four."

"Oh well, that's something." Beryl shrugged. "There are only two."

"Which ones?"

"I don't know," Beryl said sharply. "I don't recall their names—I had other things on my mind. They were Mr. Merryweather and Mr. Merryweather."

"One was Harold and the other was Joseph," Clara said. "We arrived here at nearly the same time."

"They prefer Harry and Joe," Lucy murmured, still reeling from Cameron's deception and her family's surprise appearance. "My father is Harold." She sucked in a sharp breath. "Is my father here as well?"

"No." Beryl shook her head. "At least not here at Millworth. But your mother did mention the rest of their party had remained in London."

"The rest of their party?" Lucy groaned. "That's all I need."

"Lucy." Cameron wrapped a blanket around himself, stood, and hobbled toward her. "We have to talk."

"Now is not the time." She had to dress and go downstairs. She had to figure out what she would say to her mother and her brothers. She had to . . . She whirled to face him. "You could have told me before now! You've had every opportunity to do so."

"I wrote you a note."

"Last night!"

"I tried to tell you everything before then."

"Not very hard!"

"Well, it wasn't easy." He ran his hand through his already tousled hair. "I knew you weren't going to take it well."

"Not take it well?" Her voice rose. "Not take it well!"

"Good Lord, Lucy, the problem isn't that he didn't tell you what he was doing." Clara glared. "The problem is what he did in the first place."

"Exactly." Beryl crossed her arms over her

chest. "That's what you should be so infuriated about. I know I would."

"I'm furious about all of it," Lucy snapped.

"I can understand that," Cameron said. "And justifiably so, but—"

"There is no time for this now," Beryl interrupted. "Lucy, you need to dress at once. Miss West." She nodded at Clara. "Please go downstairs and do whatever is necessary to keep Mrs. Merryweather in the parlor. I did tell her we had hosted a small party last night so Lucy was sleeping in. However, she does seem the type to take it into her head to track down her daughter herself. Give her tea or, better yet, brandy."

"I'll do my best." Clara nodded, cast a contemptuous look at Cameron, and then quickly left the room.

Lucy stared. "What am I going to say to her?"

"Ask him." Beryl gestured at Cameron. "He's the writer."

"Let me think," Cameron said.

Lucy stared. "She wasn't serious."

"Of course not." Beryl scoffed. "Although I do think your *Runaway Heiress* stories are quite clever and extremely humorous."

"Do you really?" Cameron looked entirely too pleased given the circumstances.

"Oh, I do indeed." Beryl nodded. "But I daresay

this is not the right moment to discuss your literary prowess." She smiled pleasantly. "Surely you have clothes here somewhere?"

"Somewhere." He glanced around the room. Between Lucy's grabbing the bedspread and Cameron's use of the blanket, bedclothes were now scattered around the room in a haphazard manner.

Lucy clenched her teeth. "Get out!"

He shook his head. "I'm not leaving until you hear what I have to say."

"I have no interest in hearing anything you have to say!"

"Although it's probably quite interesting," Beryl murmured.

"Nonetheless." He squared his shoulders, which would have been far more effective had they not been naked. "You have to hear me out."

"I don't have to do anything!" She tottered toward the wardrobe, threw open the doors, and grabbed the first acceptable day dress she found. She swiveled on her heel to face him. "Last night on the terrace you said I knew the truth now."

"Yes, well, not the *whole* truth." He winced.

She stared at him. "How could you, Cameron? How could you write those stories about me?"

"They weren't about you. Not really." He stepped closer. "You were simply the inspiration."

"You used me and lied to me." The full impact of his deception crashed down on her. Her stomach heaved, a lump lodged in her throat, and her eyes burned. But she absolutely would not let him see her cry. She clenched her teeth. "Get out, Cameron. Now."

"Lucy, I—"

"My lord." Beryl stepped between them, her voice calm and reasonable. "I think you are suitably attired for the short trip down the hall to your room, where you shall immediately dress, pack your bag, and leave Millworth as discreetly as possible so as to avoid awkward encounters with our newest visitors." She leaned toward him in a confidential manner. "Aside from being quite handsome, Lucy's brothers are as tall as you and, while it's difficult to compare accurately as they have their clothes on and you do not, seem to be healthy and extremely fit. I cannot imagine how protective older brothers would respond to so much as the merest hint that you and their sister—"

"They'd shoot you!" Lucy glared.

"They do that sort of thing in America, you know, or so I've heard," Beryl continued. "And I think it's best for all concerned if you return to London."

"But I'm going to marry her," he said staunchly.

Lucy scoffed. "Don't bet on it, *Mr. Aldrich!*"

"Go, now." Beryl ushered him to the door. "I shall join you in a minute to show you how to get out of the manor undetected." She opened the door and nudged him out. He cast one last look at Lucy.

"Lucy." The note of desperation in his voice nearly undid her.

She looked at him for a long moment, then pointedly turned away. After a moment, she heard the door close.

"Lucy," Beryl said briskly. "I'll help you with your dress, then you must greet your mother. This is not the first indiscretion Millworth has seen and I doubt it will be the last. Nor is yours the first heart to be broken here." She paused. "Although I will admit that having one's mother and two out of four brothers, who are supposed to be an ocean away, appear when one is still basking in the aftermath of passion does lend a farcical note to the proceedings."

Lucy uttered something that might have been a sob or a laugh.

"Lucy," Beryl snapped.

Lucy turned toward her.

"I realize that at this moment you want nothing more than to fling yourself on the bed . . ." She glanced at the disheveled bedclothes. "Well, perhaps not the bed but the chair or the chaise, anywhere really, and weep until you can weep no more. However, there's no time for that now." She moved to Lucy, grabbed her shoulders, and met her gaze firmly. "I've watched you, Lucy, and

447

you, my dear girl, are made of sterner stuff. The last people you want to know about any of this are your family. While there is a chance you might forgive Effington—"

"Never!"

"You believe that at the moment and it is entirely possible you will never be able to forgive him. But love is an exceptionally diabolical emotion and pays no attention to reason or logic. If indeed you truly love each other, you might forgive him one day." A firm note sounded in Beryl's voice. "I would advise putting him through all the fires of hell first as is your due. However, if your family knows about his writings about you and, God help us all, last night, they will never forgive him. And never accept him."

"Good!"

"Don't burn bridges, Lucy. Not when it comes to your heart." She studied her for a moment. "Keep your chin up, dear girl, and whatever you do, don't cry. Mothers, no matter how formidable they may seem, can always tell when their daughters have been crying. And they are relentless in their efforts to find out why."

Lucy stared, then drew a deep breath. "You're right. My family would never forgive him." She gathered her resolve and tried to ignore the awful ache that had settled around her heart. "And neither will I."

• • •

The sons of Harold and Pauline Merryweather were not expected to back down from a confrontation. Neither would their daughter. Even with her mother.

Lucy drew a deep breath and stepped into the parlor.

"My dear girl." Mother rose from the sofa to meet her the moment Lucy stepped into the parlor.

Clara cast her a smile of encouragement and quickly took her leave.

Lucy adopted her most brilliant smile and sailed across the room. "Good day, Mother. What a lovely surprise."

"I'm certain of that. Come here so that I may greet you properly." Mother held out her arms and Lucy obediently moved into her embrace. At once she was a little girl again and the almost irresistible need to cry and be comforted rushed through her. She summoned all her resolve and stepped away. Mother studied her closely, then nodded. "You look . . . well."

"Thank you, Mother." Lucy turned to greet her brothers. "Harry, Joe, I can't believe Mother dragged you across an entire ocean."

"Not just us," Joe, her second oldest brother, said with a long-suffering smile. "We left Cole and Parker in London."

"So you're all here. How delightful." Although

Lucy considered it anything but delightful. "Did Father come as well?"

"No," Harry said, and Lucy breathed a silent sigh of relief. "We thought someone should stay at home. It didn't make a great deal of sense for all of us to come." Harry was the oldest and not at all prone to undue alarm or jumping to unwarranted conclusions. Pity his sister wasn't more like him. "It didn't make sense for the four of us to accompany Mother either, but she was worried about you."

"Really?" Lucy widened her eyes in feigned disbelief.

Harry nodded, but curiosity shone in his eyes. "The rest of us knew there was probably nothing to be concerned about."

"After all, you've never done anything to cause concern before," Joe said, eyeing her thoughtfully.

"I do apologize, Mother, if I've caused you to worry. Although I can't imagine why."

Harry and Joe traded glances.

"Oh, and I think you can." Mother's eyes narrowed. She was a good inch shorter than her daughter, her hair still vibrant but a few shades darker than Lucy's. In her early fifties, Mother looked at least ten years younger. "I think you can well imagine my surprise when I received a letter from a, well, a long-lost side of the family, if you will."

Lucy winced to herself.

"Lady Northrup wrote expressing her delight in meeting a member of the American branch of the family. The letter was quite lovely, extolling the virtues of my only daughter. How terribly brave and independent you were, she wrote." Mother's eyes flashed. "Why, she would never have had the courage at your age to visit a foreign country accompanied only by a surprisingly youthful traveling companion."

"Have you met Miss West?" Lucy said brightly.

"As she just left, it was unavoidable." Mother's jaw tightened.

"She's very efficient and well organized," Lucy added, as if efficient and well organized would negate everything else.

"And pretty," Joe said to Harry. "Very pretty."

"And she did appear"—Harry grinned—"extremely well organized."

"I don't care if she is the most efficient and organized creature ever to walk the face of the earth," Mother said sharply. "What happened to Mrs. Channing?"

"Didn't you get her letter?" Lucy said innocently.

"I most certainly did not!"

"I can't imagine what happened." Lucy shook her head in a regretful manner, ignoring the memory of Mrs. Channing's letter merrily burning away in the fireplace in this very room.

"But you know how unreliable transatlantic mail can be."

"Nonetheless, I want to know what happened to her, and where on earth is Jackson?"

"I did write to you," Lucy pointed out.

"And in spite of the untrustworthy nature of the mails, I did receive your letters. Quite regularly until the first of the year, and since then there have only been two." A sharp note sounded in Mother's voice. "Neither of which mentioned that you were no longer in Elizabeth's company. Nor did they mention that you and Jackson had indeed parted company, which I assumed, by the way, given Lady Northrup's suggestion that her son, Alfred—"

"Freddy," Lucy said.

"—and you made such an attractive couple and perhaps we could encourage the two of you along those lines."

"Goodness, Mother." Lucy waved away the comment. "That happened before I left New York." She paused. "Jackson and I parting ways, that is, not marrying Freddy. Which I have no interest in doing, by the way."

"I was hopeful the differences between you and Jackson would be resolved when you came to England."

"They weren't because there really weren't differences to resolve," Lucy said firmly. "We were simply ready, more than ready really, to go our separate ways. You and Mrs. Channing were the only ones who thought differently."

"She's right there, Mother." Harry nodded.

Joe scoffed. "The rest of us knew by the third or fourth time they postponed their engagement that this was one marriage that was never going to happen."

"Fine," Mother snapped. "My question still has not been answered. What happened to Elizabeth and where is Jackson?"

"Shall I be perfectly honest?" Lucy asked.

"I've never known you to be less than perfectly honest before."

"Thank you, Mother. Well then." She shook her head. "I have no idea."

"What?"

Lucy shrugged. "They could be anywhere. Europe, the Orient, Persia."

Mother's brow rose. "All of them?"

"Jackson set off to travel and seek adventures with his father. His mother is accompanying them."

Mother's eyes widened. "Elizabeth Channing is traveling with her husband?"

"Colonel Channing?" Surprise sounded in Harry's voice. "The husband we all thought was dead until recently?"

Lucy nodded. "They decided to, oh, see if marriage was to their liking, I think. Something like that."

"Good Lord." Mother sank down onto the sofa. "In all the years I've known Elizabeth, she scarcely ever mentioned the man's name."

"He was dead, Mother," Joe pointed out.

"Will wonders never cease," Mother murmured, then she drew a deep breath. "So you have been alone here?"

"Not at all." Lucy scoffed and sat down beside her mother. "I had Clara—"

"The lovely Miss West," Joe said.

"And Lady Dunwell." *And Cameron Effington-Fairchild-Aldrich.* She ignored the thought. "I haven't been the least bit alone."

Mother stared. "But what have you been doing?"

"Oh, the usual sort of thing." *Flying in a balloon, baking a cake, being painted in the nude.* She shrugged. "This and that. Seeing the sights. All the expected things that tourists do."

Mother stared.

"What fun." Harry grinned and Lucy threw him a grateful glance. While all her brothers were overly protective, they were also fairly easygoing in nature. Any one of them would probably appreciate the quest she'd been on.

"All right then." Mother rose to her feet. "I assume you're ready to return to London with us. We plan on staying for the rest of the week, then we have passage booked back to New York. Passage for *six.*"

Lucy stared at her mother for a long moment. The oddest wave of resignation and defeat and sorrow washed through her. She had known this moment would come and she hadn't expected to accomplish everything on Great-aunt Lucinda's list. Certainly there was no reason why she couldn't continue her quest at home, although she doubted she would. In New York she was Miss Lucy Merryweather, the perfect, proper, and always well-behaved daughter of a director of Graham, Merryweather, and Lockwood Banking and Trust. Lucy Merryweather, who would have married the man everyone expected her to marry and lived the life she was expected to lead. Lucy Merryweather, who would never buy an elephant or wear a mustache or dance on a frozen terrace in the moonlight.

In New York she would be far away from *The Daring Exploits of a Runaway Heiress* and far away from its author. The man who had betrayed her and deceived her and broken her heart. And the sooner she could put an ocean between them, the better.

"Excellent, Mother." She cast her mother her brightest smile. "I can't wait to go home."

Chapter Twenty

"As large as Channing House is, it's beginning to look a great deal like a florist." Mother glanced around Lucy's room. "Not in here, of course."

Lucy had absolutely forbidden any of the numerous offerings of flowers that had arrived for her in the three days since their return to London to be placed in her room. It was bad enough that Mother had refused to allow her to throw them away, insisting, as hothouse flowers were so dear in February, that it would be a terrible waste to simply discard them.

"I think flowers are unnatural at this time of year," Lucy murmured. She reclined on the chaise, Albert curled by her side, and paged through a copy of *The Woman's World* magazine as she was no longer reading any publication that bore the name *Cadwallender.*

"So you've said." Mother paused, then sighed. "Are you going to tell me who this young man is and why you refuse to see him?"

"No, Mother, I'm not." Lucy turned the page she'd been staring at but had yet to read so much as a single word. She couldn't seem to concentrate on anything but the clippings of *The Daring Exploits of a Runaway Heiress* Beryl had given her. Those she had read over and over so often they were nearly committed to memory.

"Do you intend to acknowledge his flowers and the numerous notes accompanying them?"

"No, Mother, I do not." Although she had read every note as well as the one he had brought to her room at Millworth the night they had spent together. One would think now knowing everything would make his actions more palatable. Her jaw tightened. It did not.

"Yours is not the only heart ever to have been broken, you know."

"Goodness, Mother." She glanced up and forced a firm note to the lie. "My heart is not broken."

"Oh, well, my mistake then." Mother hesitated. "You know, if you and Jackson had—"

"We would have had a practically perfect life together." Lucy smiled. "However, Jackson has found the love of his life and I am quite happy for him."

"Of course," Mother murmured. "And what do you intend to do with yours?"

"I intend to return home with you and hope I never have need to step foot upon English shores again," she said with far more vehemence that she had intended. It was not the way to convince her mother that there was nothing wrong.

"I certainly don't blame you." Mother moved to the foot of the chaise and sat down. "You know," she said slowly, "I've only ever wanted the best for you. If I have been wrong in the past, especially about Jackson, well . . ." Her face crumpled. "I am truly, truly sorry."

"Mother." Lucy sat up and shifted to sit next to her mother. Albert gave an annoyed grunt and moved to her other side. "Are you crying?"

"No." Mother sniffed and a tear rolled down her cheek. "I don't cry."

"I've never seen you cry before." Lucy pulled one of several wrinkled handkerchiefs from her pocket and handed her mother one that was still dry. "Why are you crying now?"

"I'm not." Mother sniffed and accepted the handkerchief. "I have only ever tried to do what is best. If I have been overbearing in that effort, my intentions have always been good."

"I know."

"And now you've become this independent, self-sufficient creature."

Lucy widened her eyes. "I've what?"

"You needn't deny it, dear. There's an air of, oh, I don't know, confidence about you that was never there before. Lady Northrup mentioned it in her letter and even your brothers have noticed, and you know how obtuse they can be. And I can see a definite change in you."

"Can you?" Lucy stared.

"Oh my, yes." Mother nodded. "Admittedly, it's nearly obscured by your obvious distress at the moment, but it's there all the same. And I have no idea why. Nor do I know what you have done

458

here these last few weeks." She sniffed, sat up straighter, and met her daughter's gaze. "I had always hoped it would be the two of us united in a house full of men."

"Oh, Mother." Lucy's heart melted.

"I hoped you would be able to confide in me. I hoped, when you were an adult, we could be close, but it never seemed we had any common ground. You've always been so, well . . ."

"Perfect?"

"Exactly." Mother nodded. "And I've always been so . . ."

"Demanding? Expectant? Intractable?"

Mother's brow furrowed with dismay. "Have I really?"

"No." Lucy scoffed, then grimaced. "Somewhat."

"Oh dear. I never meant to be. I was just trying to do what was best. What was right. I suppose I was trying to be my mother." Mother shook her head. "After four boys you have no idea how much I wanted a daughter. Didn't you ever wonder why I never made much of a fuss about you and Jackson postponing an engagement year after year?"

"You did mention it rather frequently," Lucy said wryly.

"That's my job, dear. But I quite selfishly didn't relish the idea of your not being around every day. So as much as it might seem that I pushed you and Jackson together, believe me, I could have done far more." She sighed. "I just wanted your life to be perfect. Mine has been and I owe it all to my mother."

"Your mother?" Lucy's grandmother had died before she was born.

Mother's eyes widened in surprise. "You didn't think I wanted to marry your father?"

"Well, actually, yes, I had."

"Oh, good Lord, no. For one thing I had no desire to be Mary Merryweather."

Lucy choked back a laugh. "Who?"

"My first name is Mary. I'm surprised you didn't know that, although I never use it anymore. My mother pointed out if I married your father, I could use my middle name—Pauline. I always loved Pauline. Mother hated it. She thought it sounded like an actress." Mother flashed her a grin. "Part of why I liked it."

"Mother!" Lucy laughed.

"Your father thought the whole thing was very funny." She smiled. "He has an excellent sense of humor."

"*My* father?"

"Oh my, yes. That's what made up for his being a banker. And what made me fall in love with him." She shook her head. "I had no desire to marry a banker."

"You didn't?" Lucy said slowly.

"No indeed. I wanted a man of adventure who

would take me along on adventures with him. An adventurer or an explorer." She thought for a moment. "Or a pirate."

"Mother!"

"I know it's extremely silly but I was very young." She thought for a moment and her voice softened. "And then he became a man of adventure. During the war they all were, really. I nearly lost him at Gettysburg. Did you know that?"

She stared. "I had no idea."

"He was home right before the battle and you were born the next year. After Gettysburg, he was transferred to the quartermaster corps, the perfect place for a banker. He had managed to avoid it up till then and he was furious." She smiled. "I was delighted."

Shock coursed through Lucy. The idea of her imposing, solid father as being anything approaching adventurous was hard to accept or believe. "I didn't know any of this."

"There was no reason why you should. It was a very long time ago. Your father never speaks of those days and neither do I." She shrugged. "It's pointless really. The past is over and done with. And our lives have turned out well in the end."

"I'm so . . . glad." Lucy had never really thought of her parents as being anything other than the socially prominent Harold and Pauline Merryweather, pillars of the community. Eminently proper and extremely dull. Now, she had a glimpse of a woman in love with a husband who had gone off to war. A young mother with four sons who feared the man she loved might never return.

"As am I." Mother smiled. "It was my mother who encouraged me, no, pushed me toward your father. I've never regretted it. It hasn't been perfect, mind you. Your father can be high-handed, inflexible, and quite annoying."

Lucy snorted back a laugh. That she could believe.

"We've been quite happy, Lucy, for more than thirty-three years now, and I don't think one can ask for more than happiness. It has been the most wonderful"—her hazel eyes twinkled—"adventure."

"I never thought of you as the sort of woman who was interested in adventure," Lucy said without thinking.

Mother laughed. "Life itself, my darling girl, can be the most marvelous adventure with the right person by your side. And even if someone's life might seem rather staid and boring—"

"Oh, I have never thought . . ."

Mother raised a skeptical brow.

"Well, perhaps I did," Lucy said weakly.

"Of course you did." She patted her daughter's hand. "No one ever imagines their parents might have done anything even remotely interesting before they became parents."

Lucy wondered what she and this woman she now realized she hardly knew had missed through the years with both of them trying very hard to be what they were expected to be. She drew a deep breath. "May I confide something to you?"

"Always, but can it wait?"

"Of course."

"Good. Because I came up to tell you there's a very dashing young man downstairs wishing to see you." Mother studied her closely. "A lord something or other."

"Cameron Effington?" Her hopes rose and she viciously slapped them down. She really didn't care if he was here or not, but it had been three days and if the man truly loved her, one would think he would make some sort of effort to see her.

"I think so. He's the one who has been sending the flowers, isn't he?"

Lucy nodded.

"I can have your brothers throw him out, you know. Or give him a sound thrashing if you'd prefer."

Lucy smiled. "That would be lovely."

"Very well then." Mother stood and started toward the door.

"No, Mother, wait," Lucy said quickly. She didn't think her mother would actually set her brothers on Cameron, but she was learning all sorts of things she never suspected about her mother today and it might be best not to take a chance. "I will see him."

"Are you sure?"

"No." She blew a long breath. It might be best to have it out with him and then never see him again. There were things she needed to say. "But I'll see him nonetheless."

"Of course you will," Mother said staunchly. "Besides, your brothers can always thrash him later if you wish. I might well assist them myself." She flashed her daughter a wicked smile, then paused. "I won't press you about him, but I am here to listen if you ever feel the need to talk to someone. Someone who will always, always be on your side. But, if I may give you a piece of advice."

"You've always had excellent advice."

"Thank you. I just think you should keep in mind that there are truly bad people in the world." Mother grimaced. "But most of us are just stupid."

"I only agreed to see you for one reason." Lucy's voice rang cold and unyielding, and Cam could have sworn the temperature in the parlor plummeted the moment she walked in.

He certainly hadn't expected her to fling herself into his arms, although it would have been nice. The flowers and the notes he'd sent obviously hadn't had the softening affect he'd hoped for. It was, however, oddly encouraging to realize she looked as weary as he felt, as if she too had had no more luck at sleeping than he. And in spite of her frosty manner there was a vague sadness about her. His heart clenched. He was entirely to blame.

"To forgive me?" He smiled and didn't try to hide the note of hope in his voice.

A lesser man might have run at the withering look she gave him. "Clara heard from Mr. Chapman that you have compiled the *Daring Exploits of a Runaway Heiress* stories into a novel for publication."

"I have."

"I want it stopped."

He stared. "I can't."

"You mean you won't." Her eyes narrowed. "This is exactly what you want. This book not only makes a point to your father but to the world. Cameron Effington-Fairchild-Aldrich has at last found his calling."

"No, I mean I can't stop it." He shook his head. "Even now it's being printed."

"How convenient."

"Convenience has nothing to do with it. It was my brother's idea and I didn't think to stop him." But would he stop publication if he could? It was a disquieting question. He feared the answer and was grateful it was indeed too late. Was Phineas right? Did ambition really triumph over affection after all?

465

"I see."

"Lucy," he began.

"I trusted you and you made fun of me. You held me up to public ridicule. Public humiliation. You turned me into a caricature, an exaggeration, a stock character. The madcap heiress, found in every drawing room comedy and every over-written serial."

"What do you mean *overwritten?*" he said without thinking, and immediately knew it was a mistake.

"I mean you are not Shakespeare, you are not Dickens, and . . ." Her gaze slid over him in a disgusted manner. "You are certainly not Twain!"

He gasped. Not that what she said wasn't true, although he would dispute the overwritten comment. But even if she believed that, she was only saying so now because she was angry and hurt.

"You have made me look like an idiot and a fool. You've represented me as a stupid American female with more money in her purse than brains in her head."

"I most certainly did not," he said firmly. "No one who reads my stories or my book will ever know the heroine has anything whatsoever to do with you."

"Everyone who knows me and who reads that book will know it's me." She stared at him. "The stories were bad enough, but a book?" Her jaw clenched. "Today's newspaper is the wrapping for fish tomorrow, but a book . . ." She shook her head. "A book lasts forever."

"I took great pains to make certain no one would connect you to the heroine."

"Not great enough." She stared. "You are so eager to justify what you've done you cannot see it yourself."

"Because there's nothing to see."

"Nothing?" Her brow rose. "Even the older gentlemen we played cards with at Millworth compared me to your fictional creation. Were I to stay in England, more and more people would connect me to your *madcap heiress*."

"What do you mean if you were to stay?" He stared. "You're leaving England?"

"I'm returning to America." She paused. "We sail tomorrow."

"You can't leave tomorrow." Sheer panic surged within him. If she left England, if she returned home, any hope he had of wearing her down, of proving to her he could indeed be trusted, would be dashed. "What about us?"

She stared in disbelief. "How can you possibly think there can ever be an us?"

"You said you'd marry me."

"And you said any number of things that have turned out not to be true."

"In point of fact," he said slowly. "I did not."

"What?"

He had given this a great deal of thought. It was a tiny loophole but a means of escape nonetheless. "You're the one who assumed I was a private investigator. I never said that."

Anger and disbelief widened her eyes. "You never denied it either. You never corrected my assumption."

"Your unwarranted conclusion," he said pointedly.

"Yes." She fairly hissed the word.

"I never actually lied to you."

"You mean aside from the stories you told about your exploits as an investigator?" She scoffed. "No, in the strictest definition of the word, I suppose you didn't actually lie. You were far too clever for that. And yet you did manage to mislead me, to *deceive* me all the same. Or am I mistaken in that too?"

"I didn't mean for any of this to happen."

"Any of what?" She crossed her arms over her chest. "You didn't intend to write stories using me as your—"

"Inspiration?"

"Unwitting dupe!"

"I prefer muse."

"You may prefer whatever you wish," she snapped. "Or didn't you intend for me ever to find out?"

He winced with the accuracy of her charge. "It did seem best—"

"Best for whom?"

"For both of us!"

"Both of us?" She cast him a scathing look. "Fine, believe what you want. Whatever is convenient to salve your conscience. It really doesn't matter." She shook her head. "You used me, Cameron, and I trusted you. Worse, I trusted myself." She drew a deep breath. "From the moment we met, I never doubted that you were a good, honest, honorable man. Admittedly, there have been moments when I wondered if making amends for the regrets of another woman was no different than how I've spent my entire life. Living up to other people's expectations and ignoring or perhaps simply failing to recognize my own path. But I never doubted that I was right about the kind of man you are." She met his gaze directly. "How could I have been so wrong?"

He wanted to say she wasn't wrong, but at the moment, she wouldn't believe it. And right now, he didn't know if he believed it either.

"It didn't seem to me that it was a lot to ask. Or to expect." Her voice was quiet and far more frightening than when it had risen in anger. "That you simply be the man I thought you were."

"I am," he said quietly, and wondered if it was true.

"I have always, always jumped to conclusions. Mother long ago warned that would be my undoing one day and she was right. The way

I misjudged you . . ." Her brow furrowed. "Obviously I'm not smart enough or brave enough to be an independent woman."

"Lucy—"

"You know, through this entire quest of mine, I didn't doubt myself. For the first time in my life I was doing something for me, even if it was another woman's adventures. They became mine, you know. I knew I could do this. But if I was wrong about you, if my judgment was so flawed" —she shook her head—"then I have to wonder if I am wrong about everything."

She was shattered. He could see it in her eyes, hear it in her voice. And it was his fault, all of it. "Lucy." He shook his head. "I don't know how to make this right. I want to but I don't know how."

"Neither do I." She drew a deep breath. "It's not all for nothing, I suppose. I'm sure this will give you something new to write about."

"I'm not going to write about us. I would never—"

"You mean never again, don't you?"

He winced. "You're right, of course."

"No, Cameron. I wasn't right about anything. That's part of why it's so . . ." She paused, then raised her chin, as if she had just made a serious decision. What bit of hope he still clung to faded. "But I do owe you my thanks. You have helped me with yet another item on my great-aunt's list

I did not think I would be able to accomplish." His stomach lurched. "The one about taking a lover?"

"Oh, well, two then, I suppose." She shrugged. "No, I was speaking of the one about having a romantic interlude."

"With someone you never want to see again." His throat tightened.

"Yes, that's the one. I'm so glad you remembered." She looked at him for a long, silent moment, then cast him a wan smile. "Good day, Mr. Fairchild." She nodded and took her leave.

He stared after her for a long moment. He had lost her and had no one to blame but himself. If this was a story, he could write his way out of it. But this was his life and nothing was as simple in reality as it was on paper. Nor was he as confident that he could fix this in reality.

But he knew as surely as he knew anything in his life, if he couldn't set this right, it would be a regret that would eat at his soul for the rest of his days. A regret that no future descendant, no matter how well intentioned, could ever rectify.

Pity he had no idea how to do that.

Regrets Set to Rights

Have a romantic interlude with someone
I plan to never to see again.

Chapter Twenty-one

Lucy sank down on the bed in the room she'd occupied since childhood in the grand house on Fifth Avenue and stared at the calling card in her hand, emblazoned with the same crest she had seen on one of the references Cameron had provided for her.

It was about time.

It had been three weeks, six days, and a fair number of hours since she'd seen Cameron Effington-Fairchild-Aldrich. Practically a full month since the damned man had broken her heart. Even accounting for the weeklong voyage between England and New York, one would think he would have been here by now. What on earth had taken him so long? Why, she was just about to pack her bags and head back to England her-self.

Not that she wasn't still furious with him, but nearly a month had given her a great deal of time to consider his actions and her own. She had been a fool to think she could return home to New York and life would be exactly as it was before she'd left. She was not the same Lucy Merryweather who had sailed for England in December, nor would she ever be again. Her life

472

here left her restless and bored and terribly lonely. Even the regret of her great-aunt's she was pondering how to resolve wasn't enough to fill the endless days. She missed Clara, who had confessed her unwilling role in Cameron's deception. And worse, she missed him. It seemed she was no longer the type of woman to be content with doing the expected.

It had dawned on her slowly that Cameron's greatest crime wasn't so much that he had used her for inspiration—the idea of being someone's muse was growing on her—but that he had led her to believe he was someone and something he wasn't. Certainly, one could say if she hadn't jumped to the wrong conclusion in the first place, he wouldn't have taken advantage of the opportunity she presented him with. While she could fault him for that, it didn't seem quite fair. It did however still rankle—she had trusted him after all—and forgiveness would require a fair amount of groveling on his part. Not that she didn't intend to forgive him. She simply didn't think it should be too easy for him. Mother had once said deceit was not the way to begin a marriage, and Lucy quite agreed.

However, there were worse things in life than being seen by the world as a madcap heiress. Spending the rest of your life without the man you loved was at the top of that particular list.

She hurried downstairs, tried to ignore the eager

thudding of her heart fueled by anticipation, and stopped in midstep when the open drawing room doors came into view.

On one side of the room, Cameron perched uncomfortably on the sofa beside a very large, cloth-covered something or other. On the other side of the room, all four of her brothers sat or lounged or leaned. None of them looked especially welcoming or friendly. They had known there was a man to blame for her disposition, but she hadn't confirmed it, hadn't denied it, and indeed refused to discuss it altogether. Their presence now could be blamed on her. Ever since they'd returned from England, her brothers had made a concerted effort to raise her spirits and had formed some sort of conspiracy to make certain she rarely spent an evening alone. Which was as annoying as it was endearing.

At least her parents were out for the evening, which was a small blessing. Looking at the expressions on her brothers' faces as well as Cameron's, it was very small indeed.

She braced herself and sailed into the room as if she had just seen him yesterday and not three weeks, six days, and a fair number of hours ago. Cameron stood and offered her a tentative smile, obviously uncertain as to how he'd be received. Good.

"Good evening, my lord," she said pleasantly. "How was your voyage?"

"Very well, thank you." His manner was as polite as hers.

"I assume you've met my brothers." She gestured at the solid wall of American masculinity behind her. They did make an imposing display. "Harry, Joe, Cole, and Parker."

Cameron nodded. "We were introduced when I arrived."

"Excellent. I would hate to have to introduce you. I can never remember the right name." She smiled sweetly.

"Effington will do," he said slowly.

"Very well then." She moved to a chair near the sofa and sat down. "Why are you here?"

He glanced at her brothers. "May we speak privately?"

"Anything you wish to say to me may be said in front of my family."

He raised a brow. "Anything?"

"I told them about Great-aunt Lucinda's regrets." Not that she had told them everything on her great-aunt's list. She might not be the woman she once was but she certainly wasn't stupid. Her brothers had thought her quest was admirable if somewhat silly. Apparently everyone did. Her mother's face had paled a bit when she'd heard of Lucinda's desires to swim naked and kiss a stranger, but she had said Lucy was a smart, competent woman and well capable of making her own decisions. She had also pointed out it might be best not to tell Father about any of this. Lucy wasn't quite sure who her mother was anymore, but she did like her. "Beyond that . . ."

"Did you tell them I want to marry you?"

Murmured expressions of surprise sounded behind her.

"Well, that changes everything, doesn't it?" Cole said under his breath.

"She's going to be twenty-four tomorrow, after all," Parker said quietly. "This might be her only chance."

"Do you mind?" She cast them an annoyed glare. "If you're going to stay, then do me the favor of keeping your mouths shut."

"I have nothing to hide from anyone." Cameron smiled.

"And isn't that a pleasant change?" she said.

Harry cleared his throat. "Perhaps we should wait in the hall."

"Don't go far." She nodded toward the door. "I might need one of you to shoot him."

"Why were we here in the first place if she was only going to throw us out?" Cole asked Harry as they filed out of the room.

"Because she's mad." Parker snorted. "All women are."

"We're here in a show of family support," Joe said, glancing back at her. "Not that she needs it."

Cameron studied her, obviously trying not to grin with amusement.

476

"You haven't answered my question. Why are you here?" *And what took you so long?*

"I brought you a gift. I didn't know tomorrow is your birthday, but now that I do, this is even more perfect." He pulled the cover off the something or other with a flourish to reveal a brass cage and its occupant, a brightly colored bird the size of a pigeon.

She gasped. "You brought me a parrot?"

"It's the ninth or tenth item on your great-aunt's list, I believe. Right after a dog." He glanced around. "Where is Albert, by the way?"

"Albert is a creature of divided loyalties," she said absently, rose, and moved closer to the cage. "He has fallen head over heels for Mrs. Helstrom, our cook, and spends most of his time in the kitchen, where I believe she encourages his affection by feeding him all sorts of treats he probably shouldn't have. Only when she leaves for the day does he deign to be by my side."

"I see." Cameron smiled. "Then allow me to present Fernando. Fernando, say hello to Miss Merryweather."

"Hello," Fernando said obediently. "I'm sorry."

She stared. "You're what?"

"Please forgive me," Fernando said.

She glanced at Cameron. "Did you teach him—"

Fernando squawked. "I'm an idiot."

"I had a great deal of time on my hands,"

Cameron said in an offhand manner, and idly meandered the perimeter of the room. "The first week after you left I spent wallowing in self-pity and despair. At least that's how my oldest brother put it." He glanced at her. "I thought he was wrong but my other brothers agreed with him."

"I'm a fool," Fernando added. "I'm an idiot."

"What a perceptive bird," she murmured.

"But I did write a bit." He paused in front of a bronze statue of Mercury on a marble pedestal. "A story about a man standing on the docks, watching a ship carry off the woman he loved while his heart was being torn slowly out of his chest. He had gone to stop her from leaving England, from leaving him, but his courage had faltered and for the first time he wondered if her life might be better without him. So he watched her board but didn't know what to say."

Her heart fluttered. Then it had been him. He had come to stop her after all. She'd thought she had seen him when her ship sailed but she had turned around and when she looked again, he was gone.

"It sounds a bit melodramatic to me." She shrugged.

"Oh, it was." He continued to study the statue as if the ancient messenger held some secret communiqué for him. "All about lost love and remorse and regret."

"What about repentance?"

"I haven't finished it yet and I don't know that I will. The main character is entirely too pathetic. He was wrong, you see, and he knows it, but he's become too mired in guilt and indecision to see what he needed to do and I've grown tired of him."

"Have you?"

"I no longer like him either, so it seemed pointless to finish writing his story." Cameron continued circling the room. "The second week was a bit brighter. I presented my book to my father." He paused. "I believe I mentioned my agreement with him in the note I left in your room the night we—"

She glanced at the open door and waved him quiet. "Yes, yes, I remember." She lowered her voice. "They really could shoot you, you know."

"It's a risk I'm willing to take." He shrugged. "By the end of the second week, the book was available for sale. It's selling quite nicely, thank you for asking."

Fernando flapped his wings. "Please forgive me."

"I didn't ask, nor did I intend to, but I have no doubt of that." She paused. "The stories were rather . . . entertaining."

His brow rose. "Not overwritten?"

"Not as much as I first thought."

"Then you've read them again." He studied her closely.

She sighed in surrender. "Once or twice perhaps." Or thirty or forty times.

"I see." His tone was solemn but there was a definite gleam of amusement in his eyes. "By the third week I realized—"

"I'm an idiot," Fernando announced.

"That too." He grinned. "So I made some arrangements, bought a parrot, and took the first ship I could get passage on."

"And?"

"And here I am." He paused by the fireplace, folded his arms over his chest, and leaned against the mantel in a casual manner. "Are you giving up your quest?"

"I haven't decided yet. It won't be nearly as much fun without—"

"Me?"

"Clara," she said firmly, but she had meant him.

"I, for one, think that would be a great shame."

"Why?" She narrowed her eyes. "Because it would give you nothing to write about?"

"No, because it would give that diabolical brain of yours nothing to sort out. You could end up in a plot to rule the world."

She considered him cautiously. "Are you trying to flatter me?"

"Absolutely not," he said staunchly. "Unless of course it's working."

"It's not."

He chuckled. "You're the only woman I know

who would take being described as diabolical as a compliment."

"Diabolical is not for the fainthearted." Neither was confrontation and candor. She drew a deep breath. "Do you know the worse thing about your stories?"

"Aside from the fact that you felt I was making fun of you?"

"You made her so much better than me."

His brows drew together. "What?"

"Your Miss Heartley, your heroine. She was smarter and braver and certainly funnier than I am. Her adventures were far more adventurous than mine. Her quest had a purpose whereas mine was just . . ."

"She is fictional, you know."

"Is she?" She studied him intently. "One does have to wonder who it is you claim to love. Me or the fantasy version of me that you created. This incredible woman who is so much more than I can ever hope to be." She shook her head. "How can anyone live up to that?"

"You do have a point," he said thoughtfully.

She stared. "Is that all you're going to say?"

"No." He picked up a folder that was lying on the sofa beside the cage and handed it to her. "There is a troupe of English actors who are performing a production of readings from Shakespeare. It's my understanding that it's a very progressive sort of thing. Costumes but minimal sets and a handful of props. They are giving a special performance for some charitable cause tomorrow night."

She opened the folder and flipped through the pages. "This is the balcony scene from *Romeo and Juliet*."

"Perhaps the most romantic scene in the history of theater."

"Except that they're dead in the end," she said under her breath.

"I have arranged for you to read the part of Juliet in the balcony scene."

"You what?" Her gaze jerked to his.

"Didn't your great-aunt wish to appear in a theatrical production?"

"She did but—"

"I told you I would help you with your quest and I feel obligated to continue to assist you to check at least one more item off your great-aunt's list."

"Is that why you're here?" She stared in disbelief. "That's it?"

"I did give you my word, and in spite of what you think of me, I do keep my word. It's a question of, well, honor, I suppose."

"Honor?" Surely this was some kind of not very funny joke on his part. "You followed me across an ocean because you felt obligated?"

"I do hate to leave things unfinished."

"I don't want your help." She tossed the folder

onto the sofa. "Nor do I wish to have anything further to do with you. And I'm very tempted to have my brothers shoot you, after all."

He scoffed. "Do you really want them to shoot me?"

"Yes!"

"But I brought you a parrot."

"I'm an idiot," Fernando squawked as if on cue.

"And in the best interests of the bird I will keep him," she snapped.

"I can't believe a woman who would rescue an elephant would stand by and allow her brothers to shoot the man who has crossed an ocean to lend her his assistance." He shook his head in a mournful manner.

"Very well then. I won't have them shoot you." She picked up Fernando's cage and started for the door. "But should they wish to thrash you thoroughly in the victorious spirit of two wars with your country, I will not stop them." She squared her shoulders and marched out of the parlor, up the stairs, and into her rooms, not pausing until she had slammed the door behind her.

She set the cage on top of her desk. Fernando looked at her and squawked. "I'm an idiot."

"Yes, I know." She waved off the parrot's comment. "I may well be an idiot myself." She folded her arms over her chest and paced the room. "It seems to me I was justified in my feelings of anger and betrayal. He did make a fool out of me even if I have come to wonder if being known as a madcap heiress isn't all that terrible. And it is the tiniest bit delightful to be someone's inspiration."

"I'm sorry."

"But is being sorry enough?" She shook her head. "He did cross an ocean for me . . ." She paused and stared at the bird. "But he certainly didn't apologize for his behavior. Nor did he take me in his arms, declare his undying love, and beg for my forgiveness."

"Please forgive me."

"Exactly like that, but teaching you to say it is not the same thing as saying it himself."

"I'm sorry."

"I know you are." She continued to pace. "The man is up to something, but what? I don't for a moment believe he came all this way simply to keep his word to help me. No, he has something else in mind."

"Hello. I love you."

She paused and stared at the parrot. "You haven't said that before."

"I'm sorry."

"Think nothing of it." She shrugged. "But you should have mentioned it sooner. If Cameron taught you to say that—and I'm more than willing to give him the benefit of the doubt on that score—then he's not simply here to help me with Great-aunt Lucinda's regrets. No, thank God, there's much more to his arrival than that. Which is a relief as there are very few regrets left on her list and I would be forced to make some up simply to keep him here." She thought for a moment. "In the spirit of compromise, I shall not allow my pride to stand in the way of my happiness. And any man who would cross an ocean and present me with a parrot—"

"I'm a fool."

"—should certainly be allowed to atone for his mistakes." She nodded firmly. "Therefore I will read the part of Juliet on stage, I will check one more regret off the list, and I will wait to see what Mr. Effington-Fairchild-Aldrich comes up with next."

Tomorrow was her birthday and she was going to read the part of Juliet on a stage, thanks to the man she loved. That could certainly be called not only an adventure but a daring exploit as well. Which only brought her back to the question she still had no answer for.

Did he love her or the better written version of her?

"Brandy or Scottish whisky?" Harry appeared in the open doorway.

"Whisky, I should think," Cameron said. "And it will be much appreciated."

"I thought so." Harry and his brothers filed back into the room.

A few minutes later, glasses had been poured and passed around and all the men had taken seats.

"So." Joe studied him over the rim of his glass. "You want to marry our sister."

"I do." Cam nodded.

"She doesn't seem very amenable to the idea," Parker murmured. "Or to you."

"But I think we all agree that she cares for you," Harry said. "She wouldn't be acting the way she has been if she didn't care."

"She never acted like this over . . ." Cole grimaced.

"Over Jackson Channing?" Cam asked.

Cole nodded.

"Good." Cam sipped his drink.

"I'm assuming you have some sort of plan," Joe said casually. "Given the way she left, you're going to need a plan."

"And fortunately I have one." Cam leaned back in his chair, his gaze circled the group. Four pairs of eyes very nearly the same shade as Lucy's studied him curiously. It was a little unnerving but not especially intimidating. Not anymore. "Gentlemen, I did not follow your sister halfway around the world to give up now."

He'd been so busy feeling guilty for his deception he'd forgotten who he was for a while. Certainly he had spent entirely too much time trying to determine his path in life, but once he had recognized his true calling, he hadn't wavered. He would not waver now. He had not failed to write a book. He had not failed to prove his resolve to his father. And he would not fail to win the hand of the love of his life. "At this point, I believe a grand gesture is called for."

"You did give her a parrot," Cole pointed out.

"And that was just the beginning. This is what I have in mind."

Lucy's brothers listened to his proposal and not one said it was stupid or far-fetched or couldn't possibly work. They reminded him of his own brothers, although, of course, his brothers wouldn't be nearly as polite. They would be far more critical of his plan and far more skeptical about his chances of success.

"I would venture to say this has not been an inexpensive proposition." Joe chose his words with care. "You're not interested in Lucy for her money then?"

"You can understand why that would be a concern," Harry said quickly.

"Of course." Cam nodded. "One can always use an heiress and I did squander my funds freely in my younger days, but I also listened to the investment advice of my brothers. I can assure you my finances are quite sound. I'm certain your father, as a banker, will be able to verify that."

Harry nodded.

"The offspring in my family have for generations received substantial trusts upon their majority and there hasn't been an Effington yet who has lost it completely." Cam grinned. "And hasn't gotten it back."

"Good to know," Joe murmured.

Harry nodded. "You should know as well, we wouldn't be helping you if we weren't convinced she likes you."

"Although you should be warned, she's not the same as she was before she went to England." Cole shuddered. "She's much crankier than she used to be. Possibly mad."

"Not mad exactly." Parker shrugged. "No madder than any other woman, that is. Rather more, well, obstinate and decisive, I would say."

"But we like her better this way." Joe grinned. "I'm not sure why."

"Because she's, I don't know, blossomed, I think. Grown perhaps." Harry studied Cam curiously. "Is that your doing?"

"As much as I'd like to say it is"—Cam shook his head—"I had nothing to do with it. She was already quite remarkable when I met her. Perhaps it was because she was no longer paying attention to expectations."

"Regardless, she's not the same." Harry grinned. "And she's not going to make this easy for you."

"Bloody hell, gentlemen." Cameron raised his glass to his future brothers-in-law. "She never has."

. . . and I should have said something but I did not. It was a minor matter, really, not especially significant. Yet, if I cannot find the strength to stand up for the little things, how can I hope to have the courage to stand up for the truly important things in life?

I am ashamed of myself for my lack of strength. I am the worst sort of coward to know in my heart something was wrong and not speak out.

Still, should the chance come along again, would I have the courage to decry what I believe is wrong, to stand up for what I believe is right? I would hope so, but it does seem to me that one never knows what one is capable of until the moment of destiny arrives.

If I do nothing else in my life I should hope one day to be the kind of woman who stands up publicly for what I believe in, regardless of whether that something is truly significant or relatively minor. It seems to me if I don't, who will . . .

from the journal of Miss Lucinda Merryweather, 1807

Chapter Twenty-two

Lucy studied the short flight of open steps that led to a small, rolling scaffold with a platform no more than five or six feet across and prepared herself to ascend it. This was nothing really. At least not when compared to climbing onto the back of an elephant. But backstage at a theater was darker and far busier than she had imagined.

Excitement mixed with apprehension in the pit of her stomach and she started up the steps. The scaffold was behind a scenery flat painted to portray the front of Juliet's house. When given her cue, Lucy would step from the scaffold, through dark, sheer curtains, and onto Juliet's balcony, whereupon she would try very hard not to make a complete ass of herself.

Lucy had never been on a real stage in her life. And while this wasn't a complete play, this performance of Shakespearean readings was undeniably a theatrical production. In a real theater with, God help her, a real audience. People she didn't know although, given it was a benefit for charity, she suspected there were quite a few people in attendance who were acquaintances of her or her family. One simply couldn't avoid it and, well, she didn't really care. Apparently, she was taking this madcap heiress business to heart.

She had been accompanied by her parents and

her brothers tonight but had yet to see Cameron, although she was confident he was here. How else would she be able to graciously thank him for his assistance and forgive him as well? Her brothers had said remarkably little about their talk with him, although Harry had casually mentioned it did seem the man was not lacking financially as arranging her appearance tonight had taken a bit of maneuvering and had not come cheap. Plus there was a sizable donation to the charity involved as well. His financial stability was a relief but, while the thought had nagged at her, she had never truly believed he was interested in her money. Just as she had always truly believed he was a good and honorable man.

Lucy stepped onto the platform to await her cue. Behind her, the wardrobe mistress straightened the skirts of her blue brocade Juliet costume. With its trailing sleeves and square cut bodice, it was perhaps lovelier than it was authentic. But this was the theater after all, a world of illusion, and the moment she stepped on that balcony, she would be Juliet. A thrill ran through her at the thought. No wonder Great-aunt Lucinda wanted to be in a theatrical production.

In the spirit of adventure, while she did have the lines written in a large notebook designed to resemble an antique book, she had memorized them as well. It wasn't difficult as every school-girl probably knew the immortal words by heart.

The reading was to start with her first line, which she had pointed out to the stage manager was not the beginning of the scene. He had strongly advised her to keep her opinion to herself and read what was in front of her.

From the right wing, the stage manager cued her. This was it then.

She held the book open in front of her, parted the curtains, and stepped onto the balcony. The bright light hit her and she noted how the blinding brilliance kept her from seeing little more than endless rows of indistinct faces, relatively anonymous and therefore far less intimidating.

Lucy sent a silent prayer heavenward and drew a calming breath. "Oh Romeo, Romeo! Wherefore art thou Romeo? Deny thy father and refuse thy name, or, if thou wilt not, be but sworn my love, and I'll no longer be a Capulet."

A male voice sounded below her and off to one side, out of the pool of light, and she couldn't see the speaker.

"Shall I hear more, or shall I speak at this?"

She continued. " 'Tis but thy name that is my enemy. Thou art thyself, though not a Montague. What's Montague? It is nor hand, nor foot, nor arm, nor face, nor any other part belonging to a man. O, be some other name! What's in a name?"

"Exactly," Romeo said.

"Exactly?" She frowned and looked down at the lines. That wasn't right. Perhaps this actor was as much of an amateur as she was. After all, this was a charitable event and if her part could be arranged for, no doubt Romeo's could be as well. Still, the man surely had the lines in front of him. All he had to do was read them. She cleared her throat and continued. "That which we call a rose by any other name would smell as sweet. So—"

"Indeed, what is in a name?"

"I wasn't finished," she said in a hushed tone. "And I already said that." She scanned the lines. She was right. She had said that. Goodness, this erstwhile actor playing Romeo was going to make a mess of the whole thing. She leaned forward to peer over the balcony. All she could see in the pool of light on the stage were his leggings and shoes.

"It bears repeating." Cameron stepped into the light. She should have known the moment she heard his voice, but apparently stage fright hindered one's powers of observation.

"What are you doing?" she said in as quiet a voice as she could manage.

"Ah, my sweet Juliet, you shall see." He flashed her a grin, then turned toward the audience. "Ladies and gentlemen. As this is the last presentation of the evening, I have taken the liberty of rewriting the scene."

A murmur of surprise waved through the audience.

"It's Shakespeare," she said in a low, urgent

voice. What was the man thinking? "You don't rewrite Shakespeare!"

"I believe the bard himself would allow a few liberties to be taken by a fellow countryman."

"Well, I won't have it."

"Let him speak," a voice called from the audience that sounded suspiciously like one of her brothers.

"Fine." She waved the book at him. "Do I need this?"

"Probably not, but one never knows what might happen in the theater." He grinned. "Give me your next line."

"Not that I have a choice," she said under her breath. She paused, willed herself to stay calm, and tried again. "So Romeo would, were he not Romeo—"

"Not that one," Cameron interrupted. "The one after 'I never will be Romeo.' "

The audience laughed.

"Go on," he urged.

"Very well." She clenched her teeth. "What man art thou that thus bescreen'd in night so stumblest on my counsel?"

"By a name, I know not how to tell thee who I am." He paused.

"Don't stop." She huffed. "There's more."

"And yet try I did, fair Juliet, but I am no more than a mere mortal man, weak and fearful of loss. And in my feeble attempts to reveal all, alas, I failed in a manner most miserable. For I feared the outcome of my deception."

"Of course you did." She sighed, tossed the folder aside, and braced her hands on the balcony railing. No doubt this was not the kind of theatrical production Great-aunt Lucinda had envisioned, but then it was no longer her adventure either.

It was no longer Lucinda's adventure.

She had realized some time ago that her great-aunt's adventures had become hers, but here and now, with the man she loved making the silliest kind of grand gesture, on a stage in front of her entire family and God only knew who else, this had nothing to do with Lucinda. This was now indeed Lucy's adventure. And Lucy's life. And there would be no regrets.

She thought for a moment, then addressed the audience. " 'Tis obvious there will be no performance of star-crossed lovers here tonight."

Cameron placed his hand by the side of his mouth and leaned toward the audience in a confidential manner. "A shame perhaps, but 'tis hoped the play you see before you now will end far better than with death to all."

Appreciative chuckles ran through the audience.

"You say you feared the outcome of deception and yet, noble Romeo," Lucy continued, "the truth might well have served you better than deceit, for did not the playwright himself say in yet another play we shall not perform tonight . . ." She swept her arms in a wide gesture toward the audience. "Truth is truth to the very end of reckoning."

" 'Tis not the soundness of the truth I ran from so much as its revelation. And in that, as all else, I was a fool." He stared up at her. "And I was wrong."

"And have you now learned a lesson about the virtues of truth and the consequences of deceit?"

"I have indeed, fair Juliet." He clasped his hand over his heart. "And I swear to you from this day forth, none but the truth shall fall from my lips."

" 'Tis a nice enough vow and yet . . ." She heaved an overly dramatic sigh and turned toward the audience. "Romeo has sworn his regret, an apology that, in truth, might well be seen as lacking. His remorse appears cursory, his regret more flippant than sincere." She addressed the audience. "Ladies of the theater, what say you? Has he earned forgiveness?"

A polite smattering of applause sounded from the audience.

"Or, like a truly repentant man, should he be made to grovel?"

Enthusiastic applause erupted, accompanied by more than a few cheers.

She leaned forward, rested her elbow on the railing, and propped her head in her hand. "Well,

Romeo, as all truly repentant men have done before you, you may proceed to grovel."

"If groveling is the price to be paid for the forgiveness of the fair Juliet, so be it." He leapt onto the trellis that ran up the flat to the balcony and started to climb. "I shall grovel for the rest of my days at your feet if you wish." He reached the balcony, his head now level with hers, and met her gaze directly. "But I would rather worship at them."

A definite sigh arose from the ladies in the theater.

His tone sobered. "I would move the heavens above and the earth beneath my feet were it possible to undo what cannot be undone. But note, fair Juliet, that knowing my misdeeds have wounded you has shattered my heart, and while I pray for your forgiveness for this wretched cur, I shall never forgive myself."

"Oh." Her heart caught and words failed her. For a long moment she could do nothing but stare at him.

"Surely there is more you wish to say?" he prompted.

"Yes, of course. Although I'm not sure . . ." she said quietly, then cleared her throat. "Ah, Romeo, thy words have touched my heart and while words have no more substance than the air we breathe, 'tis in your eyes I see the truth." She leaned forward to kiss him, the crowd would love that, but he pulled back.

He jumped onto the balcony and took her hands. "Then, fair Juliet, declare your love for me."

"Here?" she whispered.

"I am giving you the opportunity to stand up publicly for what you believe in," he said in a quiet voice for her ears alone. "It's on your great-aunt's list. You believe in true love and soul mates and destiny. Can you do it, Lucy? Can you stand up for love?"

She glanced at the audience. They were obviously getting restless. "Goodness, Cameron, you've made your point. This is silly and—"

"The woman I made up, the character I modeled after you could not have been as wonderful as she was if the woman I based her on was not the most wonderful woman I have ever met. She is my creation, Lucy Merryweather, but you are her soul. As you are mine."

"You do realize this is incredibly embarrassing?" She glanced again at the audience.

"I thought it might be. But that is one of the risks of standing up for what you believe. Do you really believe in true love, Lucy? Now is your chance to prove it."

She stared at him. Did she?

He addressed the audience. " 'Tis an opportunity not to be missed, to stand forth before the world in declaration that thou believest in with your heart and soul. And what better to believest in than love, true and eternal and everlasting."

He turned to her. "Will thee stand forth, Juliet? Will thee stand for love? And for me?" he added under his breath.

She studied him for a long moment. "I . . ." She raised her voice. "While it has been said the course of true love does not run smooth, 'twould be foolish indeed to not seize opportunity once presented. And so, dear Romeo, I do indeed stand up to proclaim to all far and near, that I do believe in love, true and eternal and everlasting, and in spite of your faults, little worse than any other of your gender, I believe, as well, in thee."

He grinned and turned toward the audience. " 'Tis now the end of our play, no longer sorrowful and sad, but joyous and happy and glad. And so we bid you good night and good rest unto you all."

He swept an overly dramatic bow.

She raised a brow. "And we are then at an end?"

"Well . . ." He paused. "Yes. Thou knowest, all's well that ends well."

Laughter washed through the crowd.

"If indeed 'tis the end." She shrugged. "Methinks the play is not yet resolved."

A slight look of panic shone in Cameron's eyes. He stepped close and spoke low into her ear. "This is it, Lucy. I wrote those last lines—I didn't just now come up with them. I don't have anything else to say."

"Oh, and I think you do," she murmured, cast

him a wicked smile, then gazed over the audience. "One moment, kind and gentle spectators, whilst I discuss the terms of the ending of our endeavor here this night." She stepped back from the railing and turned to Cameron. "First, while I am more than willing to be your muse, do you swear to me you will never again use me for literary purposes without my knowledge?"

"I do," he said slowly.

"And will you promise to be completely honest with me even when it's not especially easy?"

He nodded. "I will."

"And will you never again cause me to doubt the trust I place in you?"

"I would die before I would ever allow that to happen again."

"Good." She nodded. "Now," she said with a grin, "we can end the play."

"And do you have any idea how to do that?"

"You're the writer. I thought you would come up with something."

"I did and I already delivered the last lines, well thought out and well written too, I might add."

She widened her eyes. "Yes, well, rewrite!"

"Easier said than done," he muttered. He thought for a moment, then cast her a smug smile and stepped away. " 'Twould be a shame to end a play with nothing more than words." He reached out and pulled her into his arms.

" 'Tis said a story of love and romance should end with no less than a kiss and the promise of a happy ending."

"A promise?" Her heart beat faster.

"A vow then." He smiled into her eyes. "What say you, Juliet? Will you have me for the rest of our days?"

The audience held its collective breath.

"Will you be my muse, my love, my wife?"

She stared at him for a long moment. Hope mixed with apprehension in his eyes, but surely he already knew the answer. She smiled up at him. "I would be a fool not to seize an opportunity so finely presented."

Applause erupted and he laughed with a sheer delight that wrapped around her soul and she knew, in spite of his mistakes and perhaps one or two of her own, this was right and true and forever. She loved this man more than she ever would have imagined possible. And if not for the regrets of a good woman long gone and her own desire not to be who she was expected to be, they would have never found each other.

"And if there are regrets to be had in the future, let them not be of the heart." She gazed into his eyes and saw the love they shared reflected there. "For love, my good Romeo, is never a regret."

Regrets Set to Rights

Stand up publicly for what I believe in.

Postscript

In the years to come, Lord Cameron Effington continued to write as Cameron Fairchild with his muse by his side. A muse who delighted in reading everything he wrote and, on occasion when she thought it necessary, offered suggestions for improvement. He never became as successful or well known as Mark Twain but made an excellent living nonetheless and scarcely ever had to rely on the trust provided him by his family or his wife's fortune.

Lord and Lady Cameron Effington made their home in England but frequently voyaged to America and tried, whenever possible, to travel the rest of the world, finding it far easier to frolic in a fountain in a foreign country where Lady Cameron, at least, had no idea what outraged bystanders were yelling. They found, as well, it was much more enjoyable to swim naked in the moonlight in a country where the climate was far more temperate than England.

Regrets Set to Rights

Travel the world.
Frolic in a fountain.
Swim naked in the moonlight.

Lucy Merryweather Effington did on occasion wonder if she was doing a disservice to her granddaughters and great-granddaughters by not having a list of regrets to leave them that they could then pursue and have daring exploits of their own. She spent a great deal of the money left her by her great-aunt on an educational foundation, with representatives in both England and the United States, to enable young women to pursue their goals and follow their hearts in hopes they would not reach the end of their days with regrets.

While through the years the foundation did indeed help any number of young women achieve their dreams, the Lucinda Merryweather Van Burton Foundation for the Advancement of Young Women atoned as well for the last regret on Lucy's great-aunt's list, an adventure Lucy refused to keep for herself.

Make certain the world remembers my name.

And goodness, could anyone ask for more than that?

Center Point Large Print
600 Brooks Road / PO Box 1
Thorndike, ME 04986-0001 USA

(207) 568-3717

US & Canada:
1 800 929-9108
www.centerpointlargeprint.com